TRACES OF MAMMON

BUD DURAND

A FICTION IMPRINT FROM ADDUCENT

Adducent, Inc.
www.Adducent.co

Titles Distributed In
North America
United Kingdom
Western Europe
South America
Australia

Traces of Mammon

Bud Durand

ISBN 978-1-937592-12-7

Published by Adducent, Inc. under its Escrire fiction imprint

Jacksonville, Florida

www.Adducent.co (*that's right, it's not a .com*)

Published in the United States of America

ACKNOWLEDGEMENTS

I would like to thank my family for their support over the year-plus that it took me to write this book. Their encouragement and help with plot ideas was extremely helpful, and the times that I seemed to hit a wall, they helped me over it. My appreciation and thanks also go to Fortis Publishing for giving an unpublished writer a chance and for the editorial and administrative support they provided. For technical knowledge, I would like to thank Steven Metzler, Bomb Appraisal Manager for DHS/TSA at Tampa International Airport, who provided expertise in the IED arena; Farah Janjua, who helped with the Urdu interpretations; and several anonymous employees of the Federal Air Marshall Service who helped with the legal interpretations and information on their organization. Special thanks go to my good friend Vince DiPortanova for his excellent help and advice on more than one occasion.

DEDICATION

This book is dedicated to the men and women of federal and local law enforcement organizations who have devoted their lives to the protection of our country against the tyranny of terrorism.

PROLOGUE

The Badger leaned back slightly in his comfortable swivel chair and crossed his legs. Placing his elbows on the arms of the chair, he leaned his chin on his extended fingers to support his head and stared out the window. A few moments later, he leaned further back using another chair as a foot rest and concentrated on the ceiling. The late afternoon sunlight reflecting off the cloudy sky coming through his large picture windows colored the off white tiles a soothing tangerine. He soon closed his eyes and focused on the problem. *I think the good doctor has become just a little too smart for his own good. He is now a liability that must be dealt with. This would be an excellent problem for the prime cell to resolve. I'll have them get together as soon as they can set up a meeting place. Ah, but I must first decide whether accepting responsibility for this action would be more of a help or a hindrance. I obviously need to consider the ramifications of that.*

He envisioned a blank slate and then bifurcated it, methodically identifying the significant pros and cons until he had three reasons for on the left and four against on the right. After a few more minutes, when he could think of no more, he assigned each a weight and arranged them in order of descending importance. *Well, I believe it's actually too close to call, so I shall leave that up to the cell members as well. That way they'll have more leeway in their execution. I must however give them a deadline—within the week. Any further delay would be chancy, so this must be an agenda item for their next meeting, which will probably have to be sooner than they were anticipating.*

He continued leaning back for a few more minutes, reconsidering his thoughts. *Yes, that is the proper course of action. Now I need only inform the cell.* He straightened up in his chair and reached over to retrieve his minicomputer from its case. Placing it on his lap, he paused in thought for a minute, and

1

then began composing an email. When he was satisfied with the wording, he loaded it onto his flash drive. *I've been meaning to try that new little café in the shopping center, so I'll stop there on the way home to send this. The cell's progress will not be hard to monitor. Indeed, it will be very easy to determine when they have succeeded.* He pocketed the drive and placed the laptop back in its case. He then turned to his desktop. *Let's see what silly ass problem they think is important enough for me to solve for them now.*

CHAPTER ONE

Fort Belvoir, Virginia, 26 October, 2015 hours

"All right; you're all clear," said Ronnie. "Go ahead and lift off."

JT eased the throttle forward and the bird lifted straight up, slowly at first and then with increasing speed.

"I'm on my way back down to the office," said Ronnie as she exited the roof and proceeded down the stairs. Their office was in a small two-story building on Davison Air Field with the landing pad for the bird on the roof. The fixed-winged aircraft took off from the other side of the field, near the runways, of course, and this side, for the rotary-winged aircraft, was actually fairly small given the number of helicopters housed here.

When Ronnie got back to the office, JT was urging the bird to go faster. His habit of talking to the unmanned aerial vehicle, or UAV, was occasionally annoying but usually informative. JT had been an aircraft engine mechanic in the Air Force, ran a small engine repair shop for a few years after that, and now built and flew model airplanes and helicopters with his son for a hobby. What was planned as a training session for Ronnie had turned into an operation, and the boss wanted JT driving. In addition to being the Alpha Unit leader, he was undoubtedly the best UAV operator they had.

The National Security Agency had picked up a possible terrorist transmission about thirty minutes prior, which lasted long enough for them to locate it. They then informed the Fusion Team at the time when JT and Ronnie were already at Fort Belvoir preparing for a night training flight. They were now hoping to get the UAV in place in time to track what they thought was a P-STIC—a person with suspected terrorist involvement or connections. The team just called them "Sticks." Although the conversations were sporadic, they occurred often enough and long enough that NSA could give them a real-time feed. The transmissions were coming from or near a building on Naylor

Road, just off Branch Avenue in Prince Georges County, Maryland, just a few blocks over the District line. That was about fifteen miles from where they were at Davison Field with no restricted airspace between them and that location. It would take the bird just short of ten minutes at max airspeed to get there.

Ronnie had given JT the GPS coordinates, and as the bird approached them, JT hovered at 500 feet, looking for his quarry. Luckily the street lighting was fairly good here and he saw a man talking on a cell phone outside some sort of restaurant or bar. He keyed in on the conversation and compared it real-time to the input from NSA. "That's our guy," he told Ronnie. Less than two minutes later, a Honda Civic pulled up and stopped beside the man who then jumped into it. The Civic headed up Naylor Road to the Suitland Parkway and then turned north onto Branch Avenue. It picked up Pennsylvania Avenue westbound and then north on the Anacostia Freeway. JT had no trouble following the distinctive red car from his vantage point, given all the street lighting en route.

After turning west on Benning Road, the suspects' vehicle took a few more turns and ended up in an industrial neighborhood. The apparent final destination was a large and long, three-story warehouse running parallel to Benning Road.

JT read the output of the bird's GPS system and passed them on to Ronnie. "Where does that put them?" he asked.

Ronnie keyed in the coordinates to the map program and replied, "Just north of Benning Road Northeast between Anacostia Avenue and Foote Place—pretty deserted neighborhood this time of night."

The two individuals in the Civic got out and walked over to another vehicle, a cab, with two individuals resting against the fenders. The four suspects greeted each other and began chatting.

JT honed in on the plates and Ronnie wrote them and the vehicle descriptions down. Although this was all being recorded, she wanted this info readily available. JT had just maneuvered to a point where he could pick up their conversations when a third vehicle, an SUV, arrived and two more individuals got out.

JT began conversing with the bird again. "Okay, okay. Easy, easy. Back up a little. Holy shit! That's him, I know it!" The moon was more than half full and high in the sky and that, along with the ambient light that the various warehouse spotlights were casting in their direction, gave JT sufficient lighting to receive a good clear image. "I'd recognize him anywhere—that's Rasheem himself. He and his friend are obviously meeting with these other guys. Let's get the team out here now."

Ronnie keyed the mike and requested an intercept group head towards the coordinates she was forwarding. Ronnie wished that they had requested an earlier deployment, but then they weren't sure this would turn out to be anything, or if it was, where they would be going. Ronnie got a confirmation from the inbound team leader and an estimated time of arrival of less than twenty minutes. Seems he had a hunch this might be a good lead and had already the hit the road with the rest of the team.

"They are on the way JT, but I'm running the recognition software now." Ronnie keyed a few strokes into her laptop and transferred the image from the UAV into the FRS and hit enter. The face recognition software program was quite sophisticated, and with all the inputs that DHS had made lately there was hardly a foreign national or anyone here on a passport or visa who was not already in the database. And Ronnie was an exceptional analyst who could usually coax the best performance out of any piece of software. While she was waiting for it, she wrote down the data on the SUV.

Now that Rasheem was here, the six of them headed inside the nondescript three story building with four or five large garage door openings on the long side facing Benning Road, as well as a few windows, mostly on the upper two levels. The various piles of metal components lying around the yard and the three large stacks protruding from the roof led JT to guess that it was some kind of industrial assembly operation.

Ronnie fiddled with the input to the FRS but was actually paying more attention to the incoming video. After just a few minutes she said, "Well, that was pretty quick. We have positive confirmation on Rasheem."

"How can I get this hummer in the building?" JT said pretty much to himself. "I don't see any obvious entrances.... Wait a minute, there's an open, unscreened vent just below the eaves. It's pretty narrow but I think I can make it. Damn, I hit the edge." The DARPA developed UAV was actually a MAV, or micro air vehicle, affectionately called the hummingbird, and had come a long way since UAVs were first developed. While this one was not exactly one of the state-of-the-art NAVs, or nano air vehicles, it was more than adequate for this job: real-time audio and visual reconnaissance with a sixty-power zoom lens, point-and-click, single-person ground control, digitally recorded audio and video reference for analysis, a hover time of over twelve hours, an operating range of over twenty miles, and GPS capability. All this in a package with only a six inch wingspan that was not only tough but also very stable and quiet. Unless, of course, you ran into something.

"Slow down and take it easy. Is she okay?" Ronnie had picked up on the fact that JT always referred to his birds as women. "You're pretty high up, so I doubt they heard that. What are you seeing now?" Ronnie asked as she took her eyes from JT's screen to feed the live audio into the language translation program.

"She's fine. It's pretty dark inside but I can see some light coming through what looks like a door.... It opens onto a catwalk over a large open space. I see the group down about two floors and they are moving towards the back of the building. Looks like they're heading towards a small room on the, ah, north side. I'll hold position until they're all in."

"This audio is not the greatest. Sounds like there's a motor or something in the background. Can you get down close?" she asked.

"Yeah, yeah. There're all in and there's a transom over the door. They closed the door but hopefully that won't be a problem. I'm getting great video through the transom but the audio is kinda noisy. I think it's all in—Urdu? Guess we should have had an interpreter here. Isn't this being piped through to the situation room in Headquarters?"

"Yes, but that doesn't mean there's an Urdu-speaking agent there right now, or anybody for that matter."

"I thought we had a translation program."

"Yes we do, and I'm feeding it as it comes in but you know how accurate it is, especially with this fidelity."

"Do you understand any of that?" JT asked.

"Not really. My Urdu is a little rusty. I did catch something that sounded like *rail gaari,* which I'm betting translates to train, so my money is on a Union Station or maybe a Metro Center plot."

"Yeah, that would be my guess, too."

"Are you ready for a quick exit—at least high enough so they won't catch on to our surveillance? Whoa! They seem to be looking right at us and, yep, they're coming out!"

"I'm getting her out of there!" JT yelled. Then, "Holy shit they're shooting at us! Come on baby—zig zag, zig zag!" JT rotated the controller back and forth and the bird was ascending, albeit on a rather crazy path. Only two shots were fired however as the group took off for the exit. "Let the team know we've been made!" JT shouted as he tried to regain control of the UAV. He did manage to get it out of the vent he had entered through and down towards the parked vehicles. He saw Rasheem jump into the same SUV that he had come in as it headed out of the parking lot with smoking tires. The Civic stuck close behind, carrying another two of the Sticks.

Ronnie had already passed on the descriptions and tag numbers of the other two vehicles and now added that of the SUV to the list since, in her excitement, she had forgotten to do that earlier. Thank goodness the UAV could reach airspeeds in excess of ninety.

As soon as the two vehicles got to the main roads, they headed in opposite directions. JT decided to track the SUV with Rasheem in it. "He turned east on Benning so I think he's headed for 295 which is the main north-south route in that part of town. Yep. They're going up the freeway. How close are our guys?"

"They are already well on their way from Andrews Air Force Base and heading up 295 so they are only a few minutes behind." Ronnie put out a BOLO for all three vehicles to the various DC and Maryland police forces. The be-on-the-lookout notification would alert law enforcement officers from these jurisdictions to watch for these particular vehicles.

"Uh, oh! They didn't come out from under the overpass. I'm going down to get a closer look." JT brought the UAV back toward the overpass, eased it down and glided under the bridge. "I see the SUV—it's over on the shoulder and...damn! There's nobody in it! Where the hell did they go? Oh man, they must have transferred to another vehicle. They obviously had this set up as an escape route and practiced it enough to be good at it. There's no way I can tell which vehicle they transferred to or whether they're headed north or south."

"Well, that was so quick let's assume they're still headed north and I'll alert the team. You keep the bird focused on the vehicle." Ronnie informed the intercept group and they continued north on 295.

As they went past the abandoned vehicle one of the team jumped out to secure it after verifying that it was indeed empty. After thirty minutes, the team hadn't seen any likely terrorist-containing vehicles, so they called off the search and headed back to the warehouse site to look for any clues.

JT had already guided the UAV back to the meeting place and kept watch on it until the team arrived to secure it. After signing off with the team leader on the ground, he headed the UAV back to its home base with them in Fort Belvoir.

"All right, Ronnie, I'll do the post flight on the bird while you get the paperwork started." He determined that the bird had only sustained some minor scratches, so he refueled it and accomplished the remainder of the post-flight checklist before returning to the office. Ronnie had completed the flight logs and secured the rest of the shop. "Let's call it a day, shall we? We'll face the music tomorrow."

CHAPTER TWO

The Badger was more than upset. *I cannot believe what happened! How could they have figured out where and when the cell was meeting? Is it possible that we have a mole in our midst? Rasheem said they followed standard protocol, so there could not have been much lead time. We will have to look into this. Their having partially discussed the prime objective may cause us to revise some of our parameters. At least they did not discuss the secondary objective before they realized they may have been monitored. Thank Allah for small favors. But alas, the secondary is now more urgent and must be tended to with great haste. We shall have to divert some resources. Opportunities abound.*

Fusion Team Headquarters, 27 October, 1615 hours

All of the team had finally arrived and were waiting for the Captain to get off the phone with the National Counterterrorism Center. They were expecting to get some last minute information from Interpol about Rasheem that the Team had requested. That was what this relatively new organization did. They were formed as a brainchild of Hanson, the head of one of the directorates in the Counterintelligence Field Activity (CIFA), who had gotten fed up with the parochialism of the various intelligence agencies, the very thing that CIFA, created just after the September 11, 2001 terrorist attacks, had been formed to overcome. Their mistake was forming yet another government entity with its own ax to grind. Initially tasked with coordinating Pentagon security efforts, CIFA eventually got the power to investigate certain crimes within the United States, including treason, foreign or terrorist sabotage and economic espionage. This eventually triggered major concern about domestic intelligence gathering by the Pentagon against Americans. Whether it was this that brought the agency's demise after less than seven years, or the mismanagement and contract kick-back and bribery scandals that included some Congressmen, was anybody's guess, but Hanson was glad he got out when he did. The best thing he had to say about them was that "CIFA put the F in CIA."

His new outfit, the Fusion Team as they called themselves, was a focused response unit of the Department of Homeland Security, and included an ad-hoc group of individuals from various intelligence, counterintelligence, counterterrorism and law enforcement agencies that tried to cut out the bullshit and get the right resources focused on the problem fast. Operating as a DHS entity gave them federal police powers, and Hanson thought that as such, they encountered less resistance from other agencies—probably because they felt sorry for the burgeoning, seemingly out-of-control organization. After all, who is inclined to lend help to an "altogether organization" like the FBI or the CIA? So far the Team, which consisted currently of six separate units or sub teams, had gotten along very well under Captain Hanson's command, and they each contributed a good deal of data and operational expertise from their parent organizations to the specific task at hand: tracking down the possibility of a terrorist attack on one of Washington DC's train stations. The mandate from the White House and the more-than-adequate budget didn't hurt either.

Thomas (Tom) Sebastian Hanson was not really a captain, at least not anymore. That was his rank when he got out of the Air Force's Office of Special Investigations (OSI), and the appellation stuck. Although selected for Major, he turned it down and resigned his commission, figuring that there were more exciting things to investigate than some of the criminal activities he had thus far in the service. From OSI he went to the Central Intelligence Agency's Domestic Terrorist Task Force and stayed for several years before learning of an opening, via a friend, heading up a special task force in the Bureau of Alcohol, Tobacco, Firearms and Explosives (ATF). After three years with ATF he went to CIFA to head up their Operations Directorate, and then finally to DHS. He had a no-nonsense matter that generally got things done, and a personality that made you want to please him. He was six-foot-two and weighed 210, with only a trace of flab around the middle. His graying hair gave him an air of maturity beyond his forty-three years. The ladies on the team thought he looked a lot like Denzel Washington, but with lighter hair.

Hanson came into the room and the Alpha Unit quieted down. JT Dunkirk was the leader of the group, which was one of the sub units of the Fusion Team. Besides JT there were six other members: Charles Burton from the Federal Bureau of Investigation; Josh Paxton and Ronnie Hamilton from the ATF; and Juanita Singletary, Phil Ellis and Brendon Gotlieb from OSI, the Naval Criminal Investigation Service and the Army's Criminal Investigation Division respectively. JT was the only actual DHS employee in his unit—the rest of the members were on detail to his unit, but they also got DHS credentials. "Ladies and gentlemen," Hanson began, "let's figure out what's going on here. So Phil, did we get anything from the warehouse?"

Phil Ellis was a tall black man but with lighter skin coloring that hinted at some Caucasian in his background. He obviously worked out and had a smooth, friendly face that belied his no nonsense attitude—after all he was a Commander with over 20 years in the Navy. "It is owned by an *S&S Enterprises*," he began, "and they make and sell rivets and other fasteners for aircraft, including some NASA spacecraft, but they are clean as far as we can tell. In any event, the door was jimmied so we don't think there's any connection with our group. We found nothing that appears to have been left behind by any of the group, and we are waiting on forensics but are not hopeful."

"And what can you tell us about the vehicle owners, Juanita?"

"Well, Captain, as you know, the Chevy Tahoe was stolen. It's owned by a GS-12 budget analyst working for Agriculture who appears to be on the up and up. He said he was home alone last night since his wife was visiting with her sister for a few days. He reported it missing this morning when he went out to go to work. It does have a rather sophisticated alarm system that would have taken some effort to defeat. The Honda Civic was also stolen and is registered to a small business owner who runs a lawn service. This is the vehicle that our two Sticks used to get to the warehouse. The owner reported it missing late last night, about an hour after we lost Rasheem on the freeway. After walking home from a local bar, he said he noticed it 'wasn't where he left it.' His family verifies his leaving for the bar at about seven and getting back at eleven-thirty and asking where the car was."

Juanita rifled through her notes for a moment before producing a picture. "I'll get this picture over to the bar this evening to check out his alibi. Like the Tahoe owner, he doesn't have any hits in any of our systems—no wants or warrants or any record at all—so appears legit. The third vehicle is a Crown Vic cab operated by a Pakistani who is a resident alien, but it's registered to his brother, whom he lives with. I've talked to the owner, the brother, who is a citizen, and he says he hasn't seen his brother or the cab since early yesterday and did not know about it being missing until I contacted him. He doesn't have any record and his family verified that he was home last night. They weren't in the TIDE database and the ICE database went down before we could check on any of the owners or the cab driver. None of the three owners look like our six Sticks, but the cabbie's operator's license was not in the vehicle, so we couldn't check on him. By the way, the cab has not been reported as stolen yet."

"Phew, that's quite a rundown," said Hanson. "But aren't all the terrorist databases supposed to be in TIDE now?"

Juanita knew that TIDE, the Terrorist Identities Datamart Environment, was the NCTC's terror database and indeed was supposed to contain every government organization's terrorist data. "Yes, it's supposed to. But our own, the ICE data base, is apparently not quite all there yet."

"Okay. Thanks, Juanita. Ronnie, how about the locations of the vehicles?"

All eyes turned to Ronnie, who was tall for a woman and also slightly overweight, and with her somewhat rough demeanor cut a rather imposing figure. Her nose had a slightly puggish look, as did most of the noses in her family, and she kept her curly red hair short. Between the hair and the dark green eyes, you expected her to break out in Gaelic any minute. She seldom cared what people thought about her, rode a Harley most of the year, and was always up for anything.

"The Tahoe owner lives within a mile of the warehouse, so I suspect that Rasheem and his cohort came to the general vicinity of the meeting, stole the thing, and then parked their other vehicle under the overpass for the getaway," Ronnie began. "The Metro Police found the Civic this morning just a few blocks from where it was stolen near that bar on Naylor Road. It appears as though our two suspects parked a few blocks away from the vehicle they were going to heist, stole it, and then doubled back to retrieve their own vehicle after they were sure they shook any pursuit. As far as the two guys at the bar go, our surveillance started with them in front of the bar, so we missed them getting there. When we got there with the bird, we saw this guy out front on a cell phone that we were pretty sure was our intercept, and we verified that real time with NSA. As he was talking, the Civic came up and he jumped in and we followed it to the warehouse. We don't know where the cab was stolen from, but it was also found this morning only a few blocks from the warehouse, so I suspect it was stolen near there and then again the guys doubled back to get their own vehicle or vehicles. As you may recall, we never actually saw the cab leave the warehouse. Forensics has all three, but they haven't come up with anything usable so far."

"Okay, so what do we have on the feed from the UAV?" Hanson asked as he looked at Brendon.

"Well, Sir," Brendon began, "the little information that was decipherable indicates that they were discussing a train station—we are fairly certain of that. Earlier in the meeting, we did detect what could pass as the Urdu word for bomb—which is actually *bomb, bumb* or *bumm,* depending upon the background and level of education of the speaker. We also picked up what sounded like the English word *sarin,* as in sarin gas, which doesn't really translate either and is close to several other Urdu words. This could be a stretch as well. The Urdu terms for cold, or *sardi,* and weather, or *mausam,* did come through with more clarity. The rest of it was just normal conversation we think, so unfortunately we got nothing else definitive: no other details, no dates, and certainly no plan of action."

Brendon paused for a minute before going on, thought about whether or not he wanted to add anything, but then continued. "It's obvious that the persons of interest know they were discovered and probably recorded, so it would seem likely that they may alter or even abort these plans. I would not be surprised if they disappear altogether. There is a possibility, however, that their misadventure will not be relayed to their superiors for fear of any repercussions. It would behoove us therefore to consider this a distinct possibility and put the potential targets under surveillance." Brendon wasn't so much of a naysayer as he seemed, but rather precise, and chose his words carefully as if trying to eliminate any chance of misunderstanding or perhaps contradiction. He had a medium build but was pudgy, and had short, curly black hair and a rounded face. The team sometimes teased him by calling him Georgie after the character on *Seinfeld*.

"I'm not so sure people willing to die for their religion are concerned too much about repercussions," Hanson commented. "I'm *hoping—and* that may be a poor choice of words—that they will just have other folks carry on for them if they think they've been compromised, because they have too much planning invested in this already. They may think that one of them was followed, or they may think we just picked them up at the warehouse—hopefully the latter."

"Oh come on Boss," JT protested, "they fired at my damn bird! And they gotta know that we have their pictures if nothing else." He was usually this impulsive and usually right. He may have been short and weighed only 145 pounds, but his energy was boundless. His face was chiseled and handsome and his short brown hair and brown eyes gave him a distinguished look, especially when he was undercover and sporting a short goatee and mustache. If he stood still for five minutes, it was because he was concentrating deeply on something extremely important to him. He was always wise-cracking, making fun of others' foibles or his own, and people just couldn't help but like him. He was particularly good in interviews; by the time he was finished with a suspect, the poor individual had usually admitted to everything but stealing the kitchen sink. He actually did this by appealing to their better side, and a person had to be the most depraved of individuals not to respond positively to him.

"Pictures, yes," Hanson shot back. "But do you really think they believe they are compromised by that? We've had Rasheem's picture for months. And for all we know the rest of them could have been disguised. JT, is it possible they heard you bang into that vent and just fed us a line of bull? That was an awfully short meeting."

JT chaffed a little in his chair after this mild rebuke from Captain Hanson, but their solid working relationship certainly wouldn't suffer from this. "I really don't think so, Captain. And it appeared to me as though one of them just coincidentally looked up and saw my bird. He really looked surprised. This is why the meeting was cut short."

"Yeah, I'd have to agree with that," Ronnie added.

"Speaking of pictures," Hanson continued, "what do we have on these Sticks, JT?"

"Of course we know Rasheem Haqqani was identified since Ronnie got a hit on him in the FRS. To be brief, as most of you are already aware of his pedigree, he is a suspected Taliban cell leader from Pakistan, is here illegally, and on our top ten Stick list. This is a major development, as he was thought to be in Afghanistan just a few days ago. Captain, did you get anything from Interpol on him?"

"Yeah," Hanson replied disconsolately, "that he was probably either en route to the U.S. or already here. I told them we had a positive confirmation on him here. What about the rest of the crew?"

JT continued, "Mohammad Shah was one of the other attendees at last night's soiree. He is another suspected Taliban member of Iranian descent, but we really had no clue where he was before last night. The guy we got the lead on and followed to the warehouse was not in the TIDE database, but of course he is now. But all I could add was his picture, his association with the rest of the crew, and the few details we have on this meeting. We did get an eighty percent hit on a Shufu Ozawa, a suspected member of the Japanese Red Army, which has not been active for many years, and therefore quite suspect, so to speak."

If Hanson caught the pun, he didn't acknowledge it.

"As you know, some of the older pictures are a bit grainy and the FRS will give us a false positive now and then. So the guy that looks like Shufu, and the remaining two, like the guy we followed, now have their pictures and this group meeting entered in the database."

"OK, folks," Hanson said trying to sum up, "what we have here appears to be a nascent terrorist plot to bomb, maybe, or use sarin gas on, a train station, perhaps in the cold weather, which I'm guessing means January through March. I don't need to tell you that as iffy as that is, it's major, certainly given Rasheem's involvement, and it's paramount that we don't let this happen—actually capturing any of these Sticks would be a nice bonus. We've got to follow up on everything, coordinate with everyone that might be able to help, and let absolutely nothing drop through the cracks. I'm going to request increased security at both Union Station and Metro Center as the two most likely targets. So what's left to do here?"

Hanson paused a few moments while he thought about the answer to his own question and then continued. "Phil, follow up with forensics on the warehouse, and if you would also help Juanita and Ronnie check on the vehicles. I'd particularly like to get the cab back on the road as soon as we can, since that's the guy's living, assuming he hasn't skipped town. I'd also like you three to check out the Civic owner's alibi and to see what the cab driver's story is when we do locate him. Do not hang around the bar or raise any undue suspicion. Check on his alibi, make sure they know that's what you are doing, and get in and out. We don't want them to think we intercepted a transmission from there or that we suspect there's anything going on there. See if DC Metro got anything on their canvass of the neighborhoods where the vehicles were stolen—that is, assuming they did one. Brendon, ask the lab boys to go over the UAV feed again and see if there's anything else there that we might have missed. I'd love to get more clarification on what they think was said. And check on the cab driver and the vehicle owners when the ICE database gets back online. Josh, I want you to see if there are any reports of missing sarin gas. Charles and JT and I are going to rendezvous with Charles' guys on the JTTF and see if we have anything to help each other out."

The Joint Terrorism Task Force that Hanson referred to was a collaboration between the FBI and other federal agencies that was charged with taking action against terrorism, and consisted of 100 regional units nationwide. In addition to the FBI employees, the units were made up of members from the Secret Service, the Immigration and Customs Enforcement (ICE) and Transportation Security Administration (TSA) components of DHS, state and local law enforcement groups, and some specialized agencies, such as railroad, airport and harbor police. The FBI obtained written memoranda of understanding between these participating law enforcement agencies and in turn provided funds to pay for their expenses, such as officer overtime, vehicles, gas, and cell phones. The JTTFs were often helpful in providing manpower for surveillance, electronic monitoring, source development and interviews. The Fusion Team drew heavily upon them since they themselves were much smaller, but had a shorter chain of command. The FBI, the "owners" of the JTTFs chaffed at this a bit, but they were usually glad to be in on the action.

Hanson finished up with, "Any questions?"

Since there appeared to be none JT piped up with, "Boss, did you hear what happened over in the Capitol today?"

Hanson shook his head and the others turned toward JT.

"Senator Johnson from Idaho, who, as you know, is quite hot tempered and has an acid tongue, exploded in mid-session on the Senate floor and began to shout, 'Half of this Senate is made up of cowards and corrupt politicians!' All the other Senators naturally demanded that he withdraw his statement or be removed for the remainder of the session. After a long pause, Senator Johnson acquiesced. 'OK,' he said, 'I withdraw what I said. Half of this Senate is NOT made up of cowards and corrupt politicians!'"

After a few groans and one or two chuckles Hanson said, "And with that, ladies and gentlemen, we'll adjourn until tomorrow afternoon: same bat time and same bat channel. Charles and JT, if you two could hang around for a few minutes so we can discuss our visit."

CHAPTER THREE

Arlington, Virginia, 28 October, 1730 hours

"Doctor Quarles, are we through here for now?" his research assistant asked. Tamika Johnson lent credence to the rumor that DARPA hired only beautiful young women as research assistants. Her light, coffee-colored skin complemented her long, raven hair, which she had tied up in a bun—its usual configuration when she was trying to shuffle all the doctor's notes and papers. Research assistant was a euphemism for personal assistant: someone that did most of the scientist's busy work such as keeping his or her calendar, making travel arrangements, putting slide shows together and generally making life easier for them. Tamika was quite smart and thus quite bored, but the decent pay helped and she occasionally got to learn something. Assisting scientists of this caliber looked good on her resume and, as a contractor employed by *TDL Systems*, you never knew when you would need that resume.

"Did you run me a copy of those slides I wanted?" Quarles asked Tamika. He was actually quite nice to her considering his general I-can't-be-bothered attitude, but then she helped him out tremendously. Doctor C. Stefon Quarles cut an imposing figure at six foot two and about fifteen pounds on the heavy side. He had very short and thin, light hair such that he appeared bald at a distance, or even up close for that matter, and his round face made him appear heavier than his actual weight. He was brilliant and certainly deserving of his position at DARPA, but also one of the more eccentric employees in an organization that employed a considerable number of them. Most people were not worth talking to, in his opinion, and that round, full face and the way he looked down at you when he deigned to converse with you, emphasized his egoism. He also tended toward paranoia.

But then, this was not uncommon at DARPA, or the Defense Advanced Research Projects Agency, also known as

ARPA, or the Advanced Research Projects Agency, depending upon what administration occupied the White House and headed up the Department of Defense (DoD), and whether or not they thought the Agency should be engaged in general research in support of the country, or only that in support of the DoD. There are numerous research organizations in each of the services, and in general they are parochial. DARPA/ARPA was usually not so, and it often funded research that was riskier, more basic, and often difficult to link to a specific DoD benefit. It was created in February, 1958, as a reaction to the Russian launching of Sputnik the prior October. The Eisenhower administration decided that the U.S. could not be technologically surprised again and thus ARPA was born. Some, however, argue that its creation was more directly related to an attempt to reign in the various missile development projects of the services.

Nevertheless, its successes over the years have been legion, including the Saturn V rocket that helped put the first man on the moon, the ARPANET, which led to the Internet and the global information revolution, the stealth technology employed on U.S. combat aircraft, advanced body armor and today's thinking machines. Although they didn't usually bring the new idea, process or invention to fruition, they did get it to the point of potential do-ability, which usually enabled others to get funding for the remaining development. This was a direct result of them hiring the best and the brightest scientific and engineering minds in the business. Even though DARPA pioneered a number of personnel practices that enabled them to pay more than the top GS-15 salary, the scientists and engineers often took a considerable pay cut. Then again, they usually had a more-than-adequate project budget, the freedom to work on something that didn't need a likely commercial application, the government contacts that meant so much on the outside, and, of course, big travel budgets. As one clever scientist quipped, "ARPA is just a group of eclectic scientists tied together by a common travel office."

DARPA recruited Quarles in an attempt to get a handle on the currently untraceable financial transactions that were no doubt funding a number of terrorist organizations. Three earlier contracts in that area had made good progress and resulted in the award of a single follow-on contract that had even completed limited beta testing. DARPA actually had no in-house research facilities and used either other government organizations' facilities, or, more often, contracted the work out to industry, universities and think tanks. The agency was in the process of letting a new, more comprehensive contract that would be jointly funded with DHS, and that utilized advances made in the current and earlier contracts. Quarles was actually excited about potentially seeing his ideas come to fruition.

"They're in your briefcase," Tamika replied. "Along with the article by Doctor Okuru on Bayesian quantile stochastics that I downloaded from the *Scientific American* podcast. Don't forget you have a staff meeting with the Director tomorrow at eleven." The Director was Doctor Richard Briceman, head of the Information Exploitation Office. Naturally he was also brilliant, and not a bad manager for a scientist. And managing scientists at DARPA taxed even the best of them. His penchant for weekly staff meetings irritated Quarles, who figured he only called them to show that he was in charge. Actually, Briceman was playing catch up with his charges and attempting to keep the Agency Director informed and thus a little more likely to agree to his budget requests.

"Why don't you just attend for me and take notes? You know nothing ever comes of those things. Besides, I have to work with the guys in contracts tomorrow on my new acquisition."

"Doctor Quarles, you know what Doctor Briceman would say. I can't tell him what you are doing and what he needs to pass on to the front office. You have to be there." She and Quarles had been through this rain dance before, several times in fact and usually with the same result: Tamika didn't attend and Quarles did.

"Alright, alright; I'll be there. Would you update the schedule on the last briefing chart we showed, and include what we got from Jabornae over at NRL yesterday as a potential avenue of research? I'll be in by ten o'clock and we can finalize the charts then. You can head on home now if you want. I'd like to stay here and work on one of my new theories a bit. I'll see you tomorrow."

Tamika tidied up, closed and locked her safe, and called her boyfriend. It was early enough that she could probably talk him into going out for a bite. The charts would only take a half hour or so tomorrow and it was already late. "Good night. See you in the morning," she called as she went out the door.

Quarles retrieved some notes out of his brief case that he had jotted down earlier in the day and had just sat down at his desk to read them when the phone rang. "Listening," he said after he hit the speaker button.

"Doctor Quarles, *you know who* is on his way to see you," Tamika said. "I saw him heading for the elevator when I got off on the first floor and he asked if you were in. I told him that I thought you were just leaving."

"Thanks, Tamika. You do watch out for me." Quarles walked over to his office door and made sure it was locked. He then turned out his lights and sat back down. It wasn't long before he heard footsteps and someone started banging on his door.

"Open up Quarles. I know you're in there," the Assistant Director for Administration called. Mike Styles made Attila the Hun seem like Wally Cox. "I told you last week I needed this big office for an operations and surveillance room for the new security system. I have an office more befitting of your status down on the first floor. If you're not out of here by COB tomorrow, I'll have my troops move your stuff. And you damn well better not have this cipher lock on your door set to a number that's not in the security files, or you'll be paying for a new door."

By this time, two nearby research assistants had made themselves scarce, and the one scientist nearby had closed her door. Styles was of average height but well built—not muscular so much as just in good shape. He fancied himself a real ladies' man and had managed to cultivate an affair in the less than one year that he'd been there. He smiled to himself and thought how funny it was that they sent him here from the Pentagon as punishment for trying to get his job done over there. Back in A&T, the Acquisition and Technology office of DoD, he had little real power and few gofers. Here he had over twenty government employees, almost twice as many contractors, and a substantial budget to play with. These egghead scientists paid little attention to him since they were on the road or in their contractors' facilities most of the time. He just made sure the travel section was well run and he got few complaints.

Quarles said nothing. He was not actually afraid of Styles—not physically anyway—but he did wield significant power in the organization. The Director seemed to place great stock in him, probably because he got things done whatever it took or whomever it inconvenienced, and usually approved his budget requests. On the other hand, the Director had recently denied one of Quarles' budget requests for no seemingly good reason. Quarles was sure he was just being picked on and thought that he damn well would make them break the door down and move his stuff themselves. Besides, he had already cleared out all of the important things—he moved them out little by little in his briefcase so they wouldn't know he was doing it. About all that was left was the furniture. He heard the cipher lock being keyed and the latch turned, but to no avail since he had indeed changed it himself and not given it to anyone, not even Tamika.

"Damn you, Quarles! Remember, close of business tomorrow." Styles really disliked Quarles, mainly because the "IT Guru" threw roadblocks up against every improvement that he and his security guys recommended. *It will always be an uphill battle*, he thought, *with that damn supposed scientist around, since he has nothing but negative comments about the improvements and never any realistic suggestions for making them better*. Styles complained that Quarles was always off in some never-never land and did not come up with enough good ideas to justify his high salary. He figured that putting the egotistical twit in a small office on the busy first floor and degrading him in front of the rest of the staff by forcing him to move should have him considering leaving the Agency before long. That would be a sweet victory.

Quarles waited another hour before deciding to put the lights back on. The time was not wasted, since he mulled over some new mathematical approaches to his latest problem. By the time he got most of these new ideas on paper it was almost half past seven so he figured he'd just go home and deal with Styles tomorrow. *Maybe I should leave, since they don't seem to appreciate me here anyway.* But then he was unlikely to get the same kind of funding for his research anywhere else in the government, and most certainly not outside the government. *There are other research organizations however; I've worked a lot with the Naval Research Lab. But they probably wouldn't give me more than a GS-15 there, as opposed to the Senior Executive Service position I have here. Or maybe the FBI or CIA. They pay better and would most likely be interested in what I am trying to accomplish. Perhaps I should talk to some of the larger defense contractors. A few of them might be interested and I've already made some good contacts with SAIC, HP and DATEL, although I'm not really all that crazy about going back to HP. But, yes, I will definitely pursue these possibilities.*

DARPA occupied a ten story marble and glass high rise in the Virginia Square section of Arlington. The Office of Naval Research had a large office building nearby, and the Army Research Office and the Air Force Office of Scientific Research both had satellite offices in the vicinity. It was also only two short metro train rides away from Washington National Airport. *All in all not a bad place to work,* mused Quarles as he left his office, being careful to avoid the public areas. He took the stairs all the way down to the third parking level and was relieved to see it was deserted—a few cars but no people. He got into his Saturn and put a Vivaldi CD in the player. His home in Chantilly was about thirty-five minutes away this time of night and that would allow him to enjoy most of *The Four Seasons*. He slowed at the exit gate at the upper garage level for the sensor to detect his car and open the door.

He turned right onto North Fairfax Drive and headed up toward Route 66. As he took the ramp to head west bound he remembered some lyrics from an old rock and roll song: "You can get your kicks on Route 66." And of course there was the TV program with Martin Milner and George Maharis. He thought it was funny that he'd remember that today, considering that he drove this route several times a week. His thoughts then turned to his recent project and how he was having trouble integrating several subroutines. One of his AFOSR cohorts had some thoughts on the subject and he'd decided to call him tomorrow. He knew that he would have to begin thinking of a viable commercial application for his financial software if he wanted to make any real money, however, and then sell the idea to one of the Fortune 500 companies. *Wow, I sure am a creature of habit: already on Route 50 and crossing into Loudoun County.* His Poland Road turnoff loomed only a short distance ahead. *Seems as though I just left Arlington.*

South Riding, Virginia, 28 October, 2010 hours

Quarles decided, as was often his wont, to go a little further up the road to South Riding and stop at the *Starbucks* for a large vanilla decaf coffee for himself and a mocha latte for Martha. He thought about how lucky he was to find Martha and how his home provided such a wonderful respite from the idiots at work. His usual parking spot, in the third and last row near the end, was vacant, although a Ford Taurus was parked two spots over. He always parked away from wherever he was going figuring the extra walking did him good. *Lord knows I get little enough exercise as it is.* As he approached the store, the barista saw him coming and started to prepare the same two drinks he made for him every time he came there. Some routines are good. After paying for the drinks, Quarles, with one in each hand, pushed the door open with his back side and proceeded to his car. As he set the drinks on the roof of his car and reached for his keys, there was a loud explosion and the drinks, Dr. Quarles, and pieces of his car and the Taurus next to him went everywhere.

The two cars were on fire and pieces of automobile were spread in an odd pattern up to fifty feet away. A small brush fire had started in the grass median but appeared to be burning itself out. Luckily, no one else was hurt as nothing made it as far as the store fronts, and only a few scattered cars were hit, causing some dents and broken windows. People came running out of the stores but didn't approach the cars because of the smoke and heat. Someone had called the Loudoun County Emergency Rescue Services, which were only a few blocks away, and their sirens could already be heard.

"Rescue One, this is a bad one but we're only gonna need one wagon. There's only one victim here. I'm afraid he's a mess though." Senior Fireman Paulson relayed the rest of the situation to the station and then went over to watch his guys finish foaming the vehicles.

By this time, two sheriff's deputies had arrived and set up perimeter control. They started taking statements from the bystanders but nobody had seen anything—they just heard the explosion and then looked and saw the smoke and flames. The man from Starbucks said he knew the victim's name was Stefon and that he was a local but that was it.

The Accident Reconstruction Unit, which has the sole responsibility of responding to and investigating accidents that involve serious injury or death, was just starting to arrive, having been called by one of the deputies. The deputy reported to the ARU team leader who then took one look at the scene and got on the phone immediately to the ATF. He made sure that a sufficient perimeter was cordoned off to encompass all the debris from the explosion.

After a quick and easy determination that the victim was dead, the EMTs covered him with a tarp.

Sergeant Jones, the lead ARU, had worked with the ATF before and knew the drill: this was going to be a long night. It would probably be another sixty to ninety minutes before all the feds got here, and then they'd take a couple of hours getting pictures, making diagrams and gathering whatever evidence they could find. They'd take charge of the body and the cars and the County would be out of it. The two sheriff's deputies had gotten nothing on their canvass other than Quarles' first name and the fact that he was in Starbucks, and had found neither hide nor hair of the second vehicle owner or any other potential passengers. They ran the plates of the two vehicles, and they came back to Quarles, who lived nearby, and a Marvin Lester in Vienna. The deputies hung around to provide perimeter control but the EMTs went back to the station house. They'd get a call back when the ATF was done if they didn't provide their own transportation.

About thirty minutes after the ARU made the call, the ATF supervisor arrived. After being briefed and surveying the situation, he praised the work done by the county guys. The ARU had not only cordoned off a sufficient area for debris recovery, but had also erected some lights and the deputies had managed to clear a good portion of the parking lot for the feds to park and work in.

The rest of the ATF guys came in over the next half hour and started taking pictures, measurements and samples. When they were through with the body, they got the victim's wallet and verified his identity. One of the deputies copied down the information and got permission from the watch commander to make notification to the next of kin who lived just two miles away. The ATF supervisor handed the deputy his card and asked if he would call him with the contact information on the next of kin. He said to tell them that he would be in touch with them regarding identification of the remains and final release of the body, and they could call him if they had any questions before then.

The ATF called one of their own vehicles to transport the body and two of their contract wreckers to get the vehicles to their impoundment lot. The wrecker drivers and the ATF team did a good job of gathering up all the marked debris and loading it onto the two wreckers. They scene was fully documented by two-thirty in the morning, and the body was on the way to the morgue and the two cars to an ATF impoundment lot. The ARU broke down the lights, wrapped up the crime scene tape, and began cleaning up what little debris remained. When they were done, only scorch marks on the pavement and some burned patches of grass testified as to what happened there.

CHAPTER FOUR

How in Jahannam did our problem get taken care of? The prime cell disclaims all knowledge, and certainly if one of the other cells had even thought of this, I would have known. Who, then, is working for our side? Perhaps this was just a fortuitous circumstance, although one can hardly call murder that— certainly not from the victim's viewpoint. The manner of death does not suggest a personal grudge, but rather someone, or some organization, sending a message. But I should not waste time on this. And now we will not have to divert resources and can once again concentrate on our prime objective. I shall find out when the next meeting is and we can begin again in earnest.

Fusion Team Headquarters, 31 October, 1530 hours

"So, troops, what did we find out so far?" Hanson began.

JT was the first to speak: "Cap'n, before we start, do you remember that idiot defense lawyer that we had to testify for in the Williams case last year? What was his name, Forsythe?"

Hanson nodded as he remembered him well; he was one of the biggest pricks in a profession full of them.

"I heard he was grilling Doctor Hastings, the chief coroner, over in Fairfax during a murder trial, and it went something like this:

"Dr. Hastings, before you signed the death certificate, did you take the pulse of the deceased?"

"No, Counselor. I did not."

"Did you listen to his heart?"

"No."

"Did you check his respiration?"

"No."

"So, Doctor, when you signed the death certificate, you weren't really sure that the man was dead, were you?"

"Well, let me put it this way, Counselor. The man's brain was sitting in a jar on my desk. But I guess it's possible he could be out there practicing law somewhere."

Hanson and the team members could certainly imagine the supposed encounter and couldn't help but laugh at JT's latest attempt at levity.

Phil offered, "Well, Captain, I'll start with the warehouse findings. S&S Enterprises comes back clean. It's American owned and operated. The three owners have no records, and only two of the employees have some minor beefs, one for possession and one for domestic battery. One of the employees has relatives in Afghanistan and another in India. The former is here on a work visa and the Indian-American is a native-born citizen. These are not the employees with the records. There is no apparent company connection to any of our Sticks or any terrorist interests. They don't even sell to any country of interest. It looks a lot like a random choice for a group meeting."

"Thanks, Phil. Did we find anything of interest in the place?"

"No, Sir. Nothing that didn't belong there or even looked out of place, according to the manager, except for the busted door. There was nothing left behind as far as we could tell, and from the UAV feed, we could see they were all wearing gloves, so we didn't even bother to dust. The manager did mention that the alarm either was not activated when they left for the day at five-thirty, or was somehow deactivated before the terrorists entered. It's not too sophisticated a system so there are no time stamps or other help. Looks like a dead end, but we will follow up on the Afghani."

Ronnie started in next with a follow-up on the vehicle owners. "All three owners check out with no records and they are not in any of our databases, including the ICE data base which came back up this morning. The cab owner has a family alibi, the SUV owner has no alibi, and we did get a confirmation on the Civic owner's alibi at the bar. We went by there this morning, found a couple of employees stocking and setting up for tonight, and they recognized him from the picture and said he's a semi-regular. The Civic and Tahoe owners are born and bred

Americans, with no apparent overseas connections, let alone any terrorist ones. We are going to talk to the Tahoe owner again and see if we can get a feeling on whether or not he was really home. The cab owner called us early this morning and said his brother finally called him and mentioned that he 'had apparently misplaced' the car. He said his brother told him he had spent most of the night and the next day looking for it, trying to save face and avoid the embarrassment of reporting the cab stolen. We got a picture of the cabbie from the owner and checked it against the hack license issued by DC. The guy is not in any of our databases and has a clean record. We released the vehicle this morning and he came by the impound lot to pick it up early this afternoon. When we asked him about his whereabouts on the 26th, he said he was with some friends. We'll visit his friends this evening, but this really seems like the last loose end here."

"Thanks, Ronnie. Keep us apprised of any developments. Juanita, do we have anything further on the vehicles or their locations?"

"Captain, when Ronnie and I talked to the cabbie, he really was scared and embarrassed. He parked the cab only a few blocks from the warehouse, near his friends' house, and said he didn't realize that it wasn't there until the next morning. Looks like he lied to his brother about searching for it all night, but I don't think he wants his brother to know where he was all night. As Ronnie said, we'll check out his friends tonight. Captain, I think it's like we decided yesterday—all the vehicles were targets of opportunity that were in the vicinity. Forensics says the cab was broken into with a Slim Jim and hotwired, but they are still going over the SUV and the Civic. They say they can find no signs of forced entry, but they are not ruling that out as of yet. They have no prints of interest so far, either. Oh yeah, DC Metro said they didn't find anyone that saw anything when the vehicles were being lifted."

"Thanks, Juanita. Josh, do you have anything?"

"Yeah, Boss. I checked on sarin gas with my guys back at ATF. That's not something that stockpiles very easily. Sarin has a relatively short shelf life and will degrade after a period of several weeks to several months. The shelf life may be greatly shortened by impurities in what they call precursor materials, or it can also be lengthened by chemical additions. They think it very unlikely that these guys have any because it's not easy to make. Further, there have been no reported thefts or unusual purchases of the component materials. They said they'd look into it more and get back to us."

"Okay, Josh. Thanks. Charles, JT and I met with the Joint Terrorist Task Force guys and ran them through everything we had. They say that this scenario may actually be fairly common—picking a neutral place for a meeting and stealing cars to get there—but they also mentioned that they are interested in how the cars were stolen and the alarm systems apparently compromised, at least in two of the cases. They are concerned that this might be indicative of a stolen car ring, and that perhaps terrorists are using this method to finance some of their operations. We'll be looking further into that. Believe it or not, this scenario is apparently something they hadn't shared with us or the NCTC folks. On another matter, we just got word that there has been a minor car explosion that we need to investigate, so we'll have to split up the team to cover it and keep the Train Station Plot on track, so to speak."

The Team groaned at the pun and then several of them chimed in at the same time, "An explosion?"

"It's probably nothing," Hanson replied, "but the victim, Dr. C. Stefon Quarles, is—was—a DARPA scientist who was working on a highly sophisticated artificial intelligence program that promises significant inroads into the tracking of terrorist financial transactions. Since NSA thinks that his name and program codeword were mentioned within the last week in intercepts of suspected terrorist transmissions, and since his death involved an IED, we've been asked to take a look at it. I have assigned JT and Juanita to this investigation. Juanita, I want you to keep JT straight. I'll take over temporary leadership of Alpha Unit and we'll stay with the train station gig."

"When do we start Cap'n?" asked JT.

"You and Juanita will meet with a Sergeant Richard Gregg of the Loudoun County Sheriff's Office tomorrow morning at nine," he replied. "JT, keep me informed on your investigation and see if you can give me an idea how long you and Juanita will be tied up on this and whether or not you'll be able to continue to help out here. We may have to rely more on the JTTF folks if you'll be working this for a while."

JT then asked the Captain if he had anything else on the explosion, and, upon finding out he didn't, decided to see what he could learn about the DARPA scientist and his program online. Not five minutes into his research his cell phone rang. It was a video from one of his buddies in Baker Unit. After watching it JT started laughing and that attracted Hanson's attention.

"What's so funny, JT?"

"Boss, look at this video from Scotty Westfield over in Baker." JT played it again.

After watching for a few moments Hanson asked incredulously, "Is she kissing his...? Oh my god he farted. And look at her face. Oh, she is *unhappy* with him." The last scene was the guy laughing like hell while trying to run and pull his pants up at the same time while a semi-naked lady was pounding on him with her fists. Hanson was laughing as hard as the guy in the video. "You gotta send that to Charlie," he said.

"The Assistant Secretary?" JT asked with raised eyebrows.

"Yeah. You know, he's an okay guy. He'll get a kick out of it. Let me get you his private cell phone number." Hanson went back to his desk and came back with a piece of paper with a phone number written on it. "Took me a couple of minutes to find it but here it is."

JT forwarded the video. About five minutes later, JT's phone rang. His caller ID showed it as the number he just sent the video to. He answered and then heard a young girl say, "Did you just send me a dirty video?"

"Oh my gosh!" exclaimed JT. "I must have dialed the wrong number. I apologize. I'm really sorry, miss. Please erase it. Again, I'm really sorry." JT hung up and headed toward Hanson's desk. "Boss, you must have given me a wrong number. I sent that video to some little girl!"

Hanson checked it and it was the number he had for Charlie Moffet. Just then JT's phone rang and it was from the same number. He answered and Hanson could tell he wasn't happy with what he was hearing.

"Who is this?" the voice on the phone asked.

"This is special agent JT Dunkirk with DHS—"

Before he could say another word the voice boomed, "This is Charlie Moffet and you just sent a pornographic video to my ten-year-old. I'm heading out the door to catch a plane but I'll deal with you later, Agent Dunkirk."

JT heard the line go dead and then plopped down in one of Hanson's chairs. "I'm dead meat," he told Hanson as he relayed the brief conversation.

"He's really not a bad guy, JT. He must have given his cell phone to his daughter. Her name is Miranda, if I remember right. I'm sure he'll understand."

JT shook his head in disbelief and disconsolately went back to his desk. After thirty minutes or so of checking on Dr. Quarles he noticed most of the team laughing and discussing something with Hanson.

He walked over and asked "So what's up, guys?"

In a high-pitched voice, Ronnie asked, "Did you just send me a dirty video?"

The light bulb went on and JT turned to Hanson. "You son of a bitch. You set me up." He started laughing, as did Hanson and the three onlookers. "So who was that on the phone?"

"Charlie's executive assistant. You didn't recognize her voice?"

They all laughed even more.

"We thought a half hour was enough suffering for you."

JT, still laughing, looked around for Juanita but saw that she was heading out the door, probably so she wouldn't have to listen to another one of his jokes or help him plot revenge on the team. So he went back to his online searching by himself. He didn't stay too long however, as he had to get home to take Andy trick or treating. Andy had picked out a Power Rangers costume and he seemed to have extra oomph whenever he wore it. Kids are a stitch. Not to mention some of the folks he worked with.

While driving home, JT wondered what kind of revenge he could exact upon his cohorts in crime. Then he remembered how a practical joke he played on one of his coworkers in the police department came close to having a tragic ending. One afternoon, before the start of his shift, he tied a thread around a hairy, rubber spider with legs that dangled when you shook it. It was about the size of his fist and he bought in a joke shop weeks earlier and had been waiting for an occasion to use it. He ran the thread through a paperclip he stuck in the foam ceiling tile directly over the unsuspecting young lady's desk. The thread then went clear across the ceiling to the other side of this huge room that had a dozen desks and probably thirty file cabinets in it. At that point, it went into another paperclip and then down to a file cabinet drawer handle where it was tied. When the clerk got back from lunch, JT casually walked over to the file cabinet and untied the thread. He started letting the spider, which had been pulled up to the ceiling, down slowly. When it got to just above her eye level he stopped. She was typing merrily along and didn't notice a thing. So he let it down a tad more and jiggled it a bit so the spider's legs started dancing. At that point she took notice, screamed, and fell over backwards in her chair. JT was mortified.

He ran over to help her up and noticed that her head had missed by mere inches hitting an open metal drawer behind her. Now he was horrified. He naturally apologized, several times. He couldn't believe what a good sport she was about the whole thing. But he never played another practical joke on anybody again—at least not a physical one. *Perhaps I should just roll with the punches,* JT thought. *Verbal jokes, puns and stories are okay, but no physical jokes that might backfire. But I should extract some retribution--just nothing dangerous.*

CHAPTER FIVE

Springfield, Virginia, 1 November, 0705 hours

"Come on, Little Buddy, let's get a move on—get those shoes on," JT called out to his son. Five-year-old Andy attended the *MinnieLand Day Care and After-School Center* during the days his dad was working. On most days, JT went into work later and therefore got to drop Andy off at school. In the afternoons, Ms. Carmen would usually pick him up. JT lived in a medium-sized four bedroom, two-and-a-half bath split level in the Daventry area of Springfield. He and his wife Sara bought the place when she was six-months pregnant with Andy but still managed to completely outfit the nursery before he was born. JT still had bitter memories of a year and a half ago when she was killed by a drunk hit-and-run driver. *In the middle of the frickin' afternoon,* he thought. They caught the guy right away as his get-away was not exactly a smooth move, but the trial dragged on for six months and the guy got off with vehicular manslaughter—a four year sentence with loss of driving privileges for ten years and a $25,000 fine. He was a doctor with no prior convictions and will probably be out on probation in a year or less. He paid for a new car and all the funeral expenses for what that was worth. He did also set up a $50,000 scholarship fund for Andy that JT did not want to accept but was talked into by his friends. Naturally, JT had not yet recovered emotionally from all of this, nor did he think he ever would—not completely anyway. But the days were getting a little easier, and the job and little Andy kept him pretty busy. And JT's siblings and his mom and dad were a huge help, as well.

Things worked out well when he found Carmen, an absolute jewel. In her early fifties, she stood five foot two, was just a tad overweight, and had dark brown eyes and long, ebony hair that she wore in two braids. Her younger sister was Maria Reynolds, the wife of one of the sergeants JT worked for when he was with the Fairfax County Police Department. Carmen had lost all of her family in a flood in their native Panama, except for Maria, who had already moved to the U.S. After Sara died, Sergeant Dan, as JT still called him, suggested that he could bring Carmen to the states if JT would hire her as a live-in housekeeper. JT agreed. Thus Carmen was here on a work visa and proceeding toward her citizenship. Of course, Sergeant Dan would have brought her here anyway, and JT knew that, but it seemed to Carmen to be a godsend. She felt very lucky since she loved Andy and he had become quite attached to her, and she now lived close to her sister. Carmen and JT were really good for each other under the circumstances and had formed a strong bond of friendship. JT kidded Sergeant Dan about how he owed him big time for keeping Carmen out of his house, and Sergeant Dan reciprocated with the fact that JT owed him for all the after school day care, rent-a-maid, and other domestic services costs that Carmen's meager salary didn't come close to being a proper compensation for.

"OK, Andy, here's your lunch box. Are you going to eat all your lunch today? Miss Judy says sometimes you give away your sandwich. I thought you liked peanut butter and jelly."

"I do, Daddy, but sometimes the peanut butter sticks to my mouth and makes me cough."

"OK, but if you drink your apple juice that will help." JT helped Andy with his coat and they went out front to get in the car after saying goodbye to Carmen. JT let Andy fasten himself in the car seat, then checked it. "You all ready to go?"

"Yes. Is Ms. Carmen or Nanny going to pick me up today?"

"This isn't Wednesday, so Nanny won't pick you up today. Ms. Carmen probably will, but if she doesn't, I will." JT's mom and dad usually picked up Andy on Wednesdays and often kept him over night. "So, let's roll Little Buddy." JT pulled out and headed to *MinnieLand* a few miles away.

After dropping Andy off, he headed up Backlick Road to Annandale to pick up Juanita. Juanita moved there after her transfer from the Air Force Office of Special Investigations, which is located on Bolling Air Force Base in Southwest Washington, right on the Potomac River. Actually, she had spent most of her time working out of Andrews Air Force Base over in Prince Georges County, Maryland. And both Bolling and Andrews are on the east side of the Woodrow Wilson Memorial Bridge, often a major bottleneck in the local traffic patterns. On this side of the river she wasn't that far from Fort Belvoir or Arlington, and didn't have to cross that bridge.

A few minutes after eight, JT pulled up to the apartment Juanita was renting in the Kenwood section of Annandale, just north of Little River Turnpike. Sitting on her couch by the front window, she saw him pull up. She waved, grabbed her coat and backpack and locked up. "Hey," she said as she jumps in the car, "you are a little early, *amigo*. Good thing I was ready, huh?"

JT was a little surprised by her perky attitude—pleasantly, of course—so he bantered right back. "I thought you were gonna move down closer to Belvoir, *amiga*."

"I will. As soon as I find something that's affordable and decent that isn't located right on Route 1, okay? I could move in with you, you know. We could split the rent—excuse me, house payment. Then you wouldn't have to support that housekeeper. Besides, she's too old for you, anyway."

"Yeah, you wish. So how've you been anyway?"

Juanita's mom, Bonita Montoyas, had immigrated to the U.S. from Mexico in the early 50s looking for work. Her dad, Major Michael Singletary, met Bonita when she was waiting tables in Del Rio, Texas, and he was assigned to Laughlin Air Force Base as an instructor pilot. Juanita apparently inherited the best of both worlds, including looks, physical ability, quick wit, empathy and brains, and an almost insatiable curiosity. That's partially what drove her into the criminal investigations field, and with some influence on her dad's part, the Air Force. She and JT had worked a case together back when he was with the FCPD and she was still with OSI. She and Sara had hit it off together and Juanita and her boyfriend had stayed in touch with JT and Sara up until Sara's death. She broke up with her boyfriend just after that and thought it was best not to have two recently broken hearts too close together, so she kept their relationship strictly professional. "Hey, I'm doing all right—kind of getting back into the swing of things. You know I started dating again, off and on. How is little Andy doing?"

"He's a real trip, Nita. He keeps me focused and the thought of him helps me make it through the day." JT paused, like there was something more he wanted to say, so Juanita kept quiet and just stared out the window. "I'm sorry we haven't talked much these last two months that you've been with the Team," JT began again, "but, honestly, you brought back some memories. It's been a little hard with you on the team. I'm sorry if I seemed a little stiff."

"Hey, it's okay. I understand, *amigo*. I was keeping my distance too for the same reason. By the way, I'm sorry I skipped out on you last night, but I had something I had to take care of. Are we going to be able to work this together? I mean, it's a little late now, but I know the boss would understand if you wanted someone else on this with you."

"No, no. We'll be fine. It's nice to have a female friend I can talk to again." After he said that JT thought that it might have sounded a little too presumptuous, so he added, "I mean if that's all right. I don't want to come on too strong or nothing like that."

"That's okay, I'm cool with that. So what do you think about this whole thing?" she asked, bringing the conversation back to work.

"Well, I'll tell ya, I just don't see this as a terrorist action. I think it's a little too sophisticated for them—like they had a complete makeover or something. Sort of like when the Mafia got accountants and lawyers and attempted to legitimize their businesses. That just doesn't happen overnight and we've had no indication of anything like that in anything we've learned about them so far. Doesn't mean it couldn't happen, though."

By now JT had reached the Capital Beltway and was making surprisingly good time up towards Route 66. His Toyota Highlander was fairly comfortable and he had some contemporary jazz coming in on the XM Water Colors station, so the trip was actually relaxing. He also owned a Chevy Aveo sedan that he let Carmen use, as he preferred the larger car and, besides, he got reimbursed for mileage. Juanita was collecting her thoughts and putting together a list of questions for the Sheriff's guys. They reached Route 50 in short order since they were going against traffic once they left the Beltway. Just a couple of miles past the county line, they turned south on the Loudoun County Parkway and pulled up at the South Riding Substation of the Loudoun County Fire Rescue System and Sheriff's Office. They were ten minutes early so JT reviewed Juanita's list of questions.

"Okay, *amigo*?" Juanita asked.

"Couldn't have done it better myself," JT complimented as they proceeded into the building.

South Riding, Virginia, 1 November, 0900 hours

The Dulles South Public Safety Center took up 22,000 square feet and was located on a 4.7 acre site adjacent to the Loudoun County Parkway. It served as a combined fire, rescue and law enforcement station. The outside looked fairly modern with a single-story red brick bottom and a white wooden raised roof. The Sherriff's Office was on one side and the Fire & Rescue Station on the other. JT and Juanita entered through the center connecting portion that seemed to be mostly windows and a glass door. Juanita went up to the receptionist and told her who they were and that they were here to see Sergeant Gregg.

"Through the glass doors and then the third door on the right," she said and pointed down the hallway that was off to the right. She buzzed open the glass doors. "He's expecting you."

Sergeant Gregg saw them coming through his window and waved them in. He got up and, as he was introducing himself, motioned them towards three seats located on one side of his office. The chairs were situated around a low coffee table on which some police journals and other professional literature were neatly stacked. Although not overly spacious, the office did have a comfortable atmosphere for a police station.

After introducing Juanita and himself, JT took his seat and said, "This is a pretty nice building."

Gregg had the right physique for a policeman—he tipped the scales at 285, with very little of that coming from fat, and spread that out over a six- foot-seven frame. His square, strong, high-boned face and short, sandy brown hair provided him with a noble bearing befitting his Norse ancestors. "It's only a few years old," he remarked. "As you no doubt noticed, we are collocated with Fire & Rescue Station 19. We have about 12,000 square feet and they have a little less I think. Besides Second Lieutenant Brinkman, who's the supervisor here, and his deputy, me, and an assistant, we have a crime analyst and six field deputies. In addition to offices we have deputy work stations, a roll call/meeting room, interview rooms, processing areas and holding cells, and evidence and equipment storage areas. We share the exercise facility with the fire house. The way this area is mushrooming, however, we really need to expand. They are already talking about putting us in another new building going up on the Parkway north of Route 50."

"I'm not surprised," said JT. "This area has really grown the last few years. People getting away from the city, I guess."

"DC or Fairfax County?" the Sergeant asked.

"Yes," JT responded. There was a lull in the conversation, so JT decided to jump right in. "What did Captain Hanson tell you about our purpose in coming here?"

"Actually, not a lot. Said there was interest in the deceased from a Federal perspective, and that you'd fill me in on the details. While he didn't say much, I did get the distinct impression that between you guys and the ATF, we wouldn't be much involved with the case. Don't get me wrong, he was very professional—just mentioned possible ATF and FBI assistance if we needed it."

"Sounds like you already have the ATF assistance. How about if you go first and tell us what you have found out so far, and then we'll go from there."

The Sergeant handed JT a copy of the Accident Reconstruction Unit report and then began, "Well, there were no witnesses that we could find: just a dozen or so people who heard an explosion and then saw two cars smoking or on fire. The ATF guys believe this was intentional, that is, a murder, and said it looked like an improvised explosive device. They think that explosives were planted in the Taurus, which belongs to a Tom and Janice Folsom who live over in Vienna and who reported it stolen on the morning of October 24 when they got up. The car had a tag from a similar Taurus registered to a Marvin Lester, who lives in the same neighborhood, believe it or not, and who didn't realize he was missing his front tag until we pointed it out to him. I can see why you guys are interested. This certainly seems premeditated: they steal a car and replace the rear tag with a front tag from another similar car to give them a few days to make sure the good doctor has time to visit his local watering hole."

"Wow, that's some scenario," Juanita said. "How about just some accidental explosion or a case of mistaken identity?" she offered.

"Possibility, I suppose. But, given the evidence, I'd say an unlikely one. Not with the tag switching, and even more so the couple of days lag. These people appeared to know what they were doing, so I'm betting it went as they planned."

"Yeah, I guess you're right. Did you or the ATF guys get anything from the accident scene or the Taurus itself that might help us?"

"I don't know. They haven't gotten back to us yet."

"What do you think became of the driver? I mean, I'm guessing this was a remotely detonated explosion, so did anybody see any suspicious looking characters drive away from the scene?"

"We're pretty sure he was in another car, say 150 feet away or so, and just left in all the commotion without being noticed."

"Did you run the owners of the Taurus, the Folsoms I believe you said, and the guy whose tags were stolen, Lester?" JT asked.

"Yes. And we got nothing. Both clean as a whistle."

"How about their ethnicity?"

"All WASPs far as we can tell."

Juanita made a mental note to ask JT what a WASP was. Checking her list, she asked if there was anything unusual about the Saturn or the Taurus, other than them being blown up. Upon getting a negative, she gave Sergeant Gregg a brief rundown on what they knew. "Well, Sarge, if you can give us the contact info on the ATF guys, then we'll be on our way. Is there anything we can do for you on this, besides keeping you apprised?"

"No. For the time being, we're just going to list this as an explosion of an IED resulting in the death of a DARPA scientist. You guys and the ATF have the details that could lead to solving it. I did ask Fairfax County if they'd canvass the neighborhoods where the Taurus was stolen and the other Taurus' tag was lifted to see if anybody noticed anything unusual, and they told us to have at it. I sent some officers over there yesterday and I'll let you know if anything turns up there. I really would like to know how it all works out if you guys could keep us informed. And if there's anything else we can do for you, please don't hesitate to ask. We don't get cases like this out here very often. Well, hardly ever."

"Say, Sarge, I gotta mention what happened to a friend of mine who was speeding out here on Route 50 last week."

Gregg looked a little dismayed, as he figured this was going to be a request for a ticket fixing or an officer complaint.

"Well, admittedly, he was feeling secure in a gaggle of cars all traveling at the same speed when he passed your speed trap, got nailed by one of your guys with an infrared speed detector, and was pulled over. The officer handed him the citation, got him to sign it and was about to walk away when my friend asked, 'Officer, I know I was speeding, but I don't think it's fair—there were plenty of other cars around me who were going just as fast, so why did I get the ticket?' 'Ever go a fishin'?' the policeman suddenly asked the man. 'Ummm, yeah,' the startled man replied. The officer grinned and added, 'Did you ever catch 'em all?'"

Sergeant Gregg groaned like he had heard that joke or something similar a thousand times, then handed them the ATF contact information.

JT and Juanita said goodbye and thanks, and headed for the door. On the way out, Juanita asked where he got all those awful jokes.

"Online," he replied.

"Figures," she said. "And what is a WASP?"

"Stands for White, Anglo-Saxon, Protestant," JT replied.

"Oh. I noticed we passed a *Dunkin' Donuts* back on Route 50. How about we stop for a coffee and decide where to go from here."

"Sounds like a plan to me." JT drove back towards the beltway and a few minutes later pulled into the shopping center with the *Dunkin' Donuts*. He actually got a parking spot right in front of the place. He ordered a large hazelnut iced coffee with cream only and Juanita ordered a small Dunkaccino.

"So tell me," Juanita said as they settled into one of the small round tables in the place, "What did you find out last night when you reviewed DARPA and their recently deceased scientist?"

"What makes you think I did that?"

Juanita gave him a look that said "Gimme a break, campadre" and he just laughed.

"The doc was brilliant," JT began. "He made the *Who's Who in the Scientific World* list when he was a graduate student. Graduated from the California Institute of Technology magna cum laude in information technology. While he was at MIT working on an advance degree, he published several papers that were heralded as major breakthroughs in stochastic data mining, whatever that is, and was offered a job with Hewlett Packard before he finished his doctorate. He took them up on this and after two years there and a few more papers, he was hired by DARPA. MIT actually awarded him his doctorate by considering one of his published papers as his dissertation and waived the requirement for an oral presentation. Somewhere along the way, he apparently found somebody that thought enough like him to want to marry him, and they lived happily ever after until a couple of days ago."

"Or maybe she was completely the opposite of him. And what about her—anybody talk to her yet other than the notification?"

"No. We need to do that," JT lamented. "But I'd like to wait at least until the guy's in the ground before we do that, if we can. I'm thinking we need a trip to DARPA to talk to his coworkers and bosses and get any other leads we can. Then we check into his finances, lifestyle, the usual. You want to get that ball rolling? I'll call the ATF forensics guys when we get back and see what they have on the cars."

"Yeah, I'll take care of that now," she said as she punched a number into her cell phone. When finished she continued, "Do you want to head over to DARPA now, or do we need to set up an appointment or something, you know, get clearances passed or whatever?"

"I don't know," said JT. "Let's head on over there and find out." They downed the remainder of their drinks and headed out to JT's Toyota. In the car JT asked, "So, what happened between you and old what's-his-face?"

"You mean Alex? You know, he was a lot of fun at first. You remember all the fun things we did together. But then when I got a little serious about my studies, he couldn't settle down with that. He still wanted to go out every night and live it up. Then I noticed how much he—well, both of us—were drinking. So I told him we needed to slack off a bit and get serious with our lives. And I'll give him credit, I think he tried. But you remember that old country song line, 'You ain't much fun since I quit drinking?' Well, that's kind of where we were. I even mentioned one time that I thought you and Sara had a really nice life together, and he jumped all over me saying he wasn't ready to settle down with kids and a mortgage and that was that."

"So you're blaming it on me, huh?"

"Hey, what are partners for?

"I'm sorry it didn't work out, but it sounds like it might be for the better. And you're not really dating now, are you?"

"Who has time for that? They keep us hopping on this job and I'm working on my masters and my thesis. That reminds me. Think I could talk to your dad about my thesis? He's with the Citizens' Advisory Council for the Fairfax County Police Department, isn't he? I mean, that and the four or five degrees that he has kinda makes me think that he might be a good resource for my thesis."

"Which is?"

"The effect of citizen involvement in local terrorist awareness programs."

"Nita, you know he'd love to help you. And it sounds like it's right up his alley. He was going to write a book on the Federal Air Marshall Service until I quit and then he lost interest. I think his heart wasn't really in it, because now he's writing a murder mystery."

"Oh, cool. Are we in it?"

"In one fashion or another, I'm sure we will be. I'll mention it to him."

By this time, they were in the Ballston section of Arlington and approaching DARPA.

CHAPTER SIX

Arlington, Virginia, 1 November, 1130 hours

JT thought: *So this is where one of the premier think tanks in the world is housed?* DARPA: a ten story, beige, faux-marble and black glass building on North Fairfax Drive, with tiered stories that made it look like a giant monolith with a black mask hiding part of its face with its stone hands. Even so, it looked like a lot of other buildings in the vicinity, and the fierce visage notwithstanding, the only thing that distinguished it from the others up and down the street was the Arlington County Police Department car sitting along the empty curb on the east side of the building. Well, that and the three armed guards stationed at various entrances around the building. JT couldn't help himself, so he pulled up right out front, parked, and took his time getting out. The uniformed officer drove up right behind him, walked up and said he couldn't park there, so would he please move his vehicle. JT badged him and said he and his partner would be interviewing a few folks inside on national security business and could he please keep an eye on his car for him. Somewhat chagrined, the officer turned around and went back to his car.

"So, you think that they want everybody to know that there is something special in this building?" JT mused. "Hell, the DIA occupies an entire building just down the street in Clarendon and you wouldn't know that unless someone told you. And people only have rumors that the CIA has a couple of buildings a little further down in Rosslyn."

"I'll bet we have fun trying to get through security," said Juanita.

JT walked through a glass door labeled "DARPA Visitor Control Center" and asked to talk to the man in charge. It was actually a small room with a mid-chest-high counter running most of the length of the room. There were two rooms of indeterminate size, each located through a door on either side of the main room. On the other side of the counter were stools where several personnel sat monitoring computer or other video screens. Shortly, a man with a friendly smile and even friendlier demeanor approached them.

"I'm Lou Callas," he said, "How can I help you?"

"Hi! I'm JT Dunkirk and this is Juanita Singletary from DHS and we're here to see the Director."

"Yes, Sir. He's been expecting you."

Juanita glared at JT as if to say "you rotten dog."

"If I can just get you to sign in here, we'll have your visitor badges for you momentarily," Callas said. "These will allow you unescorted access throughout the building. I would ask you to return them on the way out and, if you like, we'll keep them for any return visits that you might be planning on." After just a few minutes, they had two badges, with pictures, printed out and laminated.

"When did you get the pictures, just now?"

Lou nodded and looked up at an overhead, barely-noticeable camera.

"Good thing I was smiling," kidded JT.

"If you're ready, Sir, I'll have one of my escorts take you up to the Director's suite. Have a pleasant visit."

JT and Juanita followed the "escort" out to the elevator banks and waited only a few seconds for one to arrive. They rode up to the ninth floor and stepped into a lobby that looked exactly like the one on the first floor, except a little smaller. The carpet was a beige color and the lobby walls were a faded pink color. In fact, the wall paper was actually peeling in some places. All in all, it looked like most other drab government buildings that JT had been in.

The escort badged the door open and pointed to a cubicle directly inside and said, "If you'll just see the young lady right there, she'll take care of you. Have a nice day."

JT thought they had just left Kansas and entered the Land of Oz. The carpet was a plush azure blue and the walls were a pale but nonetheless radiant blue. The first class furniture obviously came from one of the better manufacturers. There were beautiful paintings, presumably copies of famous originals, hanging tastefully here and there. The receptionist had a modern flat-screen monitor, a slim line ergonomic keyboard with wireless mouse, and a sleek, multi-line phone on her desk, but little else. "If you would take a seat over there for just a minute, the Director will be right with you," she said, and motioned them to two modern yet comfortable looking chairs.

Juanita whispered to JT, "When did you set up this visit? Last night?"

"I had a few phone calls made," he replied. "Normally I like to do opposite-sex interviews with these folks, with the non-interviewer taking notes on the person's demeanor, nonverbal indications, voice stress levels, or whatever. Except today I'll do all the talking with the Director, okay?"

"Sure," Juanita agreed. "I presume you have some master plan?"

Just as JT was about to answer, the receptionist interrupted and indicated that they should follow her. She led them down a short hallway and into a spacious office that was not only well adorned, but had a stunning birds-eye-view of the local area. There was a couch and several chairs positioned around a large coffee table on the near end of the office, and several straight-backed wooden chairs surrounding the director's desk at the other end of the office. On the walls hung several frames displaying his awards and degrees, as well as pictures of him and various politicians and other dignitaries.

The Director approached them and motioned for them to take a seat around the table. "Hi. I'm Tommy Townsend, or just plain TT. Welcome to DARPA." He shook hands with JT and nodded at Juanita. The Director, a big man, or more precisely an overweight man, had a round, red face and thin black hair that he had over-combed across his head. JT figured him for his mid- to late 50s. His jacket hung in an armoire and he had the sleeves of his white shirt rolled up. All in all, he seemed a rather unkempt person for one in such a position of authority. "I understand that you don't have the most auspicious reason for your visit, but we'll do everything to help out where we can. Awful thing about poor Stefon. Have you talked to his wife yet?"

The Director came on like gangbusters and took JT aback some. He didn't quite expect such an open and forthcoming person as the director of a $3 billion agency. But then, he didn't really know quite what to expect as he was not used to dealing with scientists and engineers whose sole purpose in life was their research. Some of the geeks he knew perhaps came close, he guessed, but they didn't work in a place like this.

"No, Sir," JT replied. "We have that unfortunate task still ahead of us. We thought we'd talk to some of the other folks that Dr. Quarles knew, and give Mrs. Quarles a day or two to process all this. Forgive me for asking this, Sir, but do you have any idea who might have wanted to harm Dr. Quarles?"

"You do get right to the point don't you, Son? I have been mulling that over and the only thing that comes to mind, if indeed there is a motive for this tragedy, is that someone didn't really want him to complete his work. And that, to me, says terrorist, as unlikely as that may seem. I really don't know much about his personal situation, but I'm pretty sure he was well off, with no monetary problems, and I've heard that he was a devoted husband. So I don't think I'll be much help there. I presume you'll want to talk with his supervisor, his research assistant and his coworkers, so I've advised them that you would be around asking questions, and requested that they extend you every courtesy. I did take the liberty of getting you cleared for the security level required to discuss his program, but you will have to sign a nondisclosure agreement that my receptionist will have for you on the way out. Is there anything else in particular that you need to ask me?"

"We thought about the terrorist motive as well. Why do you think that is unlikely?"

"I have to admit that that does seem like their modus operandi, but I can see no reason why they would be aware of what he's doing. The program is, after all, classified. That's just a personal opinion of course. However, if you do eliminate the other possibilities...."

JT nodded, indicated that they had no more questions, thanked him for his time and cooperation, and got up to leave. TT shook his hand, nodded to Juanita and turned to his desk.

The receptionist asked them each to sign a piece of paper, and then explained how they could get down to the seventh floor and the office of Quarles' boss.

As they were taking the stairs down, JT asked Juanita if this seemed to be a place with a good-ole-boys mentality, or if was he just imagining things.

She just shrugged her shoulders and said that it was nothing new.

JT badged the card reader on a stairwell door with a large number 7 on it and they ended up in an outside corridor on the seventh floor. They took a left as instructed and badged their way into another door that opened into a hallway where they could see the receptionist at the end. JT went up and introduced himself and Juanita and asked to see Dr. Briceman.

"Yes, Sir," she replied, "he's been expecting you," and showed them into a nicely outfitted corner office that looked out on a small Arlington County park with a baseball field and several picnic areas.

"Good afternoon. I'm Rick Briceman. You must be the folks from DHS. Please sit down and make yourselves comfortable," he said as he motioned them to some chairs just in front of the windows. "Can I get you something to drink?" Briceman couldn't have weighed 135 pounds soaking wet. He had short but thick red hair, including a goatee, a pleasant face and reminded Juanita of one of those little gnomes on the Keebler commercials, except skinnier.

Juanita indicated they were fine drink-wise, introduced herself and JT, and then began, "Dr. Briceman, we're sorry about the loss of Dr. Quarles. You must be really shaken up about this."

"He was a difficult person to know, but once you were around him awhile he rather grew on you. He even let down his stand-offish persona on occasion and I actually heard him tell a joke once in a staff meeting. It was awful, but we humored him and laughed anyway."

"I know how that is," Juanita offered as she cast a side glance at JT. "We were hoping that you could tell us just a bit, hopefully in layman's terms, of what he was involved in, and if you think he had any enemies, or, frankly, anything that you think might help us in this investigation. Because of the program that Dr. Quarles was working on and the possibility that the explosion was the work of terrorists, we are investigating this rather than the Loudoun County Sheriff."

"I guess that doesn't surprise me. His program, albeit a very difficult and complicated one, is one that we nonetheless have high hopes for. It involves some very sophisticated artificial intelligence programming that sifts through terabytes of data on banking and other financial transactions throughout the entire world. Just the gathering of the data is an enormously complex proposition, what with getting everything in the right format, and then mining it with sophisticated algorithms to glean patterns that do not fit normal business transactions presents another problem, or actually a whole set of problems. How Quarles managed to even get started in the right direction, let alone begin to show progress toward the ultimate goal, is beyond me, but then he was quite talented."

"You're talking like you think this is still a doable program," commented Juanita.

"Oh, absolutely. We may have to take a step or two back and probably find someone else with Quarles' abilities to help out, but I understand that Arati Jabornae over at NRL was following the program's progress and may even be able to carry on without any outside help. We really need this and are prepared to spend whatever it takes to make it work. The payoff is enormous."

"That's encouraging, because we sure could use the help. Can you think of anyone who might have had a reason to stop this work, other than terrorists concerned about having their financial transactions tracked?"

"Not really," Briceman replied. "I mean, there were three different contractors involved originally. Then we made one award recently for a decent sum of money. And there are three or four additional companies out there that have the expertise to implement this program in the follow-on contract, and most of them bid on it, either directly or by subbing. No one benefits from a program stoppage that I can think of."

"How about other programs here at DARPA?" Juanita asks. "If this one fails or goes away, doesn't that mean more money for other programs?"

"Not really. The Boss, the Director, has a significant pot of money that isn't even committed to programs yet. We can't find enough good ideas to fund. If you make a good case, even on a seemingly far out or crazy idea, you'll get the funding to run with it. No, that's not a concern here."

JT couldn't help but ask, "You actually have money left over at the end of the year? I mean, don't you lose it if you don't spend it?"

"No. R&D, or Research and Development, funding is two-year money, and that's the only type of funding we have. We do get hit with general fund reductions now and then, but we've never turned in more than an insignificant portion of any one year's funds. At least that's what I've been told."

"I can think of only one other thing we need to ask you Dr. Briceman. Do you know of anybody that had a personal grudge against Dr. Quarles or that might to do him harm for any reason?"

"No, I really don't think so."

"Then I have nothing further. How about you, JT?"

"I think that's about it. If you happen to think of anything else that might help us," JT said as he handed him his card, "please don't hesitate to call. Thank you very much for your time. Could you direct us to Dr. Quarles' research assistant?"

"I can do better than that," Briceman said as he got up from his chair and started toward the door. "Jessie, can you show these folks to Tamika's office, please?"

JT and Juanita felt dismissed, but Jessie obviously thought nothing of it and led them down the hall and around a couple of corners to the opposite side of the building—the side that looked out on North Fairfax Drive. Juanita couldn't help but notice the nice reproductions hanging all along the corridor walls. Tamika's "office" was actually just a cubicle located in front of what used to be Quarles' office. She was just sitting there more or less staring out into space.

"Tamika, these are the people from DHS here to talk about Dr. Quarles."

Tamika looked up and acknowledged Jessie and said, "Okay, thanks." In spite of her natural beauty, Tamika looked haggard. Juanita figured she was stressed out about Quarles and was about to say something when JT started in and said how sorry they were for her loss. Tamika started sobbing and dropped her head in her hands. JT and Juanita waited patiently and after a couple of minutes, when the crying subsided somewhat, JT looked at Juanita and nodded toward Tamika.

"Have you talked to anyone about this?" Juanita asked.

Tamika shook her head and started to compose herself.

"We've seen this a lot," Juanita continued, "and it really does help to talk through it. Let someone know how bad you're feeling. Someone you can really talk to, like maybe your mom or a close girlfriend."

Tamika nodded slowly, wiped her eyes with a tissue and said she was ready to begin. She added that she had talked to her mom about this and it seemed to help some.

JT started by saying, "We'd rather not do this so soon, but it is important to get your thoughts and impressions right away and follow up quickly on anything you might tell us. In general, we'd like to know if Dr. Quarles had any enemies, run-ins with anybody, or if he had been acting any differently lately—things like that. Would you like to just start talking in those general areas and let us pop in with a question now or then?"

Tamika started slowly, but then the flood gates opened. "I don't think he had any enemies, but there aren't really any people here that he was friends with, either. Like many of the scientists here, he was off in his own world and my job was to keep him connected with this one. He was stand-offish, but I don't really think that offended anyone very much, because a lot of people here are like that. There were the run-ins that he had been having with Styles, but then most everyone was in that category. However, Styles did seem to particularly enjoy picking on Dr. Quarles. And he did at times seem to be at odds with the IT guys. He did talk a lot with his cohort at NRL, Dr. Jabornae, and he was on pretty good terms with Dr. Marvin Kovnowski, a friend of his who worked at OSR."

Tamika paused at this point, like she was wondering if she had missed addressing any of the questions, so JT asked her about his conduct lately.

"He did not seem upset lately. In fact, he was excited about the new contract coming up and said he was looking forward to working out some new theories. And as far as I know, he got along very well with his wife and enjoyed family life."

"Tamika, that's very helpful," JT said after she had slowed down. "Could you get us contact information for Drs. Jabornae and Kovnowski and show us around Dr. Quarles' office? We'd like to look at his notes, his files and his computer."

Tamika agreed and said that Dr. Briceman had already reviewed Dr. Quarles' notes and files and computer to make sure there was no classified data on them, so they could be removed if they wanted them.

JT almost choked and started to say something, but Juanita placed her hand on his arm and gave him her best it's-no-use-yelling-at-her look, so he thought better of it. "Thank you very much," he said. "Do you know if Dr. Quarles had a laptop that he carried with him?"

"Yes. But he was very careful not to put anything classified on it. He had it with him all the time. He even took notes at staff meetings with it, or at least that is what he said he was doing. I'm sure he must have had it with him when he drove home that night." She started to choke up again but then managed to keep control. "I'm sorry," she said. "Is there anything else you need?"

"If you just get us those phone numbers while we're looking around in the office, I think that will be all. Unless you think there is someone else here we should talk to."

"I don't think anybody here really knew him at all." She opened the door to Quarles' office and JT and Juanita walked in. Tamika then went to get the information they had requested.

It was surprisingly messy for someone with such a disciplined mind, JT thought. Or maybe not—you just never knew about these things. Papers were not exactly scattered about everywhere, but there were many piles of neatly stacked papers and journals on almost every surface in the office. At least each stack was labeled with a post-it-note on top that JT presumed categorized the contents. When Tamika came and handed JT a paper with phone numbers and office locations for Kovnowski and Jabornae, JT asked if she could round up a few boxes for them to put the papers and journals in.

There wasn't anything of import in the desk drawers, nor on the desk itself. The white boards were clean but had obviously been used a lot based on the dust on the board ledges. The four filing cabinets were empty of anything except a few office supplies. From the dust on the bottoms of the shelves, it looked as though they were not used at all. JT figured his Rolodex was most likely electronic, as were most of his notes. He and Juanita packed up the stacks and liberated the computer tower. Tamika had thoughtfully provided a cart and helped them load the stuff up. They thanked her again, gave her a card and asked her to call if she thought of anything that might help. Tamika had also called one of the escorts to help them down to their car with the boxes. *This does seem to be a professionally run place*, thought JT.

JT closed the Toyota hatch after everything was loaded and jumped in after waving to the county cop. "I used to do the rent-a-cop thing when I was with Fairfax," he said as he was pulling off. "Mostly I sat at highway construction sites so the workers wouldn't get run over by speeding idiots. Boring as hell, but the pay was good. There probably isn't that much opportunity for that here in Arlington." He turned west on North Fairfax and drove a few blocks before making a right. "Great place for lunch here," he said, "—*El Pollo Rico*—if that's okay with you. Thought we could map out the rest of the day there."

Juanita nodded and they headed in. The lunch crowd had died down by this time and there were a few tables available.

After they got their food, JT picked a table somewhat away from the others and started eating and talking at the same time. "I'm thinking we go back to the shop, go through some of this stuff, get the techies working on his computer, get an update from the boss, and then tomorrow we go see Mrs. Quarles."

"Is that all?" Juanita asked.

"So, what did you think about all that? Did you form any impressions?"

"It seems to me," replied Juanita, "that Briceman wasn't very concerned about Quarles' demise or his family and he didn't balk at the terrorist idea. Perhaps that's the cool, calm, scientific mind at work, but I would have expected a little more sympathy, on the one hand, and a little more curiosity, on the other. Tamika, conversely, was very upset, and genuinely so. Old TT is quite another story. I don't know what to make of him. Sounds like he agrees with you that a terrorist connection is a little hard to swallow. By the way, what's with the opposite sex interviews except for the Director?"

"I was advised that he doesn't think much of the fairer sex, so I thought I might get a better interview with him. As for the others, it's been my experience that people often come up with good stuff after the interview, and a good entrée for getting back to them is the old 'I thought you might have been uncomfortable talking to a woman, or man, so I thought I'd call back and see if there was anything that you didn't say or that you might have thought of since.'"

"You're kidding me. Does that actually work for you?"

"Truthfully, I'm not sure. But I don't think it hurts. It does depend on the circumstances and the individuals, and I don't always use it. It seems to work better on the men than the women. Do we go see Mrs. Quarles tomorrow?"

"We better find out where she is with funeral arrangements first."

"Yeah," JT replied. "Guess we better head on back to the shop when we're done and brief the Captain. Maybe he has some new information for us."

Then Juanita popped up with, "Hey, we need to make sure we get his laptop. The Sergeant didn't mention a thing about that, did he?"

"No. We did ask about the Saturn, but he didn't mention any laptop and we forgot to ask, didn't we? That's another thing to ask the ATF when we get back." They finished their lunch slowly, chatting about past escapades and current events.

CHAPTER SEVEN

Fusion Team Headquarters, 1 November, 1530 hours

The afternoon rush hour was still young, so after a quick jaunt down Washington Boulevard, JT and Juanita arrived at Headquarters right at three-thirty. They found a parking space on the second underground level of the garage, parked and took the elevator up to the twelfth floor. After dropping their stuff off at their respective cubicles, they went around the corner to Hanson's office. He was on the phone and motioned for them to have a seat. His spacious office was well equipped yet not cluttered, and had a nice view of the city and the river. The doorway located on the left side connected to a small conference room that they frequently used for staff meetings. Making themselves comfortable, they got out their notes out and waited for him to get off the phone. When they were finished briefing him on their meeting with Sergeant Gregg and the interviews at DARPA, JT asked him about the intercept that hinted at terrorist involvement with Quarles' death.

"Well," began Hanson, "English names, or I guess more properly U.S. names, don't translate well into Urdu. Typically they'll just use the name as spoken here as best they can pronounce it. A couple of weeks ago, NSA passed on a large number of suspected terrorist transmissions to us, the JTTF and the NCTC. Upon analysis, they thought that something that sounded similar to *Quarles*, preceded by *daactar*, the Urdu word for doctor, was mentioned several times. More than that, they heard what sounded like *Coltrane*, as in the jazz trumpet player, which is the codeword for his program. So, these two put together are what we think may tie them to his demise. This doesn't necessarily mean our Sticks were at all involved with Quarles, and we may very well have two separate plots working, so the boss wanted us to work them both as high priorities, and he passed that on to the other two organizations." The Boss was

Assistant Secretary Charlie Moffet who reported, to the DHS Secretary, but also had collateral reporting responsibilities to the Director of National Intelligence and the head of the National Security Council.

"As far as the Quarles case goes, I don't have much for you. We did get the ME's report on him: blunt force trauma due to the explosion—no drugs or alcohol were detected. His body was released earlier today. We also got the forensics back from the ATF on the Taurus, and there were no fingerprints in the vehicle other than the owners', along with several little kids' prints in the back. They are sure there was an IED inside the Taurus that was detonated by remote control. I've set up a meeting with one of their explosive experts at their Ammendale facility tomorrow at three to give us a run down on what they found."

"We know for sure that Quarles was a target," said Juanita. "And we know that he was on somebody's radar, most likely terrorists, if you can believe what NSA thinks about the source of their intercepts. We don't have any other viable suspects at this time, but we haven't yet talked to his wife or his two cohorts--one that he worked closely with and the other one a friend. This doesn't really tie in with the train station plot, either, so I guess we have two separate cases."

"Speaking of which," says Hanson, "when Ronnie talked to the cabbie's friends, she said they were really hinky, like they were trying to make sure they all told the right story. All their scenarios weren't exactly the same, but they did seem rehearsed, she said. The forensics guys found it odd that the Tahoe and the Civic were very carefully broken into and the alarm systems defeated, whereas the cab heist was more obvious—like they wanted us to know it was stolen. It could be that they were more careful with the former two because there was resale potential, whereas there wasn't with the cab. Or maybe the team that stole the cab just wasn't as experienced. So because of the negative vibes and the questionable break-in, we decided to put the cabbie under surveillance. We checked the Tahoe owner's email traffic on the night of the 26th, and he was definitely online during the period in question, and he got a phone call at home right in the middle of that. Finally, forensics says the warehouse alarm was not defeated but rather not activated. The last person out that evening swears he activated it, but then one of the employees could have come back and deactivated it and left the door open. The owner we talked to says that only he, his two partners, and two other employees have the activation code, but that it wouldn't be that hard for any of the other employees to get it if they really wanted to. It could be that, in order to cover their tracks, the remaining Sticks that you didn't see depart the premises that night went back and 'broke the door open' before they left. We're looking more into the friends and relatives of the guy from Afghanistan, but so far we don't see anything warranting our attention." Hanson paused for a moment and then added, "I think that's all the developments on this end since you were last here. Where are you going now?"

"Tomorrow we're going to see if Mrs. Quarles is up to talking with us. We'll also meet with his friend at AFOSR and his colleague at NRL," replied JT. Just then his cell phone rang and JT saw that it was Sergeant Gregg from the Loudon County Sherriff's Office. JT answered and asked him what was up.

"As you know, our guys canvassed the neighborhoods where the Taurus and its borrowed license plate were taken from. Seems one of the neighbors saw something that could be helpful, but I admit it seems like a long shot. In any event, he gave us a partial plate and vehicle description, and we were going to run them but figured you'd rather do that yourself."

"Sure, Sarge, that'd be great. Whatta ya got?"

"There's a Bernard Szymanski that lives near the guy that had his plate stolen, and he said he saw a dark-colored, mid-sized pickup in the neighborhood a few days before Quarles bought it—black or maybe dark blue. He said he saw the rear end, which had a Virginia plate that began 'ZZY' and had two number '2's in it, probably next to each other. I sent you an email with his contact info and a summary of his statement. I thought you might want to run the plate, its owner if you can narrow it down enough, and maybe talk to this Szymanski fellow."

"Great, thanks Sarge. We'll definitely look into it. By the way, did anybody recover his laptop from his car, or anything else?"

"Glad you mentioned that. One of our deputies did say something about it. Seems he may have had it strapped into the passenger seat right next to him. I'm sure the ATF has it and are getting what they can from it, although it was covered with foam, from what I hear."

JT told the Sarge what little he got from the ATF, via Hanson, and thanked him. He then passed the information from the Sarge on to Juanita and Hanson, opened the email from Gregg and forwarded it to Juanita. He asked one of the staffers to get Quarles' hard drive to forensics and then called the ATF. Seems they did have the laptop, had already downloaded its contents and said JT could have it anytime. Apparently, it had come through the whole episode in pretty good shape.

While JT was on the phone with the ATF, Juanita accessed the Virginia Department of Transportation data base. There were only two blue or black pickups with plates that began "ZZY" still on the road in the Northern Virginia area. She accessed the owner data, and then checked for any police record. One of the guys did have a rap sheet. There were two arrests but no convictions for domestic violence—seems his wife would not testify—and one arrest for a homicide. He got off on a technicality on that one. Then there was a conviction for assault on a police officer at a DUI stop. He did a nickel on that one and served the full time, too, so he was not on parole. *Sounds like he might not have played well with others while in prison*, she thought. She noted the addresses and the tag numbers and decided to get pictures of the vehicles before they saw Mr. Szymanski. She also got the ex-con's place of work, just in case, but didn't have that data on the other guy. Two or maybe three more items on tomorrow's to-do list.

Chantilly, Virginia, 2 November, 1110 hours

Juanita had called the night before and Mrs. Quarles had agreed to see them, deciding that now was as good a time as any to get this over with. The neighborhood consisted of recently built million-dollar homes with manicured lawns and freshly planted shrubbery. At either end of the neighborhood stood a large group of mature trees with a two-acre pond on the back side, but few of the lots had anything more than saplings around them. It appeared that this was mostly farmland before being developed. The two story above ground house, like all the rest of the ones in the development, included a full underground basement. They all sported nine-foot ceilings, a spacious entryway, and a three-car garage on the side. Beautiful stone steps led up to her stone front porch, which was adorned with flower pots and some stone statuary. Juanita rang the bell. They decided on the way over that, in spite of JT's ground rule, she would lead the discussion with Mrs. Quarles.

Martha Quarles was a diminutive woman. She and her husband must have made an odd couple, given his over six-foot stature. JT would have described her as mousey, but Juanita would have been more kind, as she was after all in grieving. Her long brown hair hung down almost to her waist, and seemed darker than it was against her plain beige housedress. "Hi," she said, "I'm Martha. Please come in and have a seat."

"Martha, I'm Juanita, the one that called you last night. This is JT. We're both very sorry for your loss and hate to have to bother you at a time like this. I know you must be busy making funeral arrangements and trying to cope with all this. Do you have anyone here to help you?"

"I can't believe it's been almost a week," she said, "and yes, they finally released him, so we're going to have him buried the day after tomorrow. My sister and her husband, that is. They are down from New York to help out. And my mom and dad will be here tomorrow. Can you answer a question for me before we start?"

Martha's thought processes seemed a little disjointed, so Juanita thought she had better answer her question. "Yes, Martha. What is it?"

"Was my husband murdered? From what the police told me it did not seem like an accident."

She asked this in a very calm manner, and like she expected a positive answer, so Juanita thought she would play it as straight as she could with this woman. "Our investigation so far points in that direction."

"And do you have any idea whom yet?"

"We are working on that. That's why we are here. So far I'm afraid that all we can say is that it appears to be terrorist related, given the facts that we know now and your husband's involvement with some anti-terrorist work at DARPA."

"Okay, I guess I'm ready for your questions. JT, is it?" she asked as she looked at him.

JT nodded.

"I have a nephew, John Thomas, who goes by JT. What do your initials stand for?"

JT gave Juanita his how-did-I get-into-this look, and she just gave him a nice questioning smile back. "It's just a kind of nickname that my Dad called me when I was young and it stuck. Not sure where he got it."

"So Martha," Juanita began so as to get things on track, "I know these may seem like crazy questions, but did your husband have any enemies? Any recent run-ins with creditors, neighbors, maybe even family members? Any gambling debts? And please forgive us, but as you can tell, we really don't know you or your husband and need all the help we can get in solving this." She added that last part as she could see Martha was starting to react slightly to the type of questions being asked.

Martha took a breath, apparently considering the validity of the queries, and then answered. "Stefon is a very private man, and a very proud one. He doesn't have many friends and—" she paused and then corrected herself, "I mean was or didn't. Oh, you know what I mean." She paused again then seemed to collect herself. "We really don't know the neighbors very well, since we've only lived here a few months. We have met the ones on either side and they seem very nice. We've even borrowed a few things from each other and had a barbeque with them, the three families together, a couple of weeks ago. Stefon had colleagues but no friends, except for Dr. Marvin Kovnowski over at the Air Force research office. We were even out to his house once. His wife was delightful and we had a wonderful conversation about normal things while Stefon and Marvin talked business or whatever it was. He knew Marvin from MIT." She paused to catch her breath. "We do have a few creditors and are a little behind in our mortgage payments, because our last house has not sold yet. But nobody's been nasty or even overly persistent. Not yet, anyway. Stefon has mentioned, several times, a nasty, brutish man at DARPA, something Styles that he really disliked. Apparently, the feeling was mutual. I really don't know what that is all about however."

Martha paused again so Juanita prompted her, "What about family members? You mentioned your sister."

"Actually I have two sisters. One, Beth, is out in California, and we don't see her often since she travels a lot. She's single and works for Marriott in some sort of quality control position, so she really gets to see the country. My other sister, Sally Ann, is here with her husband, Tom. We've only seen them a couple of times since we were married, usually when we were up at mom and dad's. They live in upstate New York also and we do see them every couple of months. Stefon got along quite well with them, and in fact, dad really liked him. He's in the computer business, too, so I guess they had something in common."

"How about Stefon's folks?"

"They are retired and live over in Rehoboth Beach. We'd visit them several times over the summer and fall and spend time at the beach. Sometimes his sister Mary Gayle would come too, from Rockville, with her husband and little boy. We all got along fine and the only tension, if you could call it that, would be about who was the more successful, Stefon or Mary Gayle. She's a microbiologist and works at the National Institutes of Health. We were really a big, happy family. And now our baby will never know his daddy."

Martha needed a few moments here so Juanita waited and then asked, "You have a little one there?" nodding towards Martha's midsection.

Martha patted her stomach, dropped her head and started a low sobbing.

Juanita went over and sat beside her and rubbed her back. After a few minutes, she managed to regain her composure. "I am so sorry, Mrs. Quarles. Would you like us to come back another time?"

"No. I'd rather do this all now if I can," she replied. "And please, do call me Martha. So what other questions do you have?"

"What about gambling or any other vices?" Juanita asked sheepishly.

"Not Stefon. He thought gambling was stupid and didn't even like it when I played the lotto. I have never seen him take more than one or two drinks at a time, usually at parties or when we had company. Although we did occasionally have a glass of wine with dinner. To completely answer your question I can't imagine him with another woman. It was all I could do to get him interested enough in me to get married."

"I know this seems insensitive but I have to ask it. How about insurance?"

"I understand," she said. "Yes, there is a $250,000 policy which will really help until the other house sells. I'm afraid Stefon and I did not put much away in terms of savings, and he moved around enough that there is only about $150,000 in his 401K. I will definitely have to go back to work. I was a paralegal for a firm in town, so hopefully I can get back there."

"Martha, you've been great, and we really appreciate your talking with us. If you think of anything else that might help us, not matter how small, please call us. And we wish you well with your pregnancy. It sounds like you'll have a lot of help from both sides of the family." With that, Juanita handed Martha her card as she got up to leave.

JT thanked her, as well, as she showed them to the front door. "That's a nice woman," he remarked as they walked over to his car. "And she seems to be holding up pretty well under the circumstances. What a rotten break—losing her husband like that and being pregnant. On the positive side, I guess she's young enough, and apparently strong enough, to start over. I hope that insurance will see her through until she can get a good job."

"Yeah. By the way, why didn't you tell her what JT stood for?"

"Didn't seem appropriate at the time."

"Oh, okay."

"Where to now?" JT asked.

"I thought we'd run by this Jonathan Furlong's place in Fairfax first, to see if his truck is there and get a picture, surreptitiously of course. If it's not there, then we'll head on over to his place of employment in Falls Church and try to get it there. On the way, we can swing by Vienna, where the other truck is registered. That one is registered to a Walter Roberts, who is sixty-three, so I'm hoping he's retired and he and his truck will be home."

Given the time, they thought they'd stop for a bite at a Pizza Hut on Route 50.

"So Juanita," JT queried between bites, "how's that dating thing going? That's something I haven't done in a while."

"I guess not all that well. Actually, most of my spare time I spend on my classwork."

"So how's that going? Isn't that the masters in criminology from Maryland?"

"It's with the University of Maryland Extension School. I started it when I was stationed at Andrews, which was really convenient since some of the classes were held there. Some I can do online. I don't actually have to go to the main campus except for three courses and a lot of that is on the weekend."

"How close are you to finishing?"

"Three classes and my thesis to go."

"Yeah, you mentioned your proposed thesis title yesterday. I thought a thesis was strictly a Ph.D. thing."

"Actually, a dissertation is the Ph.D. thing. For a masters you can do a thesis or not, depending on whether you concentrate more on theory or practice. I thought I'd go the theory route and maybe try for a teaching position down at Quantico."

"Wow. Good for you. And this is your excuse for not dating?"

"It's not an excuse, *amigo*, it's a reason."

"Ah, I see why you chose the theoretical route. You ready to go check out Messrs. Furlong and Roberts?"

"Let's hit the road, Toad."

Fairfax County, Virginia, 2 November, 1330 hours

When they arrived at Furlong's brick, three-story townhouse in Burke, there was no truck in the driveway, so Juanita climbed the steps up to the neighbor's entryway where she could see into his garage through the small windows in the top of the door. The single-car garage had a nice looking, fairly new Porsche in it. The neighbor didn't answer the door, so she didn't need to go through her I'm-looking-for-so-and-so routine.

Hoping they wouldn't strikeout at the next place, they headed up Ox Road, ending up at a charming little place in the southwestern section of Vienna on Tapawingo Road. One of the older sections of Vienna, the houses here were 1960s and '70s vintage. It was a clean neighborhood with reasonably good-sized yards, and most of the carports had been converted into one- or two-car garages. Lucky for them, that didn't include the Robert's carport. There sat the truck with the ZZY plate, and Juanita snapped a quick picture of the back end as they cruised by.

Juanita had found out that Furlong worked for QPUDS, LLC as a delivery man out of their distribution center in Falls Church. According to their website, it stood for Quick Pick Up and Delivery Service. Apparently, one of their main services was flower deliveries. As they headed back towards D.C. along Route 66 and down Route 7, which was also called Leesburg Pike after the famous Civil War general, Juanita considered her American heritage. She was exceptionally proud of it and probably knew more than most about United States history. She mused that Virginia never could figure out whether it was for or against the War. Sure it was south of the Mason-Dixon line, but it was also the birthplace of the nation, home to eight presidents, seven of those before the War, and two of the major constituents of the Union Army were the Army of the Potomac and the Army of the Shenandoah. It was also damn close to the center of the federal government, except when that was in Philadelphia. On the other hand, the Army of Northern Virginia was the primary military force of the Confederate States, and Robert E. Lee was a

Virginian. Like she always said: Virginia is schizophrenic. It probably ought to be two states—North Virginia and South Virginia—well actually three if you count West Virginia. And the "Tidewater" section and the lower Delmarva Peninsula might constitute "East Virginia." "Northern Virginia" is always complaining that they contribute the lion's share of state taxes and don't get a fair return on it. Right now she couldn't remember "Southern Virginia's" come back to that.

JT brought her out of her day dreaming by remarking that he needed directions to the QPUDS distribution center. After pointing out a few turns, they were cruising through the parking lot. She located the truck with the plate they had run on their second pass through the lot. Luck was still riding with them, as it was parked facing in so they could just snap a picture of the backend on the sly as they drove by.

"Okay," she said, "we better hustle if we're going to get over to Beltsville in time."

CHAPTER EIGHT

Ammendale, Maryland, 2 November, 1505 hours

The ATF's Forensic Science Laboratory is located just off Ammendale Road between Routes 1 and 95 in Beltsville, Maryland. Appropriately enough, it is not that far from Old Gunpowder Road. The complex is large and spread out, and therefore not really distinguishable from the other government and university facilities located nearby. JT and Juanita got there just a little bit late, but Captain Hanson had only just arrived himself. Ronnie and Charles, the only other regular Alpha Unit members besides JT and Juanita who could make it, had arrived early and were chatting with Ron Masters, the explosives expert, who was giving the briefing. The rest of the crew were busy chasing down clues or otherwise employed. Ronnie knew Masters from when they had worked together in ATF, and she mentioned to Hanson that he was one smart dude when it came to explosives. She didn't mention that the ATF folks used to tease them and call them Ron and Ronnie.

Since they were all here now, Masters led them up to the conference room to get them settled in. Ronnie formally introduced him to the team and gave a short bio. Masters was a little embarrassed at this as it was not expected, but it was okay because it was Ronnie. He offered them something to drink and they helped themselves to coffee and soda while he got himself some bottled water. After a brief organizational description, he took them on the fifty-cent tour, ending up in the lab where he would make his presentation.

Masters had a slight build and maybe weighed in at 140 pounds. With his khaki uniform and utility belt on, if you looked at him from the back, he reminded you of Barney Fife. You could just picture some comedy routine where Barney was shaking while trying to defuse some explosives. He handed a DVD to Ronnie and asked her to load it into the computer hooked up to the fifty-two inch plasma overhead. "From an analysis of the damage radius, the debris, the scorching and other items from the scene of last Friday's explosion," he began, "it was actually fairly easy to determine the type of explosives and the firing device used. Nice little bugger, too. Remote controlled, using a pager as the firing switch. Who ever made this really gets it."

Masters nodded to Ronnie, who flashed the first picture on the screen, showing several very small pieces of electronic components, including a small resistor, a part of a capacitor, and numerous other pieces which offered absolutely no identifying features anyone on the team could recognize. What they did recognize though, was that the pieces were mangled and broken, and most had obvious signs of undergoing a very hot thermal event.

"See what I mean?" asked Masters.

The team members all stared intently at the screen hoping to decipher its meaning.

After a few minutes, Captain Hanson said, "Okay, I give up. Tell me what I'm supposed to be seeing."

Masters pulled a laser pointer from his pocket, and deftly pointed it at the screen. The red dot only wavered slightly as it highlighted a small sliver of an item which, to the untrained eye, meant nothing. "There it is, folks. Right there," Masters said with controlled excitement. "That, my friends, is an SCR, or Silicon Controlled Rectifier—absolutely a requirement for this type of initiation."

Masters continued to look at the screen, drifting away into some past experience, when Ronnie spoke up. "Ron, I'm sure this is bringing back some found memory of yours, but we have a homicide to solve, remember?" Masters continued to stare at the screen for just a second more, and then, as if not hearing Ronnie's complaint, asked for the next slide, apparently unaware of the team's growing restlessness. Ronnie went to the next slide, which was a diagram of the required components for an IED.

"The killer wanted to insure that the IED exploded when the victim was at the exact position to maximize the effects, so he used a pager to act as a receiver. He builds the bomb, places it where he knows the victim will be, sits back and waits. When the target is within the estimated kill zone, the guy simply calls the pager number, and BLAM! One less dude!" Using the laser, he continued, "These are the required components for an IED: a power source, an initiator or blasting cap, a switch and explosives. It can either be electrically or non-electrically initiated. In this case, it was the former, which is most common for terrorist assassinations. This device," here he nodded to Ronnie to project the third slide, "was command activated using a pager, and consisted of a nine volt battery, a silicon controlled rectifier acting as the switch, a small container of the explosive material, and two blasting caps. The first four items, including the explosives themselves, are relatively easy to obtain. The blasting caps are more difficult to come by but can be purchased on the black market, or stolen from construction companies, rock quarries or other places. Believe it or not, there are still some Vietnam era veterans living on the fringes of society who are a source."

Masters was smiling with a wide, almost childlike grin. He was clearly in his element, and the team allowed him a moment. He glanced around, caught the look on everyone's face, and realized he needed to break it down. "You see, anyone can go to the internet now and learn how to build a bomb. The thing is, to use an electronic component like a pager, or even a cell phone for that matter, you just can't hook up a blasting cap to the system. If you do, even though the pager receives the signal and goes off, you know, beeps, the cap won't initiate!" Again, the team looked puzzled, but Masters continued, clearly enjoying teaching the seasoned team of special agents. "Safety. It's all about safety! You see, when they first started making electric blasting caps, way too many operators were getting blown up due to stray voltage and even static electricity causing the caps to fire prematurely. Can't have that—bad for business you know. So, they began to design electric caps with a failsafe system incorporating a mechanism to convert electrical current into the heat necessary to initiate the explosive content of the shell. It's normally performed by the use of a bridge wire or foil material called the fuse head. Basically, the energy required to make the cap function is specific in the duration and amperage required—insufficient current, or for insufficient time—no BANG!"

Masters stood with that same childlike smile, reminding the team that the man's only true love was indeed explosives. "Okay, here's the really cool part. The SCR, man, is a small, self-contained, electronic switch: all packaged, ready to go. Even though the current duration and amperage is insufficient to fire the electric cap, it is sufficient to close the internal leg of the SCR switch, and once closed, it stays closed even if you remove the current. I did an analysis of all the electronic components we were able to locate, and when I saw the SCR, I knew right off we were dealing with some serious players. Hey, did I mention I pulled the SCR piece out of the victim?" He could tell from the raised eyebrows that they didn't know that. "Sure enough, found it about one inch inside the guy's right ventricle. That, and about four pounds of car pieces and other scrap metal and glass throughout his body, at least what was left of his body. I know you guys are all hopped up on this info, but you aren't going to believe the really neat find I made—TATP." Masters spoke those words in almost quiet reverence. "TATP, or triacetone triperoxide, is mostly hydrogen peroxide, about 90%, and the rest acetone and a strong acid, in this case muratic." Masters nodded and Ronnie showed the next picture illustrating the combining of the three components along with their chemical formulas. "These are all easy to obtain and, from our experience, have proven to be the explosives of choice of al Qaeda and other terrorist operatives."

The team looked to one another, then back at Masters. Masters stood with a wide grin, his eyes sparkling. JT was the first to speak, "And that is...what?"

Masters said, with a look of satisfaction, "Only the latest and greatest improvised explosives out there. It's commonly accepted that explosive materials, like fuel, are highly energetic compounds that, upon initiation, release their energy content in a fast, exothermic reaction. Accordingly, excessive heat of formation has been considered to be the key property of all explosives. Although that statement is probably correct for most known explosives, particularly those containing nitro groups, including nitroaromatics, nitrate esters, and nitramines, it may not necessarily be the case for less studied families of either conventional or improvised explosives. Of particular interest has been the group of peroxide based explosives, including triacetone triperoxide (TATP), diacetone diperoxide (DADP) and hexamethylene triperoxidediamine (HMTD). TATP is one of the most sensitive explosives known, a property that allows its employment as both primary explosives--that is, it's used in the blasting cap and in the main charge. It has a power close to TNT. For instance, a ten gram sample gave a 250 cubic centimeter expansion in the Trauzl test as compared to 300 cubic centimeters for TNT. The problem with TATP is its low chemical stability, its sensitivity to mechanical stress and open flame, and its high volatility, all of which results in about a two third weight loss within two weeks at room temperature. This is why it hasn't been used extensively. You would only need a few ounces of this mixture, say five or six at most, to assure a sufficient blast to kill everybody within fifteen to twenty feet. If you added fragmentation material, such as bolts, ball bearings, nails and other metal materials, you can increase the effective kill zone to about thirty-five feet, depending upon the location, whether you are indoors or out, et cetera." Ronnie flipped to the next slide, which was a diagram with circles showing various damage levels.

"Okay, it's a dangerous, sensitive, improvised explosive that isn't widely used," Charles said. "So why was it used now and by whom?"

"That's the really important aspect of what I'm saying. It isn't used, routinely at least. Not here. Not by our everyday bad guys. This stuff is so hot, so unstable, it's only been used by the baddest of the bad, terrorists!" When Master finished, he sat down, pulled out his PDA, and began concentrating on something. To the team he appeared to be lost in his own, private world of formulas and statistics. Ronnie could not recall him even one time talking about anybody and wondered if he ever had a real relationship. The team fell silent, each in their own thoughts, contemplating the significance of what they were just told.

"Masters! Masters!" Charles had to raise his voice to get his attention. When Masters looked up from his PDA, Charles continued the probe. "Okay, improvised explosives, bad, very bad, I get that. Terrorist. Get that too. So far, although this has been educational, it really hasn't given us anything new to go on. I'm starting to feel you've left something important out."

Masters, now fully alert, thought back into his mind, and suddenly, as if struck by electricity, jumped from his seat. The movement was so sudden and unexpected that the team actually jumped slightly. "Ronnie, could you show the next slide, please?" he asked. This was a photograph of the scene of the explosion taken from far enough back so that you got the full impact of the blast. "The device and the fragmentation material were placed on the passenger seat of the Taurus, which was the side closest to the victim. The Taurus was in the second parking space from the victim's car. If another vehicle had parked between them, then the bomb may or may not have been as effective, depending upon a number of factors, but most likely would have produced the same result." Masters summed up with, "Given that the victim was standing only eight feet away from the device and was only separated from it by the car window and door, there was no chance that he would survive the blast. From all indications, this was most likely a terrorist incident initiated from probably 150 feet or more from the intended victim by a perpetrator that sent the pager the initiating signal, watched the blast, and then drove off from the scene unobserved."

The team was silent, and Masters again stepped back into his world of explosives computations, molecular structures and elements of residual electron density. Hanson was first on his feet. He looked at the others, at Masters, and back to his team. "Okay, here's what we know. The target was selected for elimination. The IED was small, powerful, well-designed and well-placed, and used materials most common to known terrorist groups. A pager, modified with an *SCR*," Hanson placed heavy emphasis on the SCR acronym while looking directly at Masters, "was used to initiate the device at the exact time and moment when it was most devastating. We have one completely unsuspecting but unfortunately very dead victim. Do we have any more questions for Mr. Masters?"

"Were you able to trace any of the components back to their source?"

"No, Ronnie, we couldn't," Masters replied. "It is possible that we could trace the pager to the seller, but most likely not the purchaser. Without pictures of potential buyers, we would never be able to get a positive ID. The blasting caps we may be able to trace, and we are still working on that. Even if we can trace the source however, it is most likely that they were stolen, but we will let you know if we come up with anything. Are there any other questions?"

"I guess just one last one," Hanson replied. "Can you say with any certainty that this was a terrorist incident?"

"That's the thing, Sir. When I did the post blast analysis, I began to get a feel for not only the IED, but, well, this may sound strange, but I kinda got a sense about the bomber. I looked at the positioning of the device, the blast damage, not only to the victim, but also the car it was placed in. I surveyed the area, and located what I believe was the location of the bomber while he waited and then detonated the IED. I ran through all the information, estimated the explosives weight, the fragmentation pattern, overpressure wave, and when I put it all together, something didn't quite add up." Masters had everyone's full attention now. He continued. "A well placed IED using TATP, with adequate fragmentation, placed in a known location where the target would be, and detonated with a remote controlled electronic device using rather sophisticated electrical components: this has all the markings of a terrorist. But, you know, and I'm just talking off the top of my head here, but man, terrorists, they usually stuff a vehicle full of explosives, usually hundreds of pounds, and BLAM! They wipe out everything. That way, they are assured of getting their target. They never care about collateral damage. It's just not something that concerns them. This--I don't know. It's nothing I can put into my software algorithm to verify, but well, let's just say that my hunch is that this terrorist is an anomaly."

"Okay, thanks very much. Can we get one of your cards before we go?" asked Hanson.

Masters handed him a business card and proceeded to gather up his DVD and notes. He and Ronnie chatted for a while, no doubt catching up on office gossip. On the way out, JT and Juanita briefed Hanson on their interview with Mrs. Quarles and found out from him that there was nothing new on his end on either the Quarles or the train station case. They decided that when they got back to the office, Juanita would start working on the Quarles' financials while JT began processing the family members. Looked like it would be a long afternoon.

CHAPTER NINE

JT's house was on the way to Bolling Air Force Base from Juanita's place, so she agreed to drive. Since the three-hour-morning-traffic-rush was not yet over, she was talked into having breakfast with JT, Andy and Carmen. Andy said he remembered Ms. Juanita, but he was not very convincing. Carmen had not met Juanita before but that did not stop them from getting along famously. Sometimes JT wondered if he should even try to get a word in edgewise with the two of them, so instead he conversed mostly with his son, which was probably better anyway, because he found out about Andy's part in the upcoming open house for the MinnieLand Day Care Center. He was going to be a talking tree and needed an appropriate costume. Hopefully Carmen was already working on that.

At eight-thirty JT suggested that they should get started since they did have to traverse the Capital Beltway and cross over the Wilson Bridge. Although it was considerably better than it used to be before it became six lanes in each direction, the bridge still served as a perennial bottle neck in the area because the traffic just grew to keep pace with the improvements. Speaking of traffic, JT preferred his bigger, more comfortable Toyota, but didn't mind not driving occasionally, even if he had to ride in a PT Cruiser.

On the way Juanita asked, "JT, what's your take on this case? Are you really inclined to think it was terrorist related and does it tie in to the warehouse incident of the other night?" She discussed cases with partners almost incessantly. It was her way of thinking through the aspects of the case and asking questions that needed answering. It helped her get things straight in her own mind, and often her partner's as well.

"Well," JT began, "it looks a lot like a terrorist assassination, to use the word loosely, I guess, or somebody really wants it to look that way. I believe that terrorists would have been better off staging an accident, and even if it was a little fishy, it wouldn't have pointed to them. The guys at DARPA are going to redouble their efforts now—thinking they are on the right track if the terrorists are trying to derail the program. On the other hand, they may not have thought of that, or may not care if we think they did it, and may even want to flaunt it. They are, after all, terrorists, probably not that sophisticated as far as murderers go, and thought their best chance for success was one of their tried and true methods. But then, like Masters said, they usually go for the big bang. So if not terrorists, I guess the question is who would benefit from Quarles demise besides them, and who would want them to take the credit for it thereby deflecting suspicion from themselves?"

"Damn, *amigo,* I can't fault that logic. We need to get on possible motives. Maybe we'll get something from Quarles' computers or his cohorts over on Bolling. We sure didn't get much from his family history or financials. Besides, I can't see anyone with a motive stemming from the last two knowing enough to make this look terrorist related."

"What about his wife?" JT asked.

"She did impress me as a smart lady, in spite of her seemingly scatter-brained responses to some of our questions. That could have been a ploy, but she's one damn good actress if that's the case. No, she seemed genuine, and my money's not on her. Trouble is, I don't know whom to bet on."

"Anybody at DARPA?"

"Based on what we heard the other day from his boss, Briceman, there doesn't seem to be any benefit to stopping the program from that end, either."

"We just need to keep digging."

Juanita thought about the case for a while and then asked JT, "So, what made you become a cop? And what was it like working for Fairfax? I mean, you had some good stories, if I remember, so why did you leave?" Juanita had a habit of asking more than one question at a time.

"Nita, I'm not sure. Being a cop is just something that I always wanted to do. I loved working as a street cop. I had even more fun when I went undercover working for the drug task force. Not only was that a real community service getting those death dealers off the street, but I made some very, very good friends. You've probably heard me talk about RJ, Deke, Ryan and Scotty. I talk to at least one of them every day, and we still get together a lot to go fishing, for birthdays and other holidays, and just goofing off. Did I tell you what Larry, my first training officer, did?"

Juanita shook her head.

"My first day on patrol with him, he has me take the cruiser through a McDonald's drive thru. As we are getting our coffee he says, 'Pay attention, Rookie, because you'll likely be doing this in a couple of weeks.'"

Juanita laughed and then said, "And the answer to my last question?"

"What? Oh, yeah. The money, mostly. Plus I could work a better schedule and be home more often. Or so I thought at the time. Sara and I talked about it and thought it would be better for Andy, at least until he got into high school. What about you? What made you want to be a cop? If I recall, your dad influenced you."

"Actually, my dad wanted me to be a pilot, like him. I think I got into it because I like helping people. When I was a teenager, we were stationed at Scott Air Force Base in Illinois, and I was friends with a girl whose dad was a staff sergeant. He got into some kind of trouble and the MPs came and took him away. I was at her house when that happened, and even though one of the guys was a captain they treated my friend's dad with respect, didn't cuff him, and told his wife what she needed to do. Plus the Air Force is like a family, and my dad said if I insisted on being a cop, that at least I could keep it in the family."

By this time, they were heading north on 295 and approaching the turnoff to the base.

Bolling Air Force Base, DC, 3 November, 0930 hours

Bolling Air Force Base is one of the smallest Air Force bases, due to its location on the east bank of the Potomac River in the most southwestern section of the nation's capital. It is wedged in between the river on the west, highways on the east, the Anacostia Naval Station on the north, and, much to everyone's chagrin, the D.C. Blue Plains Waste Treatment Facility on the south. Across the river, you can see a good deal of Alexandria, including the Masonic Temple and the Torpedo Factory, and parts of Arlington County such as the plethora of high-rises called Crystal City, and Reagan Airport, also known as Washington National Airport. Bolling is home to a number of organizations and provides base operating support to nineteen tenant units, including the Air Force Office of Scientific Research, the Defense Intelligence Agency, the Naval Research Laboratory, and the Air Force Office of Special Investigations. The DIA built its Defense Intelligence Analysis Center there, or DIAC, and moved many of its operations there in 1987. While once a fully operational airport facility, the only aeronautical facility still operational today is a 100-by-100-foot helipad.

In spite of their credentials, it took a while for JT and Juanita to get clearance at the front gate on Malcolm X Avenue. They wondered if that had something to do with the DIAC being there, or perhaps the small nuclear reactor located at the southern end of the base that had been used for NRL research, or maybe something that very few people knew about that was somewhere in one of those nondescript buildings. In any event, they just made it to the AFOSR building in time for their appointment with Dr. Kovnowski.

Building 47 must have been built during World War II and couldn't have been any bigger than 16,000 square feet. It was rectangular shaped and had one corridor running down the middle and three perpendicular corridors dividing the building into eight equal sections. Six offices occupied each section, all neatly labeled with a room number and personnel names. There was no foyer or receptionist to get past, so JT and Juanita wandered around until they saw Kovnowski's name plate with another plate below that that said "Energetic Materials Division." Located in the first office on the left, he was sitting at his desk typing away on his desktop's keyboard and did not even notice them standing there until JT said something.

"Oh, oh, hi," he said as he looked up from his work. "How long you been standing there?"

JT noticed the odd-shaped pieces of metallic and ceramic debris located here and there throughout the office. On the walls there were an easy twenty plaques, many of which were glass encased boxes that held even more materials, while others displayed diplomas and awards.

"We just got here," said Juanita. "I'm Juanita Singletary and this is JT Dunkirk. We're from Homeland Security and, as I mentioned on the phone, we are investigating the death of Dr. Quarles. We'd like to ask you a few questions."

"Yes, yes. How can I help?"

Kovnowski didn't look like your typical lab scientist, if there is a stereotype for that. He had on khaki slacks and a dark, long-sleeved shirt with the sleeves rolled up several times. He was of medium build, had short, black hair but a full beard that was turning gray, and what you could see of his face was not remarkable—all in all a pleasant looking fellow.

"Dr. Kovnowski," Juanita began.

"Please, please, call me Marvin," he interrupted.

"As you know, Marvin, Dr. Quarles was killed in a car explosion almost a week ago. The evidence we have right now points toward this being a terrorist incident. We are, for the time being, making that assumption because of his involvement with the development of some software that might be instrumental in tracking the transfer of monies to fund terrorist operations. To begin with, can you tell us how you knew him?"

"Wow. I've never been involved in anything like this before. I wouldn't say we were close friends, but I think we were going to be. We met in grad school at MIT and helped out each other with some projects. Nothing serious. Actually, he helped me more than I helped him I think. I was glad to see the school chose to award him his doctorate, for he was certainly brilliant and really knew his stuff. Hell, he could have taught most of the professors there a thing or three. He was a bit arrogant, but not with me for some reason. When he moved to the area, he looked me up and we renewed our friendship, which kind of surprised me since he was mostly a loner. I think his wife talked him into

80

it. We had them over one Saturday and we had a good time. Our wives really seemed to hit it off."

"We'd like to know if you have any ideas as to why he might be a target—financial, marital or family related, vices that might have gotten him into trouble, enemies in the business, whatever. We're open to suggestions or any information that you think might be useful in our investigation."

"Like I said, he was a little arrogant, but I don't think enough to elicit that kind of behavior. I know they were a little stretched financially because of the two houses, but I think their folks were going to help them out there if they needed it. I don't think he had any serious rivals for his job. He was working with Dr. Jabornae, who's just down the road, but I seriously doubt there was any bad blood between them. I talked to Jabornae once and I think she was glad to be on board and felt she was learning a great deal from Stefon. As for vices, I don't think he had any. Unless you consider his work as one. He and his wife seemed well matched and quite happy. I don't think I missed anything, did I?"

"No, Marvin. I believe that that just about covers it. Unless there is anyone we should talk to other than Jabornae. We already talked to the people at DARPA."

"Are they going to continue with his work, or do you know?"

"According to his boss, Dr. Briceman, they plan on continuing with the project, and may be looking for a replacement, or they may just continue with Jabornae running things."

"Okay, okay. Thanks."

Kovnowski paused like he was considering something, so Juanita asked him if he was *sure* there was nothing else he wanted to add.

"Well, I guess one other thing. Stefon did mention this one butthead at DARPA that was always bugging him. He thought maybe it was because this guy thought that Stefon was the one that reported him to the IG. He said the guy was falsifying TDY vouchers, taking unnecessary trips, having an affair with one of his subordinates, stuff like that. But I seriously don't think it rises to the level we're talking about."

Juanita knew the Inspector General was a DoD in-house police force without arrest powers. They usually investigated accusations of minor crimes and then presented their findings to the individual's management for disposition. "Was this guy Mike Styles?" she asked.

Kovnowski nodded rather sheepishly so Juanita pressed a little further. She was pretty sure that the IG investigation was not public knowledge. "*Did* Quarles report Styles to the IG?"

Kovnowski paused but then said, "Yes, but he swore me to secrecy, which I don't think matters now. He was rather paranoid about it and asked me to mail the complaint when I went TDY to Houston, which is someplace that he had never been. He even told me to wear gloves so I wouldn't leave any prints!"

"Did you?" JT asked incredulously.

"No. I seriously doubt the IG dusts the written complaints they receive for prints. I could have told him that nothing would come of it—the IG is somewhat of a joke in DoD, but he was serious about doing the right thing and was convinced that DARPA management wouldn't do anything. This was only a couple of months or so ago, so I don't think any investigation has even been started."

"Did anyone else know that he filed this complaint?" asked Juanita.

"Stefon said that we were the only two that knew about it. He said he didn't want to mention it to Martha because he didn't want her to worry."

Sensing that the interview was over and to lighten the mood a little, JT piped up with, "Marvin, did you hear about the young materials scientist, who upon learning that he was denied tenure after six productive years at a University in California, requested a meeting with the Provost for an explanation, and a possible appeal?"

Marvin shook his head, unsure of what was coming.

"At the meeting, the Provost told the young man, 'I'm sorry to say that the needs of the University have shifted during the past six years leading up to your tenure decision. In point of fact, what we now require is a female, condensed-matter theorist. Unfortunately, you are a male, high-energy experimentalist!' Dejected but not defeated, the young scientist thought for a moment about the implications of the Provost's words. 'Sir,' he said, 'I would be willing to convert in two of the three categories you mention, but ... I'll never agree to become a theorist!'"

Marvin laughed heartily and said that was a good one.

Juanita thought he was just being polite. She thanked him and handed him their cards and gave the usual spiel.

Marvin got up and saw them to the door and then watched as they went up the corridor toward the exit. He couldn't take his eyes off Juanita and thought, *man, that's a really nice package.*

When out front and out of earshot, Juanita asked how long he had searched the internet for that joke.

JT just grinned.

"Did you ever hear 'I think' said so many times in such a short period?" she asked in a somewhat more serious vein.

JT shook his head and grinned again. "That's what they get paid for. These scientist types are certainly an odd lot, aren't they?" he asked rhetorically. "What about this IG complaint thing, however?"

"Guess that's one more thing we need to look into," she said as they got into her car and headed down Duncan Avenue towards NRL.

The Naval Research Laboratory serves as the corporate research laboratory for the Navy and the Marine Corps. NRL's Information Technology Division, in which Jabornae worked, was actually a descendant of the Laboratory's Radio Division, one of the two original research divisions making up the Lab when it was commissioned in 1923. Today their research programs cover areas such as Artificial Intelligence, Virtual Reality, and High Performance Computing, to name a few. Jabornae directed the Center for Computational Science, which participated as a partner in DoD's High Performance Computing Modernization Program and in DARPA's sponsored National Consortium. This was how Jabornae got involved with Quarles. DARPA sponsored her program in this area and paid for three contracts for the "improved collection, transmission, and processing of information to improve the conduct of military operations." When financial tracking became more of a priority, Quarles got involved and the COLTRANE program was born. The acronym stood for collection, transmission, and analysis enterprise.

Dr. Jabornae worked in Building 14, which Juanita remarked looked strikingly similar to the one they were just in. At least parking was not a problem. They found her office in short order and introduced themselves. Dr. Arati Jabornae earned her Ph.D. in information technology at Caltech, and then worked for the Navy at China Lake before coming to Washington. She was born and raised in India, but her parents emigrated to the U.S. just after she finished high school. She stood five-foot-seven and probably weighed about as much as he did, or 145 pounds, JT guessed. She had medium-brown skin and a full face with a shortened, almost flat nose, and her jet black hair was hung in a pony tail that reached down to her waist. Her office looked similar to Kovnowski's but had several PCs instead of chunks of various materials. There were also a dozen or so charts on the walls that JT couldn't make heads nor tails of.

JT gave the same introductory speech to Jabornae that Juanita gave to Kovnowski and she asked to be called Arati, pronounced 'Arth-ee.' "So, Arati," JT began, "we have been cleared on your program, as I'm sure you know, so we have some idea of what you are doing here. Our question is how will Dr. Quarles' demise affect the program?"

"There is no doubt that it will slow us down a little," she responded in perfect English, much to JT's delight, "but Stefon laid out a detailed, and we believe comprehensive, set of scenarios that we are pursuing in the current contract. The few difficulties that we foresee, which involve two or three widely varying parameters that we have several potential algorithms for, will be overcome. I am convinced that we will have a full beta program within two months."

"So you are confident that you will be successful even without Dr. Quarles?"

"Yes, and not because we are brilliant. Rather, Stefon has anticipated all the pitfalls and left us with definitive paths for their resolution. I believe that to a substantial degree he had it all worked out in his head when he wrote the statements of work for the contracts. I could see where he was going and from my many discussions with him, I am sure we will get there."

"Arati, is there anyone else but you that believes this?" JT asked.

"I do not think so. Stefon was very closed-mouth about this, except with me. I believe that he was indeed confident of success, but did not want to predict it too strenuously. He feared that if there were unforeseen difficulties that resulted in a less-than-anticipated product, it would reflect poorly on him. Since the follow-on contract will emphasize terrorist financial transactions, they decided to make it black, and he coined the acronym TOMFOOLERY. He said TOM stood for Traces of Mammon, and the foolery part meant that anybody would be a fool to think they could get away with hiding financial shenanigans in the future. Although the new program has a higher security classification, it actually faces only the normal procedural and operational problems of implementing any undertaking of this magnitude with myriad interfaces."

"Is there anyone that would benefit from a program interruption or failure?"

"As you know, if successful, the program will be an enormous help in pointing out financial transactions that are of a suspicious nature. This includes not only the ones that may divert monies that could fund terrorist activities, but also those used for other criminal activities, such as drug buys, illegal automobile sales, contract kickbacks, murder-for-hire, and so on. Actually, the terrorist algorithms are the smaller set."

"Is this well-known?"

"I do not see how it could *not* be, at least among the DARPA people involved with the program, your people in DHS that are partially funding the work, the handful of contractors involved, a few people here at NRL, the contracting organization at CIFA--the managements of those organizations, and, finally, all those that have been cleared for this program, including you two. That adds up to over fifty, but you should check the clearance list. The Director of DARPA would be able to get that for you. Unfortunately, there are a lot of people on the periphery that could surmise the program's usefulness, which probably at least doubles or even triples your list."

"I just have two final questions, Arati. First, can you think of anyone who might want to harm Stefon, or who would somehow benefit from his death?"

"I am not that familiar with Stefon's personal situation, so other than those I mentioned that would benefit from a program stoppage, I cannot think of anyone."

"Second, did he mention anything to you about an IG complaint or trouble with anyone at DARPA?"

"No, but that is interesting. He seemed most concerned about the program's potential for uncovering contract irregularities, and I do not believe that that was because that part of the program was any more difficult than the rest. It may have indicated a personal interest."

"Arati, thank you very much. You have been most helpful and we appreciate it. If you think of anything else later that might be of use to us please don't hesitate to call." JT and Juanita handed her their cards and got up to leave. "Good luck with the program," JT added as a final comment.

"Was she impressive or what?" asked Juanita as they walked over to her car. "And not because I almost understood everything she said, but did you read her bio?"

"Yes," JT responded. "I was impressed not only with her bio, but also by the way she managed to explain the program so I could understand it. At least I think she did. Her English was excellent, certainly better than mine. What impressed me more, though, was the fact that she didn't have an 'I love me' wall, like the other scientists we've visited. I believe she's very comfortable with herself and her accomplishments."

"Smart enough to pull off a murder?"

"Oh, absolutely. But I just don't see the percentage for her. Since she's government, there's no financial payoff. She could grab the credit for the program success, which could be money in the bank later, I guess, but after what she told us about him and the paperwork trail indicating his involvement, I just don't see that. I really think she's a straight shooter. God, I wish I was that smart sometimes."

"Ah, but then you probably wouldn't need me to work with you," Juanita chided.

"Well now there's an incentive," he kidded back. "Let's head on over to Reston and see what Mr. Sha-man-ski has to tell us. And I made a note to check on those selection boards she mentioned."

"So why didn't you expose her to one of your jokes?"

"You know, it just didn't seem right. She was so...smart."

CHAPTER TEN

Reston, Virginia, 3 November, 1215 hours

JT enjoyed having Nita drive for a change, since that way he got to concentrate on the case. And she was kind enough to let him. He mulled over the conversations they had with Kovnowski and Jabornae. *Kovnowski was reluctant to mention the IG investigation. Maybe he thought that reflected badly on Quarles. I know there's a severe reluctance—a stigma, even, depending upon the jurisdiction-- among police officers regarding cooperating with their own internal affairs divisions, but I don't believe that same reluctance applies to the IG in DoD, at least not to the same extent. Anyway, I can't see Kovnowski being involved in anything like this, nor Jabornae, either, for that matter, but she did seem more capable and had more motive, maybe. Then again Kovnowski is no dummy, either.* He remembered what Sergeant Reynolds whom he used to work for over in Fairfax always used to say: criminals are stupid. *But ole Dan was dealing with a different element than this case's suspects. At least the ones so far.*

Juanita interrupted his thoughts with, "What's that address again, JT?" Juanita had chosen to come back down 295 and around the Beltway up to the Dulles Toll Road. She was now coming down Wiehle Avenue and knew she had to turn left on to Sunrise Valley Drive, but didn't remember the address.

"It's the third left," JT said. "There it is, *Spry Systems, LLC.* He told me he'd meet us in the lobby at twelve-fifteen and we should be right on time. Said he'd be wearing a black suit with a black tie, and sitting on the bench just inside the lobby."

Juanita found a close-in parking space and they headed toward the building. A typical glass and marble structure like many of those built during the dotcom boom, the building had glass entrance doors and a fairly spacious atrium just inside the entrance.

JT had described himself and Juanita to Szymanski so he had no more trouble identifying the two of them than they did him.

After mutual introductions, during which he insisted on being called Bernie, Juanita began the questioning. "So, Bernie, can you relate to us what you saw and reported to the Loudoun police?"

Approaching his late fifties and graying around the temples, Szymanski was nonetheless in good shape for his age, due no doubt to his walking habit, and spoke with considerable animation. He sported a black suit, black dress shirt and black tie. Even without the black hat, he reminded JT of Johnny Cash. "This officer came to the door one evening saying he was investigating a crime in the neighborhood and asked if I might have seen anything unusual in the last week or so. You know, suspicious characters, people acting funny, things like that. I told him not really, but that I did see a strange vehicle just down the street from my house one morning. I get up at three-thirty on weekdays, stretch for a while and then spend an hour walking around the neighborhood. So naturally I got to know my neighbors' cars as I walk the same five-mile route every day. Well, one morning I saw a dark blue or black pickup truck that I didn't remember seeing before. Besides, it was parked in front of some common property and not directly in front of one of the houses, and I noticed the license plate. See, I have this thing for plates and know all the different series of Virginia plates and their numbering sequence. This truck had a plate that began ZZY. That was one of the first plates issued after Virginia went to the seven character plates in 1993. For some reason, the state decided to go backwards and began with ZZZ-0000, then ZZZ-0001, up through the first 10,000 numbers, and then ZZY, then ZZX, through all the ZZs then ZYZ, ZYY, et cetera. Well, they went down to the XU series and then stopped to cut the Jamestown commemorative plates five years before its 400th anniversary in 2007. Actually, they've gone back to the old series now, so we've been seeing the X plates again. So a ZZY plate is pretty old and you don't see many of them anymore. That's why I noticed and remembered it."

"Where was this and was there anything else you noticed about it?" asked Juanita.

"It was close to Marv Lester's house. I'm with the homeowners' association, so I know a lot of the folks in the neighborhood. And yeah, the one other thing I noticed was that it had a '22' as part of the four numbers in the plate."

Juanita first showed him the picture of the truck belonging to Roberts, the retired guy. His plate was 'ZZY-', and then four numbers containing a '22' in the middle.

"Yeah, that could be it. I thought there might be a '22' in the number."

Then she showed him the picture of Furlong's truck with the plate 'ZZY-' and then four numbers with '55' as the last two digits.

"That's it!" Szymanski exclaimed. "I recognize those fancy tail lights. They must be aftermarket lights because they sure stand out. I guess the '22' I thought I saw was a '55.' I'm really positive I saw that truck in the neighborhood that morning." Indeed, he had identified a 2000 Toyota Tacoma with aftermarket chrome taillights.

"And what morning was that?" Juanita asked.

"I remember the officer came by on Halloween, because I thought he was an early trick-or-treater. Which would make it the thirty-first, and it was pretty close to a week before that. Sorry I can't be more specific."

"Did you see anybody or hear anything when you saw the truck?"

"No, nothing. And at four in the morning, I would have heard anything unusual. You know, I got pulled over one morning last month."

"You mean a cop pulled you over for walking around the neighborhood at four A.M. in the morning?"

"Yeah. So I asked him if I was walking too fast."

Both JT and Juanita laughed. When Bernie still looked serious Juanita asked "This is a joke, right?"

"No, seriously. I had heard helicopters earlier and he asked me for some ID and said that they were looking for somebody. I learned later it was an auto theft suspect that had dumped his stolen car nearby. You know, the cop didn't even laugh. I think he was nervous."

Getting back on point Juanita said, "Bernie, this is a 2000 model truck. How could it have a 1993 or 1994 license plate on it?"

"Oh, you can transfer your current tags to your new car as long as they are in good shape. Must be what this guy did."

"Bernie you've been a big help. Here's my card if you think of anything else that might help us. We appreciate it."

"Hey, I hope it helps you. What is this all about anyway?"

"We believe that the owner of this truck stole the front license plate off of Mr. Lester's car and put it on a similar car he used to commit another crime. Sorry, but that's all I can tell you. Thanks again for your help."

As they walked out to Juanita's car, she remarked that there are certainly some odd people in the world.

"That's what makes it so interesting," said JT. "Let's stop for a bite then head on back to the shop. We've got some homework to do. Can you call that Lester guy that had his tag stolen and see if he has any connection with Furlong, or if there was any reason that he would be parked in front of his house that morning?"

Juanita checked her notes and made the call. "Mr. Lester has never heard of him, so it certainly appears as though he stole the plate used on the exploding Taurus. You thinking we should request surveillance on Mr. Furlong?"

"My idea exactly."

Juanita called Hanson on speaker phone and briefed him on what they had found out from Quarles' friend at AFOSR and his colleague at NRL, and from Mr. Szymanski.

"This neighborhood walker was really positive, huh?" he asked.

"The guy was very convincing," JT said. "There's no doubt in his mind or mine that he saw Furlong's truck that morning. Furlong had no reason to be there so the only explanation is that he stole that tag or this was one big coincidence, and neither you nor I believe in the latter. He was either working for somebody and gave the tag to them or used it himself to swap the tag with the other Taurus. I think it would be worth the resources to put him under surveillance, Boss."

"What about you, Juanita?"

Juanita indicated her agreement with a vigorous head nodding.

"She's shaking her head up and down, Boss," relayed JT.

"So what you have is an ex-con whose truck happened to be at a location where a license plate was stolen, who has no alibi and seems to be living above his means because he owns a Porsche, right?"

"When you put it that way, it doesn't sound quite so convincing," admitted JT.

"All right, I'll authorize GPS units for his vehicles, and maybe some occasional real-time coverage depending upon our workload. But I can't spare guys for around-the-clock coverage. Send me the info on him and I'll take care of it. JT, can you request the IG file on this guy, what's his name, Styles, and see if that yields anything?"

JT agreed.

"If you run into any flack there, let me know. By the way, Josh's ATF cohorts got back to him and said the sarin gas thing is pretty much a dead end as far as they are concerned. I presume you ran Quarles' buddies?"

Juanita answered: "Kovnowski was a friend with no other ties that we can see. They met back at MIT. Jabornae was helping Quarles with the program and I guess she could get some credit for it now that he's gone, but I just don't see her doing that, Sir. She's smart as hell, lives modestly, and does not seem to have a big ego. She didn't even have her Ph.D. hanging on the wall like most of her cohorts and the other Ph.D.'s we saw at DARPA."

Hanson asked JT what he thought.

"I agree a hundred percent. But we won't write her off, either."

"Okay, thanks. Keep me posted."

"Boss, before you hang up, did you see that email from Tom in Charlie Unit about that new scam that's going around?"

Hanson said he hadn't.

"Let me read it to you." JT pulled a piece of paper out of his briefcase. "This is a heads up for those who may be regular *Home Depot/Lowe's* customers," he began. "Over the last month, I became a victim of a clever scam while out shopping. Simply going out to get supplies has turned out to be quite traumatic. Don't be naive enough to think it couldn't happen to you just because you're in law enforcement. Here's how the scam works: Two seriously good looking twenty-, twenty-one-year old girls come over to your car as you are packing your shopping into the trunk. They both start wiping your windshield with a rag and *Windex* in their skimpy shorts and T-shirts. It's impossible not to look. When you thank them and offer them a tip, they say 'No' and instead ask you for a ride to another *Home Depot*. You agree and they get in the backseat. On the way, they start undressing. Then one of them climbs over into the front seat and starts crawling all over you, while the other one steals your wallet. I had my wallet stolen October 17th, 19th, 20th, 24th, and twice on the 27th. Also three times last Saturday and very likely again this upcoming weekend. So, hey, be careful out there."

Hanson and Juanita laughed at that one.

"JT," Hanson said, "you and your jokes are going to be the death of me. Speaking of which, I can just see you offering a eulogy for your best friend and half the place is laughing and the other half is groaning. Get off the phone and go to work."

"Yes sir, Boss," they both said in unison.

CHAPTER ELEVEN

Downtown Washington, D.C., 5 November, 2010 hours

A nice, warm sixty-eight degrees but with a breeze coming up the river from the south meant it wasn't exactly Indian summer, since it was too early for that, but it wasn't exactly fall, either. Not the worst night to be on a surveillance mission. Brendon Gotlieb looked over at the sour face on his partner, Sal Dominico, behind the wheel of their department issued Chevy Caprice and laughed. "Come on Sal, forget about ole what's-her-face and enjoy the ride." They had paired up a member of the Fusion Team with a JTTF member in order to spread the resources better. In his regular JTTF job, Sal dealt mostly with computers and paper work, so he really didn't mind the surveillance work. Luckily for Sal, Brendon was a lot less formal in the field than in the office.

"Yeah, well, she didn't stand *you* up at the stadium holding two tickets."

"I told you to pick her up instead of meeting her there. At least you got to scalp the ticket and recover your loss. And you got to see the best three-quarters of the game with the Skins climbing all over the Giants. Hell, it was so embarrassing by the fourth quarter that I almost turned it off."

"Okay, so it wasn't a total loss," conceded Sal. Salvador Dominico had an Italian-American upbringing, second generation, and was proud to be serving his country as a member of the JTTF. He couldn't believe how much more he enjoyed football than soccer. It rankled his dad to no end, or so his dad said. He liked to think of himself as a "good-looking Al Pacino." "Thank goodness our boy is finally next in line for a fare," he commented. Sal grew up in Little Italy in New York and didn't start driving until he reached nineteen. Thus, he always wanted to drive and Brendon didn't mind at all, since he was the more senior agent and didn't have the nervous energy that Sal seemed to. In fact, right now Sal was getting a little antsy, as he and Brendon had been sitting outside Union Station for almost thirty minutes waiting for Ashan Khadija's cab to make it to the front of the line. They had been following him since he started hacking a few hours ago and this would be only his fifth passenger in that time. They had taken over surveillance duty from Ronnie from the Team and Chuck Forsythe of the JTTF. The Team had put him under surveillance a few days ago when his alibi for the night of the 26th didn't satisfy Hanson. Ashan seemed to intersperse personal trips with his normal fares and it was hard to tell sometimes whether he was working and had no shows or was delivering messages. The Team had been taking down all the addresses he visited and checking them out as soon as they could. So far, nothing had clicked.

"Did you hear what the boss' son told his mom the other day?" asked Sal.

Brendon shook his head.

"He said, 'I couldn't sleep last night, so I went into your room. Why were you jumping up and down on daddy?' His mom, thinking quickly said, 'Well dear, I was pushing the air out of him.' The boy responded with, 'Well, then, I guess you're wasting your time. The lady next door blows him back up every day.'"

Brendon chuckled in spite of himself, but turned when Sal said, "Hey, it looks like our boy has another fare. The guy has a small carry-on type bag, so I guess he could be a businessman either closing out his day and going home or heading for a hotel to begin business tomorrow. Guess we'll know when we see where he takes him."

Ashan pulled out into traffic and headed west on Massachusetts Avenue. Sal started out and decided to hang back about a block. They had placed a GPS tracking device on the cab, so they weren't too concerned about Ashan getting ahead of them. There was still considerable traffic even this late at night, so it was slow going.

"I love this city," said Brendon. "There is so much history here." He seemed lost in the buildings they were passing and the organizations that were housed therein.

"You ever been to New York?" Sal said, trying to start up a conversation.

"Been there, done that."

"Come on. That's all you've got to say about it?"

"All right. I took a senior class trip there in high school and don't remember too much of that. My wife and I went up for a long weekend a couple of years ago and we did a lot of sightseeing. And I've been there a couple or three times TDY. So what I can say about it is from that perspective."

"Which is?"

"Oh, it's really a fascinating place—very diverse, multicultural, lots to do. We really enjoyed it. However, I wouldn't want to live there, because we both found it too crowded and too noisy. And we didn't go into any of the bad areas. So you grew up there, right?"

"Yeah. And although it's a great place—very much like you describe—I'm glad to be gone. I don't even think of the D.C. area as crowded with that as a background, and the weather is nicer, too. Where do you hail from?"

"Right here in River City. Well, the other side of the river anyway. I grew up in Springfield, Virginia. Went to Lee High School and then to Virginia Tech. Actually, JT and I went to high school together, but we didn't realize that until I joined the Team last year."

"So, you mean you and JT are the same age?"

"Within a couple of months."

"Yet he doesn't have a degree, he's a pay grade or two ahead of you, and he's your boss?"

"While I was having fun in college and maybe learning a couple of things, he was out there getting experience. Plus, as you know, he was a Fairfax County cop for several years. That, plus the fact that he's smart as hell and can read people like a book more than qualifies him for his position. And he's working for his degree. Actually, I think he contributes more to his classes than his instructors. I've been in a few of his training classes and he knows where it's at. Looks like our boy is turning right on 22nd Street. I think we may be getting close, so I'm gonna drop back some more."

Right after turning, Ashan pulled into the first available space a couple of car lengths past the Marriott entrance. Luckily, 22nd Street was one way northbound, so Sal could pull over on the other side of the street.

"Looks like he's getting paid," Sal remarked as he noticed the fare leaning over the front seat.

The passenger then exited the cab but turned back to say something to the driver, waved like he was saying thanks, closed the door, and headed back down the street and into the hotel.

Brendon noted the time and location in the log book given to him by Ronnie. He remembered the instructor back in the academy saying that surveillance was hours and hours of boring and either very cold or very hot sitting, followed by a few minutes of boring but usually more comfortable driving. So far, he was right. "Now it looks like he's taking inventory or something, maybe calling in."

After a few minutes of no movement, Brendon decided he'd better go check it out, since this was not usual behavior for this cabbie, who, for the most part, hurried to get the meter running again. Brendon walked up the left side of the street just in case Ashan decided to pull off. That way, Sal could pull up and have him jump in without losing the subject. As he got almost perpendicular to the cab, he noticed that Ashan's head was slumped over. "Oh shit!" he yelled as he raced across the street, dodging the oncoming traffic.

Sal, figuring something was amiss, jumped out of the car and headed up towards the cab.

"Sal, I think we just lost him!" Brendon yelled as he motioned Sal toward the Marriott. "Follow that guy into the Marriott and apprehend him!" As Brendon approached the cab, he saw a splash of red all over the front of Ashan's shirt. He pulled open the driver's door—almost causing an oncoming car to hit it—and reached for Ashan's throat. Through the thick, gooey flow of blood, he felt a thready pulse. An attempted murder committed right in front of them! He quickly ripped his own shirt off to use as a compress to stop the bleeding.

A passerby yelled, "Can I help?" and Brendon asked him to call 911. Brendon was applying pressure to the wound—

97

hopefully enough to stem the bleeding but not cut off his air supply. Ashan was trying to say something but Brendon couldn't understand a word, if they were words. He heard sirens in the distance and hoped they were coming here and coming fast. He couldn't feel a pulse anymore but didn't think CPR would be of any use at this point, so he just kept pressure on the wound trying to stop the bleeding. Brendon looked around and saw Sal running up.

"No luck, man. He disappeared into thin air. Nobody saw him in the hotel or on the street. He just melded in and walked off, I guess. Is our guy gone?"

"Yeah, it looks that way. We have to call the Boss," said Brendon. "I think maybe our Afghani subject is in danger. I hope it's not too late already."

"Okay. You take care of that. I'm going back to the hotel lobby."

By the time the paramedics arrived and took over a few minutes later, Ashan was dead. Brendon explained what happened and then said he was going into the hotel to wash his hands and would be right back. He stopped by the car and got out a JTTF jacket from the trunk and put it on. It was cold out here with just a tee shirt on. After a quick trip to the restroom, he got back on the scene and pulled out his cell phone. He called Hanson at home but the call went to voice mail. He then tried his cell phone when he noticed an in-coming call—it was Hanson.

"What's up, Brendon?"

"Sir, our cab driver just had his throat slit by a passenger. His wallet is gone, so it could be a robbery, but this seems a little brutal for that. The suspect disappeared into the night and left only the knife behind on the front seat. It happened so quickly there was no way we could have prevented it."

"I'm sure not, Brendon. Do you have any sort of a description?"

"He was medium build, dark-skinned, I think, wearing a dark-colored overcoat and a hat so we couldn't see his hair, but he was clean shaven. He blended right in, Sir, and acted like any run-of-the-mill passenger. We're not too far from the Dupont Circle Metro station, or he could have had a buddy waiting nearby with a car. Whoa! Sal's coming over with what looks like the guy's bag. Hold on. There's a black coat and hat in the bag that Sal found in the restroom of the hotel. We've definitely lost him now. Based on this, I think we should reconsider the surveillance on our Afghani subject."

"I agree. Actually, I'm thinking protective custody. I'll get two agents on it right away. Send me your route and I'll have the D.C. guys check for cameras along the way. Are the Metro Police there yet?"

"Yes. Just arriving."

"Okay, let them handle it but you stay there and get what you can. I'll see you back at the house tomorrow." Hanson made a couple of phone calls and rousted the troops. JT said he was available and Hanson also got a hold of Brian Canterbury from Delta Unit to take on the new task. After a brief description of events, Hanson gave them directions to Mustafa Yousef Ahmadi's place and told them to step on it, pounce him out of bed if they had to, explain the situation and their concerns, and offer him protective custody.

Brendon and Sal hung around long enough to give statements and talk to the detective that would be working the case. They briefed him on their activities and exchanged cards. It was pretty late by this time, so they were glad to call it a night.

CHAPTER TWELVE

Northeast Washington, D.C., 5 November, 2255 hours

JT and Brian met at Fusion Headquarters to get a company car and then proceeded to the Benning Road area of D.C. Brian Canterbury was a DIA employee on assignment to the Fusion Team's Delta Unit. He had served in the Army as an MP for nine years while he worked on his degree in law enforcement. After he graduated, he got a job with the Defense Security Service as an investigator, where he spent three years before landing the job as a special agent with DIA. When they formed the Fusion Team, he requested and got one of the detailee positions, hoping for a permanent position if things worked out. Although only thirty-six, he had almost seventeen years in law enforcement. His dark hair, including a large but not obtrusive mustache and wide sideburns, and prominent nose with high cheekbones gave him that smarmy Mediterranean look. He worked out regularly and often ran marathons. He hoped his knack for seeing the big picture would get him into management someday.

Mustafa lived with his cousin and some other relatives in a row house on Brooks Street just a couple of blocks from Benning Road. A man of obvious middle-Eastern descent who spoke in broken but understandable English answered the door. They asked for Mustafa and were greeted with the attitude often reserved for USCIS agents. After explaining that he was not in trouble but in possible danger, they were asked to wait outside. They hoped that their message was taken at face value since it was too late to get to the end of the block to watch the rear of the house. Mustafa appeared a few moments later along with his cousin who acted as an interpreter. JT recognized him from his visa photograph. Although communications were difficult, JT felt that he got the message across. Mr. Ahmadi clearly did not want to come with them. His agitation and nervousness also stood out. JT tried a few more times, rewording his arguments, but to no avail. He thanked both men and offered his card which they refused.

As they walked back to the car Brian asked, "Now what?"

"Let's drive off, circle around and look for a good surveillance position. I'll call the Boss and see if that's what he wants us to do." When JT got Hanson on the phone, he asked them to sit there for a couple of hours until he could get another team together. "Guess I could use a little more overtime," said JT.

Brian laughed, since 1811s, or law enforcement officers, got a standard amount of overtime pay, usually twenty-five percent, no matter how much, if any, overtime they put in. They picked a good spot near the end of the block with Mustafa's place only five houses up on their side of the street. Brian broke out the surveillance gear from the back seat.

"Did Hanson say when the relief would get here?" asked Brian. "I really don't think I could do this for more than a couple of hours." Brian had played racquetball for an hour and a half after work, and then had a big dinner and a few beers with his opponent, his brother-in-law.

"He mentioned maybe a couple of hours until he could round up some fresh troops. Does our guy have a car registered in his name?"

"I doubt it, but I'll run him through the D.C. data base," offered Brian.

"*S&S* is only about ten or twelve blocks over, so he may actually walk to work from here if he couldn't get anyone to drive him," said JT.

Brian punched in the data but came up blank. "You have the cousin's name?" he asked JT.

JT handed him the data on the cousin to see if he had a registered vehicle. The inquiry on him came back positive, showing one registration on a gray Toyota Camry with D.C. tags.

Brian read out the tag number and JT checked the cars up and down the street that he could see from his vantage point.

"Got it," he said. "Third car up from us on the other side of the street. Well, at least we'll have one entrance and his cousin's car covered until we get some more troops here. You want to try and get some shut-eye while I take the first watch?" JT offered.

"Yeah, if you don't mind. Not that this is the most comfortable place to sleep, but I'll give it a shot." Brian put the seat back and hunkered down as best he could.

JT scanned up and down the street with the infrared scope, trying to keep away from the one street light that was working near the end of the block. He started wondering how he got into this line of work and then remembered reading *The FBI Story* and *The New Centurions* when he was in high school and how much he had enjoyed them, as well as the cop shows on TV, especially *Hill Street Blues*. The lawyer shows, while interesting and often a challenge, just didn't cut it for him. Actually, he found episodes of the *Law and Order* and *CSI* shows quite interesting and always learned something from them. After about twenty minutes, JT nudged Brian awake.

"What's up?" Brian said.

"That's twice the same car has circled around the block, and I don't think he's looking for a parking space. Something's up. If he makes another trip around, we should see him any time now. Yep. Here he comes. Get ready to write down the make, model and plate and then call for backup." When the car drove by the third time, JT called out the data and Brian copied it down.

As Brian dialed his cell phone, the car approached Mustafa's place and slowed down. The individuals in the front and the right rear passenger seats got out and approached the residence. "It looks like they're throwing—whoa!"

With that last word, two front windows broke—one on the upper story and one on the lower story of the row house—as Molotov cocktails plowed through them. Two rooms of the place became engulfed in flames. The two perpetrators jumped back into the car.

JT yelled at Brian to call 9-1-1, but he was already on it. They both jumped out of the car, Brian still talking to the emergency response folks. About half way up to the flaming house, JT held out his arm to stop Brian. "Brian, these guys are still here. They are—shit! They've got rifles sticking out of the car windows. They're waiting for the residents to come out. Open fire!"

Both JT and Brian pulled their weapons and each fired two rounds into the back of the vehicle sitting in front of Mustafa's residence. Its rear window shattered at just about the same time that two people ran out of the front of the house. They fired another two rounds each and the car's tires started smoking and it jerked forward. As it pulled forward, they got off a few more shots at the driver's position and apparently hit him, as the vehicle swerved off to the other side of the road and ran into a parked minivan. Three of the doors opened and two of the occupants emerged with rifles in hand. A third occupant, the one that came out of the back passenger side door, had his hands in the air. The guy behind him grabbed him around the neck to use him as a shield and turned his rifle, which JT could now see was a shotgun, toward the two people that had exited the blazing house.

"Brian, take out the guy on the left," JT yelled and then, using the light from the blazing house, took careful aim at the head of the rear assailant on the right. He was about thirty yards away, so it was an iffy shot, but if he missed, he was going to employ the training he learned at Artesia and close the gap. He'd only fired seven rounds and had six left. He was going to race up to the man while firing away and pepper the guy if he had to. It wasn't necessary, though, as his marksmanship training paid off and his shot found its mark. JT saw the rifle drop and the human shield fall to the ground. The man he had just shot teetered back and forth, fell to his knees, and then keeled over on his face.

At this point, the assailant on the left had taken a bullet from Brian in his upper-left torso, which jerked him around toward the other two assailants. As he started to fall, his shotgun went off, sending a load of buckshot down toward the ground and into the lower back of the only man so far that hadn't been shot by one of them. Three more people had run out of the house by this time, and it looked as though all five of the escapees were having second thoughts about jumping out of the fire and into the firing line.

"It's okay! It's okay!" JT yelled at the frightened victims as he motioned them down the street towards his car and away from the flames, meanwhile running up to check on two of the fallen assailants. The guy he had shot in the head was probably dead before he dropped his shotgun. Unfortunately, whether it was intentional or a lucky shot, the guy Brian shot had severely damaged the back of the one assailant that apparently wanted to surrender. He was alive, but unconscious; whether he fainted, hit his head when he fell, or passed out from the gunshot wound JT wasn't sure, but his backside was a mess although not bleeding profusely. JT made sure this "innocent victim" wasn't armed and then grabbed the shotgun of the man he'd just shot.

At the same time, Brian ran up to check on the man he'd hit while keeping an eye on the driver's position. He found the guy on the ground in bad shape, his front torso covered with blood, but still breathing. Brian picked up the injured man's gun and then carefully approached the driver, whose head was scattered over a good portion of the steering wheel and windshield. After checking to see if JT needed any help, he went back and cuffed the guy on the ground, helped him to sit up against a car, and then grabbed a compress that JT had retrieved from the trunk of their car to apply to the assailant's wound.

JT was assisting his wounded assailant in the same manner.

From the sound of the sirens, the fire department would be there shortly, so JT, catching his breath, made sure Brian had control of the prisoners, and then found Mustafa's cousin. JT asked him if there was anyone left in the house and was told that everyone had made it outside. After ascertaining that, miraculously, no one from the house was injured, JT huddled them all into his car. The temperature had dropped to fifty-four degrees outside, but none of them had managed to grab a coat before running outside.

Brian was still working on the guy he shot when the paramedics arrived just moments after the fire company. The fire department contained the blaze within twelve minutes. Even with the fire, smoke and water damage, the place looked like it would be salvageable. It's doubtful that the occupants would fare as well after this ordeal.

"JT, you seem to be making a habit of waking me up tonight," said Hanson after taking the second call from JT. "What is it this time?"

"Well, Boss, there's bad news, good news and better news. The bad news is that we just lost two apparent terrorists. The good news is that we just lost two apparent terrorists. The better news is that there are two others still with us, and hopefully, although they are both shot, at least one of them will make it." JT outlined the recent events and suggested that Mr. Ahmadi may change his mind about protective custody.

"Take him," said Hanson, "but make him think it's his idea."

"You got it, Boss."

JT went back to the company car, which was filled with five frightened people, and asked Mustafa's cousin to roll down the front passenger side window. "Is your name Ahmadi also?" he asked.

"Yes, I am Younis Ahmadi. What will happen to us now?"

"We can get you and your family into a shelter until you find another place to live. Were you renting this house?"

Younis translated the questions for his family and the answers for JT. His English had improved to something not quite so broken and more understandable. "Yes, do you think I will get any rent back or maybe I would have to pay for this damage?"

"Whether or not you get any rent money back will be up to you and your landlord, but I wouldn't count on it. This was not your fault, so no, you will not have to pay for any restoration. Do you have any insurance on your furniture and other stuff that may be ruined?"

After a pause for more translation, he answered, "No. No insurance. What will we do?"

"We can probably get you some help in that area as well. Do you know what happened here tonight?"

Younis looked at his cousin and they exchanged words for a few minutes. He then turned back toward JT and said, "I think maybe these people were here to harm us. I know that they set our house on fire, not you, and I saw their guns pointed at us. It is a good thing that you were here and you could stop them. My cousin thinks that they were here for him and he wishes to maybe go with you to a safer place."

JT told him that that was probably a good idea and asked them to wait there in his car while he talked to the local police who were now there in force. The paramedics had stabilized both men, and Brian got a commitment from two of the Metro PD guys to follow the ambulances to D.C. General Hospital and keep an eye on the injured assailants until the Team could get someone over there. He had just about finished explaining what had gone down when JT walked up.

After introductions, JT asked if the Metro guys could get the Ahmadi family to a shelter and was told that, if they had no friends or family that they could stay with, they would be housed in a homeless shelter nearby. The Metro guy said that someone from the Office of Victim Services and the Office of Human Services would be taking care of these people. JT told them that they would be putting the one man under protective custody and asked the battalion chief if he could let him back into the building yet to get his things. The chief said they needed a few more minutes and he would let them know when it was safe.

JT went back to the car and relayed this to the Ahmadi family through Younis. He asked Younis to tell Mustafa that he'd be taking him back into the house to get any of his things that he would need for the next few days, and then to a safe house where he could rest up and where they would have an interpreter. Then the others could go into the house, get their things, and then they would be taken to a nearby shelter. Younis had indicated that Mustafa spoke very broken English and would need an Urdu interpreter. JT called the Boss one more time and found out that he had already taken care of the protective custody arrangement and that JT was to take him to the safe house.

One of the firemen came up to JT and told him that he could enter the damaged house now, so he got Mustafa and they went in through the charred living room. Mustafa's room was upstairs and they went there and he got some clothes and other personal items that were not damaged. He put them all in a grocery sack and indicated that he was ready to go. He and JT left just as the other family members were entering the residence.

Mustafa and his cousin hugged and exchanged some words and then bowed to each other. JT got the impression that this was a goodbye. Mustafa nodded to each of the other family members and then turned toward JT and motioned that he was ready to go.

JT led the way back to his car and asked Brian if he wanted to come along or go back to headquarters first to get his car and return home.

"They're not that far apart," Brian responded, "so let's go get him settled. Besides, I've never been inside the safe house and would kinda like to see it." An MPD detective had arrived by this time and JT checked out with him before leaving. Brian drove and nobody said much on the trip back to Arlington.

When they were almost there, Brian's cell phone rang. "Canterbury," he said. "Really?" A few minutes went by with Brian listening intently. "Okay, thanks, man."

JT looked expectantly at Brian.

"Seems the guy I shot found enough strength to knock out the attendant, undo himself from the gurney, open the back door and jump out of the bus—right into the path of the police car following them. I guess right about now he is finding out about the shortage of vestal virgins for terrorists."

"And the other guy?"

"They didn't say, so I assume he's being worked on by now. Some night, huh, partner?"

"Amen to that."

CHAPTER THIRTEEN

I guess I should consider it good news and bad news, like many of these people here do. The cab driver was definitely a liability and at least that is no longer a problem. The job was no doubt performed with great precision and, so far as we know, has resulted in no ramifications. The Mustafa thing is a whole other matter, however. We weren't even sure if he knew anything compromising, and now we've lost Khalid and Mahmoud and two others —three dead and one injured in the hospital under police custody. That may have been a bad decision, but we could take no chances. Perhaps if we had acted quicker, this might not have happened. Then again, Khalid may not have participated in the planning of the second operation as much as he should have. We must get to Farooq before they can get any useful information from him--which means that we will have to follow Rasheem's advice and change some things based on Farooq's knowledge of our operations. And we are not sure just how much, if any, compromising information Mustafa is aware of. They obviously had him under surveillance, and probably the cab driver, but we'll never know for sure, since Khalid is no longer with us. He will be very difficult to replace. I fear the accomplishment of our prime objective is delayed until we can train some of the new recruits and that we must regroup. I will have to change protocol and meet with the cell. I see no other option at this point.

Crystal City, Virginia, 7 November, 0910 hours

The Fusion Team's safe house was located in an apartment high-rise in Crystal City, or the concrete jungle, as JT called it. He met with Hanson in the lobby to discuss their interrogation strategy before meeting with Mustafa. Hanson was leaning toward the good cop-bad cop routine, but JT disagreed. "Boss, he was really scared and concerned for himself and his family. Based on this and the good treatment that I understand he's received from our folks yesterday and this morning, I really think he'll flip on his former associates. Also, we cashed in a chip or two with our D.C. friends and got his family into a good shelter, and Mustafa has talked with them about it. We do need to decide how much protection we're willing to provide them and have that in our hip pocket as a bargaining chip, however."

Hanson thought about this for a few minutes and decided he'd trust JT's instincts. Besides, if they didn't get the cooperation they needed, they could flip to the other routine. "What time is the interpreter supposed to be here?"

"Twenty minutes ago," JT replied, "but she did call and say she was running about a half-hour late."

"She?" Hanson asked with raised eyebrows.

"I know you think it would be better to have a man given the Middle-Eastern background of our guy, but there just isn't one available. We even talked to the Agency, but they couldn't get us one until tomorrow. I really think this will work out. His family didn't strike me as the orthodox kind, perhaps because they've been here for a while."

"Well, we're sure not waiting for tomorrow. Is this our interpreter coming in now?"

"That's her—Maryjo Myers." JT recognized her from a course he took last year at The Centre for Counterintelligence and Security Studies, or the CI Centre, located in Alexandria, Virginia. Plus, she was a DHS employee and he had checked her credentials with headquarters when he requested assistance with Mustafa. He also knew that she was fluent in Farsi, Urdu and one other Middle-Eastern language he couldn't remember the name of. "Over here," he called as he waved her over. MJ, as she insisted upon being called, had long dark hair, brown eyes and slightly olive complexion that hinted at her Turkish heritage. The few extra pounds she carried was spread out nicely over her tall frame.

JT remembered her as being quite attractive, and he wasn't disappointed—her no-nonsense black pantsuit that made her look like an executive notwithstanding. After introductions, they proceeded to the elevators. One opened right away and JT pressed button number ten. They traded small talk on the way up, with JT confirming that she was still guest lecturing at the CI Centre.

JT knocked on the door of the appropriate apartment and an agent let them in after seeing JT's badge. Mustafa was sitting on a hardwood chair at an oblong table in the dining area, right in front of a picture window that provided a view of Route 1, part of the river, and Washington National Airport. He seemed to be mesmerized by it and didn't take notice of his visitors until they moved in close. The Boss had already talked to the FBI and they mutually agreed to a relocation for Mustafa's cousin and his family—if his cousin agreed to take a job as an interpreter, a deal he readily accepted. They were less inclined to help Mustafa himself, pending his cooperation and what verifiable information he had for them.

JT heard MJ introduce herself and them. They conversed for a while longer in Urdu and then she turned to JT and Hanson and said Mustafa had some questions before he was ready to talk. Hanson fielded the questions and basically got the message across to Mustafa that his family was safe, but that *his* disposition depended upon what happened in the next few hours. And they were indeed at it for several hours, with JT doing most of the inquiring, and occasionally checking on the recorder and referring to his list of questions.

Mustafa had been recruited while attending an "Afghans in America" meeting. This was a national organization with a D.C.-based chapter that helped Afghan immigrants assimilate into their new community by helping with job searches, group meetings and English and other classes. He didn't know where the recruiter came from or how he knew about his background, and he only saw him at one of the meetings. The recruiter, Khalid, had played on Mustafa's patriotism for his homeland and said that he only wanted the use of the building where Mustafa worked for an occasional meeting. Khalid also hinted that it would be "good" for Mustafa and his relatives here and back in-country if he cooperated. Mustafa had met two other "patriots" and had names and contact information. He said he was contacted three times about the use of the building, the last being a few days before the aborted meeting on the 26th. He had disabled the alarm system and left the door unlocked, and had intended to arrive early the next day to reset everything. He didn't know if they actually used the building the other two times. He did attend two meetings with his new "friends" in the last six weeks in two other locations where Afghan independence and other homeland issues were addressed, including a potential plan to bring about more recognition of Afghanistan's problems by the international community. He gave them the two meeting locations and as many names and dates as he could remember. Unfortunately, he did not seem to know anything about a train station plot or the murder of Dr. Quarles.

"Okay, I think that's about it for now," Hanson offered, and JT agreed. "How about we reconvene over in my office?"

MJ explained to Mustafa that they were done for now, and that they would get back to him regarding his future. The three of them bid him and the resident agent goodbye and took the elevator to the street level. They walked two blocks to the underground and then through several long tunnels containing a host of shops. They stopped at the food court for lunch before going back to Hanson's office.

Fusion Team Headquarters, 7 November, 1315 hours

After offering his visitors two of the comfortable chairs in his office and taking one himself, Hanson turned the recorder back on. "I'm going to tape our impressions of the interview, as well," he stated and then began the discussion. "So, what's your take on Mr. Ahmadi, MJ?"

MJ started by addressing Hanson as "Sir," was informed he preferred Tom, corrected herself, and proceeded. "I think he was being very honest with us. He was a little nervous at first, but he warmed up and, I'm sure you noticed, became quite loquacious and animated towards the end of our discussion. I don't think—"

Hanson held his hand up and interrupted her with, "Hold that thought. JT, is he a terrorist or a terrorist supporter?"

"Boss, I think he was being roped in by a terrorist group and felt like he didn't have much of a choice when he started to realize who he was in with, if he did get to that point in his thinking. From what MJ said, he might have been concerned that they had some influence over what might happen to his family, but that was vague. It reminds me of the situations where the mobster asks the cop to run a plate for some minor favor, and it goes downhill from there."

Hanson looked over at MJ and nodded expectantly. "Tom, I think JT's nailed it. I was about to sum it up pretty much like JT just did, and I think you knew that when you stopped me. I do think he is smarter than I was originally willing to give him credit for. Mustafa, that is, not JT," she said as a smile crossed her face. "When he mentioned the 'Afghan independence and other homeland issues,' I got the impression that he didn't think you needed to have a secret meeting to discuss that, unless it was something more than we'd be okay with."

"I'm leaning in that direction too. JT, what do you recommend?"

"We know they tried to kill him. Who 'they' are is still being checked on by our guys, and maybe we'll get more from Mustafa's attacker that made it to the hospital, but it's obvious that they thought Mustafa had information that might help us and that we'd already figured that out or would eventually. He is of no use to them now, but may be to us. I'd keep him on tap until we can check out all the info he gave us, and then relocate him with his cousin or deport him, his choice."

"Sounds reasonable to me. I'll see if Charlie agrees and then go from there." He turned off the recorder, looked at JT and asked, "Will you get the tape over to transcription?"

JT nodded.

"MJ, no offense, but we'll have another interpreter verify your input. Do you want a copy of the transcript?"

"Yes, please. I understand that's standard procedure and I'd appreciate the double check on my take."

Hanson got up, indicating the meeting was over, and JT proceeded toward the door.

"Could I have a word with you before I go?" MJ asked Hanson.

He replied in the affirmative and sat back down.

MJ waited until JT was out of earshot. "I thought JT was the one that lost his wife in that hit and run accident a year or so ago, but I see he's wearing a ring. Have I got the wrong guy?"

"No. That's him," Hanson said with a slight smile creasing his face. Are you interested? You know he does have a little boy and a live-in housekeeper."

"I was just wondering. He really seems like a nice guy." She paused as if considering her next words and then asked, "Oh, what the hell, is he dating?"

"Actually I don't think so—gets kinda wrapped up in his job and his kid, you know."

"Got it. Hey, thanks for letting me work with you on this. Can we, ah, keep this conversation to ourselves?"

"My lips are sealed. Thanks for your help. We'll be in touch."

MJ got up, shook Hanson's hand and headed out the door.

He watched her walk away and noticed that she went out of her way to stop by JT's desk on the way out. After she left, Hanson fielded a phone call and then called JT into his office. "JT, I just talked to the shooting review team and they cleared you for full duty. So, I want you to give that tape to Bravo Unit to get transcribed. I also want them to check out the info we got from Mustafa. I need you back on the Quarles case."

"Thanks, Boss. I was just going to check with Juanita and see how we're progressing. How 'bout we give you an update tomorrow?"

Hanson gave him a thumbs up and then decided to catch up on his messages while JT headed back to Juanita's desk.

"So, what's up, Nita?" Juanita had been working on the Quarles' family financial history.

"Hey, *amigo*. How'd it go in there?"

"I gotta process it. How about I fill you in later? By the way, I'm back on full duty. What do you have?"

"Almost everything that Mrs. Quarles gave us is spot on: the $250K insurance policy; the 401K is worth only a little more than the $150K she mentioned; she's the only beneficiary; and they have two mortgages but no other debts. I talked to both sets of parents and hers were going to help with payments until the house sold. Quarles didn't drink much and didn't gamble. He was a devoted husband and looking forward to being a father. Sounds like the ideal young family."

"You said almost?"

"She did forget to mention the copyrights that her husband had on three software programs that he wrote. Whether they are worth anything or not, I don't know. They haven't made any money off of them yet, but I guess there's potential."

"Did she know about them?" JT asked.

"Don't know. But it would be an easy thing to forget since they haven't made any money off them."

Just then JT's cell phone started ringing and he didn't recognize the number. "Dunkirk. Yes. Damn. Okay, thanks. That was one of our guys over at D.C. General. Our Stick still isn't talking, but was apparently either delirious or having some sort of nightmare at one point. The Farsi interpreter said he thinks the guy was ranting something about a transportation system or something similar. Sort of confirms the train station plot but other than that, looks like we're striking out everywhere."

"Maybe not. You got a package from the DoD IG. Hopefully there's some good news in there."

JT opened the thick manila envelope, which contained copies of a complaint and interview transcripts. The complaint was against Mike Styles of DARPA—the Assistant Director for Administration and the guy that Quarles had had at least one run in with. The complaint was anonymous, but of course JT knew that Quarles had told his buddy Kovnowski that he had submitted it. According to the complainant, Styles had falsified TDY vouchers, taken unnecessary trips for personal reasons, improperly spent government funds on food, drink and other items, had his Facilities Director transferred so he could promote a lady he was sleeping with, and accepted bribes to steer government contracts to selected companies. The IG personnel had interviewed ten individuals, mostly government employees who worked for Styles and the contractor personnel that supported them, and gotten reasonable confirmation for all of these transgressions but the latter, more serious one. JT thought that Quarles probably had not mentioned that one to Kovnowski or he would have mentioned it to them. Perhaps he was not as sure about the contract irregularities, especially since all the former allegations were stated more like facts than accusations. Quarles himself had not been interviewed by the IG personnel. It would have been interesting to see how he handled himself in the interview and how he answered their questions. While reading the interviews, JT got a picture of not only a crooked individual, but a very vindictive one with a short temper who was prone to petty acts of vengeance. One of the interviewees reported having seen Styles and his lady friend going at it in her car in the parking garage! This man was a little Caesar with serious self-importance issues. That could be an interesting interview.

"Hey, Nita, did we ever get Quarles' laptop from the ATF?"

"Yeah. One of their guys dropped it off a few days ago. I forgot to tell you. You want it now?"

"Yes, please. Then you need to read this stuff."

As Juanita handed the computer to JT she said, "By the way, they said this thing was password protected and it took their best guy two days to get through all the protocols. And apparently neither the explosion nor the foam from the firefighters damaged it. But they said they didn't find anything of interest—to them, anyway. However, they did say that we might find it interesting so they left it 'open' for us."

As JT perused the laptop contents, he cast an occasional glance at Juanita, who was reviewing the IG file. He saw her shaking her head in disbelief. She saw him watching and said, "If half of this is true, this guy is a real loser. How could anybody work for him?"

"Sometimes if you want to keep your job, you gotta put up with some shit. As you probably noticed, when the IG folks asked the people they interviewed that question, or why they hadn't said something to someone, they all said basically the same thing—that they thought management wouldn't do anything about it anyway and it could come back and affect them. The 'nobody likes a whistle blower' syndrome, I guess. Quarles' notes on this guy paint an even bleaker picture. Not only does he think Styles was accepting contract kickbacks—at least on the Quintrax contract for the security system at DARPA, and that he was living above his means as a result—but also that he was altering the security codes at DARPA to 'prove' that he was at work when he wasn't."

"Senior executives don't get overtime, do they?" Juanita asked.

"No. Must be some other reason he wanted to appear to be at work. You're right, this guy is a piece of work. I think we have some homework to do on him, and then an interview. In the meantime, I'm going to review the UAV tape from the other night."

After twenty minutes, JT called Juanita over. "Look here at this cab, Nita. What do you see?"

As JT played the video in slow motion, Juanita narrated: "I see two men leaning on it discussing something or other. Then the Civic pulls up, two more guys get out, and they all greet each other. Then the Tahoe with Rasheem and his buddy in it gets there and the six of them all go inside. What do you see?"

"Concentrate on the cab," he said as he replayed the DVD and focused it for the best picture of the cab.

"It's hard to tell from the angle of the UAV shots, but— there might be a driver in that cab that never got out." The light bulb came on for Juanita. "The cab was there when you guys got there and you followed the Tahoe when it pulled out. You never saw the cab leave or the remaining two guys get in it, most likely neither one of them into the driver's seat. Ashan could have been sitting in the driver's seat the whole time!"

"Exactly. My bet is that he was told to provide transportation as part of his acceptance into the group, but not attend the meeting itself—just act as a lookout. Most likely, he was supposed to steal a car but didn't get around to it, or didn't want to, so he used his own cab without the ID placard in it, of course. After he dropped off the other two Sticks, he parked his cab where it was found and 'broke into it' so it would look like it was stolen, and then hightailed it over to his friends' house. Damn! If we had better video, we could have gotten to him before they did. Why don't you ask the Boss over here and we'll show him."

After seeing the tape, Hanson agreed with their assessment but didn't think there was sufficient cause at the time, even if they had noticed the apparent presence of a driver, to bring the cabbie in—just tail him, which is what they did. Nor, under the circumstances, was there time to get better video of the event. He encouraged them to just keep on trucking.

"By the way, Boss, how's the tracker for Furlong coming?"

"Sal got one on his truck while he was at work. I understand that the data's been coming in regularly since Monday, but I don't know if there's anything interesting there so far. And I don't think they have one on his Porsche yet, since they have to wait for him to take it out of his garage. You need to talk to Sal."

They couldn't find Sal, so they left him a message and then pressed on for another hour working the data before calling it a day.

CHAPTER FOURTEEN

Annandale, Virginia, 8 November, 0835 hours

"So, JT, looks like we're off to DARPA land again," Juanita said as she got into his car in front of her apartment. "I'm liable to start liking the place if this keeps up. Are we talking to anybody besides Styles?"

"I guess that depends upon what he has to tell us," JT replied, "although I want to talk to their security guys, as well. But, I don't want anyone there to know that. What's your take on this Styles guy?"

"If he is into fraudulent contract activities to the extent that Quarles indicated, and if Styles thought that he was about to report this, then I think he has motive. Most of the rest of the stuff about him paints him as a slime ball but isn't motive. Now, if he's having an affair, that's a horse of a different color."

"Paints and color? You're in a descriptive mood today."

"I'm always colorful. You only notice it sometimes. I did run his financials, and while he makes a great salary, he lives high on the hog. There's no way he could make it without his wife's income. Who, by the way, kept her maiden name: Elizabeth Falworth."

"What's she do?"

"She's vice president of a telecommunications services company and brings home about twice his salary, plus substantial bonuses. Her share of the company, based on current stock values and a recent takeover offering, is probably over three million. *She* owns a two-million-dollar-plus house in Potomac, several nice cars, and a considerable portfolio. *He* owns an SUV and a townhouse in Alexandria. Their son goes to a private school and they've taken a few nice cruises. And he's paying child support for a teenager from his prior marriage. I think the bottom line is that he'd be willing to get serious about protecting the lifestyle that she has enabled him to become accustomed to. Based on the descriptions of him that were given to the IG, I wouldn't put it past him."

By this time, they were cruising up Sleepy Hollow Drive headed for Wilson Boulevard. "I've been thinking about the security tampering that Quarles mentioned. That's why I want to talk to the security folks first. If we can get a confirmation out of them, then we'll have something in our hip pocket on this guy." JT was interrupted by Juanita's cell phone.

"Singletary," she announced. "Yes, how are you?" Juanita paused, then said, "Yes we can. Okay, we'll see you then. That was Arati over at NRL. Said she has something for us and wants us to stop by tomorrow morning at ten. Actually, she seemed a little excited, but said she didn't want to say anything on the phone. That's an interesting development."

"Excited? Indeed," JT replied.

"Okay, so maybe I was more excited than she was."

"I love police work. Can you call Lou Callas at DARPA and have him meet us at their Visitor Control Center? Tell him we want to see the person in charge of their electronic security and badging system, but that we want that kept on the QT."

Juanita found his card and made the call.

Arlington, Virginia, 8 November, 0915 hours

JT once again parked in front of the building, again much to the chagrin of the local gendarme. Lou Callas was in the visitor control center, as usual, and gave them their badges. "Who you seeing this time?" he asked.

"We're here to see Mr. Styles," JT replied.

"Let me see if he's in." Lou typed a few strokes on his keyboard, waited, and then replied, "He's in a meeting in the tenth floor conference room, but should be out in less than ten minutes. I'll escort you up." He led JT and Juanita to the elevator bank, walked over to the last one and inserted a key, and the elevator door opened. "We keep this one available for special guests," he said smiling.

"Is the Director in today, Lou?"

"Yes, Sir. All day." When they exited the elevator, he led them down a corridor on the south side of the building and then badged them through what looked like a security vault door. "Your badges wouldn't work on this one," he explained. "This is where the system is controlled from. Jeremy, you have some guests," he called out. "This is Jeremy Johnson," he said to JT and Juanita as the man approached. Then he looked at Jeremy and said, "The old man said to give these folks whatever they wanted." He then turned and headed out, winking at JT and Juanita as he exited the room.

JT and Juanita showed Jeremy their badges as they introduced themselves. "We'd like to ask you a few questions about your badging system," Juanita began.

"I'll have to call Mr. Styles up here for that," he responded. Jeremy's black hair, thin physique and baby face made him look like a teenager. "I have strict orders not to discuss the workings of our security system with anyone outside this office."

"Well, now, you see, that's a problem. We're investigating a murder case and really need to ask you some questions in confidence. You don't have a problem with that, do you?"

It was obvious that Mr. Johnson was getting nervous, perhaps caught on the horns of a dilemma. He looked around as though he might see someone to help him solve his problem, and seeing no one came back with, "I'm sure Mr. Styles could help in this matter, as well. He actually knows a lot about how it was purchased, the cost, and a number of the features used in other locations that we didn't purchase."

"We'll talk to him next," Juanita assured him, which really seemed to upset Jeremy.

"I really think he should be here," Jeremy requested more than said, his nervousness apparent even to himself.

"We can talk to you here, alone, or we can take you to an interrogation room at our facility. Either way, it's going to be you alone."

"If you are concerned that Mr. Styles will find out that you talked to us, than we can keep this in strict confidence. The more you protest, the more I think you might have something to hide."

"You don't understand. This could mean my job. He's not the most forgiving person. And one of the other guys, or even Styles, could walk in here at any moment. And even if that doesn't happen, he reviews the security logs periodically and would find out anyway."

"Couldn't they be altered?" JT interrupted.

"Yes, but—" Jeremy stopped. He knew he'd been caught.

"All, right," Juanita said in a conciliatory tone, "I think you realize that you have no choice in this matter now. While neither Mr. Styles nor you are suspects at this time, this is an on-going murder investigation, and there are the potential charges of impeding an investigation and withholding information that could be brought to bear. And in this case, those are felonies. So, how do you want to play it?"

Jeremy's face fell nearly to the floor. He spaced out for a minute, imagining his whole life going out the window. "Look. I'm a contractor here. Not only could I lose this job, but my company could fire me and I wouldn't find work in this town or even this business again. Can't you give me a break here?" he pleaded.

"If you answer all our questions fully and honestly, and if you haven't broken any laws, then I don't see any of the dire consequences you mentioned occurring. Nor do I see the need for anyone to find out about this. So how about you just come out with it and we'll get this over with."

"Styles asked me to fake some entry data for him. He's messing around with one of his employees and wanted to have it appear as if he was here when he wasn't. At least that's my take on it. He didn't actually come out and say that but it is rather common knowledge. I got the impression that someone knew one of the guys here in security and would check on him."

"And that would be...?" asked Juanita.

"Don't know if he was talking about his wife or the husband of his girlfriend."

Juanita posed another open ended question: "And you did this because...?"

"As I said, I'm a contractor, and he's an Assistant Director. One word from him to my boss and I'm out of here. I didn't think it was illegal, just immoral, I guess."

"Can anyone else alter the data?"

"No, just me. And the guys that put the system in, of course: a company called Quintrax. But they only come out when we have a problem, which we've only had once in the two years that the system has been operative."

"All right," said Juanita, "is there anything else you want to say about this?"

"Well, you guys suspected this before you came in here, didn't you? That's why you wanted to talk to me."

"We had an idea," admitted Juanita.

Jeremy looked at her with raised eyebrows and held his hands out with palms up.

"Quarles."

"I should have guessed. I wouldn't be surprised if Quarles hacked into the system. Everyone knows there was no love lost between those two."

"Can that be done?" asked JT.

"Supposedly not. It's not connected to the other systems and has its own server. But I wouldn't put anything past Quarles. That guy was a genius." Jeremy paused like he was remembering something, so JT and Juanita waited for him. "Come to think of it, that was one of the differences they had. Quarles didn't think this was a very good system and really badmouthed it. But obviously Styles prevailed, since that's what we put in."

Juanita handed Jeremy her card. "Here's what you're going to do, Jeremy. My email address is on there. Send me all the dates that Styles asked you to falsify data on, and I think we're done. If the record of our visit here just happens to disappear as well, I think we can live with that. Lou is one of the good guys and he won't bring this up. So we're out of here before anyone else sees us. And Jeremy, we're going down to talk to Styles now, so I want that data sent to my computer now. And it had better be there when I get back to the office this afternoon."

Jeremy ushered them out quickly. "Thanks, guys. I'll get right on it."

Juanita just nodded. They proceeded down to the eighth floor and Styles' office and introduced themselves to Styles' secretary, Sharon. She said he should be back any moment, as his meeting was due to be over ten minutes ago. While they were waiting, they noticed the sign on Styles' door: Assistant Director for Administration. Juanita remarked that she didn't recall seeing any other signs on doors in the agency, even the director's.

Styles charged in ten minutes later. As he proceeded towards his office, Sharon motioned to JT and Juanita and said that they needed to talk to him.

"I don't have time now. They'll have to come back," he said without acknowledging them as he went into his office.

JT got up and said, "No, sir. It will be now."

"And who the hell are you to talk to me like that?" Styles blared as he turned around to face JT.

JT showed his badge and mentioned the Quarles investigation.

"You've got five minutes," he barked, as he walked over to the chair behind his enormous desk.

With Styles back turned towards him, JT looked at Juanita and pointed to her with a nod of his head and a smile on his face, indicating that he indeed wanted her to conduct this interview. Before beginning, they both took their time closing the door, making themselves comfortable in two of the chairs around the conference table that was butted up against his desk, spreading out notes, and getting writing implements ready.

"Three minutes."

"We understand that you didn't get along with Dr. Quarles," Juanita offered as a beginning.

"I don't get along with anybody here. It's a thankless job."

"In particular, we know that you had a serious disagreement over the security contract for the badging system. You selected the current contractor over his objections."

"He only had a recommendation in that. I was the source selection authority and I chose the best contractor for the Agency. End of story."

"And the disagreement you had with him the night of his death?"

"I needed his big office. We've only got limited space in this small building. I'm in charge of the facilities around here and he had to move but didn't want to. I told him I'd move him if he didn't move himself. He was just being an asshole, as usual."

"Where were you later that night, the 26th?"

"I was here until after ten, and you can check the security logs on that."

"We understand that you've been jimmying those logs."

Styles was caught off guard, but recovered quickly. "That's it. We're done here," he said with finality as he got up.

JT got up and Styles paused. Styles was bigger and better built and had a nastier demeanor, but JT had a gun. JT walked over to the door as Juanita looked on, wondering what was coming next. Surely he wasn't leaving or he would have indicated that to her. JT opened the door and called out to Styles' secretary, "Sharon, could you tell TT that I need him to step in here for a moment please?"

Before she could react, and neither Sharon herself nor JT knew quite how that would be, Styles composed himself and yelled, "Never mind, Sharon, that won't be necessary." JT nodded at her, closed the door, and sat back down and looked at Juanita.

"The security logs, Mr. Styles?"

"Yes, I had the log entries faked. I was someplace else that night and didn't want my wife to know. She's got a spy in the Agency and has them check the logs whenever I'm late. I know who it is but I let them play their little game."

"And who do we need to talk to in order to check out this alibi of yours?"

"Martha Ventura, my Facilities Director."

"Cozy little organization you have here, *Mister* Styles. Any other peccadilloes you'd like to reveal before we talk to *Mrs.* Ventura?"

"No," he said emphatically. "We done now?"

"Yes, but do stay in touch," Juanita said as she gathered up her things. JT was out the door first and asked Sharon to get Ms. Ventura on the phone. As Juanita was leaving, she turned to Styles and said, "I know you want to know, and I think it's ironic, so I'm going to tell you: Quarles knew you were messing with the security data. He mentioned it in his laptop that we reviewed yesterday. Kind of a comeback from the grave thing, huh? Oh, by the way, does TT know?" With that she made her exit.

Styles slammed his door and they could hear him yelling in his office.

Juanita turned to Sharon with an apologetic look on her face and the secretary just grimaced.

In the meantime, JT had found out that Ventura was in a meeting with her staff and had gotten directions to her office: get off the elevator on the second floor and go toward the windows overlooking the lobby, and then through the door on the right.

Juanita thanked Sharon and then she and JT exited into the hallway. In the elevator, she grinned at JT, "Damn that was fun! I hope he's guilty, because I'd sure love to fry his ass. I see why you asked about the Director. Smooth move."

"The only thing an asshole like that understands is power. At that level, his job is totally dependent upon the Director, and he's having much too much fun playing in his sand box here to have anyone mess it up. I mean, they wouldn't fire him—just put him in a do-nothing job where he can't cause any trouble. By the way, thanks for protecting Jeremy. I was going to mention something but wasn't quite sure what. That was nicely done. You seemed to enjoy it, too."

Her grin got even wider.

Martha was still in the staff meeting in a small conference room around the corner from her office. They had her secretary get her out. Upon seeing JT and Juanita, she looked put out. When JT badged her and mentioned that they were there to talk about the Quarles case, the look turned to confusion. They went into her office and JT closed the door behind them. While her office looked almost as nice as Styles', you didn't get the same view here as you did from the upper floors. Juanita noticed that every government employee they had talked to had a nice outside office with a reasonable to great view, while the contractors usually had a cubicle located in a hallway or an inside office. Martha was a slim blonde, actually skinny, but fairly nice looking. Juanita thought she looked, well, artificial. The colored hair, the makeup, the clothes—it reminded Juanita of someone trying to be something she wasn't. When JT mentioned that Styles was a potential suspect in the Quarles case and he had used her as an alibi, Martha became extremely nervous.

"Look," said JT, "the fact that you are sleeping with him is really none of our concern, and doesn't need to go anywhere outside our confidential files. So, if you just tell us where you were on the night of October 28, the night Dr. Quarles was killed, we can make this short and sweet."

Martha gulped, paused for a moment considering whether or not to come clean on this, and then sighed realizing she didn't have a choice. *Maybe this could actually be a release for me*, she thought. She'd been trying to figure out a way to break it off with Styles but hadn't so far. *Maybe this is my chance.* "Yes, I was with Mr. Styles from about six-thirty or seven until late, maybe ten-fifteen, ten-thirty or so."

"Can you be a little more specific, Ms. Ventura? Where, for instance?"

"The Days Inn in Arlington. It's right at Route 50 and North Pershing Drive. We had dinner in their restaurant and he had a room rented."

"Did you pay cash or use a credit card?"

"He used his government credit card."

"Okay. If this checks out, then I guess you won't be hearing from us again." Juanita got up and she and JT headed for the door. Before exiting, Juanita turned to Martha with a questioning look on her face and asked, "Why? He's such and asshole."

"He's a powerful man. And he *was* useful."

Now back in JT's car they headed to the office. "Do you believe them," Juanita said shaking her head. What a sorry couple. I see what he's getting out of it, but do you think he was that 'useful' to her?"

"He's an SES, Nita, and she's a direct report, so I'm guessing she's a GS-15. As you know, that's a pretty nice salary and, if we can believe the accusations in the IG report, she owes her job to him."

"Yeah, I know that. It's just that—he's such a slime ball," she said as she shook her head and shoulders in disgust. "You want to check out their alibi on the way back to the office?"

"Good idea."

CHAPTER FIFTEEN

Bolling Air Force Base, D.C., 9 November, 1000 hours

Once again, they had trouble getting through the front gate. JT simply *had* to get one of those DoD stickers. The Air Force tried to do away with them since there was a one-hundred percent ID check in progress at all Air Force Bases, as well as other military installations, but the other services balked and it never was implemented. At least, having been there once, they knew exactly where they were going. And Arati was waiting for them at the door to her building. She greeted them and asked if she could ride with them to another building. They got into JT's Highlander and Arati directed them a few blocks over to another nondescript building, number 51. She explained that since the COLTRANE program went black, they had to work on it in a SCIF, or sensitive compartmented information facility, and that that was located in this building. They parked right out front and Arati showed her badge to the guard who made her sign in. He then asked for picture IDs from JT and Juanita, from which he took some information that he entered into his security system database. It took a few moments, but then he announced that they were cleared to enter. Arati led them through an inner door, then down a long corridor with locked doors on either side. Each door had a card reader and a keypad for entrance. After Arati waved her card in front of the reader located outside room seven, the red light went out and the yellow light lit. She then keyed in an eight-character code and the green light next to the yellow one came on. She opened the door, turned on the lights and invited them in.

The room was completely enclosed, with no windows. There were tables all along the walls, with the exception of the entrance way, supporting various electronic equipment, mostly computers, thought JT. A small conference table occupied the center of the room with several wheeled chairs around it that were obviously used to access the many computer stations. The indirect lighting bathed the room in a comfortable, very pale blue light. "Actually, I didn't bring you here to show you anything," Arati commented, "for, as you can see, it is mostly equipment. Since this is a SCIF, I can talk at the compartmented level which I thought necessary to explain what I found." Arati had seated herself in one of the swivel chairs around the table and JT and Juanita followed suit. "As you know, Dr. Quarles was working on—and I am continuing to bring to fruition—a financial tracking program that will help us to identify illegal financial transactions. It processes enormous amounts of data, much of which is piped in through normal banking channels, at least for the U.S. institutions, and a lot of which is 'pirated' by capturing the encrypted electronic transmissions sent over the airwaves. Decrypting them is actually the easy part, as NSA does that for us. Organizing them, correlating them with each other, determining which are worthy of scrutiny as they fall outside the norm of standard business practices, and determining how to go about that is what his program accomplishes. It requires terabytes of data storage capacity and the use of very sophisticated artificial intelligence programs."

"Can you put terabytes into something we can understand?" JT asked.

"I will try," Arati said. "The Library of Congress is said to have over 75 terabytes of data on its shelves. That covers over 150 million items: books, pictures, videos. YouTube claims to serve up over 110 million user-submitted videos a day, and their office holds only 50 terabytes. The total amount of email information generated in a year is estimated to be 14,000 terabytes, or 14 petabytes. That is in the whole world, not just the U.S. But this is more than just data crunching. The clever part, and the part that is Stefon's contribution, is making sense out of that. What we have so far is a preliminary program that we can run on a limited set of data, the source of which I can control to some extent. When the project is complete, there will be very little data that is not included. Based on your mention the other day of Stefon's concern with contract irregularities, I choose Mr. Styles' various accounts as a subject, added in several of the DARPA contractors, and then a number of various off-shore banking institutions to see if there were any correlations. I thought it would be a good test run. I found that over the last eleven months, which is how far back our data goes right now, a total of $82,000 was transferred in multiple small installments into an offshore account that I am ninety percent certain belongs to Styles. $37,000 of this was transferred eight months ago from a corporation that was a subcontractor to several DARPA contractors. Then $45,000 was transferred into this account in the couple of days following Stefon's demise, and then out of this account into one belonging to an individual who banks in the local area, again in multiple small installments. Exactly where this forty-five came from, I am not sure. It appears to be a dummy corporation, but I cannot verify that."

JT and Juanita were stunned. "And you can prove this?" asked JT incredulously.

"No, I cannot. This is actually a pre-beta program that has not been fully tested. It likely contains many bugs that need to be worked out, and I am sure at this stage it would not be admissible in a court of law, in spite of my high confidence in the data. Hopefully, it will assist in obtaining a warrant, however. This will be a tool that enables further investigation into suspected illegal transactions."

"Oh my god," said Juanita. "It's like the Boss said: follow the money. Arati, have you mentioned this to anyone else?"

"No. Nor shall I. I thought it would be a useful bit of information to assist you in your investigation. By the way, Mr. Dunkirk, I was interested to see that your initials stand for James Tiberius."

If JT was stunned by the previous revelation, he was flabbergasted by this one. He sat there with his mouth open unable to form a response. Juanita was in much the same condition.

Enjoying the moment Arati continued, "I was not about to entrust you with this information without checking you out first. I hope you both will forgive my invasion of your privacy. JT, I gather your parents were *Star Trek* fans?"

JT, recovered somewhat, answered, "Ah, yes, my dad still is. Arati, you are something else."

"I will take that as a compliment. I thought you might also like to know the composition of the source selection evaluation board for the COLTRANE program, so I forwarded the names to your email account with DHS. That is the board that I served on. I do not know the names of all of the current, or TOMFOOLERY, SSEB members, but I do know that Stefon was not on that board. Although Mr. Styles was not on my board, nor I believe the TOMFOOLERY one, you might want to check with DARPA for any previous boards that he served on. Is there anything else with which you could use my help?"

"Do you have anything else on that transfer to a local bank?"

"I can tell you it was a Bank of America branch, and I will email you the address and the dates and amounts. But I strongly suspect that it is an account set up under a false identity."

"How do you know that?"

"That would be difficult to explain I am afraid."

"Thank you so very much, Arati," Juanita said as she got up to leave. "Do you want a ride back?"

"No. I will be running a few test cases the rest of the morning. I will have to see you out, however."

JT bowed his head to her in gratitude and she escorted them back out front. "Do you believe that woman?" he asked Juanita as soon as they were headed toward the car. "She is scary. I hope to hell she's on our side. We have some work to do back on campus, don't we?"

"Yes, we do," replied Juanita. "By the way, *amigo*, James Tiberius? I can't believe that I've known you all these years and didn't know what JT stood for."

The conversation was interrupted until they got into the car. "Well, yeah. What can I say? Actually, dad said he named me after all of his heroes."

"All?"

"Well, in addition to James Kirk, there was James Bond, James West, James Brown, James Dean, Jim Phelps, Jim Bowie and Jim Patterson."

"I know Kirk, Bond and Dean, of course. And I guess he meant Jim Bowie of frontier fame, but who were the rest? It couldn't be James Patterson of Dr. Alex Cross fame, as he didn't start writing until after you were born."

"James West was a fictional Secret Service agent and was the hero of the TV series *The Wild, Wild West*. James Brown was an early rhythm and blues singer whose most popular song, I guess, was, "Papa's Got a Brand New Bag." Jim Phelps was the hero's name in the TV series, *Mission Impossible*, and, you're right, Jim Patterson was not the writer, but a construction worker he know when he was a bridge inspector working for the D.C. government."

"Well, that's a lot to live up to, especially the latter. He was serious?"

"Yeah, particularly about Kirk. He said he was the perfect leader: he didn't know everything and depended upon others to help him. Mister Spock supplied the rational decision making; Bones, or Doctor McCoy, was his advisor—much like Counselor Troi on *Star Trek: The Next Generation*—and supplied the emotional or human input; and Scotty was his engineer whom he depended upon for his technical help. He took their inputs and made the command decision. He was their leader and they looked up to him."

"Sounds like you've bought into this as well. I have to admit, you never acted like you knew it all."

"I'll take that as the compliment I'm sure you intended it to be," he chided back.

"I presume he was thinking that you just might display the good characteristics of these characters and people. It's not too hard to guess the famous ones, but what about this Jim Patterson fellow? What was his good point?"

"Well, according to dad, he was a good ole West Virginia boy—hard working, hard drinking, good humored, live for today kind of fellow. He was a pile driver on a construction crew and worked for eight or nine months of the year and hunted and fished the rest of the year. Dad said he needed to put some down-to-earth characteristics in there to round me out."

"Oh, that's a stitch. I love your dad."

Having had enough of this self-exposition, JT changed the subject back to work, observing, "We need to look into all the contracts that Styles has been involved with lately. I asked Tamika to send us a list of all the members of the contract review committees that Quarles or Styles had anything to do with. I guess she was out for a few days and I kinda forgot about it, but she finally responded to my email and referred me to a DARPA contracts person, a Roslyn Stapanski. Also, things are looking more and more damning for Mr. Styles. Wait till the Boss hears about this. By the way," he said, changing the subject again, "what do you know about Maryjo Myers?"

"Maryjo Myers?" echoes Juanita. "Oh, the interpreter that helped you with Mustafa. I know she works for DHS and teaches at the CI Centre."

"Nita..."

"All right. I hear she's a very nice lady. Currently unattached. Slightly anal, but then she is an instructor. And she's hot for you."

"Can't you be serious for even a minute?"

"All right, seriously. I did hear she's a very nice lady. I understand that her ex was cheating on her and that she tried to get him into counseling but he wouldn't go. She doesn't have any kids but I certainly can't say whether or not she would like to. If I recall, besides having a love of languages, she is quite an outdoor type. I think she runs marathons. This, mind you, is all second-hand from Tracey in Charlie Unit, who used to work with her. And that's what I know about that, *amigo*. You're interested I take it?"

"Well, I was thinking about maybe asking her out for drinks. I'm really out of touch with this dating thing, and actually not really sure I'm ready for it."

"Well, when you are, give her a call, if she's still unattached." By this time, JT had crossed over the Wilson Bridge, turned north on the parkway and was pulling into the parking lot for *Faccia Luna*. "I was wondering where we were going," Juanita said. "I should have known."

"Well, it is past lunch time, after all."

CHAPTER SIXTEEN

Alexandria, Virginia, 9 November, 1335 hours

JT and Juanita both ordered sandwiches and iced teas and discussed the case. "Nita," JT said between mouthfuls, "I talked to the techies, and according to them, there was absolutely nothing on Quarles' hard drive but work stuff. They did say that a lot of stuff was permanently erased, but that doesn't really prove anything, especially not with a paranoid person like Quarles. Although I did find a list of the source selection board members for a number of his contracts, which agrees with the list I got from Roslyn via email. Quarles actually had a bio on each of them stored in there, as well, even the DARPA members. Apparently, Styles only served on the one board." JT showed her the annotated lists he had made.

Security System source selection evaluation board:

Mike Styles—DARPA, SSA and procedural (agency operations)
Dr. Stefon Quarles—DARPA, technical (IT)
Sam Thorson—DARPA, technical (security)
Don Crenshaw—CIFA, contractual

COLTRANE SSEB:
Dr. Richard Briceman—DARPA, SSA and technical (IT)
Dr. Stefon Quarles—DARPA, technical (IT)
Dr. Arati Jabornae—NRL, technical (IT)
Charles Johnson—N SA, procedural (IT)
Don Crenshaw—CIFA, contractual

TOMFOOLERY SSEB:
Dr. Richard Briceman—DARPA, SSA and technical (IT)

Joel Henning—DIA (ex-CIFA), procedural (terrorist ops) and technical (IT)
Lt. Col. (Dr.) Wilson Fuller—NSA, technical (IT)
Thomas Westman—SEC, procedural (financial)
Don Crenshaw—DIA (ex-CIFA), contractual

"I take it that SSA means the Source Selection Authority and SEC stands for the Securities and Exchange Commission?" Juanita asked.

JT replied in the affirmative.

"What's with the military person?"

"Well, it is a DoD project, and according to his bio, he's supposedly one of the top men in his field—the name of which I can't pronounce—but which obviously has a lot to do with the project. I think they had trouble finding the right people who had the clearances. I was surprised to see an SEC individual on the committee until I read in his bio that he's a former Air Force comptroller and vice president for finance for a large military contractor. This certainly expands our list of suspects."

"Weren't there three other contracts that preceded the COLTRANE one?"

"Yes, but Roslyn said that they were all awarded using a 'broad area announcement,' I think she called it. In any event, since they were smaller contracts and open to everyone, they didn't require selection boards. Hey, did you ever get that data from your friend Jeremy over at DARPA?"

"Yes. Over two dozen times in the last year, Styles asked him to falsify the security tapes. One was on the night in question, and there's also one subsequent to that but before our discussion with him. What a slime ball. I also verified his credit card charges at the *Days Inn*."

Just then JT's cell phone rang. "Hey, Brian, what's up? Yeah, I was cleared a few days ago. They did ask about you and I told them you were one hundred percent. I had no indication whatsoever that you'd had a few and that's what I told them, but it would have been better for you if you had mentioned it to me. No problem. Later." He saw Juanita looking over. "They're giving Brian the third degree about having a few beers before he came out for the surveillance the other night, but I'm sure it will be okay. It was definitely a righteous shoot."

"I'd have said something," she said.

"Yes, and I would have asked you if you were okay, you'd have said yes, and that would have been that. Still, he should have said something. I'm gonna work on these contract committee members when we get back to the office. How about you?"

"I'll call Charles," Juanita said, "and see if they have learned anything about Furlong. Then I'll check on the Union Station footage and see how that's coming."

JT nodded in response. "Oh, I almost forgot. That list of people cleared for Quarles' program came in from DARPA. Arati was right: there are over fifty people on that list."

"Anyone interesting?"

"All the usual suspects," he replied, "so nothing that stands out. I think we should check out our other leads before we get into them."

JT's phone rang again, but this time it was Hanson. He asked for an update on everything so far on the Quarles case, so JT and Juanita brought him up to speed. When they were done, Hanson said, "You're kidding, right? This guy admitted the affair and you verified it?"

"Yeah, Boss," JT replied. "We stopped at the *Days Inn* and verified that Styles and his 'companion' had been there the night of October 28. They checked in at five of eight and there was no way that Styles could have made it out to Loudoun County by the time of the explosion. In fact, the night clerk is now on days and identified them from the pictures that Juanita had downloaded from the Maryland and Virginia DMVs."

"No, that's not what I meant. I didn't really think you doubted his alibi. I just meant he had the balls to admit the affair just like that, and she agreed?"

"You wouldn't believe his ego. He's a real manipulator and doesn't think he can be hurt. She acted like she didn't have a choice in the matter, like it was a career move."

"She probably didn't, so I'm glad you nailed it down."

"We're waiting for verification on the credit card he used but that's taking a little longer since it's a government credit card."

"Once again you're kidding, right? His government card?"

JT nodded with a smirk on his face, forgetting that Hanson couldn't see him, then responded positively.

"So where are you two going on this now?"

"There's a couple of things we need to check out based on the IG report, particularly the contract fixing that Quarles really came down strong on in his laptop notes. All the people the IG interviewed claimed they didn't know of any contract issues, but the IG didn't press the issue on that, just the more provable accusations. I don't know where they plan on going with that. You want me to check with them?" JT asked, he hoped rhetorically.

"No way. Conduct your own investigation. If they come up with anything, they can verify their data with us. Any other suspects so far besides Styles and potentially this Furlong fellow?"

"Nita and I have pretty much ruled out the wife and Dr. Jabornae, and with Styles alibi-ing out, that would leave us with the original assumption of terrorists, except that we did talk to Dr. Jabornae this morning and she says she's fairly certain that funds were transferred to an offshore account belonging to Styles and then back into a local account right after Quarles' murder."

"That's interesting. Maybe the scumbag had some help. Is she trying to verify this?"

"Said she'd work on it."

"Okay. But I have a question on his program. If it's cancelled, would the money for it go to someone else at DARPA?"

"According to Quarles' boss, and Jabornae for that matter, they'll probably continue the program, but even if they don't, they have money begging for good R&D programs. TT, the director, is tight with the bucks, and if you can't convince him, which is often the case, the money just sits there waiting for the next good idea."

"And then they lose it at the end of the fiscal year?" queried an unbelieving Hanson.

"It's what they call two-year money and it is usually used up by the end of the second year. Apparently they have even lost money, but not often."

"You remember Deep Throat's advice, right?"

Remembering what Juanita had said just this morning he responded with, "Yes, Sir. We'll follow the money. Do you have anything you can tell us on the four terrorists that were in the shootout the other night?"

"Yes. Hang on a minute while I get my notes."

They heard drawers opening and closing and papers shuffling.

"So far we have identified three of them—one of the men that died at the scene, the one that died jumping out of the ambulance, and the guy that's still in the hospital. The one who was driving and died at the scene was a Pakistani and a resident alien by the name of Talat Iqbal. The guy in the hospital is an Afghan here on a work visa by the name of Farooq Husna. Who, by the way, has been very reluctant to talk to us. I'm still hoping we can get something out of him. His sponsoring family is not related and we have no data on him from his homeland. Prior to this, we had nothing on either of them, not even any suspected ties to anything. We're thinking that they were new recruits and this was some sort of initiation for them. We'll check out where they worked in case those were some of their meeting places."

Hanson paused at this point, and shuffled through his notes. After a minute he continued: "The guy that jumped off the bus was Iranian and also here on a work visa using the name Mahmoud al-Sadr. He was also one of the Sticks from the meeting at S&S Enterprises—what, two weeks ago? The fourth guy, the one that JT shot as he was threatening Mustafa and his family, was one of the individuals that we also got on tape at the *S&S* meeting. This was the one who was using the cell phone that we traced them on. When we showed the pictures of the assailants to Mustafa, he identified him as Khalid, the guy that 'recruited' him. Other than that, we have nothing on him. Mustafa did not recognize any of the other assailants, nor the ones from the meeting at S&S Enterprises, except Khalid. I was kind of surprised he didn't say something about Khalid being the one that attempted to shoot him when we first debriefed him."

JT responded with, "Things were a little hectic out there, Cap'n. Did we get anything on the other meeting places that he identified?"

"Both the NCTC and the FBI are very aware of "Afghans in America" and neither has a problem with the organization. It's not their fault that others use it as a recruiting ground. All their meetings are held in public in places like libraries, schools, and the like. The FBI in particular feel it is a completely above board and legit outfit. I got the impression they know this because they've checked out their financial dealings, had undercover agents attend their meetings, and so forth."

"I suppose the ATF checked out the explosions?" queried Juanita. She had pulled out a checklist of open action items that she was working from.

"Yes. And there was nothing for them to go on, since it was just gasoline used in the cocktails. They did finally get back to us on the blasting caps used in the Quarles murder. They traced them to a rock quarry in Loudoun County, located, coincidentally, perhaps, very close to where he was blown up. The quarry had completed a routine inventory check two days before the ATF boys got there and had just reported the missing caps. It appears as though there may have been a break-in, which could explain why they went missing, so they're checking into that and will keep us advised. Is there anything else I can do for you, Juanita?" Hanson asked with an impish smile on his face that Juanita could see even through the phone.

"Well, now that you mention it, Sir, did we get anything from the cameras along Ashan's final fare route, or perhaps from Union Station itself on our missing perp?"

"We got him on three cameras on the way, but of course we couldn't see his passenger. We just got the Union Station coverage and the boys are checking that. The hotel cameras were not working at the time, so nothing there. And, honestly, Juanita, I can't think of *anything* else."

"The surveillance on Furlong?" she asked sheepishly.

"Actually I can't answer that one," replied Hanson. "You'll have to check with Charles on that. Are we done now?" He didn't wait for an answer and hung up the phone, shaking his head. Sometimes he considered them two of the biggest pests he had ever known.

JT and Juanita went back to their lunches and continued discussing their leads.

CHAPTER SEVENTEEN

Fusion Team Headquarters, 10 November, 1410 hours

Charles briefed them on the Union Station coverage that they had obtained. Based on the time sequencing, the video analysis guys were convinced they saw Ashan's last fare enter a restroom with a briefcase dressed in casual clothes, and then come out with the same briefcase but dressed in the dark suit and hat that Ashan's killer had on. It looked like Khalid, but whoever it was kept a low profile. Charles apologized that he couldn't offer them more, but, as he said, "It is what it is." Further, there was nothing to report on the surveillance of Mr. Furlong, a suspect in the murder of Dr. Quarles, since he had done nothing other than go to work and perform other normal everyday routines. At least they managed to get a GPS unit on the Porsche when two of the guys from Delta Unit sat on him over the weekend and he took it out and made a stop long enough for them place it on the car. Although JT was pretty sure Furlong had received $45K in blood money, that was not provable since his regular bank account showed no unusual deposits and they had no way to trace any bogus accounts of his in spite of Arati's suggestion. Furlong had been out of jail for almost three years now, but this was not long enough for him to request a restoration of his civil rights in Virginia, given the violent nature of his crime. It was highly unlikely he'd ever get back the right to bear arms, since this would require a petition approved by the court, so he probably didn't have a gun—not legally, anyway. They were maintaining surveillance, however.

JT and Juanita thanked Charles and went back to their cubicles.

"So, what do you think, *amigo*?"

"I think that Ashan was a victim of his own cohorts, most likely because he was not an accomplished car thief and used his own cab to provide transportation to one of their meetings. Like I said before, he was probably supposed to steal one for them as part of his acceptance program, but he didn't, and his buddies didn't know the difference since his hack license was removed from the cab. I suspect that they figured he was being tailed after that and therefore couldn't participate any further and was useless to them. However, he probably knew some of their operations, meeting places, other terrorists, or whatever, and couldn't just be cut loose. What do you think?"

"That makes sense. I'll ask the Boss if he wants us to check further into Ashan's brother, just in case he was more involved than we thought. Did you get anything on the SSEB members?" she asked.

"The only one out of all those guys that has any sort of record is, surprise, Styles." He handed Juanita his list with his notes, which were rather cryptic, so he narrated for her.

"As you know, Michael David Styles is the Assistant Director for Administration for DARPA. There was one domestic violence charge against him by his former wife. No surprise they separated. He moved out and agreed to a divorce, so she dropped the charges. He's been to London a couple of times with his second wife. The two of them do have a lot of bills, but their combined income is more than keeping the wolves away from their door. He does have a little boy with the second wife and two kids from the first marriage. One of those is a teenager, and I think I mentioned before that he's paying child support for her. He's fifty-one and worked for the government most of his life: Navy, DOD, and DARPA mostly.

"Thomas Westman is the Director for Intergovernmental Relations for the SEC. He has a lot of speeding tickets but nothing else worth noting. He worked for a number of banks and other financial organizations, including a stint as vice president for finance for a large military contractor, before coming to the government as deputy comptroller for the Air Force. He did work for Lloyd's of London at one time and was stationed over there for four years. He is forty-four, not married, and quite well-off."

Juanita got a big smile on her face and cooed, "Wild, well-off and 'available.' My kind of guy."

"Let's stay on track here, Nita. Lieutenant Colonel/Doctor Wilson Fuller of the U.S. Army is currently assigned to NSA. He's been to Bosnia and Iraq for regular Army assignments. He's divorced and has three teenage kids by his first wife. He remarried and has no kids by the second wife. His first wife remarried also, so he pays no alimony. He and his wife make regular trips to the casinos in Atlantic City, New Jersey, and the racetrack in Charlestown, West Virginia, but apparently their gambling is within reason. Thirty-nine-years old with no debt, not even a school loan, but does have child support payments of $900 a month. Got his doctorate in finance paid for by the Army.

"Joel Henning is an interesting case. He's the Deputy Director of DIA's Joint Intelligence Task Force for Combating Terrorism and the ex-deputy director of CIFA. He was adopted by the Henning family when he was only ten, and I couldn't go any further back on him with the time that I had, although he and his adoptive family checked out okay. He was valedictorian of his high school in Philadelphia, which apparently earned him a full ride to the University of Pennsylvania, where he got a degree in information science and technology. He worked for some contractors for four years and then joined the FBI, where he got a masters in counterterrorism studies. Spent eight years there and then he went to CIFA. He's thirty-six and has no family except his adoptive parents. He's rather young for someone in his position.

"Charles Johnson is the NSA Program Manager for the INFER program. That stands for the International Financial Enterprise Referendum program, whatever that is. He's actually a National Counterterrorism Center employee on loan to NSA. His father had a name change from Mohammed al-Maliki to James Johnson just before he went into high school. I should say his whole family did. James married a Caucasian and I'm guessing that his kids were fair-skinned enough that they thought they would fit into the community better and increase their chances of success in school, job hunting, et cetera, by doing this. Not sure why they picked Johnson other than it's a very common American name. Charles himself is thirty-eight, but his wife is only twenty-seven and they have two young kids.

He's a third generation American with no traceable relatives in Iran, and, as you know, works for NSA and has a very high DoD security clearance."

"Did you go that far back on all those guys?" asked Juanita.

"No. I only go back one generation unless I see something, like his family's name change; then I go back a little farther. So who does that leave?"

"Looks like, uh, Crenshaw, Briceman, Thorson and Jabornae."

At that point, JT's computer beeped as he received an incoming email. "Speaking of the devil, one of them anyway. I just got an email from Dr. Jabornae. She says there is a DARPA business conference next week up in Baltimore and that we ought to drop in and catch a few of the presentations. She believes it will help us better understand the organization and perhaps aid the investigation. She included a contact point. What do you think?"

"Good idea."

"So, back to our SSEB members. Don Crenshaw looks pretty clean. He's a DIA, and formerly CIFA, contracting officer. Seems he took a job with the government early on and has had a mediocre career with several DoD agencies ever since. Married with no kids, close to retirement at age fifty-four."

"Hey, wait a minute. The boss worked at CIFA, didn't he? Does he know this guy or that other ex-CIFA guy, Henning?"

"Yes, he knows Henning and Crenshaw, as they were both there when he was. I mentioned it to him and his take on Henning was that he was pretty smart but rather reserved. The boss actually reported to Henning and he said he made a good deputy as he was into details, but could never be the front man and run anything. Crenshaw, on the other hand, was outgoing— in fact, kind of a gadabout. The boss called him the typical contracts type, whatever that means. Says he told a lot of inane jokes and was always looking for candy or other freebies on everybody's desk."

"That sounds a lot like someone I work with."

"To continue... Dr. Richard Briceman, who we talked to at DARPA and was Quarles' supervisor, is the Director of their Information Exploitation Office. He has quite a pedigree, almost as impressive as Quarles. Has a Ph.D. from Rensselaer and has been in and out of government with a couple of sabbaticals here and there—one of them in Israel. He's worked for three contractors, two think tanks, and this is his third government organization. He's forty-eight and on his second wife. No kids by the first wife, but three step-kids from the second. He spends a lot but has quite a bit put away given his fairly high salaries, especially at the think tanks. Took a pay cut to come to DARPA."

"Guess they can't pay government people as much, huh?"

"Believe it or not, he gets more than most as he's what's called an IPA, or Intergovernmental Personnel Act employee. They have the same authority as a fed but not the same benefits, and their salary can be negotiated higher than that of the regular employees."

"How do you know this stuff?"

"Dad worked for a few DoD organizations and hired a few of these. Back to my list. "Sam Thorson is the Head of the Security Division at DARPA. He looks pretty clean, also. Has an undergraduate degree from Maryland University and is working on a masters in security studies, also with Maryland. He's thirty-two and has been with the government for eleven years; outstanding ratings; recently married with a new house. No debts between them except for the mortgage and a small school loan from the wife.

"I was almost afraid to check on our good Doctor Arati Jabornae. Thought maybe I'd get one of those happy faces pop up on the screen telling me that that was a no-no. Before becoming the head of the NRL Center for Computational Science, she earned her Ph.D. in information technology at Caltech, and then worked for the Navy at China Lake. Born and raised in India, she came to the U.S. after high school, and became a naturalized citizen when she was twenty-three. There's not a good deal of data on her besides her schooling and government career, but then she's only been living here since she was eighteen. Single, thirty-two, no family here other than parents, but lots of relatives in India. Her parents, however, are living in Anaheim, California, and are both naturalized citizens as well."

JT closed with, "Th, th, th, that's all folks."

"Okay, then. While I go check out our attendance at the DARPA conference with the Boss and ask him about Ashan's brother, why don't you call the contact point and get us invited?" Juanita suggested.

JT nodded his agreement, so Juanita headed over to Hanson's office. He okayed their going and said he'd get one of the other units to check on the Khadija family. Juanita then went back to her cubicle to help JT go over the information on the SSEB members.

JT looked for the tenth time at the listings of the members he had drawn up. "Nita," he said with exasperation, "the only wrongdoing we have any inkling of so far on any of these folks is that Styles might have been getting kickbacks from Quintrax. And that we got from Quarles' laptop, and his complaint to the IG, which he didn't mention to his buddy Marvin over at AFOSR."

"And Dr. Jay mentioned Quarles' interest in the contract algorithms, and the 'fact' that $45,000 was transferred to a local bank out of an account she thinks belongs to Styles," she said.

"Dr. Jay?" JT asked with raised eyebrows.

"It's easier than her name," Juanita retorted. "I'm going to look over the information in the laptop again. Why don't you review the notes from our conversations with Marvin and Dr. Jay?" After scrutinizing the information several times, Juanita put the laptop aside and then looked at the SSEB lists one more time. She went back to the laptop again with the SSEB lists in her hand and then called out, "Hey, JT, look at this. Right here where Quarles talks about Styles accepting a contract bribe, he has this notation 'DC2.' What if those are initials and he's saying 'Don Crenshaw too,' as in 'also'? You know, like Crenshaw knows or suspects that Styles is skimming off the top."

"That's not a bad idea. He abbreviated a lot of stuff in there—I remember seeing 'AJ' quite a bit, which of course would be Dr. Jay. He might have also been saying that Crenshaw was cooking the books too. I think we need to pay a visit to Mr. Crenshaw. Besides, I need to get out of here. After we talk with him, I think I'm going home for a long weekend, since tomorrow's a holiday. You doing anything this weekend?"

Juanita shook her head.

"Want to come over for a cookout Saturday afternoon and maybe help Andy and me fly one of our model airplanes?"

"Yeah, that'd be great. I have some things for Carmen and something I think Andy might like, as well. Let me go tell the Boss what we're doing and make sure the long weekend is okay. I'll meet you in the garage and we can head on over to Bolling." Juanita had met JT at the Dunkin' Donuts on Backlick Road, and she had driven from there.

"Okay. I'll call Crenshaw and tell him to expect us. See you downstairs in a couple."

Bolling Air Force Base, DC, 10 November, 1650 hours

Don Crenshaw now worked for the Defense Intelligence Agency, since that organization absorbed most of the employees of the Counterintelligence Field Activity when it was disbanded. While the Pentagon is officially DIA headquarters, the DIAC, or the Defense Intelligence Analysis Center, which is located on Bolling Air Force Base, is the largest of their facilities. JT figured that most of its twelve thousand employees must be here, given the size of the complex. He knew it was also the headquarters of the National Defense Intelligence College and the Defense Intelligence Operations Coordination Center. Since DIA is a member of the United States Intelligence Community, they report to the Director of National Intelligence (DNI), whose office and headquarters staff used to be located in the DIAC before they moved to their Tysons Corner location. The National Counterterrorism Center also reports to the DNI, and they too are located at Tysons. JT was working on a degree in intelligence and counterintelligence studies at an online university, so he was well aware of the intelligence and counterintelligence agencies in the government from his classes, but he had the

147

counterterrorism ones down cold from personal interest and work contacts.

"So, you said you got nothing unusual on Crenshaw when you ran him, right?" asked Juanita as she turned into the base from Route 295.

"No. Like I said before, he's squeaky clean," replied JT. "The boss thought he was a good contracts person, but his PEs aren't that good."

"I'm guessing that's proficiency evaluations," Juanita offers. "We can get those from the database?"

"Only if you ask the right people. But after reading them, I think his boss tried real hard to make it sound as bad as he could."

"And his boss is...?"

"*Was* none other than Joel Henning, one of our SSEB members. They're not in the same chain of command now at DIA, but Henning was his second level supervisor at CIFA. Most of the CIFA personnel were transferred to the Defense Counterintelligence and Human Intelligence Center at DIA, but Henning was sent to the Directorate for MASINT and Technical Collection, and Crenshaw to the Contracting Directorate. And, before you ask, MASINT stands for Measurement and Signature Intelligence. This is what they call technical intelligence. If you read their mission statement, it doesn't include the type of data that they'd be collecting from Quarles' financial data collections program, but I think that's so new they haven't figured out where to put it yet. I understand that Henning is supposed to head this program for DIA once they get it up and running. I have a feeling that if they do get this up and working however, the FBI or maybe even our guys will take it away from them."

"You know, I always thought I did my homework, but you are definitely one step ahead of me here, *amigo*. You think maybe I could make a case study of this and include it as a paper in one of my courses?"

"Sure, if you take out all the classified. But then what would you have left?"

"I could fake it."

"Kinda like your love life, huh?"

Juanita tried to smack him but he blocked it easily, since she was driving. They were both laughing so hard that the gate guard looked at them funny, but passed them through anyway after checking their credentials. Juanita had a DoD sticker on her Cruiser. JT reminded himself again that he had to get one of those.

The DIAC sat only a few blocks from the gate, so they arrived at the center main entrance in short order. The signs pointing to the visitors' parking area were helpful, but when they got there all the parking places were taken, so they headed back out toward the north forty. Fifteen minutes later they finally made it to the front of the building. The entrance foyer reminded Juanita of the DARPA Visitors Center, only a lot bigger. One of the visitor control personnel checked their badges and called Crenshaw, who arrived six minutes later to escort them upstairs.

Crenshaw had no trouble spotting them sitting in the visitors' chairs and apologized for the wait as he walked up to them. "It's a long walk to my office," he said after they had introduced themselves. Crenshaw had long, wavy brown hair that flopped down over a pale, round face. His average five-foot-ten frame forced his 188 pounds to bulge slightly over the belt holding up his wrinkled, dark pants. Although his flower-strewn tie was knotted, it was pulled loose and the top button of his light blue long sleeve shirt was undone. He presented a white collar working man image if there is such a thing. "If you just follow me, we'll head on back there," he said and headed past the guards towards the elevators.

The clutter in his office had been neatly arranged, and you got the impression from the three groupings of paper stacks that he had several acquisitions going on at once. Before JT and Juanita sat down in the two visitor chairs, Crenshaw waved toward the window and offered, "The office is a little small, but at least I have a view of the two rivers and the Capitol in the background. If you press up against the window and look left you can see National." He was, of course, referring to the Potomac and Anacostia rivers, at the crux of which lay Hains Point, the lower end of East Potomac Park and its golf course. He offered them coffee but they both declined, so he just fixed himself one.

"Mr. Crenshaw," began Juanita, "as you are probably aware, we are investigating the death of Dr. Quarles. The explosion that he died in was a deliberate one, so we are looking for anyone with a motive: someone he owed money to, someone whose wife he was having an affair with, professional jealousy, all the usual reasons. Can you shed any light on that?"

"I knew him professionally, not personally. He was very smart and a lot arrogant, but I think most people liked him in spite of that. He had a childlike presence about him that enabled you to easily forgive his ill manners. And I never knew him to be wrong about anything technically, but procedurally his opinion was probably just as good as a lot of differing ones. He was picky about qualifying potential contractors, too much so, and I had to loosen some of the criteria that he wanted to use in their evaluation. These weren't disagreements, mind you—we were both just doing our jobs, and I'm sure he understood and appreciated that."

"So, he thought the criteria were such that unqualified contractors could be selected?"

"He may have thought that, but he never said it. I was leveling the playing field. Any contractor selected would have been qualified to do the job. Maybe not the best technically, although that usually has the highest rating factor, but the best overall considering their on-time performance on other contracts, their management and technical teams, accounting practices, and a host of other qualifiers."

"Was there room for anyone to stack the deck in one contractor or another's favor?"

"Many of the rating factors were subjective and an individual could slant the numbers in favor of a particular contractor. To make a difference however, unless it was very close, you'd really need a couple of the SSEB members doing that to affect the outcome. If you are asking if that was done on any of the two contracts that I worked on with Quarles, I'd have to say I don't know. I suspected that the security system contract, the one won by Quintrax, was, shall I say, mishandled by Mike Styles. He seemed to have a preference for them that I do not think was supported by their capabilities. But the system they put in is apparently adequate, but certainly not state-of-the-art enough for an organization like DARPA. The second one that I worked with Quarles on was the COLTRANE contract, which was won by American Vision Quest, or Avique, as I believe they call themselves now. It was certainly the more difficult of the two, and I couldn't say if that one was mishandled or not."

"What were their values and did Quarles have any suspicions of wrongdoing?"

"The Quintrax contract basic was awarded at $1.5M, with one option for another $1.5M and two for $500K each. DARPA has exercised one of the $500K options and there have been two ECPS submitted but none approved." He noticed Juanita's quizzical look and explained, "ECPs, or Engineering Change Proposals, are changes to the contract that we weren't planning on when we set it up. The Avique contract basic is $3.8M, with four options varying from $200K to $650K each, two of them exercised, and there have been four ECPs submitted for an average of about $150K, all approved. Quarles mentioned to me that there might be some 'criteria fudging' on the Quintrax contract by Styles, and, while I think he might have been right, it was not provable. I suspect he had misgivings about the Avique contract too, but he did not mention that to me."

"By the way, why did your organization, CIFA at the time, award these contracts rather than DARPA?" asked JT.

"DARPA, although it's been around since 1958, did not have its own contracting authority until the late eighties. They used other organizations to award the contracts, usually the one that would develop the technology once proven feasible by DARPA. That way, they avoided the not-invented-here syndrome and got buy-in from the beginning. It also made for an easier transition, of course. CIFA, recently formed at the time, was interested in a security system, as well, and had heard what DARPA was doing, so we contracted that effort for them. For the second one, we had already established a relationship, we had an interest in the technology as the potential implementer, and so we awarded that one, as well."

"Did CIFA get the Quintrax system as well?"

"No. That was the more expensive option that was not exercised. We were constantly moving around on various floors of the building we were in, then there were rumors of a move related to BRAC, then there were rumors that we would be disestablished, the latter rumor proving to be true."

JT knew that BRAC was the Base Realignment and Closure effort that looked at shutting down and/or consolidating DoD assets in a giant money-saving activity that was effective to a considerable extent, in spite of numerous dissenting Congressmen.

"Is there anything else that you can think of that might help us in our investigation?" Juanita asked.

"Not that I can think of offhand. If I come up with something," he started to say as Juanita and JT handed them their cards, "I'll let you know."

As they got up to leave, JT asked, "Did you hear about the three contractors who were bidding to fix a broken fence at the White House—one from New Jersey, another from Tennessee, and the third from Florida?"

Crenshaw shook his head.

JT continued as Crenshaw led them back the way they had come in, "They go with a government contracting official to examine the fence. The Florida contractor takes out a tape measure and does some measuring, then works some figures with a pencil. 'Well,' he says, 'I figure the job will run about $900: $400 for materials, $400 for my crew and $100 profit for me.' The Tennessee contractor also does some measuring and figuring, then says, 'I can do this job for $700: $300 for materials, $300 for my crew and $100 profit for me.' The New Jersey contractor doesn't measure or figure, but leans over to the White House official and whispers, '$2,700.' The official, incredulous, says, 'You didn't even measure like the other guys! How did you come up with such a high figure?'" Just as the elevator opened on the lobby level JT delivered the punch line, "The New Jersey contractor whispers back, 'One thousand for me, one thousand for you, and we hire the guy from Tennessee to fix the fence.' 'Done!' replies the government official."

JT wasn't sure who groaned louder, Crenshaw or Juanita.

CHAPTER EIGHTEEN

Springfield, Virginia, 12 November, 1550 hours

JT, Juanita and Andy got back to the house just before four. They had been at a local soccer field flying one of JT's hybrid planes. He had probably bought a dozen models in the last few years but lately had been building his own out of parts from ones that weren't totally destroyed in crash landings. Juanita turned out to be a pretty good "pilot," and JT kidded her about applying for UAV duty. Andy had two really nice landings and only crashed once. Just as they got cleaned up, Dan and Maria Reynolds, who were also invited to JT's for the cookout, arrived right on time at four o'clock. Maria didn't get to see Carmen, JT's housekeeper, and her sister, that often, so they spent the time when they were somewhat alone talking about lost family members and Panama. And naturally, there was the update on Dan and Maria's children—two of whom were out in the work world and one who was still in college—and little Andy, who Carmen treated like her own. The state of world affairs and local topics, such as the immigration issue, transportation problems and school overcrowding were thoroughly and sometimes vehemently discussed. Sergeant Dan tended toward the conservative side and his wife and sister-in-law favored the liberal side of the issues. JT and Juanita would take sides as the arguments moved them.

Sergeant Dan had met Juanita when she worked a case a few years ago with JT when he was still a Fairfax cop. "So Juanita," Sergeant Dan said, "did you hear what the squad did to JT during his first week on the job?"

She shook her head and turned an attentive ear towards him, as did Carmen and Maria.

"While he was out, the guys got a small cardboard box and a little kid's folding chair and labeled them 'Dunkirk's Desk' and 'Dunkirk's Chair.' Not that they thought he was shorter than your average cop or anything. When he came back, we got him to remove his boots and kneel down in them and snapped a picture. He looks like he might be three-and-a-half foot tall. Got the picture hanging in my office to encourage other vertically challenged recruits."

They all laughed, especially JT, and the story motivated him, as well. "How about what we did to Scotty Long?" he reminded the Sarge. "Scotty was always wearing tennis shoes instead of the regulation boots," JT began. "Now they were nice looking black *Rockports,* so unless you looked closely, you really didn't notice. So one day, just before an inspection, we decided to try and break him of the habit and got an old pair of boots, painted them with white stripes, and swapped them for his shiny boots that he kept in his locker just for inspections. So he comes in five minutes before inspection, sees what we've done and has no choice but to wear his tennis shoes—after looking around frantically and giving us all hell first, of course. So we're all lined up and in walks the Captain and the Major for the inspection. Scotty is sweating bullets standing there with his *Rockports* on. They both pass right by him without saying a word or even noticing his shoes. As they exit, however, the Major turns around and says, 'Officer Long, I'll expect a three page report on my desk in the morning explaining the importance of complying with departmental dress regulations. And I'll thank you to retrieve your boots from beneath my desk before you begin your shift.' Long replied with a sheepish, 'Yes Sir.'"

After a few minutes of laughing, Juanita came up with, "Oh, that's nothing compared to what they did to me." With all eyes riveted on her she began, "So, I'm at the Federal Law Enforcement Training Center in Glynn County, Georgia. This is where all OSI recruits go to get their basic law enforcement training. Towards the end of the course, you get a taste of various areas of specialty that you could chose to go into, like antiterrorism, counterintelligence, cybercrimes, photographic services or polygraphy. So I hook up this local Georgia boy, Willie John, who is a volunteer for the polygraph testing. I begin by asking him all the normal baseline questions, like his name, age, et cetera, and then some specific questions that they predetermined from talking to him about his recent activities.

He's told to answer some truthfully and to lie on others, and I have the correct answers in front of me. Reading from the script I ask him if he was in his barn last night. He responds with 'Watcha wanna know that fer?' I say, 'Just answer the question, Sir.' We were told that some of the test subjects were instructed to be difficult. He responds with, 'They didn't tell me you'd be askin' 'bout them horses.' Perplexed I ask him, 'What horses?' And he comes back with, 'The ones in heat, and I didn't touch 'em. 'Sides it was all Jimmy Bob's idea. I didn't want nothin' to do with 'em.' At this point I threw up my hands and decided that the test was over. It was then I heard peals of laughter from outside the booth, and 'Willie John' starts laughing too."

"Oh, that's a stitch," the Sarge gets out between laughs.

"I thought that was bad until I heard what they did to JT the other day," said Juanita. JT winced as he recalled the stunt. The weather had decided to cooperate, so they were all out on JT's patio. Juanita checked to make sure that Andy was still in the house playing video games, then relayed the incident with the cell phone video. Sarge nearly choked on his beer he was laughing so hard. And the stories went on for another hour. By this time, JT had cooked hotdogs, hamburgers and some kielbasa on the grill and served them up to the hungry crowd. Carmen had prepared some potato salad from one of Sara's recipes, and Sancocho, a soup made with chicken, corn and rice. Maria brought some Carimañolas, or stuffed yucca fritters. Juanita brought a couple of bottles of red wine, and, of course, JT had a cooler full of Miller Chill and Sam Adams, his two favorites.

Right then, JT's mom and dad, Hal and Mary Dunkirk, showed up—a little late due to a previous commitment, but just in time for dinner. They had actually met everyone before and knew Sergeant Dan, Maria and Carmen quite well. After a relatively quiet period when everyone was eating, Carmen turned to JT with a sparkle in her eyes and asked "JT, how was your date with MJ last night?"

JT scowled at her like she'd just broken a promise not to bring that up, and then decided that he might as well come clean. JT's mom looked especially interested.

Before he could respond, Juanita piped in with, "MJ? That was quick, *amigo*. She must really be on the rebound, huh? So why isn't she here today?"

"I didn't want to scare her by introducing her to my 'family' too soon," he retorted. "And before you ask, we went to see Pearl Jam at the Verizon Center and then out to eat at Hooters."

"Hooters!" Juanita and Sergeant Dan exclaimed at the same time.

"Gotcha! Actually we were in the mood for Chinese so we ate at the China Doll, which is only a few blocks away. It was excellent, and according to MJ, very authentic."

"And what time did you get home?" teased Juanita.

"Carmen promised she wouldn't tell and neither will I."

Juanita could see she wasn't going to get much more mileage out of this, especially with Mary there, so she asked Sarge what the big problems in Fairfax were this year.

"Well, besides the immigration problem that we talked about earlier, it's our manning levels," he said. "The troops are making a fair salary if you add in the overtime, but they can do better with the Feds, particularly if they have a degree. We're losing good, young guys like JT to DHS, ATF and the other three-letter organizations in town. They can make more money, have a less dangerous job, keep better hours, generally have better promotion opportunities, and earn that federal retirement. We've been after the legislature to drop the DROP plan and to lobby our congressmen to let local law enforcement participate in the federal TSP." Juanita was not familiar with the deferred retirement option plan, so Sarge explained it. "It's a scheme where officers and deputies who reach retirement tenure on the force agree to 'retire.' That is, you get your twenty-five years in, or whatever amount of time your normal pension requires. You then sign papers that say you are effectively retired, meaning you get no more raises or promotions, but you can work up to three to six more years, or however many are the maximum for your plan. So during this five years, say, you keep earning your regular salary, but the money you would have received in pension payments goes into your DROP account to be invested like a

401K. Of course, the operational guys love it, because they get to keep experienced cops longer and don't have to hire and train new guys. The finance guys love it because the caps on your sick and annual time are much lower, and they say it costs more to train recruits, double them up with training officers, pay for their lawsuits and the higher percentage of damaged vehicles, et cetera. The older cops like me love it because you're not bucking for promotions or trying to impress anyone anymore, and, depending on how well you invested—and a hundred thousand a year is not a gross exaggeration—you retire in a few years and hope that you don't die soon and have to think about one of your cop buddies sipping margaritas with your wife on some tropical island spending all his drop money *and* yours. Now the other shoe drops: the younger guys are shafted. Their normal path to promotion and transfer is significantly curtailed. Further, there's no guarantee that the DROP program will be around when they're eligible for it. Finally, and perhaps worst, many DROP participants—although more experienced—aren't always the same 'go-getters' they used to be. Unfortunately, these deadbeats are allowed to participate in the program because there's no screening process. And that's all I have to say about that."

"I think I see how dropping it would help, especially if you had an alternative like the federal thrift savings plan," said Juanita. "But what will those older guys do instead of sticking around?"

"Go find private employment. Hell, the military guys have been doing that for years. They have good training and an up-or-out policy that we'd do well to emulate." Sarge then changed the subject by asking, "So, how's your terrorist case going?"

"You know, Sarge," JT began, "we don't know if it's a terrorist case or just plain old murder." He explained where they were on the case, and how more and more what used to look like terrorist incidents seem like regular old greed or envy-motivated crimes and vice versa.

"This financial program sounds like something you should try to utilize more often," Sarge offered.

"We're following the money," JT told him, remembering what Hanson had suggested and Juanita had explained earlier.

The conversation then turned to famous people they had met. Carmen said she used to work for Manuel Noriega but he probably fit better in the infamous category. Sarge mentioned that he had helped provide security for Vice President Chaney when he had visited Fairfax Hospital once. Juanita related that she was standing right next to President Bush, the second, when he addressed the graduates of an OSI class. As they turned toward JT, he looked at his dad and said "I can't top your stories, Pops," so they all turned to look at Hal.

"Well," Juanita said.

"I used to work for NASA and was a flight controller during the Apollo missions."

"So you knew Armstrong and Aldrin?" queried Sarge.

"Oh yeah. Not knew so much as worked with. My favorite astronaut though was Pete Conrad. He was supposed to be the first man on the moon, but NASA decided that for political reasons, they didn't want the first man on the moon to be military, so they switched the eleven and twelve crews so Armstrong, Aldrin and Collins replaced Conrad, Gordon and Bean. When I worked the Apollo XII mission, the one Conrad commanded, I had the graveyard shift, the one when the guys were out on the surface. The whole time that Conrad was out there he kept whistling 'Hi ho, hi ho, it's off to work we go.' The guy was very cool. He fell down once and Al thought that was it—ripped suit—no more Pete. But he just gets up, brushes himself off and continues whistling."

"Wow. I'll bet you have a lot of stories like that," said Juanita.

"I guess I have a lot of NASA stories," replied Hal. "But my favorite is when I was coming back from a simulation in the mission control center and got on the elevator on the third floor. Each story was about fifteen feet high, what with all the false flooring, and the elevator was huge and slow so it took a while between floors. When the doors opened on the second floor, in walks Wernher von Braun. Here was the father of the Saturn V rocket alone in the elevator with me. Now, this guy had a reputation for being rather gruff, but I had to say something and damned if I wasn't tongue tied. Finally, and I have no idea where this came from, out pops, 'Dr. von Braun, may I have the pleasure of telling my grandchildren that I shook your hand in the elevator of the mission control center?' He looks at me, gets a big smile on his face, shakes my hand and says in his deep voice, 'Oh very good. It's my pleasure, Sir.' Well, I was beside myself and told everybody about it. And now the funny thing is that I have grandchildren that I can tell that to and they have no idea who he was, even the older ones."

They went on for about another hour and a half before JT mentioned that he needed to get Andy off to bed. Twenty minutes later, he was back and walked in on a discussion of the efficacy of the off-year national elections held a week ago. "I know the chief of staff for Congresswoman Hamilton from Ohio," Sergeant Dan was relating, "and she says that her boss is relatively effective for the first year after elections, but the second year is spent mostly trying to get reelected. At least it's a little better in the Senate."

Carmen mentioned that in Panama it was a unicameral legislature made up of seventy-eight members who served five-year terms. She thought that, although the judiciary still had a way to go, the rest of the government had progressed quite well since the 1989 Operation Just Cause and the ouster of Noriega. The long-standing U.S. ties and its continued financial aid were helping the country progress toward a true democratic republic.

JT opined that the U.S. would do well to adopt that election strategy, and then make sure that the legislators only got one term with limited pensions based on that.

"So, Dan," Hal said, "surely you must have heard some good lines that your guys used when they pulled over various traffic violators."

"Oh, you bet. Let's see, there was, 'You know, stop lights don't come any redder than the one you just went through.' Or, 'Relax, the handcuffs are tight because they're new. They'll stretch after you wear them awhile.'"

JT piped up with, "How about 'If you take your hands off the car, I'll make your birth certificate a worthless document.' And two of my favorites, given that I love rabbits, 'If you run, you'll only go to jail tired.' And 'Can you run faster than 1200 feet per second? Because that's the speed of the bullet that'll be chasing you.'"

Juanita added two she heard on Air Force bases: "'You don't know how fast you were going? I guess that means I can write anything I want on the ticket, huh?' And, 'Warning! You want a warning? Okay, I'm warning you not to do that again or I'll give you another ticket.'"

"I remember two that I used manning a DUI check point," JT offered: "'The answer to this last question will determine whether you are drunk or not. Was Mickey Mouse a cat or a dog?'" Sergeant Dan really liked that one. "And, 'How big were those "two beers" you say you had?'"

"I love the quota ones," Sergeant Dan offers: "'Yeah, we have a quota. Two more tickets and my wife gets a toaster oven.' Or, 'No sir, we don't have quotas anymore. We used to, but now we're allowed to write as many tickets as we want.'"

"I especially like it when they try to pull the 'I know someone routine,'" JT chuckled. "'I'm glad to hear that the Chief of Police is a personal friend of yours. It's good to know someone who can post your bail.' But my favorite was one I used after pulling over this one woman: 'You didn't think we gave pretty women tickets? You're right, we don't. Sign here.'" Juanita nearly choked on that one.

By this time, Sarge's comments were becoming less and less coherent and Maria thought it best to get him home. They said their goodbyes and Carmen promised to go over Maria's house tomorrow and help with the sewing on some dresses that she was making. JT's parents really had to go also since they were leaving early in the morning for a couple of days' jaunt down through the Williamsburg and Tidewater areas. Juanita started to leave as well, but Carmen convinced her to spend the night in the spare bedroom. Once Carmen left the patio, Juanita asked, "So, *amigo,* how *did* it go with MJ? I see that you have taken your ring off."

"She is really a nice lady and we had a great time. We seem to have a lot in common: we're both in the same business; we both lost a loved one; we're both horny...."

"Spare me the graphic details—just the romantic stuff."

"Come on, Pearl Jam and Chinese romantic? We're just getting to know each other. Her only family is a brother out on the west coast, and they're not very close. They hardly ever get in touch in spite of her trying. I think she's finally given up."

"And you didn't invite her over today?"

"Yes, I did. But she promised an officemate that she'd help her move today and tomorrow. Say, you want to flex some muscles tomorrow?"

"Sure. You have her cell number? Let's invite ourselves over." JT had programmed her number into his phone and rang it up. MJ said they would be delighted to have some help as the job turned out to be bigger than they thought and another friend had had to go out of town, so they were really short on help. They all planned to meet at her friend's house in Herndon at eight the next morning. JT and Juanita discussed MJ and other friends and acquaintances until after midnight and then turned in.

CHAPTER NINETEEN

Baltimore, Maryland, 15 November, 0725 hours

JT and Juanita had driven up right after rush hour the day before, because they knew they'd never make it for the opening of the conference the next morning if they fought the AM rush hour traffic through DC. When they got there, Juanita wanted to see the National Aquarium and JT wanted to tour the Maryland Science Museum, so they compromised and did both. Between those two excursions, they took the water taxi ride over to Fort McHenry for that tour. They finished up with a fabulous seafood dinner at the Blue Sea Grill. All in all, it was a really nice day and they discussed very little business. They checked into the conference hotel, the Baltimore Marriott Waterfront, late in the evening and certainly could not complain about the accommodations. JT considered it only fitting that they get a perk once in a while.

Since they'd already registered for the conference the night before, they had plenty of time to take advantage of the free continental breakfast. They dallied a bit, not wanting the ambiance to end, so they ended up with seats near the rear and were barely in time for the introductory remarks by the conference coordinator and then a welcome by the DARPA comptroller. The latter's last act was to introduce the agency director, Tommy Townsend, or TT as JT knew he liked to be called.

"Good morning, everyone. You all look bright eyed and bushy tailed." There were as many groans from the assembled audience as there were chuckles. "I know you are raring to go, but before we start, I'd like to thank all the DARPA folks for putting this together, and I'd especially like to thank all the agents out there for doing such a good job for us over these past many years. We simply could not function without you and greatly appreciate your helping us get things on contract and for taking our projects to the next step in their development. As you can tell from the agenda in your handout, we have a lot of informational briefings for you, but also included in there are some brochures explaining all the things to see and do in this beautiful place. We've scheduled a short free period here and there for you to take advantage of the many attractions here so we don't go into information overload, a perennial problem at DARPA." This one got a few more laughs. "I am sorry that we couldn't offer a golf outing like we did last year at our conference in Phoenix. I do have to admit that I went out there a day early for some golfing. There was a nice plush country club nearby and I enjoyed the luxury of a complimentary caddy. Since I don't get too much practice, I wasn't hitting worth a damn all day. I actually played so poorly that on the seventh tee, I sliced my shot deep into a wooded ravine. I took my eight iron and clambered down the embankment in search of my lost ball. After many long minutes of hacking at the underbrush, I spotted something glistening in the leaves. As I drew nearer, I discovered that it was an eight iron in the hands of a skeleton! I immediately called out to the caddy, 'I've got trouble down here!' 'What's the matter?' the caddy asked from the edge of the ravine. 'Bring me my wedge,' I shouted. 'You can't get out of here with an eight iron!'" Half the audience thought that was a great one, most likely the golfers in the group. TT continued, "'Round about the 18th hole, I spotted a lake off to the left of the fairway. I looked at the caddy and said, 'I've played so poorly today, I think I'm going to go drown myself in that lake.' The caddy looked back at me and said, 'I don't think you could keep your head down that long.'" The audience really enjoyed that one. TT had a few more words to say, and then he introduced the first speaker, whose topic was organizational conflict of interest. JT commented to Juanita regarding the appropriateness of that.

During the first break, JT and Juanita went back to his room and phoned the office on speaker phone. Hanson answered and after a few preliminaries, he asked, "Guess who just got transferred to the Pentagon?"

JT and Juanita peered at each other with a how-in-the-hell-should-we-know look on their face. Was the boss getting transferred, or was it somebody from the team, they wondered.

After letting them think about it a bit Hanson relented, "Your good buddy Styles. According to the IG findings, he was 'no longer effective in his job at DARPA because he had: (1) failed to exercise proper fiscal management; (2) made questionable personnel decisions; (3) exhibited poor leadership qualities; and (4) was an all-around asshole.' Okay, so I added the last one. He also has quite a bunch of money to pay back after amendments were made to his TDY vouchers. The Director must have given him the bad news yesterday and said he couldn't attend the conference you're at. Shame, too, because his girlfriend is there."

"So what's he going to do now?" asked Juanita.

"Probably nothing but sit around and draw his paycheck. Actually, it sounds like the job is gofer for an assistant secretary. I think they should've fired his ass. I'd even think about taking his pension away. Let me know if you guys come up with anything serious on this contract angle so we can forward it to the appropriate law enforcement authorities." He had nothing further of any interest on either case, so let them get back to the conference.

"Thanks, Boss," they both called as JT hung up the phone. They decided to get some more coffee before attending the next speaker's presentation.

Fusion Team Headquarters, 15 November, 1215 hours

"We've been keeping tabs on this Furlong guy for what, almost two weeks now, and things have been nothing but quiet. I mean, this guy doesn't have much of a life. Besides work, he hasn't been anyplace but the grocery store and Midnight Video. And he hasn't had a single visitor the whole time." Sal was reviewing the GPS tracking data and the surveillance logs on Furlong from the past four days, which included a Friday federal holiday and the weekend.

"Maybe he's got a honey that works at Midnight Video. Besides, what do you expect from a guy with two counts of domestic violence and assault on a police officer on his sheet? Not to mention the murder rap he beat on a technicality. It's no wonder he's divorced. How do you suppose this guy can afford a Porsche driving for QPUDS?" Brendon queried.

"Well, I doubt if he's paying any alimony and he doesn't seem to have any other expensive habits, so it's not unreasonable I guess. Does make one wonder, though." Furlong's townhouse was near the end of the block, so the surveillance teams that were there over the weekend positioned themselves on another cross street that had a lot of parking. "Here's something interesting," Sal said. "He took a Metro train ride last Saturday. Seems as though he drove to the Vienna/Fairfax-GMU station and boarded the train, got off at the Metro Center station, and the then the team lost him in the crowd. They picked him up again back at the Vienna Metro station just after five in the afternoon and can only speculate where he went or what he did—hopefully just sightseeing. Did your guys come up with anything else on that cab driver that we watched get whacked the other night?" Sal knew that Brendon felt bad about an assassination happening on his watch, but they'd gone over and over it and did not see how they could have prevented it.

"JT and Juanita checked out his family pretty thoroughly and came up empty. As for Ashan himself, it's fairly certain that he was a newly recruited terrorist and was killed because we were on to him. Apparently, he hadn't been schooled in the fine art of grand theft auto and that cost him."

Sal interrupted Brendon with, "Hey, look at this. He took the Porsche out last night after eleven and went to Baltimore—the Inner Harbor. Say, aren't JT and Juanita going up there for a conference this week?"

"I'm pretty sure they went up yesterday," said Brendon.

Hanson was walking by just then and what he heard piqued his interest, so he stopped and asked Sal and Brendon what was going on. From the GPS data, they could see that Furlong's Porsche had left his residence at 11:06. Assuming Furlong was driving, he proceeded around the Beltway and up Interstate 95 toward Baltimore, arriving at the Inner Harbor and only two blocks from the hotel at 12:17 in the morning. He was there for forty minutes and then returned home. Hanson told them to get in touch with JT and Juanita and let them know that Furlong had paid them a visit. This was no coincidence and they needed to know about it.

"Where is he now?" Hanson asked.

"We're showing his truck at his work place, Boss, and his Porsche in his garage."

"All right, then. Make that call." Brendon reached for the phone.

Baltimore, Maryland, 15 November, 1335 hours

JT felt the vibrator on his cell phone. He pulled it out and saw the call was from the office. He showed Juanita the phone and motioned that he was going out in the hallway to take this call. "This is agent Dunkirk. Yeah, Brendon, what's up?"

Juanita was not particularly interested in this session, so she joined JT in the atrium just in time to see the surprised look on his face.

"You got to be kidding me. Here?" JT exclaimed. He looked around as if he expected to see Furlong standing right there in the lobby. "All right, thanks." JT relayed Brendon's information to Juanita. They looked at each other and then said at the same time, "Crenshaw!" JT told Juanita to check for him in the session while he walked over to the nearest house phone. "Can you connect me with Don Crenshaw's room, please?" he asked the operator. It rang five times and then went to voice mail.

Juanita came back shaking her head, saying she had also checked the drinks and fresh fruit table set up around the corner.

JT told her to get Crenshaw's room key while he checked the men's room. He came out of the restroom and got to the elevators just as Juanita arrived with a desk clerk that insisted it was hotel policy that he escort them into another guest's room.

They got off the elevator on the eighth floor and went directly to Crenshaw's room, 837, and saw that it had the do not disturb sign hanging from the door handle. Juanita knocked loudly on the door while not actually standing in front of it but got no response. She knocked again.

JT took the key from the clerk and told him to get back as both he and Juanita drew their weapons. He swiped the key, got the green light, then pushed the door open while standing back and holding it there with his foot. There was a person sitting on the floor just inside one half of the closet with his or her legs extending out into the room. From the clothes, it appeared to be a man, fully dressed, and he wasn't moving.

Although the room seemed otherwise unoccupied, JT and Juanita checked the rest of the place with their guns still drawn. The door to the bathroom was immediately inside on the left and JT went in. "Clear!" he called.

Juanita had proceeded far enough into the room to see that it was clear. She turned back to see Crenshaw sitting in a pool of thick, dark red blood on the floor, mostly in the closet. She checked the other half of the closet while JT cleared under the bed. She felt for a pulse but knew there wouldn't be one. Juanita could see two entrance wounds in Crenshaw's chest, sustained either when he answered the door or had entered the door. Then he must have fallen backwards into the closet. From the state of the body, she figured the murder happened either late last night or very early this morning. Juanita asked the clerk to call the Baltimore Police and report a dead body.

By the time the BPD detectives and the coroner got there, JT had relayed everything to Hanson. He told JT to let the Baltimore guys handle it but to keep them informed. JT could tell them why they thought Crenshaw might be a target, and thus why they came up to check on him, but not that they had any definitive suspects in mind.

The detective in charge didn't like that much and felt that the "feds" were holding out on him. He had found scratch marks on the door however, and Crenshaw's wallet and watch, if he had one, were missing. Given that and the position of the body, he was inclined to consider this a burglary gone bad, but was disturbed by the fact that no one had reported any gunshots or even any loud noises, and that it had happened at a time when the rooms would most likely be occupied. He got what information he could from JT and Juanita, including their statements and that of the clerk who had let them in. He did agree to let them handle the next-of-kin notification, however, and gave them his information and that of the morgue.

Juanita said that she would also notify Crenshaw's place of employment and, given his clearances, mentioned that the BPD would most likely be visited by some representatives of DoD.

JT thought that they should notify the DARPA director and located his aide just outside the briefing room. The aide said his boss had already returned to his room to prepare for dinner. So he buzzed TT, explained that some federal agents wanted to see him, and then asked JT and Juanita to go up to his room on the top floor. TT occupied a suite of three rooms—two bedrooms divided by a nice sitting room big enough to host a small party. Two baskets of fruit were located in the center room, which also sported a nicely stocked mini-bar. TT offered them a drink, which they politely refused, saying they were on duty, so he poured himself one: a rather stiff scotch.

"To what do I owe the pleasure?" he asked. "Our last encounter was not under the best of circumstances. Have you found out anything from your investigation so far that you can tell me?"

"I'm afraid, Sir, that we have more bad news." They explained what had apparently transpired last night or this morning, right here in the hotel, actually one floor down and two rooms over from TT's room.

TT was flabbergasted when he heard what they had to say. He almost spilled his drink. "Should I cancel the conference?" he asked. "And what about the program? I mean, there's a lot of people working on the program."

"Sir," JT began, "I don't think Mr. Crenshaw would want you to cancel the conference. As for the program, well, there were items missing from his room, including his watch and wallet, so it could be that he interrupted a burglary in progress. I really don't think that this is related to the program. I do want you to know that we'll notify his family and the DIA."

169

"Okay. Thank you. If there's anything that we can do to help, please let us know."

They thanked him, offered their condolences again, then got up and let themselves out. They could hear TT calling for his aide as they exited the suite. It was almost five o'clock by this time, so they decided to eat dinner in the restaurant and wait out the traffic before making the trek back to D.C.

The hotel eatery, located on the top floor, afforded a magnificent view of the inner harbor. They had just missed the sunset, so the harbor glowed a beautiful reddish-orange shade. "Wow. This is some development," offered Juanita.

"I presume you agree with me that these two deaths are related," he asked Juanita rhetorically after they had placed their dinner orders. "Someone or some group wanted Quarles and Crenshaw out of the picture. Their connection is that they both served on the source selection board for the security system contract and they both thought that Styles might be accepting kickbacks. They also were tied together on the financial tracking program, again both serving on the source selection board."

"Yes, both SSEBs," offered Juanita and added, "and they were both involved in the follow on contract: Quarles because it was his program, and Crenshaw because he was going to award it. I wonder why Quarles wasn't on the SSEB for the follow on contract?" she mused. "I don't think that eliminating Crenshaw would have any substantial effect on the latest contract. They'd just have another contracting officer take over and pick up the pieces. So, it seems to me like the connection is Furlong and maybe Styles. I certainly don't see terrorists involved in Crenshaw's murder."

"I agree," said JT. "But if these cases are related, then the timing seems off. Quarles was killed on the 28th of October; today is the 15th of November. That's almost three weeks. And the first one was—or someone wanted it to seem—terrorist related. And this one was, or someone wanted it to seem, burglary related."

"Maybe Quarles found out something incriminating on someone back then, and they didn't find out or suspect that Crenshaw knew until later. Or maybe he didn't find it out until later. Or maybe they decided to wait a decent period between the two and used different methods so they'd seem unrelated." All this speculation hurt her head so much that she shook it.

"This is just too much of a coincidence to think they're not related. It's possible that some folks knew that Quarles suspected Styles. Hell, I suspected him. But I don't think too many were aware of Crenshaw's suspicions. We think that Quarles knew about Crenshaw's thoughts on the matter based on a cryptic note that he wrote. But, according to Crenshaw, Quarles mentioned his suspicions about the Quintrax contract but not the Avique one, and didn't take any action because he thought the allegations were not provable. That doesn't mean he didn't discuss it with anyone. Perhaps we should talk to the various legal counsels that he may have discussed it with, or maybe Crenshaw's boss at the time."

They continued discussing the case while they ate. When they finished, they went back to their rooms and got their stuff together. The desk clerk thought their checkout time was a little unusual, but did not charge them for the extra day. JT drove back listening to some jazz CDs while Juanita made some case notes and tried to tie all the data together in her mind. He dropped Juanita off at 8:50 and got home just in time to read a story to Andy before he fell asleep.

CHAPTER TWENTY

Arlington, Virginia, 16 November, 1015 hours

JT suggested that he and Juanita put some more pressure on Styles and confront him with Crenshaw's murder, and the boss agreed. They decided it was easier to Metro up than try to drive, especially since it was only two stops away from their building. "Have you ever been in the Puzzle Palace before, Nita?"

She shook her head.

"It's really an interesting place with history written all over its walls. One corridor has short blurbs on all the NATO countries, including their flag and an outline of their country shape. Another has pictures of all the Secretaries of Defense. Another has World War I displays with artifacts, newspaper articles, and the like. And so on. I try to walk through as many different corridors as I can whenever I get over here."

"You never worked there did you?"

"No. But I do feel a definite connection with the place. My great grandfather was a plasterer and helped with the original walls when it was being built, and my grandmother worked there as a clerk typist during WWII. Then my dad was stationed here for thirteen years while he was a reservist in the Air Force. My Uncle Joe was an iron worker and helped build the Metro station there. And finally, my sister worked on the PenRen, or Pentagon Renovation program, after the 9/11 strike."

"I see what you mean. Kinda like a family affair, huh?"

They got off the Metro at the Pentagon station. Just past the turnstiles, they took escalators that led them up to the southeast side of the building. On the outside of the building, they encountered two armed guards behind bullet- and blast-proof shields who checked their NCR or National Capital Region badges. JT knew that these were standard DoD building passes that granted access to most Department of Defense facilities in the Washington area and was glad that Hanson had made sure they were issued to several of his agents. Being an AFOSI employee, Juanita already had one of these before coming to the Team. Juanita noticed that either end of the outside area contained more ballistic shields and guards with automatic weapons.

They entered the building through what JT figured must be at least twelve-foot-high wooden doors, and then passed through a second set of seven interior doors that were four-foot-wide each. These were opened and closed variously to control traffic. They passed through a bank of security gates that scanned their NCR cards. On this level, there was a visitor's area, a waiting room and a credentialing room on the south side. There were up and down escalators on either side with a guard control area between them to oversee the entrance. At the top of the escalators was another ballistic shield with a guard with an automatic weapon. On the north side of the entryway, there was a red, white and blue striped quilt that Juanita figured was at least twenty-five feet square or larger. On it were printed photographs of the faces of the 184 September 11, 2001, terrorist attack victims: fifty-three passengers and six crew members on board American Airlines Flight 77, and 125 military and civilian personnel inside the building. JT liked to come by here every once in a while to remind himself why he joined the organization that he did. He could tell that Juanita was moved by the quilt. Maybe now he could tell her the real reason that he left the police force.

As they took the up escalator, they walked through another set of four doors side-by-side in pairs. Long gone was the open mall area with a *CVS*, fast food restaurants and various other retail outlets. In their place were narrow passageways of sheet rock painted flat white and other indications of on-going construction. They headed off to the right past the Pentagon Federal Credit Union and what remained of the mall. To the left they saw the DoD Office of Reserve Affairs and the ramp to the third floor. Taking the ramp to the right, they ended up on the second floor in an open area that flowed into the A-ring. The Pentagon was aptly named, and in addition to its five concentric rings—A through E, with the latter being the outside ring—it had ten corridors. The E-ring had the offices with a view, at least on the outside of the ring, and it is where all the high ranking officials resided. Most Pentagon offices, if they had windows at all, viewed the next concentric ring.

"You know this place has five sides..." JT remarked and then paused.

Juanita looked at him expectantly.

"....on every issue: Army, Navy, Air Force, Marines and DoD," he finished.

Juanita laughed and said, "One thing's for sure, this place is huge."

JT nodded and said, "The late newsman David Brinkley told a story about a woman who told a Pentagon guard she was in labor and needed help in getting to a hospital. And the guard said, 'Madame, you shouldn't have come here in that condition.' And she said, 'When I came here, I wasn't.'"

As they walked, they viewed various signs, posters and displays, which JT knew were random and were changed day-to-day or week-to-week. Directly ahead, two glass doors off the A-ring led to the center court yard of the Pentagon. Outside the glass doors were stairways on either side leading down to the burgers, sandwiches and soda grab-and-go style eatery located in the center and open except for the coldest months of the year. But JT and Juanita stayed on the inside, turned right on the A-ring, and walked down a narrow corridor past what would have been Corridor 10, except it was covered over by construction dry wall. They passed Corridor 9 and continued to Corridor 8½, an addition not there in the past. They transited down Corridor 8½ to the stairway between the B and C-ring and took it up one floor to the third floor. Because various corridors and rings were blocked with new offices or on-going construction, getting from one place to another proved a challenge to anyone not familiar with the building. On the third floor, they exited the stairway and turned left, headed toward the E-ring and a few paces down, they reached their final destination, Room 3E890. They couldn't believe that Styles had gotten a room on the E-ring, but at least it was not on the view side.

This was certainly a comedown for the egotistical Mr. Styles. His receptionist was shared with three other people, and his office, although it did have a window, looked out on the outside of the offices across on the D-ring and was not nearly as spacious as his previous one at DARPA. And JT knew that he basically had no authority here, as they had given him a can't-get-into-too-much-trouble job. Both JT and Juanita were smugly satisfied with this but felt it was only the first step in his well-deserved comeuppance. Unfortunately, he was still a year and a half from retirement or that might have been an option they wouldn't have allowed him to refuse. The receptionist merely nodded toward his office when Juanita requested to see him.

"Mr. Styles, how nice to see you again," Juanita greeted him in a less-than-convincing tone as she and JT entered his office.

"What the hell do you want this time?" he bellowed. "Haven't you two screwed up my life enough yet?"

"Screwing up seems to be what you're good at, or do you prefer the top position?" Juanita was really enjoying this.

"Ha. Ha. I presume you came here to ask me the same questions over again, so please do so and then get the hell out."

"Actually, no. We came to ask you about your whereabouts last night."

"Somebody else got killed and you need another scapegoat, right?"

Juanita didn't quite expect that question, but his reaction to her response would be more telling, hopefully, now that he had phrased the question like that. "Yes—Don Crenshaw."

The look of surprise on his face meant he was either a consummate actor or he really didn't know what had happened last night. Neither JT nor Juanita could tell which with any degree of certainty.

"When? I mean, obviously it was last night, but how? Wasn't he up at the DARPA conference in Baltimore?"

"You nailed two of those for us, Mr. Styles. Would you like to try for the third one and tell us how?"

"I was here. I was with someone last night." Styles realized that his presence or absence in the building would be easy for them to check. You have to enter and exit through the various check points with your NCR card. You could get someone to swap cards with you and establish a different arriving or leaving time, but Styles didn't know anyone here he could browbeat or blackmail into doing that for him. *Damn it, I have so little control here,* he thought. *Besides, it doesn't really matter, since my wife doesn't know anyone here she could use to check on my comings and goings anyway.*

"Miss Ventura, I suppose," posed Juanita.

"No, actually it was another lady."

"We'll need her name and contact information."

Styles wrote it down on a piece of paper and handed it to Juanita.

"And from when to when?"

"From about 4:30 yesterday afternoon until ten or so. And before you ask, we were at her place over in Rosslyn."

Juanita looked at JT and said, "Not much of an alibi for 12:30 this morning, is it?"

JT shook his head.

"Well, shit. You didn't say that. I was home with my family at that time."

"If your wife is not a sound sleeper that may be an alibi, so we'll certainly be talking with her. Should we mention your earlier whereabouts?"

"Fuck you. Are we done now?"

"Yes. But please don't leave town. And thank you for your cooperation."

They got up and walked out. Juanita kept waiting for the sound of a slamming door but didn't hear one this time. Perhaps he was not as secure in his position here as he was in the one at DARPA. Or maybe his door didn't work. As they retraced their path through the building back to the Metro, Juanita asked, "So what do you think?"

"He had motive in both murders—the risk of exposure for contract fixing. Much as I hate to admit it, I think he has an alibi for both. However, if we can believe Doctor J., he may have transferred funds to a hit man for the first incident, and we can ask her about the second. If that proves out, it would be strong evidence against him. But unless we can get better evidence than that, I don't think we could get a conviction. We've got to make the connection between him and Furlong."

"I can't believe that we pretty much know what's going on but can't make a case. I am glad that you didn't let me throw the financial transactions in his face. Probably better if he doesn't know we know about that yet."

When they got out of the building, JT called the office and got a pleasant surprise: the ATF had a suspect on the blasting cap disappearance. Although at first blush it appeared that there had been an unauthorized entry into the alarmed storage room where the caps, explosives and other items requiring special handling were kept, their forensics team determined that the break-in was faked and therefore had to be an inside job. While they had no specific evidence to point to the culprit, they did find that three of the employees were related to known felons. When the ATF passed this to the Fusion Team, Hanson realized that Furlong was the ex-brother-in-law of one of the employees. Now they had his probable presence at the scene of the license plate lifting and the possibly related murder of Crenshaw in Baltimore, no alibi for either murder, his rap sheet, his expensive toy, and finally his knowing a possible source for the blasting caps. They also had Arati's belief that there were fund transfers corresponding to a "contract" payment. Although Hanson knew the financial transfers were too iffy to include, since they couldn't be traced directly to Furlong, he still felt they had more than enough for a search warrant. He told JT to prepare the request when he got back to the office, and to make it as inclusive as he could.

When JT finished the call, they went down into the Metro station to catch the train back. Juanita remembered that she needed to call Sergeant Thompson of the Baltimore Police Department, the detective in charge of the Crenshaw murder, to see what they had uncovered in their investigation. As soon as the train came and they got above ground, she placed the call. She learned that they had recovered two .38 slugs from Crenshaw and were waiting for the FBI to run them through NCIC or the National Crime Information Center. This system had recently added all available data on guns and ammunition used in crimes, in addition to the data that had been available for some time on stolen guns. As far as Crenshaw himself, one bullet had pierced his heart and the other his lung, so he had no chance and died quickly, according to the ME. He placed the time of death at 12:30 in the morning. BPD found a number of fingerprints other than Crenshaw's that they had run through AFIS—or the Automated Fingerprint Identification System, another FBI crime fighting tool—but so far all the hits they got back belonged to previous occupants of the room or hotel employees. Some foreign material, also waiting analysis, was found on the slugs removed from the body—plastic or something similar—possibly a remnant from something used to muffle the gun shots.

"Were there any witnesses?" Juanita asked.

Thompson informed her that the hotel night clerk remembered someone fitting Furlong's general description entering the hotel about 12:15 carrying a tote bag, but he did not recall anyone leaving within the next three hours. However, someone could have taken the stairs down and exited the side door of the building without being picked up by the cameras. The hotel surveillance cameras did capture the entry and elevator ride but showed the individual exiting the elevator on the floor below Crenshaw's and proceeding to the end of the hallway where the stairs were located. From there, the assailant could have walked up a flight and entered near the eighth-floor west side surveillance camera. This was likely, since from the time stamp on the film from that camera, which was the one covering Crenshaw's side of the floor, they determined that it had been spray painted at about that time. Unless they were actually watching the camera at that exact moment, which nobody was, this would appear as a simple camera malfunction.

"When was the last time that anybody saw Crenshaw?" she asked.

"He had dinner with some of his cohorts and they finished up at about 8:30. One person remembers him saying something about an errand to run, but he didn't say what or where. Nobody remembers seeing him after that. His room was entered at 8:47 with his key, and then we believe it was jimmied open sometime after that but before he entered with his key again at 12:33." Notwithstanding the information he received from JT and company, Detective Thompson's assessment was that this was an attempted burglary that resulted in a confrontation that ending in a shooting. "There were, after all," he said, "items stolen from the room. The forced, though nevertheless stealthy, entry at a time when the victim's wallet would be in the room was not an uncommon MO for hotel burglars. They could often hit several rooms before being detected, and then, usually just by waving a gun around, could usually lock the victim that caught them in the act in the bathroom with a door latching device. The burglar, now upgraded to a robber, would make sure there was no phone in the bathroom or disable it. By the time the victim recovered enough nerve to make some noise, the perpetrator would have made an exit. It could be that in this case, Crenshaw was the first victim of the evening and the perpetrator left after the shooting to avoid detection."

"Plausible," said Juanita, "it fits the facts we have." She thanked the detective and said goodbye. After she relayed his comments to JT, he suggested that Detective Thompson, like most good detectives, was not willing to complicate a case without significant cause, and in his view he didn't have that yet. However, he was not privy to all the data the team had, but merely a summary from JT. "So, where do we go from here?" she wondered out loud.

"Furlong's place," replied JT, "as soon as we get our search warrant, hopefully tomorrow. Which reminds me, but don't ask me why, that I checked with the General Counsel and the head of the Contracts Management Office at DARPA, and neither one of them recalled talking to Crenshaw about any suspicious activity with contracts awarded for DARPA. I also talked with the former General Counsel and the person who used to head the Contracts Office at CIFA, Crenshaw's former employer, and neither one of them had any discussions with Crenshaw regarding that either. So in other words, he apparently kept his suspicions to himself."

"Another dead end," Juanita commented.

"One more thing. I got a call from ole TT this morning."

"The DARPA Director?"

"Yes. Seems they are developing a new automatic weapon, and he asked if I would like to test fire it down at the FBI range day after tomorrow. Wanna come along?"

"Are you kidding? Of course. What's it called?"

"The HK MP3000. Guess we impressed him or something. He did ask if you'd be available to come as well."

"Are you shittin' me?" she asked before noticing his impish grin.

CHAPTER TWENTY-ONE

Burke, Virginia, 17 November, 1600 hours

Neither Hanson nor anyone else on the team aware of all the details on Furlong thought Furlong was aware of their interest in him, so waiting for a warrant was not deemed a problem. JT wanted to request the warrant from Judge Harold Krolick, since he was quick and usually sympathetic to the difficulty of getting evidence on terrorists, however Hanson vetoed that. "This one does not seem to be terrorist-related anymore, and I think we have a very good basis for it," he said, "so let's go with whatever judge is up. We should save the Honorable Judge Krolick for when we need him."

JT finally called at 4:12 and said he had it. Since Furlong got off work at four o'clock, JT suggested that it would probably be best to wait for him to get home before they approached his house to serve the warrant. Hanson agreed and asked the Team to make final preparations and plan on executing as soon as Furlong showed, but no later than 5:30. They went over to one of the consoles to check the GPS tracking data and saw that Furlong was already on the move. He made a short stop, apparently at a grocery store, and then proceeded home, arriving at 4:55.

JT arrived before the Team, since the courthouse was not that far away. Hanging back a few blocks, he waited for the rest of the team to arrive. As prearranged, JT would serve the warrant and keep an eye on Furlong while the other three team members searched the premises. "Alright, Team, let's go." At 5:03, JT knocked on the door while the other three remained out of sight. "Mr. Jonathan Furlong?" he asked.

"Yeah. Who wants to know?" he asked after opening the door.

"I'm agent Dunkirk with the Department of Homeland Security and we have a search warrant for these premises." He handed the stunned Furlong the warrant and motioned for the rest of the search team to come forward. This included a JTTF employee, a member of the Charley Unit of the Fusion Team, and a Fairfax County Detective that JT had "borrowed" from the department. All three were highly skilled in the execution of search warrants.

JT started to enter the premises when Furlong stammered, "Wait, I haven't read this yet!"

"Sir, we don't have to wait for you to read it, but if you make it quick, I will. And that's yours to keep so you can peruse it to your heart's content."

Furlong looked over the warrant and then asked, rhetorically, "You think I may have been involved in rigging an explosion and you're looking for blasting caps? Aren't those things really small?"

"Yes, Sir, they are. That means this will be a long and very thorough search. And I'm afraid that I'll have to ask you to stay right here in my sight while my colleagues execute this warrant."

"Well, how about I get a beer then and watch the ball game? Just so happens the Skins have a Thursday night game. Can I offer you one?"

"Thanks, but no thanks. I'm on duty. 'Though I'd be glad to watch the game with you."

Under JT's watchful eye, Furlong grabbed a beer from the fridge and then sat down on his couch and tuned his fifty-two-inch plasma TV to the Redskins game. The pregame program led into the game itself and, for the next two hours, the Team searched the premises while JT and furlong watched TV. Towards the end of that time, they asked them both to move while they searched the couch and chair they were sitting in. Then they went into the garage after spelling JT for a bathroom break. At just past three hours into it, Melissa Barnes, the FCPD officer, indicated that she wanted to talk to JT in another room. Melissa's long brown hair accented her brown eyes, and JT thought she was pretty. She certainly was easygoing—not to mention very good at her job. The other two watched Furlong, who by this time had consumed four beers, half a bag of potato chips with sour cream dip, and two slices of a leftover pepperoni, mushroom and jalapeno pizza.

"His house is clean and so are his car and truck. The only thing that we found of interest is this." She showed JT a key. "We think it's a storage locker key, but as you can see, there are no identifying marks on it. It was in a small, concealed, wooden compartment located under the built-in workbench in the garage. I almost missed it," she said with a smile on her face.

"Thanks, Melissa. Let's see how he reacts to this."

Melissa had put a string through the whole at the top of the key so it could be handled without destroying any prints on it.

JT went back into the living room. "Mr. Furlong, we found this key in your garage. Can you tell us what this is for?"

"In my garage? Where?"

"Is it yours?"

"Never seen it before," he said as he grabbed for it. "Where the hell was it?"

JT quickly removed it from his reach. "It was in a hidden compartment under your built-in workbench in the garage."

"Must be from the former owner. I've never seen it." Furlong could not remember if he had wiped it clean before he put it under the bench, but he was pretty sure he didn't, because he never thought this situation would arise. "No, wait a minute," he said, "that's where I hid the key to the kitchen door in case I forgot my keys. I could use the automatic garage door opener and then use that key to get in the house if I had to. I guess I forgot about it because I changed the kitchen door lock a few years ago."

"Fine. Then you don't mind if we take it do you?"

"Well, ah, you can't take it, can you?"

"Sir, it's an item of interest in the search."

"Well, ah, then sure. I guess it's of no use to me anymore. Are you taking anything else?"

"Nope, that's it. Are we all done here, Team?" JT asked.

"Yes, Sir," the JTTF guy replied.

"Okay. Then we're out of here. Thank you so much for your cooperation, Mr. Furlong. We'll let you know if we need anything else." Once outside, JT got in his car, which he had parked in one of the visitor spaces directly across the street from

Furlong's place, and called the Boss. "We're all done here, Cap'n." JT then gave him a summary of their findings. "Melissa has a local storage locker key collection that she says will provide us with the locations of the companies that use that type key. She took pictures of the key and has already left. Her info combined with the GPS data should pinpoint the place for us unless he hasn't visited it in the last week or so. I presume you want us to keep an eye on this guy until we can locate the locker and get a warrant for it."

Hanson agreed.

"So, can you please send in a relief man for me so I can get home at a decent hour tonight?" JT pleaded.

Hanson mumbled something about pantywaists and told JT to hang tight for an hour or so.

Less than thirty minutes later, JT's cell phone went off and he saw it was Melissa's number. "Oh, sweet Melissa, whatcha got for me?"

"This particular key is used by two self-storage companies in the area—True Blue Storage and StorageRight. I can send the locations to the email address on your card if you'd like."

JT heartily agreed and asked her to include Hanson as an addressee on the email. He thanked her for the quick response and then called the Boss and let him know what was coming. A few minutes later, JT took an incoming call from Brendon. "I see you guys are still working the night shift."

"That way we can sleep and get away with it," Brendon quipped. "We're en route to some storage place. So what do we have on this guy?"

"There was nothing in the house but a hidden locker key. We're trying to locate the locker now and get a warrant for it. Furlong obviously knows we're on to him, so we need to make sure he doesn't get there before us. I suspect he'll check his vehicles for tracking devices if he's smart and probably figure his phone's been tapped. Let's hope he didn't leave a key with an accomplice who might be able to do that for him, but I'm betting he works alone—no sharing of the profits that way. Yeah, okay. Well, you guys have fun and I'll check with you later."

As soon as Hanson had finished talking to JT, he decided that he'd better not leave anything to chance, so he ordered a team to the storage location nearest to Furlong's place, figuring he could relocate them quickly if need be. One location was a mile north of Furlong's and the other about four miles south, both on Ox Road. Those were the only two within a five-mile radius. A quick check of the GPS data indicated that Furlong hadn't used his cars to approach either one of them, at least not within the last two weeks that he was under surveillance. In particular, a few days before and the day after the Baltimore murder, there was no indication that he had made a stop at any storage location. He must have picked up and dropped off stuff from the locker, if he needed to, while driving around on his QPUDS route. As soon as Hanson got the names of the companies from Melissa, he was sure it was the southern one that Furlong was using, and he redirected the team there. He completed the emergency search warrant from his stored electronic template in less than ten minutes after getting the storage locker information. He thought it was now time to call Judge Krolick.

The Judge agreed they had probable cause and told him to send it. The Judge filled in his portion of the document and forwarded it back to Hanson in nine minutes flat.

Brendon and Sal got to the storage location at 9:43. The place was lit up fairly well at night so they could park half a block away and still see anyone approaching it. They settled in for a long night. Three minutes later, Sal saw a man fitting Furlong's general description and dressed in a jogging suit with a backpack on approach the StorageRight office. He grabbed the binoculars and took a quick look. "Isn't that our man heading for the office there?"

Brendon looked through the binoculars. "Sure looks like him. Guess he needs the manager to give him a key."

"Who's at his place?" asked Sal. "Do you think we should apprehend him?"

Brendon was already dialing JT's cell phone. "JT, we think Furlong's here at the StorageRight."

JT ran up to check the townhouse. "He doesn't seem to be here but both his cars are. He must have hightailed it out the back on foot. How far away are you?"

"About four miles."

"I saw him look out his window damn close to nine. It was after nine. He must have hiked down there."

"Right. Call the boss and let him know what's happening. We're going after him. " Brendon hung up and looked at Sal. "There's no time to call for backup. As soon as he comes out with the key, we'll nab him!"

This was not a climate-controlled facility and the lockers were located on either side of three alley-like passageways running parallel to them. They got out of the car and proceeded toward the first row of lockers. Unfortunately, there was not much cover for them, so they tried to look casual and still hurry. Since the key was sufficient indication of where he was going, they didn't want him inside where he could destroy or plant evidence. They were about fifty yards away when Furlong came out of the office.

Furlong headed for the front row of lockers, so Brendon motioned Sal to go around the second row to cut him off if need be. As they started to cross the street in front of the storage facility, a passing car beeped at them and Furlong turned and saw them. He knew he was made. He tossed the backpack down and started running towards the back of the place.

Sal yelled, "You get the car and go around the block! I'll take after him on foot!" With that, he sprinted in Furlong's direction.

Brendon ran back to the car and headed south on Ox Road, in the same direction that the car was parked. Unfortunately, the block extended for half a mile with no left turns. He remembered from the map that after he turned, the first street on the left would be a court, Pyracantha Court or something like that. He found it and took the turn at about thirty-five after braking just before it. As he approached the end of the court, he saw Sal running across the street headed for the other side, so he turned around and headed back out to the intersection and made another left.

Furlong's familiarity with this neighborhood meant he had no trouble navigating it on foot. He always kept himself in good shape and could run five miles easily, even though he had just jogged almost four. After he climbed the fence at the back of the storage facility, he quickly ran through a couple of back yards, climbing over fences near the rear of the yards. After three houses, he spotted a cul-de-sac in the front of the house so ran out the gate and sprinted across the street to the houses on the other side. He started the fence hopping again and after he entered the fifth backyard, he made a sharp left and went up towards the house and through their side gate. He ran across that street and into the backyard of that house. Luckily, only a few dogs got wind of him and as best he could tell, no residents. He jumped their fence and landed in the backyard of the house behind the one he was just in. He paused for a moment to look back and see if he had shaken his tail. He could see his pursuer crossing the street and heading for the yard he had just vacated. *Shit, this guy can run,* he thought, *so I'm not getting away from him on foot.* He ran through the yard and then the gate and out onto the street.

A motorcyclist coming towards him started slowing down as he approached his driveway. Furlong ran up to him, grabbed him by the collar and flung him off the bike, which continued to the curb before falling over. Furlong ran over and grabbed it, righted it and jumped on. About fifty yards down the road, he looked in the rearview mirror and saw the rider still on the ground and his pursuer approaching the fallen victim. *That was close. I'm pretty sure that if I head west on this street, I'll end up on Ox Road. Looks like I'm home free now.*

"Hey, Buddy, you okay?" Sal asked the man who by this time was getting up and shaking his head.

"Yeah, just some scratches maybe, but I'm really pissed. Glad I had my leathers on. Who was that guy?"

"He's a murder suspect. What street is this?" With that information, he called Brendon who was about two blocks away. Sal told him what happened and asked Brendon to put out a BOLO for Furlong and the motorcycle. He described Furlong's attire and the color, make and plate number for the bike. Thirty seconds later, he reached Sal's location.

Police Officer First Class Juan Delgato of the FCPD had just decided to turn south onto Ox Road when he saw the bike heading north on Ox Road doing twelve miles over the limit. No big deal, but the rider also wasn't wearing a helmet. He decided to cite the guy. Just as he got close enough to light him up, the bike did a wheelie and the guy took off like a bullet. Delgato didn't get close enough to see the plate, but he called it in as a pursuit.

The dispatcher alerted other patrol cars in the area and asked for a description of the rider. "We just got a BOLO on a motorcyclist fitting that general description in your area. He's a murder suspect and possibly armed. Maintain your pursuit and distance until backup arrives. Keep me posted on your route."

Furlong was now doing about eighty, weaving like hell and blowing through red lights. *If I can only make it to Fairfax County Parkway, I can weave around up to I-66 and head for West Virginia*, he thought. Then he almost bought it at the intersection with Popes Head Road. He saw the flashing blue lights close behind and realized that there would be more joining the chase shortly. He figured the only way he was going to get away was to take off across country. He looked around and saw his opportunity—an apparent bike path off to the left. He came to a quick stop, walked the bike across the median and up the curb on the other side. It was then that he noticed the second set of blue lights, this one coming down Ox Road right towards him. He couldn't believe these guys caught up with him so fast. *Good decision to leave the road now.* He crossed a short plot of grass to reach the path, which was about five-feet wide and ran perpendicular to the road. He accelerated up to thirty just to get into the woods and out of sight quickly. The path turned fairly sharply to the left about thirty yards in and Furlong slowed slightly to negotiate the curve. Then his headlight hit it not fifteen feet ahead—a fallen tree across the path. Before he could react at all, the front tire hit the tree and Furlong went flying over it. He landed flat on his back on the other side of the tree, the wind knocked out of him and his head spinning.

Delgato had been joined by Master Police Officer Dale Remington, who was headed south on Ox Road when he heard the pursuit on the radio. With no traffic in sight, Delgato crossed the median and the southbound lane and drove over the curb right where Furlong had left the road.

Remington pulled in right behind him.

They both heard what they thought was a crash over the sound of the dying sirens and saw a shining light on the tree tops, probably the bike headlamp. They figured Furlong could still be in shape to attempt a getaway on foot, so they both headed down the path with guns in one hand and flashlights in the other. When they reached him, he was sitting up in the middle of the path facing away from them on the other side of the fallen tree, holding himself up with his hands, moaning and shaking his head.

"Put your hands behind your head!" Delgato shouted. Furlong just sat there shaking his head, so Delgato yelled at him again. He still didn't respond, but since Delgato could see his hands and Remington had a bead on him, he holstered his weapon and withdrew his cuffs. Once the cuffs were in place, Delgato frisked him. "Damn, that was fun," he said to Remington. "Guess you got the BOLO on this guy?"

"Yeah. We don't get to chase murder suspects every day." By this time, Furlong seemed semi-coherent. "Are you hurt bad?" Remington asked.

The suspect responded by shaking his head and moaning again.

Since they weren't sure what that meant or how bad he was hurt, they decided to let Furlong sit there. "I'm going to call this in and let dispatch know we got the guy and ask for a bus and a wrecker. You okay here watching him?" Remington asked.

"No problem."

By the time Furlong came out of his daze, he was in an ambulance headed to Fairfax hospital. He looked at the cop sitting next to him and knew he was in big trouble. As a convicted felon who had just committed another two at least, he figured on a long sentence, especially when they got the stuff in his locker. He did not want to go back to jail, but that sure seemed in the offing now. He thought about making a break for it and then realized he was cuffed. *Maybe I'll just die tonight.*

Brendon and Sal had reunited and called the locals to take a report from the biker Furlong had tumbled. When Sal finished giving the officer his statement, he and Brendon proceeded back to the self-storage place to talk to the manager. They showed him Furlong's picture and he positively identified him. He said that Furlong had been renting the place for a couple of years, and tonight claimed he had lost his key and needed to get into the locker. The manager had charged him $20 for the extra key to locker A-17 that he gave him.

Brendon called Hanson with an update and asked if he could send some evidence technicians out to the site while Sal recovered the bag that Furlong had dropped at the storage site before taking off. It contained a crowbar and a five pound sledge hammer. He figured Furlong wasn't taking any chances in case a spare key wasn't available. Sal pulled up the warrant on his laptop and showed it to the manager, got his last key to the locker, and then he and Brendon settled in to wait for the techies. In the meantime, Brendon decided to monitor the FCPD frequencies and heard that Furlong was apprehended and taken to a hospital.

Two evidence technicians from DHS got there a couple of minutes before midnight. Furlong had rented the smallest walk-in you could in this facility: four-feet wide and eight-feet deep. His locker housed two roll boxes, a Craftsman with twelve drawers and a Waterloo with eight, plus a small work table and chair. The table supported a laptop and some writing material. In two of the roll box drawers, they found six blasting caps, wiring, a multimeter and other electrician's tools, SCRs, batteries and other IED materials, but, luckily, no volatile explosives. There were also some common tools, a set of lock picks and a Slim Jim, as well as clothing and various makeup and disguise materials. A watch and digital camera and five grand in twenties occupied another drawer. Finally, there was a box of .38 ammunition, but no firearms. The blasting caps alone would put him away for quite awhile, but the combination of material located here just might give them a slam dunk. It took them about an hour, but they catalogued and carefully packaged everything. Not a bad haul for an evening's work.

CHAPTER TWENTY-TWO

Fusion Team Headquarters, 18 November, 0910 hours

"Glad you folks could make it in today," chided Hanson, as JT and Juanita had just rolled in a few minutes earlier. "Come into my office and we'll review where we are with Mr. Furlong. Brendon and Sal and Bill Hastings from Bravo Unit will be joining us." The six of them gathered around the conference table in the room just off Hanson's office. Everyone brought a cup of coffee or tea with them and settled down at the table. "Furlong's injuries were minor, so they took him to the county West Springfield Station. We had him transferred from there to our detention facility in Fullerton early this morning." Fullerton was a business complex just west of I-95 and south of the Fairfax County Parkway. In addition to many small businesses and a *Costco*, there were several government agency offices located there—identified only with Department of State or Department of the Interior logos on the doors, and some were not identified at all. Furlong was now in a building labeled, **Atherton Research and Development, Inc.** behind an eight-foot concertina wired fence.

"I know it's early yet, Captain, but did we get anything from the watch or camera or blasting caps?" Brendon asked.

"He was apparently smart enough to wipe the watch and camera clean. The only solid prints we got from the camera and the watch itself were his. However, a lot of amateurs don't know that there is a relatively new procedure that can uncover prints from metal surfaces even after they've been 'wiped clean.' Sweat reacts with some metals to corrode them slightly. So, if we apply a very fine, charged sensitive powder, then apply an electrical current that causes the powder to collect in the corroded tracks, we can get a good print. By using this technique we got one pretty good print and one iffy partial on the watch battery that were not his. Unfortunately they were not Crenshaw's, either, nor did they show up in AFIS. We asked Mrs. Crenshaw if maybe she changed the battery for him, but she said she never did that, and no one else lives with them. She also said that her husband usually changed watch batteries for both of them, but sometimes he'd ask the jewelry store person do it. So the print probably belongs to some clerk that sold the battery to him. The camera had a tag missing off the bottom of it that most likely had a serial number on it. And there was no memory card in it. It would have been really nice to recover one with pictures of Crenshaw's family on it. So, while these match the items missing from his hotel room, this is all circumstantial. If the caps come back as the ones missing from the quarry, and therefore a match to the ones used in the murder of Quarles, that still doesn't mean he did it. He could have sold them to a third party. Finally, I've asked Charles to visit his workplace to see if there's anything there that might help us."

"So now what?" Juanita asked.

"He won't be arraigned until later this afternoon, but given his high flight risk, I'm confident that he will be held without bail. He has retained a lawyer and has given us nothing. I have a meeting with a prosecutor from the Department of Justice in another hour and I'd love to be able to recommend life without the possibility of parole in lieu of the death sentence, *if* Furlong cooperates and gives us what he has on his employer. I doubt if he'll go for that with what we got, but maybe Furlong's locker or desk or whatever these QPUDS drivers have at work will yield the smoking gun. Otherwise I'm afraid all we have is a string of felonies that will keep him in jail for a while but probably not forever. JT, I'd like you to interview him, or I should say talk to him, and make him the offer, if the Justice guy approves. If so, I'll have that in writing before you talk to him, but that's not likely to happen before early Monday morning. I think sitting in jail over the weekend and having some time to think about the hopelessness of his situation may soften him up a bit. All right, enough on Furlong. Is there anything else on the Quarles case before we switch to the terrorist plot?"

"Two more things, Boss. First, we did verify Styles' alibi for the time of the murder. Do you believe he actually tried to say he was in the Pentagon and then realized he couldn't fake that data?" Juanita asked rhetorically. "His second honey is more of a bimbo than his first one, but she seemed sincere in her statement. Second, we got another call from Arati over at NRL, and she said there were more fund transfers similar to last time. This time $45,000 was transferred into what she's pretty sure is an offshore account belonging to Styles, and then from there into the same local Bank of America account. She's not sure where the money came from that went into Styles' account, but it was different than last time. The timing is within seventy-two hours of Crenshaw's murder. We need to work on making that more solid so we can nail him along with Furlong."

"Tell us how you really feel, Juanita," said Hanson. He smiled and then asked, "Are we through with the Quarles case for now?" When JT and Juanita nodded in unison, he asked, "Bill, could you tell us what you found out about the names and places that we got from Mustafa?"

Bill Hastings led the Fusion Team's Bravo Unit and was a DHS employee, as were JT and Hanson. He also came to the Team from CIFA—where he met Hanson—and was with the CIA before that. Hastings actually looked like a spy, or so they all told him. He was average height, not bad-looking but not remarkable either, had short, dark hair, was clean shaven, and, to complete the image, dressed very unobtrusively. "Well, Tom, first off we took the tape of MJ's interview with Mustafa to one of the CIA interpreters, and she agreed completely with MJ's translation. She also agreed with JT and MJ's assessment of his state of mind and his complicity with the terrorists, so I'd say everyone was right on there."

"Did we get anything useful from the names and places that Mustafa gave us?"

"Not really," replied Hastings as he stood up and passed around a sheet of paper. "The two meeting places for *"Afghans in America"* that he gave us we were already aware of and in fact the FBI had checked out. The names of the attendees that he gave us were part of the meeting records that the organization keeps. He did indicate that he thought he saw Khalid talking to one of the attendees out in the parking lot after one of the meetings. He gave us the guy's description and we had a sketch drawn up. When we showed that to one of the meeting coordinators, he identified him as Naseer Qalzai, and that's his picture and resumé on the handout. As you can see, he's a naturalized citizen, has a wife and two kids, and has a job as a mechanic and car inspector with a *Sunoco* gas station in Annandale. He rents a place nearby. Doesn't seem like someone who would be a terrorist sympathizer but, as you know, we put him under surveillance. So far that hasn't been fruitful. We did find out that he has some family back in Afghanistan that he's trying to get over here. Think that's about it, unless anyone has a question." Seeing they didn't, he sat back down.

"Thanks, Bill. JT what did you get on the Khadija family?"

"Ronnie and I spent some time checking them out and they all seem legit. Ashan's brother has been in the country for almost eight years and has worked for *Federal Express* for the last five. He's a manager at one of their *FedEx-Kinko* locations. He was square with us about his brother's whereabouts and called us as soon as his brother contacted him. There are no ties to any suspect groups. His wife is a stay-at-home mom with a three-year-old and a kid in kindergarten. Their only debt is their mortgage and one car. They have put the cab that Ashan was killed in up for sale. Apparently they had to put a new front seat in it first because of the blood stains on the old one. Except for the lack of any credit card debt, they seem pretty middle-class American. I don't think there's anything there for us, Boss," JT concluded.

"How's our guy in the hospital doing?"

"A lot better than he was," offered Juanita. "He lost a lot of blood, not to mention suffering considerable internal damage from the shotgun blast. The pellets mutilated his left kidney, nicked his spleen and punctured his colon. The kidney is gone but they think they got the rest under control. He did develop an infection in the hospital that kept him listed as touch and go for awhile, but that's improving as of yesterday. If you recall, they reported some ranting on his part about a transportation system. The doc says he should be up to talking soon and MJ knows Farsi and is on call. As you know, we have him under guard."

"Let me know as soon as we get something there or figure out we're not going to. I don't know how long I can keep the MPD in there guarding him, but I do know it's not helping my overtime budget. All right, folks, unless there is anything else..." He looked around and seeing that there wasn't, he charged them, "Carry on!" as the meeting broke up and everyone went back to their desk.

"Hey, Nita, you still going down to the range with me? I need to requalify before the end of the month anyway, so I thought I'd kill two birds with one stone, so to speak. Hey, that reminds me of a joke about Chief One Stone."

"Forget it—it's terrible. I have to requalify in two months so if you don't mind we can both do that. I'll drive if you like."

"That'd be great. I need to make a phone call or two and then I'll tell the Boss where we're going. Can you give me an hour?"

Juanita gave him a thumbs up.

"How about if I drive over to the Dunkin' Donuts on Backlick in Springfield and meet you there? That way I won't have to come all the way back here to pick up my car."

"Is that the one just north of the Fairfax County Parkway?"

JT nodded.

"No problem. Meet you there in about an hour and a half, say 11:30?"

"Great."

Springfield, Virginia, 18 November, 1135 hours

Juanita had only been sitting outside the store for two minutes when JT pulled up in his Highlander. She headed into the store with JT on her heels. As usual, he ordered a large hazelnut iced coffee with cream only and Juanita ordered a small decaf latte. They each ordered one of their flatbread sandwiches, as well. "All that caffeine is bad for your heart, you know."

"I only get two caffeinated drinks a day, both around lunch time. I don't think that's going to kill me," JT rebutted. "All that sugar you ingest is probably worse for you."

"I don't—oh, never mind. Neither one of us ever changes our habits after these little discussions, so let's drop it," Juanita smirked. They finished their lunch in less than twenty minutes and were back on the road in Juanita's PT Cruiser. In short order, they were on I-95 South headed toward Quantico. "So JT, how come you don't use the standard *Glock 23* with the .40 *S&W* cartridge that the FCPD issues? I figured they'd let you keep the same gun and not make you switch to the DHS firearm."

"Well, as you know, I was a Federal Air Marshall for almost four years and I got used to the *Sig Sauer* P229 with the .357 round. I spent eight weeks in Artesia, New Mexico, in the FAM camp living, breathing, eating and sleeping with that weapon. One thing they taught you how to do very well was to shoot from any position: prone, standing, falling, with a terrorist on your back, behind you, you name it. On that airplane, the important thing was to completely disable the hijacker with no collateral damage. So I have to admit that I became very attached to it and I'm a pretty good shot. I came in second two years in a row in the FAM national shootout, as they called it. And as you pointed out, it's the same firearm that DHS agents use. So how do you like that *Glock*?"

"I think it's fine. It's what OSI uses and I didn't want to have to get used to something new, either. What was it like being a FAM? I know we talked about why you left Fairfax and became a FAM, but why did you quit the FAM Service?"

"I enjoyed it for a couple of years in spite of the ridiculous rules we had to follow. They actually made us wear suits, sit in first class, stay clean shaven, use the cheapest hotels, et cetera, et cetera, et cetera, as Yul Brynner used to say. When they ramped up the FAM Service after 9/11, the agents came from most every department of the government, but the top layers were heavy with ex-Secret Service guys. And they had this image of what a federal agent should look like and couldn't be persuaded otherwise. Well, common sense did finally prevail, but by that time I was working the airports. After two plus years of nonstop flying, it was getting pretty old, and airport duty reminded me of my days as a Fairfax cop and how much more I really enjoyed that. Don't get me wrong—we did some interesting things in the airports, but it still wasn't like being a street cop. Anyway, this job is much better. And I don't have to fly three or four times a week."

"You're kidding, three or four times a week?"

"Sure. Unless you had an international flight—those could be two or three days in length."

"I seem to remember you telling us that you flew to England, France, Japan and a couple of places in South America."

"Buenos Aires, Sao Paulo, Caracas, Rio, and a few I can't remember right now. Also Ireland, Portugal, Mexico, Haiti and a few other places in the Caribbean."

"What was your favorite place?"

"I was actually most impressed with Japan. The people there are so respectful."

Juanita gave him a look.

"Seriously. In spite of their crowded conditions, or maybe because of them, they are very neat and orderly. We flew into a pretty big city south of Tokyo, Nagoya, and spent about a day and a half there, not counting airport time. I didn't see any graffiti or trash anywhere, and I walked around the city for several miles. Almost all the residences had neat little gardens with pruned trees that were obviously very well cared for. I felt completely safe even though I was in a foreign country and stood out like a sore thumb. Late one evening, I was walking and came to an intersection with lights and walk signs. Dozens of Japanese were standing on the corners waiting for the walk sign even though there was no traffic. Here we would have been all over that street, but they were waiting for that walk sign."

"What was your least favorite place?"

"Paris. I just don't like the French, mainly I think because the feeling is mutual. They must have originated the weekly shower idea, and they all have this hoity-toity attitude and a non-existent work ethic. But they do have good wine." JT was interrupted by the ringing of his cell phone. "Special Agent Dunkirk. Hey MJ, what's up? No kidding!" JT listened intently for several minutes. "Okay, thanks. Yeah, you bet. See you then. Bye." He looked at Juanita and smiled.

"I recognize that grin. What's going our way?"

"Seems they gave our survivor from the shootout the other night a new sedative, some derivative of scopolamine, and it apparently loosened his tongue."

"What a coincidence. And what did his loose tongue wag about?"

"He identified one of the guys from the *S&S Enterprises* incident, the guy driving the Civic that our buddy Khalid was in. They have a bead on him already and the boss agreed that we could pick him up for questioning. He also mentioned some other names and places. Says she'll give us more details in an email message."

"Excellent. We were practically running on empty in that area. But what was the 'see you then' part about?"

"You are a nosy bitch, aren't you?"

"I'm just looking out for the welfare of my partner, Partner."

"MJ and I are going out tomorrow night. Want to join us?"

"Yeah, right."

"No, I'm serious. We're going out for dinner and then to a night club. I wouldn't mind at all if you wanted to come along. With a friend of course."

"You're serious, aren't you?" The way JT looked at her answered her question, and then she felt bad. Well, almost. "Gee, thanks but not this time. I mean, I wouldn't know who to ask." After a minute she asked, "How about I just come by myself?" JT started to say something then Juanita piped in with, "Just kidding."

"That's it. I'm asking for a new partner."

"Forget it. The Boss is not going to authorize field duty for MJ." They both started laughing. "Oh, wait, I got it. How about if I ask TT if he wants to join us? You said I got a special invite from him, right?"

"I believe he's married, Nita, but you go for it if he's your type."

"He's not actually going to be at the range today, is he?"

"He didn't mention that, but I guess we'll find out soon enough."

CHAPTER TWENTY-THREE

Quantico Marine Corps Base, Virginia, 18 November, 1245 hours

The Marine Corps Monument—a 210-foot stainless steel spire that soars over the tree line and cannot be missed from I-95—came into view. The shape and direction of the spire emulate the iconic image of the raising of the American flag over Iwo Jima. Others may say it evokes notions of swords at salute, or aircraft climbing towards the heavens, or a howitzer at the ready. "If we finish up in time, maybe we can stop by the Museum," suggested Juanita. The National Museum of the Marine Corps was collocated with the monument.

"Okay, but I don't want to be too late getting home tonight. I promised Andy that we'd watch one of the *Shrek* movies. I can't remember if it's the third or fourth one."

As they came to the second Quantico exit, Russell Road, Juanita took it and headed west toward the Quantico Fullbore/Highpower Facility, which was collocated with the FBI Academy. Juanita pulled up to the entrance and showed her creds and JT's to the guard. "We're going out to the shooting range," she said.

"Yes Ma'am," the guard said as he gave them a snappy wave through.

"Think he might be available for tomorrow night?" she asked JT. "Not only is he good-looking and really built, he's damn respectful, as well. Something you don't find in most men nowadays."

"I think maybe he's just a tad young for you," JT quipped.

Russell Road turned into MCB1, then MCB4, and then J. Edgar Hoover Road, which went right in front of the main complex of the academy. Juanita veered off on Browning Road just short of that and turned into the parking lot for the range. They checked in with the range master and found out that the

DARPA folks were already on the range, so they trekked a couple of hundred yards over to the high-power section as quickly as they could.

Dr. Roger Downing, the DARPA program manager for the MP3000, was there with his team, which included two engineers from Heckler and Koch, a camera man, and the doctor's research assistant. After a round of introductions, Downing said, "You may not be aware of this, but DARPA was instrumental in the development of the AR-15 rifle in the early sixties. This was later renamed the M-16 and was ultimately adopted by all the military services. I presume you've shot other automatic weapons?"

JT mentioned that he had shot several different submachine guns in the past and gave the impression that he was not impressed. While they certainly delivered a lot of fire power quickly, they jammed occasionally and also had quite a recoil.

"I believe you'll be pleasantly surprised," Downing said, as he handed JT one of the test weapons. The *H&K* MP3000 consisted mostly of an aluminum alloy and some kind of plastic and weighed less than five pounds, even with the thirty-round magazine full of .40 Smith and Wesson rounds. It had tritium illumination sights and a flash suppressor for night use, laser sighting and a wrap-around recoil compensator that also served as a noise reducer. It accepted modular barrels: the ten-inch one when used as a submachine gun and the eighteen-inch one when used as sniper rifle. After a brief tutorial and with the camera rolling, they shot a magazine each at ten, twenty and thirty yards, and got more than ninety percent of the rounds in the targets. It had ambidextrous controls, which JT appreciated since he was a lefty. Both JT and Juanita were impressed with the accuracy and lack of noise and recoil. After a few more discussions, Downing asked if he could use their testimonials he had captured on film to promote his new invention. They heartily agreed, thanked Downing, and asked him to pass that on to TT. Anticipating JT's question, he said, "Just a few more trials, then some demos to the services and I think we'll be in production by the end of the year."

"And the non-DoD customers?" Juanita queried.

"I believe they'll be coming to us and we'll have a hard time meeting the demand."

"Well thanks again," JT said as he and Juanita gathered their stuff to depart. Downing and crew were already setting up some more tests. They proceeded back to the main building to get a spotter/verifier so they could qualify with their weapons. The small arms range was in the building and they both qualified in short order—JT with a perfect score and Juanita with a 290 out of 300. Happy, they collected their certifications from the range master, thanked him, and headed back out to I-95. This was actually Juanita's first time with an automatic weapon of this sort and she was beaming. Not to mention she got her qualification out of the way.

Once on track back to the freeway, she looked at JT and asked, "What, you didn't have a joke for the range master?"

"Damn, yes I did. I forgot."

"So let me hear it."

"Nope, wouldn't be the same now." After a few more minutes, Juanita turned onto I-95 north ramp when JT's phone rang. "Agent Dunkirk. Yes, Sir. No shit! Yes, Sir, we would. In less than an hour...got it." With that last statement, JT had scribbled an address on his note pad. He looked at Juanita. "Seems Charles found a key for a safe deposit box in Furlong's work locker. The Boss got a warrant for it and wants us to meet Charles and the evidence tech there. So much for the Marine Corps Museum."

"Safe deposit box trumps museum any day," Juanita quipped.

Burke, Virginia, 18 November, 1605 hours

Juanita dropped JT off in Springfield so he could retrieve his car, and then he followed her up to Fairfax. The Bank of America branch where Furlong had his box was the one on Burke Center Parkway almost at the intersection with Ox Road, not far from Furlong's place. As they pulled into the parking lot, they saw Charles get out of his car. He came over and jumped in JT's car and Juanita joined them. "So, Charles, how'd you find this thing and where's the evidence tech?" Juanita asked.

Charles Burton was the Alpha Unit team member on loan from the FBI. At thirty-one, he was one of the younger members; nonetheless he considered himself a more experienced law enforcement officer than the others. He tried not to show it, but it often crept through in his "professional" demeanor. His clean-cut appearance, business attire, and erect posture helped foster this impression, and his baby face, deep blue eyes and blonde hair made him look even younger. "To answer your last question first, she's on her way. As for finding it, you know Hanson asked me to check on Furlong's place of employment. We didn't think that we would find much there, so I told him I would handle it. The QPUDS manager there was very helpful. I got the impression that he wasn't happy about having to employ and ex-con and was hoping this would be a chance to get rid of him. In any event, he let me into Furlong's locker. I kept the manager there the whole time as a witness and looked through everything, none of which was incriminating. There were two shelves at the top of the locker, one at eye level and the other about eight inches below that. I noticed the bottom shelf was further toward the front of the locker than the other one. Sticking my head in there and looking up I could see there was a gap between the back of that shelf and the back of the locker. I showed the manager and then popped it up. Someone had taped a key to the back of the shelf." He held it up for them to see. "I called Hanson, who said he wanted Melissa to track the key and then be there when we opened whatever it fit. He also said he'd let you know about it. I sent her a picture of the key and she identified it as belonging to a BOA safe deposit box and traced it to this branch from the number on it. I talked to the bank manager already and she'll let us in whenever we are ready. They are open until five today but she'll stay later if need be. Melissa said she'd be here close to 4:30."

"Fantastic!" exclaimed JT, just a bit sarcastically, thought Juanita, but Charles didn't seem to notice. "I'm glad Melissa's coming. She's really good." She was pretty sure he picked up on the sarcasm the second time. "So, Charles, you can head on home if you'd like. I think there's enough of us here, what with Melissa and all."

"Oh, no. I got it this far. I'm here for the duration. Besides, I want to see Melissa Barnes in action. Why does Hanson bring in the locals on this, anyway?"

"I think he's just trying to build the best case he can," piped in Juanita. "Besides, it doesn't hurt to watch an expert at work." She was interrupted by JT's phone ringing.

"Yeah, Boss." For once, JT remembered to look at his caller ID before giving his standard "Agent Dunkirk" response. "All right. Are we going to talk to him? Sure, can do. That's probably a good idea, Sir. Okay, Cap'n. Thanks." JT looked around and saw that he had a captive audience. "As you heard, that was the Boss. The ATF had the Loudoun Sherriff arrested Furlong's ex-brother-in-law for the theft of the blasting caps. Their team found his fingerprints in an area where, according to the quarry management, they should not and could not have been unless he was up to no good. He hasn't copped to the crime yet and doesn't have a record, so he'll probably be out on bail later today or tomorrow. The boss wants to see how this thing with the safe deposit box works out and then maybe we'll sit down and strategize how to go after him and Furlong."

"Tell me he meant Monday," said Juanita. "I'd like to have the weekend off and, not to complain, it is late Friday afternoon and we aren't done yet."

"Yeah. The Captain postponed the meeting with the DOJ guy until we get a better handle on this, and— A knock on the window startled them, as none of them saw Melissa approaching.

"Hi guys," she said after JT rolled down the window. "I'm ready to roll if you are." JT really liked her as she was always upbeat. He didn't know her when he was on the force but had worked with her several times since leaving. Sergeant Dan suggested it after JT complained about a nearly botched search he was involved with. When the Sarge asked his boss, Captain Rawlings, if she could participate, he said no problem. After all, there were eight police districts in Fairfax County and each had an evidence technician, so she wasn't fully employed. Nor did the force mind her getting experience with the federal cases.

"The manager is waiting on us," Charles said, "so let's get to it."

After introductions, the manager, Ms. Indrasena Pattnayak, mentioned that she had already seen the warrant provided by Mr. Burton, and that he had already completed the appropriate paperwork. She had her key ready and they proceeded to the safe deposit box vault.

Charles and Indrasena keyed the box, and Charles pulled it out. "We'll go into one of the viewing rooms to document this," he said as he led the way. Indrasena told them to take their time and to leave the empty box and key in the room when they were done. She then went back to her desk to finish up the day's work. Melissa asked JT if he wouldn't mind capturing the event on her digital camera as she brought out, tagged and bagged each item. And what items they were: a U.S. passport in the name of John A. Mumford, with none other than Jonathan Furlong's picture; a passbook for a BOA savings account with the Mumford name and a Burke post office address that showed a balance of $132,418.63; five stacks of $50 bills that looked about 100 bills thick each; and, finally, a SanDisk four-gig flash drive. When they were done, Melissa handed the bags to Charles and they all filed out of the viewing room. JT thanked Indrasena and she opened the door and let them out.

"I'm going back to the office anyway, so I'll drop this by the property room and call Hanson to let him know what we got," offered Charles.

"Appreciate it," said JT, "and thanks for letting us in on this. It will really help when I talk to Furlong to be able to describe this stuff in detail." They all said their goodbyes, jumped in their cars and took off, Charles to the office and the rest of them home.

CHAPTER TWENTY-FOUR

Upper Marlboro, Maryland, 19 November, 1530 hours

Charles and Josh were up for extra duty, so Hanson had assigned them to this sting. They made an odd couple, considering Charles came across as the "clean cut" professional FBI agent, while Josh was the easygoing, down-home country sheriff type. Even though Josh stood six-foot-two and weighed 195 pounds, when he wanted to, he could get the Columbo persona going for him and folks were easily fooled into thinking he didn't know what was going on. He and Charles were here today because Farooq, the injured Afghani hospitalized by Brian in the shootout at Mustafa's place, finally got around to talking—with a little pharmaceutical help—and identified the other men in the car with him when they went to take out Mustafa. The Team already had IDs on them by this time and were in the process of or had already completed checking them out. When shown the pictures from the S&S Enterprises meeting, Mustafa identified the Stick that had driven the Civic that he and Khalid rode in to the meeting at *S&S* as Najam Aimal. This guy was a second generation Afghani-American who worked for Dell Computer Corporation as an on-line support technician. Although they had his picture from the S&S caper, he hadn't come up on the TIDE data base because of his longevity in the country and lack of a record. When given the name, however, he was easy to trace, and the boss agreed to have him brought in for questioning based on Farooq's ID, even though that was somewhat fuzzy given his medicated state. Besides, his name appeared on the attendance list at *"Afghans in America"* as a regular. Hanson didn't want to take any chances of this guy getting away, so he also had JT and Ronnie put a bird up to follow him just in case he ran for it. His driver's license listed his address as Old Mill Road, just off Old Marlboro Pike in Upper Marlboro, Maryland. Charles and Josh got there first and called JT to check his whereabouts. Fort

Belvoir was about twenty-five miles as the UAV flies from Upper Marlboro, and Ronnie had launched at three o'clock sharp. She did have to detour a bit south to avoid the approach to Andrews Air Force Base, and she kept the speed at a conservative, fuel efficient fifty miles per hour. JT informed the pair that the bird was due at their location in nine minutes.

Aimal's place sat right at the end unit of a group of eleven townhouses arranged in a horseshoe shape on one side of a large parking lot. The other side contained the community center for the development and another eighteen units. Josh had parked in the middle of the lot so as not to be conspicuous until the bird arrived. When JT informed him that they were overhead, Josh drove back toward the entrance and parked right in front of Aimal's residence. Ronnie positioned the bird just above the unit so they could observe the front and back simultaneously. Charles went up the front steps and knocked on the door. When he got no answer, he tried again but louder. Still getting no answer, he leaned over the railing on the front porch and peered in the window through the blinds that were partially open. There was no furniture in the front room or what he could see of another room. This did not look good. Through his earpiece, he heard JT report no movement out back. Josh went to the unit next door and knocked. An elderly black lady answered the door and said, "Whateva you selling, I ain't buying."

"No Ma'am. We're from the Department of Homeland Security and we're trying to locate your next door neighbor," said Josh as he pointed to the Aimal residence.

"What, them folks? They been gone for couple a three weeks now. Loaded everythin' in one of them box trucks I thinks they calls 'em one night, and took outta here lickety-split. Don't even know if the landlord knows they is gone yet."

"Did the truck have any markings on it?"

"Not that I 'member."

"I don't suppose you know where they went do you?"

"They wasn't the most sociable folks I eva met, Mista."

"So somebody else lived there with him?"

"I seen a couple other of them Arab peoples over there, but they all looks alike to me. Don't know if they was family, but I ain't neva seen no womin or chillin' over there."

"Well, thank you Ma'am; you've been most helpful," said Josh as the woman closed her door. He looked over at Charles and asked, "Didn't I hear that our guy in the hospital mentioned a bunch of names, and not just this Aimal person?"

"Yes, and he was the only one that we had on file anywhere," replied Charles as he got in the car and slammed the door. "With all the other names we found no drivers licenses, no tax returns, no file in the ICE or TIDE database, nothing. I think that the names we got, except for Aimal, we either didn't hear right, or the guy really didn't know the right names. I can't believe none of them were on our radar. Do we have a make and plate on this guy's vehicle?"

"Yeah," said Josh as he pulled out on to Old Marlboro Pike, "a green 2006 Toyota Corolla, Maryland plate 2AD-B93. Which, as you saw, was nowhere in the lot. Well, what that old lady told us certainly jives with the fact that his company says he hasn't been to work in over three weeks now. You think perhaps we got the information a tad too late to investigate? And didn't we put out a BOLO on the car?"

"You bet. But they probably switched plates or got rid of the car by now. We're S-O-L on this one Josh."

"I'll tell JT so he can head on back to the barn. Guess we should call this in and head home ourselves."

"Might as well. Can't dance," said Charles.

Josh started chuckling.

"That's a common expression, Josh. It's not that funny."

"No, it's that old lady. She reminds me of my grandmother—Granny Paxton, on my dad's side, of course. She talked very much like that and had that no-nonsense attitude as well."

"Where did you grow up?" asked Charles.

It surprised Josh that Charles had actually displayed a human side and asked about Josh's very different upbringing, and he was happy to accommodate. "Macon, Georgia. Nicknamed the heart of Georgia. My dad worked at Robins Air

Force Base as an aircraft instrument mechanic in the Warner Robins Air Logistic Center, and my mom was a school teacher. A lot of the time, especially in the summer, we were home with Granny. I'm sure I get a lot of my good points *and* my biases from her."

They discussed their backgrounds most of the way back to the shop.

Fort Belvoir, Virginia, 19 November, 1605 hours

"I don't want to bring the bird home yet, JT, since this is a training flight. How about if I just snoop around a bit here and there?" pleaded Ronnie.

"Okay, but start heading back to this side of the river and don't forget to give Andrews a wide berth."

"I want to bring her in over Tantallon Country Club just for a look see and then over to Fort Washington for some slow and tight maneuvers if it's clear. Then maybe on to Mount Vernon to cruise the fields out back. What do you think?"

"Sounds like a plan, Ronnie."

She had the bird cruising along at fifty enjoying the scenery when JT heard, "Oh, wow! Look at this flock of geese I'm coming up on." Ronnie had overtaken a flock of over fifty Canada geese and decided to fly in formation with them. She altered her direction fifteen degrees to the south and slowed down to forty-one miles per hour so she'd stay behind the two end geese. "These dudes are booking at over forty miles an hour," she exclaimed. "How totally cool!"

JT had as much fun watching her as she did flying with the geese.

Then Ronnie nudged the UAV up toward the last goose on the right side of the wedge.

"I know what you're thinking, Hotshot," he cautioned. "You scare that creature and it alarms the whole flock and you'll be dodging feathers and goose shit. You mess up my bird and you'll be in big trouble."

"Loosen up agent Dunkirk," Ronnie suggested. She nudged the UAV very slowly up to the rear goose on the right wedge, which had two or three more geese than the left wedge. There was a good deal of buffeting and it wasn't an easy task. These really had to be strong animals to endure this, she thought. If the geese noticed anything, they weren't reacting, although there was a good deal of honking clearly audible over the wind noise. The goose was actually moving up and down with each wing flap so Ronnie came in a little high and let the goose flap up into the UAV. The goose honked and broke formation by dropping down a few feet while Ronnie raised the UAV up and back about ten feet. It apparently didn't perceive a threat as it got right back into formation but not without a good deal of honking. "I've never goosed a goose before!" she exclaimed. She hung with the flock for another five minutes then broke formation by dropping back even more. She adjusted her heading twenty degrees more toward the west and increased her airspeed back to fifty.

As the UAV approached Tantallon, they could see golfers on almost every hole. It was a mild day for late November, which may or may not have made a difference to the players below. "Okay, at least allow me to get under somebody's drive and help it along fifty or sixty yards."

"That I'd like to see," offered her partner. "Actually, I'd like to be down there playing myself. I only got out three times this past year, and naturally I shot in the nineties."

"I thought golfers were happy to break 100."

"For as often as I play, that's probably true. Look, isn't that the Fort over there?" JT had visited Fort Washington many years ago with his Boy Scout troop and knew that it was actually a stone and wood structure and was for many decades the only defensive protection for Washington, D.C. Built in 1809, it was located on the eastern shore of the Potomac River just north of Mount Vernon and situated such that it had a good cannon shot down the river. During the War of 1812, the Fort was actually destroyed by its own garrison during a British advance. JT remembered reading that the National Park Service had to shore up the crumbling outer wall for the third time in preparation for the Fort's 200th anniversary. "It looks like the south wall is clear. Why don't you cruise over it and practice your slow turns?"

Ronnie moved the bird up and down and around the ramparts. She spied an upper entrance to the back wall and proceeded in a ways.

"If I recall, it's really dark in there, and without better lighting it'll be too risky for us. Not to mention the possible loss of signal."

Ronnie had come to the same conclusion herself and backed the bird out. Checking again for any bystanders, she continued to maneuver around the upper fort. "How we doing on fuel, Boss?" she asked JT.

"We've got lots of fuel, but we're running out of light soon. I'll be sunset in another ten minutes and fairly dark in less than an hour. Besides, I really would like to get home and spend some time with my kid. So how about we head back now?"

"Like I'm gonna say no now?" Ronnie whined.

JT looked over at her and saw a big smile.

"Okay. Up, up and away and over the river we go. Be home in less than fifteen minutes." And she was.

CHAPTER TWENTY-FIVE

Fairfax County, Virginia, 20 November, 2330 hours

"Josh, you awake?" Charles queried in a low voice.

"Yes, I'm just resting my eyes. Are there still lights on in there?" "There" was the residence of Sattar Omar, a suspected terrorist that they had been keeping under surveillance for several days now. He was one of the Sticks whose name Mustafa had overheard at an "Afghans in America" meeting. He wasn't an attendee at any of the meetings, at least as far as Mustafa knew—just

a name that he'd heard mentioned, he thinks by Khalid. In any event, it was the only name that they managed to connect up with a real person.

"Oh yeah. Must be watching the late show or something." A couple of minutes later, Charles said, "Lights out now. Looks like another quiet and boring evening. Oh, wait, someone's coming out the front door. Our boy must be going out for a midnight snack."

"Good. Beats sitting around here." In short order, Omar was headed up Backlick Road. "I'm turning the GPS back on," Josh said as he manipulated the tracking device. Charles was hanging back two or three blocks since the traffic was rather sparse. "You know, there is not much open this late on a Sunday night. Wonder where we're going?"

"Guess we'll find out. Let me know when he makes any turns," Charles requested.

A short time later Josh offered, "He's coming to the end of Backlick where it meets Little River and Columbia Pike. Looks like he pulled over." Omar was driving a light blue Aveo that wasn't too hard to spot from a distance. "Pull past so we can see what's going on. I got him—in the Fuddruckers parking lot. He's pulling off now and somebody's in the car with him. Go past a block or two until I see where they are headed." Charles complied and Josh kept his eye on the GPS display. "Okay, they are headed west on Little River Turnpike. Let's get back over there behind them." A couple of quick turns and Charles was back on Route 236 a few blocks to the rear. "They're sure not breaking any speed limits tonight. I'm thinking they are headed for another meet and greet. What do you say?"

"That's as good a guess as any," replied Charles. "I'm pretty sure they are up to no good, in any event. Have you got the infrared binoculars ready?"

"Indeed I do, indeed I do. By the way, did I hear you telling one of the guys that your dad was in the Bureau? "

"Yeah, he just retired last month after thirty-six years of government service, all with the Bureau. Finished up his career teaching down at Quantico. Believe it or not, my great grandfather was in the Bureau, as well. He worked for them during prohibition and was part of the John Dillinger and Machine Gun Kelly cases, and he took part in some Ku Klux Klan investigations."

"Wasn't that in the early thirties? I thought the FBI was formed in the late thirties or early forties."

"Actually, it was formed as the Bureau of Investigation in 1908 and went through several name changes before finally becoming the FBI in 1935."

"What kind of cases did your dad work on?"

"He is a computer geek and worked on cyber crime prevention, mostly. I think I belong to a minority of agents, and people in general probably, whose parents are more computer literate than they are."

"I can believe that. I just got my folks to start using the text messaging feature on their cell phones that I bought for them and pay for, by the way. Hey, our boys are turning right on Prosperity Drive. I think that will be the next light." A minute later they approached it and turned north. "There's not much on this road until you get up to Route 50—some parkland on either side and a few housing developments."

About four minutes later, Josh said, "They're turning right on Crestview Drive. They stopped, I'd say about 150 yards in. Turn your lights off just before Crestview and then turn the corner and pull over." A minute later, Charles pulled over and shut the engine off. Josh grabbed the binoculars.

"Anything?" Charles asked.

"The passenger is out of the car and standing next to an SUV—an Escalade, I think. He's got something in his hand and appears to be fooling with the door. He's got it open now and he's getting in. Somehow I get the feeling that that's not his car. There doesn't seem to be any action there now. No, wait, he's pulling off with no lights. His buddy is following him, also with no lights. Let's hope they stick together. Okay the lights are on now and they're turning right." Josh checked the map. "I think they are going back the way they came. Hang loose for a minute. They are—they're heading back down Prosperity." Charles did a U-turn and then turned left on Prosperity. "Okay, let's see where we go next."

They did backtrack east along Route 236 and south on Backlick Road. On Backlick, Charles got close enough one time to see that the Aveo was still following the Escalade. With the regular binoculars Josh managed to get the license plate of the Escalade when it passed by a street light. "Damn, that really makes me dizzy," he complained. "I hate using binoculars in a moving vehicle."   Josh had actually done quite a bit of surveillance at his regular job with the ATF before coming to the Fusion Team.

"So it's easy enough to figure out how I got into the FBI. What possessed you to join the ATF?" queried Charles.

"You probably remember that I grew up in Macon, Georgia. Well, in order to afford college there, I had to stay close to home so I wouldn't have to pay room and board. The Georgia College and State University filled that bill, so I went there and majored in business. An ATF recruiter came to the campus during career week late in my freshman year. He made catching bad guys and fighting organized crime seem kinda glamorous, so I switched to criminal justice and here I am. I was in the Alcohol and Tobacco Diversion section of the agency, which fights terrorism by depriving them of that illegal revenue source. When I saw the opportunity to be more directly involved by joining the DHS Fusion Team, I jumped at it."

By this time, they had traversed most of Backlick Road and Josh said, "He's turning right onto Fullerton. This is an industrial slash business center and completely deserted at night. If he goes all the way up to Rolling Road though, he'll be back in another residential area. Now he's turning left on Twist Lane. I think we are at the end of the Escalade's journey. That street dead ends so pull over onto one of the right side streets when you get about a block away." Charles did and Josh jumped out with the binoculars. He did a radio check and Charles said he could read him loud and clear. He crossed the street and walked no more than fifty yards up to Twist Lane before he could see them in the parking lot of Ron's Auto Repair and Body Work. He watched them put the Escalade into one of the bays, lock the place up and then get back into the Aveo. "They're coming back out, Charles. I'll keep out of sight and join you as soon as it's safe." He ducked down behind a parked truck where he wouldn't be seen and waited for them to turn back down Fullerton. When he saw the lights disappear over the hill he ran back to their car.

"Isn't our detention center right near here?" Charles asked.

"Yeah. Only a couple of blocks away I think. My bet is they'll be taking the passenger back to the parking lot at Fudds." And indeed Josh was right and Charles got close enough to see what vehicle Omar's buddy got into. "We know where Omar lives, so let's follow this guy," suggested Josh.

"My thoughts exactly. But you better keep those binoculars on him because I don't want to get too close."

"You got it, partner," assured Josh. The new guy didn't leave them in suspense long as he pulled over and got out only a couple of miles away, still in Annandale. Josh noted which house he went into. The lights went off in twelve minutes and Josh waited another twenty. He figured that would be enough time for him to settle down so he walked up close enough to get the make and model of the car and the plate, and the address of the residence. He came back to the car and mentioned to Charles that they might be in for a long night: it was now almost 1:30 in the morning and they had no idea if or when Omar's partner in grand theft larceny would be leaving for work or whatever. Josh called Hanson's cell phone, which luckily went to voice mail. He described what had just transpired and asked for relief when Hanson could manage it. He also told him he'd call as soon as there was any movement on this end.

They spelled each other in hour shifts, and at one point Charles left Josh there on foot and went out for some coffee and snacks at an all-night 7-11 on Backlick. At 6:20, Hanson called and said he was rounding up a relief team. At 6:55, Josh called him back and said their guy was on the move and to stand by. He had gotten a good enough look at him last night to be pretty sure that that was the same guy who was heading out now. They followed him to a Subs Are Us sandwich shop only a few miles away in Springfield. It was obvious he worked there as he opened the store up and began getting it ready for business. Josh called the Boss again and suggested that they had this guy pegged, so he agreed to their reporting back to the office.

CHAPTER TWENTY-SIX

Fusion Team Headquarters, 21 November, 0710 hours

JT got to work early and went over everything that they had on Furlong. He wanted to have everything at his fingertips when he talked to him. To help him organize his thoughts, he laid out what evidence he had against Furlong on a sheet of paper:

For the murder of Dr. Quarles:
His truck seen at the residence where the license plate placed on the
rear of the demolished Taurus was stolen
Possession of six blasting caps from the quarry, same as those used in
the explosion of the IED that killed Quarles
No alibi for that evening
Burglary tools for car break-in
His brother-in-law with access to blasting caps
Various equipment and tools for making an IED
Bank account showing a $45K transfer right after the murder

For the murder of Don Crenshaw:
His Porsche documented at the scene/time of the murder via GPS
No alibi for that evening
Burglary tools for hotel break-in
Watch and camera similar to Crenshaw's missing ones
.38 ammunition
Bank account showing a $45K transfer right after the murder
Makeup and disguise material for hotel entrance

<u>For both murders:</u>
A rap sheet showing violent tendencies, including an arrest for murder
A fake passport and driver's license for get-away purposes
His living above his means, plus $30K in cash and $132K in a hidden bank account
<u>A list of other crimes for which he is now guilty:</u>
Possession of false documents
Battery against motorcycle owner
Convicted felon possessing ammunition
Possession of blasting caps
Grand theft auto for motorcycle
Fleeing and eluding a police officer

We may not have a smoking gun for either murder, JT thought, *but the preponderance of evidence is probably enough to convince a jury. Well, maybe. Since he was already convicted of one felony, assault on a police officer, and every crime in the last list above is another felony, he is probably going away for life with Virginia's three strikes and you're out law. So, basically, I have nothing to bargain with unless a jury convicts him of the first degree murder of Quarles or Crenshaw. If he's tough, he may follow his counselor's advice and go for the trial and hope for the best. Even if convicted, with appeals and whatnot, he may never fry. We need something else.*

Hanson interrupted JT's thoughts and called the team together to bring everybody up to speed on where they were with the various surveillance missions and to pass on some good news. "Okay, folks, settle down. We have a lot to cover. Phil is going to brief us on what we've got so far on the Sticks that were in the shootout the other night at the Ahmadi residence. It's all yours, Phil."

"As you know, there were four terrorists involved. Three of them were killed and one is in the hospital. Actually, one killed himself when he jumped from the bus. We positively identified three of the four: the driver and the two guys in the back seat. Mustafa told us that the fourth guy, riding shotgun with a shotgun, called himself Khalid, a supposed Afghani who recruited Mr. Ahmadi at an "Afghans in America" meeting. Of course, he's dead and we had nothing on him in any of our databases, either prints or pictures, except his involvement with the meeting at S&S Enterprises, so he was in the country illegally. Nobody from "Afghans in America" could or would identify him. So that led nowhere. As far as the other two dead guys go, one was here on a work visa and one was a resident alien. We checked out their records, what little we had on them—where they had worked, known contacts, their family here and overseas, you name it—and again, came up with nothing. As best we can tell, none of their work places were used for meetings like the S&S one. These guys were either very good at hiding what they were doing or maybe they only just got started. Now the guy in the hospital, Farooq Husna, was staying with a sponsoring family, not related, so we couldn't get much from them on where he was from or his family back in Afghanistan. I thought it was kinda strange that they 'sponsored' him without really knowing much about him, but they did get some rent from him and a stipend from "Afghans in America" for putting him up. They had some data on him but it didn't check out with our boys over there, so it appears to be made up. We think this may be a way that they are getting trained agents over here."

"What's his condition now," Josh asked.

"Yesterday the doc said he was finally responding to the treatment and the medication and may be getting out of the hospital in another four or five days. According to JT and Brian, this guy did seem like he wanted to surrender at the time of the shootings, but then he sure clammed up in the hospital. Finally, last Friday, he started talking and identified one of the guys from the pictures of the S&S Enterprises caper named Najam Aimal. Saturday, Charles and Josh went out to Upper Marlboro to pick him up and found that he'd flown the coop with no trace left behind. The next door neighbor said that he'd been gone for weeks."

"Thanks, Phil. And now for some good news for a change, here's Josh."

"As you probably remember, when we interviewed Mustafa, he was very cooperative and gave us some names that he had overheard at the 'AA' meetings."

The assembled team groaned at the shortened term for the Afghan organization.

Josh continued, "We spent three or four days checking them out and one of those names turned out to be a real person—Sattar Omar. We put him under surveillance and last night that bore some fruit. About midnight, Omar drove from his place in Springfield and met up with the individual that we had tentatively, and most likely incorrectly, identified as Shufu Ozawa from the S&S caper. He was one of the guys at S&S in the cab with the cabbie, Ashan, who was subsequently murdered in his cab, and Mahmoud al-Sadr, the guy shot by Brian at the Ahmad residence. Omar picked up this Ozawa character, or whatever his real name is, at the Fuddruckers on Rt. 236 in Annandale. They then drove out to Fairfax and stole a Cadillac Escalade. It was dark and we were some distance away, but it looked like Ozawa used some sort of electrical device to disable the alarm system. He then drove the Escalade—with Omar following him in his Aveo—to what we suspect is a chop shop in—guess where—Fullerton, not two blocks from our detention center. They put the car inside a bay of Ron's Auto Repair and Body Work and then Omar drove Ozawa back to Annandale. Ozawa had left his car in the Fuddruckers parking lot there. Since we knew where Omar lived and worked, we switched surveillance to Ozawa and we now know where he lives—in an apartment just a couple of miles away from the Fudds. We stayed on him all night and found out he works in a The Sublette Shoppe in Springfield after we followed him there this morning. We didn't have a chance to check whose name is on the rental agreement yet, but the car he was driving is registered to a naturalized Iranian by the name of Shahzad al-Hardar. Since we got his residence and workplace and got a real good look at him, the boss told us to come on in, so we didn't talk to his employer yet either. When we pulled up al-Hardar's DMV picture this morning, we pegged him as the Ozawa Stick from S&S. Any questions?"

When no one else said anything, Juanita piped up with, "Just one. How long you guys been up?"

"Since before noon yesterday," Josh replied wearily.

"Wow! Good work guys," said Phil. "This may be the break we've been hoping for. What about the chop shop?"

Josh looked at Hanson.

"We now have it under surveillance and we're trying to determine what the best time to hit it would be" Hanson replied. We figure one more day of data and then we finalize our request for a warrant. We'll probably raid the place in the afternoon when we think it will have the most workers there, but that will depend on what we find out during our surveillance. It looks like Omar and al-Hardar are procurers, so they most likely will not be there during the raid. We'll pick them up at the same time wherever they are, so we may have three simultaneous operations. I have to admit I was sorely tempted to wait so we could identify a few more participants, but I didn't want any more cars boosted. The boss agrees, so I'm thinking this will be tomorrow or the next day at the latest. We do have to get three warrants. The one for Ron's Auto Repair and Body Work will include everything, especially the financial records, so we can see who is benefiting from this. Charles and Josh, go home and get some rest. The rest of you get to work."

JT was back at his desk for less than fifteen minutes when his phone buzzed. It was the receptionist saying that Mrs. Crenshaw was here to see him. He had forgotten all about asking her to come in. "Could you show her in please, Veronica? Juanita, can you come over her for a minute? I've asked Mrs. Crenshaw to come in for a chat and she's here now."

Mrs. Crenshaw was a tall, big-boned lady and probably weighed at least 160. She was attractive with blonde hair and strong facial features which suggested a Scandinavian heritage. Her dark pant suit emphasized the impression. After introducing himself and Juanita, JT said, "I know it hasn't even been a week yet since your husband died, but I was hoping to ask you a few questions that may help us with your husband's case." He then proceeded with his standard barrage of questions, apologizing that some may seem offensive, but explaining that they were trying to eliminate all possibilities but the right one. "One last thing, Mrs. Crenshaw, and then we can wrap this up. I asked you come in here particularly so we could get your fingerprint. We have an unmatched print on the button battery that was in what we think is your husband's watch and we'd like to eliminate the possibility of it being your print." She started to say something but JT politely interrupted her with, "I know you told the police that you never changed the batteries in his watch, but we just want to be sure. Please bear with us just a few more minutes."

She nodded and offered her hands. Juanita got the print kit, took all ten impressions, then helped her get cleaned up in the ladies room.

When they got back, JT was smiling. "I think we have a match," he called out excitedly. "I've asked Sam from forensics to come up here and verify this for us. It appears to me that your right thumb print matches the one we found on the top of the battery in the watch that we recovered from Furlong's locker. The partial print on the bottom could be from your right index finger. Can you think back again to the last time that he may have changed his watch battery and maybe come up with a scenario that would explain that?"

Mrs. Crenshaw sat there for a moment collecting her thoughts. Then suddenly she exclaimed, "Oh my gosh!" And then again, "Oh my gosh! Don always had trouble opening packages and refused to put on his glasses to help himself out. He'd end up losing patience and ripping the package open and usually whatever was inside too. I was always telling him that he had to be smarter than the package. I remember that I didn't want him fussing over nothing, so I opened the little package with the batteries in it and he grabbed one of them. If I remember right, he grabbed the battery by the sides and dropped it in the watch which is why his prints weren't on it I guess. That was less than a year ago, I think, so I guess it's the same battery. I am so sorry that I didn't remember this before."

"That's not a problem. It isn't too late at all," said JT. Sam Kenilworth from forensics had arrived and heard the latter part of the conversation. "What do you think, Sam?" JT asked as he handed him the copy of the print from the watch and Mrs. Crenshaw's print card.

He mulled it over for a few moments all the while shaking his head and frowning. "They're definitely the same print," he finally said smiling. "No doubt about it."

JT started breathing again and was about to call Sam some four-letter word, realized what company he was in, and ended up saying, "You had us for a moment there, Sammy boy. Will this hold up in court?"

"Let me print her thumb and then there will be no doubt about it." Mrs. Crenshaw gladly consented to another printing. "I'll go run these on the machine, JT, but if they are not the same I'll quit my job." He gathered up the fingerprint card and JT's copy of the battery print and headed back downstairs. "Call you in a few," he hollered back.

"So this is good news, then?" Mrs. Crenshaw asked, rhetorically, she hoped.

"This proves that that's your husband's watch. Unless you work in a jewelry store, there is no other explanation for him having a watch like your husband's with your print on it. With that and the camera and all the other evidence, I'm sure a jury will look at it the same way. Now if this actually goes to trial, you'll probably have to testify. You okay with that?"

"If it puts this man away, you damn right I am."

"Thank you very much, Mrs. Crenshaw," JT said as he got up. They both thanked her again and Juanita showed her back out to the restroom to clean off her thumb and then to the lobby. When she got back, JT was chomping at the bit to go see the boss and almost didn't wait for Juanita. "Wait until he hears this, Nita," he grinned.

The boss was indeed happy with this development. "I've got the interview with Furlong set up for four this afternoon, so this is good timing. But, I'd like to get one more nail for Furlong's coffin if we can. Why don't you go over and talk to his brother-in-law and see if you can't get him to commit to copping the caps for Furlong." Hanson smiled at his alliteration which was a takeoff on the Jack Webb/Johnny Carson copper clapper skit. JT and Juanita thought it was cute but didn't realize its origin. "I've talked to the CA and, given his clean record, they're willing to consider giving him a break if he comes clean. Check with him before you go, but if I remember right, the guy could get up to ten for stealing the caps, ten for distribution, ten for giving them to a known felon, and another ten if he had reason to believe they would be used in a felony. The last ten are nonconcurrent, I think he said. Of course, if he was in on it we can get him for accessory to murder, but that'll be hard to prove I imagine, even if it were true, which it probably isn't."

"You got it, Boss, we're on it," Juanita said as they left his office. "And I thought we were going to have to sit around here all day. So where we going anyway?"

"Leesburg."

"Leesburg? Is that where he lives? Because I remember he works down in Chantilly at the quarry."

"For some reason, he didn't get a bail hearing, so he's still in the detention center. Been there all weekend, so I imagine he's anxious to get out."

Leesburg, Virginia, 21 November, 1330 hours

Juanita offered to drive again, and that was okay with JT. She took Washington Boulevard up to Route 66, then the Dulles Toll Road out to Leesburg. The Adult Detention Center for Loudoun County was located on Sycolin Road, southeast of downtown Leesburg and right across from the Leesburg Airport. On the way out there, JT had called John Watson—the Commonwealth's Attorney whom Hanson had talked to earlier—to verify what his boss had told him. Then he called Sergeant Gregg, who had originally worked the Quarles murder for the county, and gave him an update on the case. He was glad to hear it was drawing to a close and apparently not terrorist-related. JT told him he'd call again when it was all settled.

Juanita found Loudoun Center Place and drove a block and half up to the jail. It was quite a modern facility as detention centers go, having only been completed in 2007. They checked in at the front desk and left their weapons, and were shown back to the visiting rooms. Furlong's ex-brother-in-law, Ronald Charles

Macey, was a gaunt young man of thirty-two, with blond hair and a pasty complexion to match. Juanita wondered what his sister, Furlong's ex-wife, looked like. The guard let him into the room with them and asked if they wanted him cuffed. JT said that wouldn't be necessary, so the guard sat him down in a chair and said he'd be waiting outside.

"I said I wasn't talking to any cops unless my attorney was here," Macey growled as soon as the guard closed the door.

JT had decided to violate his opposite sex interview rule once again, but only because he had prepped for it and Juanita had not. "I'm only going to ask you one question that I'd like an answer to, Mr. Macey, and that is, can I call you Charlie?"

Macey nodded.

"Okay then, Charlie, we don't need you to talk at all, just to listen to what we have to say. Then you can discuss it with your attorney and get back to us. Okay?"

Macey nodded his head again, apparently not realizing that he had just been asked a second question.

"I suppose it has already been explained to you that the ATF has recommended you be prosecuted on three counts, each of them a federal felony: stealing explosive material, distributing it, and giving it to a known felon. Each of these can carry up to a ten year sentence. The Commonwealth's Attorney, having a different mindset than the ATF, is considering two additional counts: distributing them with a reasonable cause to believe they would be used in a crime, which is another ten year sentence that isn't concurrent, and possibly accessory to murder."

Macey started to protest but JT stopped him with, "Remember, my turn to talk, your turn to listen. Here's my take on this situation, Charlie. You've got no connection to the man who was killed, so I'm confident that you weren't an accessory to that. But I have to admit, I believe you knew Furlong was up to no good. I mean, come on, why else would an ex-felon want blasting caps? And I'm pretty sure a jury is going to give you more credit than that, as well. Oh, by the way, I suppose you heard that we have your brother-in-law under arrest and found the caps in his possession. Now I'm thinking that he doesn't give a shit about you and would have no problem telling me where he got the caps when I talk to him this afternoon. In fact, I suspect he isn't exactly fond of your sister, either, since she tried to get alimony in the divorce proceedings, which she filed while he was in prison. My guess is that you only did this because he threatened you in some fashion."

Again Macey started to say something and JT held up his hand. "So here's what I'm thinking, Charlie. If you were threatened in some way, that would be a mitigating circumstance, as would be your cooperation with us in this investigation by telling us how you disposed of the caps. With these mitigating circumstances, the CA might just be inclined to drop the nonconcurrent charge of distributing to someone who you believed was going to use them in a crime, *and* to recommend much less than the maximum sentences for the other three charges that *would* run concurrently. Now I'm not going to lie to you, you're gonna do some time, but how much depends upon you. And you know you're going to lose your job. But I can guarantee you one thing: by the time Mr. Furlong gets out of jail, if he ever does, which I doubt, I bet he won't even be able to remember his name, let alone yours. Here's my card. I'd advise you to give this some serious thought and to do it quickly. If Furlong decides to give you up, then you've got nothing for me and I've got no reason to help you."

JT and Juanita got up and knocked on the door. The guard let them out. Before the guard could return to the room, JT motioned to him and shut the door. "I think it will end up being a huge help to us if you let him contact his attorney right away."

"Understand," the guard said as he headed back into the room. Just as they were about to exit through the next set of locked doors, the guard stuck his head out the visiting room door and called to JT, "Excuse me, Agent Dunkirk." JT looked back at him and the guard said with a smile on his face, "Mr. Macey said he'd like to talk to you again." JT and Juanita came back to the room and the guard held the door for them. "Be right outside."

"Agent Dunkirk," began Macey, "I've decided that I want to cooperate as best I can with you. I have to admit I don't see any percentage in trying to fight it, and maybe some in cooperating. How do you want to do this? Can we tape it?"

JT nodded and he looked at Juanita. She got up, knocked on the door and the guard let her out. After a minute, she came back in and said they'd have them set up in a jiffy. A few minutes later, a guard arrived with a tape recorder, plugged it in, tested it, and showed them the controls. "You're good to go," he said. "Call if you need anything else."

JT turned the tape on and got all the preliminaries out of the way, including the waiving of the right to an attorney by Macey and mentioning that he was promised nothing but possibly some consideration for his cooperation. "Okay, Charlie, it's all yours."

"Jon came to me..." he started but was interrupted.

"Full names and details, Charlie."

"My ex-brother-in-law, Jonathan Furlong, comes to my house around mid- to late October, maybe the 21st or 22nd I guess, and says he needs some blasting caps. I tell him no way, as that is a serious felony and I could lose my job and go to jail. He says he only needs them to get rid of some huge rocks in his buddy's place up in the mountains where they go hunting. They are going to build a cabin and need to clear out the area. Well, I don't believe him and I tell him so. I mean, he was in jail for beating up a cop, and he got off on a murder rap because of a technicality. He is not a nice guy. Then he says, 'I don't care whether you believe me or not, Charlie. I need the caps. If you don't want any harm to come to Lizzy,' that's my sister and his ex-wife, 'then you better find a way to get me some.' Well, Jon's a pretty scary guy, and he had already hurt Lizzy several times before they got divorced, so *that* I did believe. I figure if I call the cops he'd just deny everything and end up hurting Lizzy or me anyway. Maybe not right away, but eventually. So I tell him I'll do it, but only if he agrees to leave us alone after this. I realize now how dumb that was. Like he wouldn't come back the next time he needed something anyway, because then he'd have something on me. So a day or two later, when I'm at work and the opportunity presents itself, I took a package of caps, which is ten. I didn't wear gloves so as not to look suspicious in case anybody saw me, and I thought I only touched what I took— obviously not. When I leave that night, I put a small scratch mark on the entrance door in order to make it look like someone had broken in but tried to conceal it so they'd have time to use them before they were discovered missing. I give the caps to Jon that night. The next night, I approach the storage building from the rear, avoiding the cameras, and throw a small two-by-four over the fence toward the building where I know it will set off the motion detector. I knew they'd check it out, see the place was secure, and figure it was some animal, but then have cause to wonder if it wasn't something else when the caps showed up missing at the end of the month check a few days later. And there you have it. Oh, and I know this was a dumb and really stupid thing to do and I'm really, really sick at the thought that somebody may have been hurt or killed with those caps that I supplied to him. Do I need to add anything else?"

"No, Charlie, that about does it. We're going to get this typed up so you can sign it. This was the right thing to do, and it's going to be your best way out of this. We'll be in touch." As they left, Macey put his head in his lap and started sobbing.

Back in the car Juanita said, "You're really a softee, aren't you?"

"What?"

"Furlong just possessing those caps is a major felony. We didn't need to know where he got them."

"If you recall, Nita, this was the boss' idea, not mine."

"Yeah, right."

"Women."

"Men."

CHAPTER TWENTY-SEVEN

So they went looking for him, did they? It's certainly a good thing that I pulled Najam out of there when I did. He was too valuable a player to lose—a little surgery, a new identity and he was back in the game before they knew he was gone. He had to have been compromised by Farooq, just as we suspected might happen. That is a loose end that we must tie up soon, before he gives away anything else. Hopefully Rasheem is right and Farooq knows nothing else of import, but we cannot take a chance. I believe I'll put Rasheem in charge of getting around the surveillance they have Farooq under, and eliminating that problem. Surely causing a death in a hospital cannot be so difficult.

Fullerton, Virginia, 21 November, 1600 hours

JT and Juanita arrived at the Fullerton detention center at the same time as Hanson. He wanted to be here for Furlong's "interview." Furlong's lawyer, Michael Benning, was also there and conferring with his client in the interview room when they arrived. "Mr. Furlong," JT began after he and Juanita were settled, "I really enjoyed our time together last Thursday. I'm sorry we couldn't be meeting under better circumstances this time." When Benning gave him a quizzical look, Furlong explained that JT was referring to the time they searched Furlong's place while he and JT watched a Redskin's game. "If you remember, I'm not much of a bullshitter, so I'll be as succinct as I can. We suspect you of the murders of Dr. C. Stefon Quarles and Mr. Don Crenshaw, and in fact, we think these were murders for hire rather than anything personal between you and them."

"I don't know who you are talking about!" Furlong exclaimed.

His lawyer held his hand up to stop him and then addressed JT. "I've seen the evidence you have against Mr.

Furlong for those two incidents, and it's all circumstantial. I thought we were here to discuss the other charges against him."

"Mr. Benning, that's a stack of felonies committed by a known felon. He's looking at the possibility of life without parole. When the jury hears about what we found in your client's possession, they're most likely going to think that he was fleeing to avoid conviction on a more serious felony."

"Those items are irrelevant and we'll move to disallow them."

"If we decide to charge Mr. Furlong with either one or both of the murders, then these things we found are relevant and will be heard by the jury. And even if we decide to only charge him with the felonies that we know he committed, and they are ruled inadmissible, you know and I know that the jury will be wondering what he was fleeing for. They *will* take that into consideration when they try to decide whether or not to keep him out of circulation for a long time."

"That would be two separate trials and we'll take our chances on a fair judge and a decent jury."

"Mr. Furlong, we were really expecting a bit more cooperation from you. I'm sorry that—" At that point, there was a knock on the door and JT stopped. He went back to the door opened it and was motioned out by Hanson. "Excuse me. I'll be back in a second."

Benning turned to Juanita and gave her a what's-going-on look.

She shrugged her shoulders.

Eight minutes later, JT came back into the room. "Well, Mr. Furlong, I'm afraid that I have some good news and some bad news."

Benning looked at JT doubtfully and said, "We'll take the good news first, Agent Dunkirk."

"Mr. Furlong will not have to face the death penalty."

Benning and Furlong both grimaced in confusion. "That was never on the table," said Benning. "What's the bad news?" he quickly asked, quite sure he didn't really want to hear the answer.

"I can prove you killed Don Crenshaw."

"Everything you showed us is circumstantial," exclaimed Benning. "Do you have something new you'd like to offer?"

"How about a fingerprint?"

Furlong suddenly went pale. *I wiped everything off. I know I did,* he thought.

"I know what you're thinking," said JT. "I wiped everything clean. Well guess what—you didn't." He paused here.

Furlong's mind was racing. He looked a thousand miles away, probably trying to reconstruct his actions in the storage facility.

"You see, we have this new procedure that can recover fingerprints from a metallic surface, you know, like a watch battery. Seems your sweat reacts with the metal and etches your print in it—something that can't be wiped clean. And guess whose finger print we found on that battery—Mrs. Crenshaw's. Now, unless she has been moonlighting as a jewelry store clerk, which she hasn't, the only way that print could have gotten on that battery is if the watch belonged to Mr. Crenshaw. The watch that went missing the night he was murdered and that we recovered in *your* storage facility not two days later."

Furlong started slumping down in his chair and Benning began shaking his head.

"I just don't think that there is any wild ass story that you can come up with that will explain that away. Now add that to all the other 'circumstantial' evidence we have pointing in the same direction, and we have one hell of a case. So from my point of view, we're back to the good news—no death penalty. You give us who contracted you for these hits and we might consider life without parole; otherwise your ass fries. You want some time to confer with your counselor here?"

Furlong was speechless so his attorney spoke up. "Yes, we'd like a few minutes."

"No problem," JT responded, as he and Juanita got up and walked out.

After about fifteen minutes, Benning stuck his head out and asked them to come back in.

"So, you gonna cooperate with us on this, Mr. Furlong?" JT asked.

Benning said, "We'd like to see your proof and a statement from the DOJ prosecutor taking the death penalty off the table in consideration for Mr. Furlong's cooperation in this matter."

JT handed him the paperwork.

"You were apparently counting on this," Benning remarked snidely.

"We had an inkling."

Benning reviewed the fingerprint report and the plea bargain agreement from the Department of Justice. "This stipulates cooperation on the matter of Dr. Quarles' murder in addition to Mr. Crenshaw's. You have no proof that implicates my client in the Quarles murder."

"Mr. Benning, he knows he did it and we know he did it, and while we don't have the proof right now, we will get it. If he doesn't talk about it now and take the deal, and we get the proof later, then the death penalty is back on the table for a second trial. You might call this a two-for-one sale. He'll be in jail for the same amount of time whether he confesses to one or both murders. And that's the deal we're offering, Counselor. You want some more time? I guess that's a double entendre isn't it?"

Benning nodded and turned toward Furlong, who also gave a resigned nod.

In the hallway Juanita queried, "Double entendre? I'm impressed."

"I do a little reading now and then, Nita." They were no sooner out then in again, with barely a three minute lapse this time.

"Mr. Furlong will go along with your deal with two amendments to the plea bargain agreement: first, you stipulate that, in addition to the two murders listed therein, the death penalty will not be sought for any capital crimes that Mr. Furlong may have committed in the past; and second, you grant him a new identity and incarcerate him somewhere where he won't be found by his former employers."

"I must admit that thought of the first possibility and discussed it with Justice. We'll grant immunity from the death penalty for all for those capital crimes that Mr. Furlong identifies to us in our debriefing. The second request is reasonable and I don't think that will be any problem."

Benning looked at Furlong and he nodded.

"Well, we'll get the agreement changed and be back here tomorrow, say nine o'clock?"

Benning agreed and said he needed another couple of minutes with his client. JT and Juanita excused themselves and met Hanson outside.

Hanson congratulated JT and said, "Let me call Justice and get that change made. I can probably stop by on the way home and pick it up. I'll see you guys tomorrow."

Fullerton, Virginia, 22 November, 0900 hours

After Benning reviewed the agreement and told Furlong it was indeed what they had agreed upon, JT had a tape recorder brought in. Juanita turned it on and JT went through the preliminaries, identified those in the room, read the DOJ agreement, and got Furlong's verbal approval of the deal. "It's all yours, Mr. Furlong, and remember, as many details as you can recall—dates, times, places, and names. Let's start with the Quarles incident and then proceed to the Crenshaw one. After we're done with those, you can add any other incidents that you want on record for our agreement."

"Around the beginning of October, maybe the 9th or 10th, I was contacted by an acquaintance who I had done some work for in the past. Like usual, I got an email from this hotmail account that told me to go to a webpage that was one of them political blogs. One of the comments on that page was from my contact— the one signed by James Blessing—and said that I should meet him at noon the next day at the *McDonald's*—the one on Braddock Road in Burke. To an outsider the blog just sounded like some guy ranting on about the current administration. When I met him the next day, he gave me five big ones, but instead of getting a package with all the details like usual, he told me I'd be getting a package in the mail in a day or two with all the directions for the job. He said payment would be in the usual amount but the rest of the dough, instead of cash, would be sent directly to my hidden bank account after I completed the job. I wasn't sure how he knew about that, but damned if he didn't 'cause that's what happened. So anyway, I got the package the next day. It had Quarles' name and a picture of him, where he worked and lived, what his usual working hours were, and what kind of car he drove. It said to make it look like a terrorist incident by using an IED, but to do it in an isolated place so as to 'limit collateral damage.' It also listed a couple of web sites where I could learn how to construct one of those things. Within two weeks was the requested time frame."

Furlong paused at this point to catch his breath and gather his thoughts. "All of the IED materials were easy to get, except for the blasting caps. For those I had to threaten Charlie, my ex-wife's brother. Of course, he caved and got me the caps in a few days. What a wimp. Anyway, that was the trickiest part of the whole thing, working with those caps. I put together two test devices and set them off in a field way off of Route 340, not too far from Front Royal. Once I was sure I had that down, I started following Quarles when he left his office in Arlington after work. He didn't exactly keep a strict schedule and I got a lot of ass time in Arlington. Anyway, I noticed he stopped at the Starbucks near his home almost every night, so now I had the place and the device. I needed a car to use in the explosion, so I stole a Taurus, because I knew where there were two identical ones. That way I could steal the front tag from the second one to put on the back of the stolen one to give myself a couple of days leeway in case he didn't stop off at the Starbucks right away. When he came out that one Friday night and went to get in his car, I sent the page and blew the IED. Over the next several days, the other forty-five gees appeared in my Mumford account in several smaller payments. That's pretty much it. Can I get something to drink?"

"Just a couple of quick questions first," said JT, rather put off by Furlong's calm account of the murder. "Did you have any help with all this?"

"Nope. I work completely alone. I did have to use Charlie to get the caps, but he didn't know what they were for. I made up some story that he didn't believe, so finally I had to threaten to hurt his sister in order to get him to cooperate. What a wimp."

234

"How did you manage to steal the car and to get it in place without someone else driving for you?"

"I used my bike. I can put seventeen miles on that sucker in less than an hour if I have to—at least on fairly level ground."

"What can you give us on Blessing and how you get in touch with him?"

"I can describe him but don't know how to get in touch with him, and I'm pretty sure that's not his real name either. He's a big man, probably about 200 pounds, and my height, six foot. He wears this funky disguise when he meets with me—a black mustache and wig, big yellow sunglasses and a wide-brimmed rain hat with REI on it. I mean, it's obvious, but I guess it serves the purpose. Holy shit, I just realized—he's a blessing in disguise!" Furlong was so proud of his joke he started laughing. JT and Juanita didn't think it was quite so funny. Benning was still shaking his head. It was a few minutes before Furlong could continue. "The email I got from him is probably still on my flash drive, but I doubt that's gonna help ya any. They came from a different account every time. And I destroyed the letter and the picture I got."

"Okay for now. We'll take a short break while I get you something to drink." While JT turned the recorder off, Juanita asked if Benning would like anything to drink; he mentioned that water would be fine. JT and Juanita got up and stretched and left the room to get the drinks. Once outside, JT said, "What a character. But so far the details seem to fit."

"The guy gives me the creeps. I don't even like being in the same room with him. We sure meet some weird ones in this job." They got the drinks and returned to the room. Juanita turned the recorder back on and JT asked Furlong to relate the Crenshaw incident.

"It was only a couple of days after the Quarles job that I got another email from Blessing. Like I said, it was from a different account but signed Blessing. It sent me to a different web site, as usual, but it was the same ole routine telling me where to go for the meeting. At the meeting, which was at the Starbucks in Tysons, I got another five gees and was told to standby for another package. This one described Crenshaw, had the picture, home and work details, but said to hit him at a Baltimore hotel while he was at some conference in the middle of November. The instructions said to make it look like a robbery gone bad. I got rid of that letter and his picture, as well. I rode the Metro and the train up there one Saturday to case the joint. I drove up there for the actual job on the 15th, which was the first day of that conference, I think. I put on a disguise and rode the elevator up to the seventh floor, got out and took the stairs up to eight. I spraypainted the camera at that end of the hallway and then knocked on Crenshaw's door. When no one answered, I scratched the lock to make it look like an amateur entry and then used an electronic card entry device that I had built from instructions that I got off the internet. I also had my electric pick gun and a feather-touch, coil-spring, magnetic tension bar in case I needed to unlatch the deadbolt or a swing-bar. My gun was ready and inside a plastic bag surrounded by two thick cushions to muffle the noise. I've been trying to find a silencer but they ain't easy to come by. I took a quick look around the place and grabbed his camera, which looked like the only thing worth taking, and then waited for him in the john. He showed up just a few minutes later. After he was in and closed the door, he turned toward me and I plugged him twice. It was quite a bit louder than I thought it would be, so I quickly grabbed his watch and wallet and hightailed it down the stairs and out the back. I got the rest of the money a day or two later in the same fashion as before. And that's that one." Furlong took a swig of his drink and then leaned back in his chair, obviously proud of how cleverly he pulled off those two crimes.

"Do you know if these were ordered by the same person?" asked Juanita.

"No, I don't. I mean my contact's the same, but he's just a go between. I doubt he personally needed those guys whacked, but who knows."

"Okay," said JT. "Before we start on the additional incidents, I'd like to ask how you got started in this 'business' in the first place."

"Blessing, at least I guess it was him, sent me a letter saying he was aware of my unusual talents and asking if I wanted to make some extra money for some 'unusual assignments.' If so, I was to show up at some place, I forget where now, and meet him. I went and no one showed. I was a little frustrated because I'd only been out of jail for a month or so and didn't have the job with QPUDS yet and I really needed the dough. I got another letter saying they were making sure I didn't ask the authorities along and to show up at the bench in front of the *Coastal Flats* restaurant in Fairfax at noon on Saturday. I did, and a guy showed up and handed me a package and then walked off. The package had a thousand bucks in it and a cell phone along with instructions to walk east away from the restaurant. The phone rang and this guy on the other end described my rap sheet and said he thought I might be interested in some 'delicate' assignments for substantial amounts of money. I said yes and he asked for my email address and said I might be getting a message in a week or two if the person I just talked to was not followed or picked up by the authorities. I told him I didn't have an email account yet so they said they'd send me another letter. A couple of days later, I did get a letter explaining how to figure out messages that were disguised in blogs on a web site. About a week later, I got another letter sending me to a web site which it said I could access from the library or a couple of cafes in the area. I went that evening and figured out where and when I was supposed to meet this Blessing guy. I showed up but some other guy, who was not Blessing, showed. He handed me a package that had a note written on the outside. It said to look in the package and then nod my head at the guy who was then going to walk off, but that I was supposed to stay there until someone else showed up. Ten minutes later the 'real' Blessing showed and I got my first assignment. He gave me five gees and said he'd get the other twenty-five to me after the job was complete. I think it was just a test case, because I couldn't see why anyone would want this old lady whacked, but hey, what do I know. Can I go into these jobs now?"

JT indicated that that would be a good idea, so Furlong went on to describe one other hit he had completed for a total of four, including Quarles and Crenshaw. All pretty much contracted for in the same manner. He also gave them the URLs for the web sites that he had used and generally described how he interpreted the disguised information therein. By this time, it was after noon and Furlong went back to his cell for lunch.

Benning looked at JT and Juanita and shook his head. "I'm glad I won't have to be defending him in court," he said. "What a callous person. You guys know how to get in touch with me if you need me." He gathered up his stuff and JT showed him to the exit.

When he got back, JT looked at Juanita. "What do you think, Nita? Sound like the real thing or do we have a 'Usual Suspects' scenario?"

"I don't see any bulletin boards or broken Kobayashi coffee cups in here, so I'm thinking it's as accurate as Furlong remembers. I guess he could be creative enough to make that all up, but it does agree with most if not all of the facts that we have. My only problem is that he says he did it all alone. I mean, he rode his bike?"

"I was wondering about that too. But let's say he's got a bike carrier and he loads it in the back of his truck along with his bike. He then drives to a secluded spot within walking distance of his intended heist, walks to the scene of the crime, boosts the car and drives it back to wherever he parked his truck. He then puts the bike carrier on the back of the stolen car, loads the bike on it, drives to a nice safe place where he can keep the car until he's finished with it, then bikes back to pick up his truck."

"Cumbersome, but I guess it'd work. Particularly if you want to keep all the profits for yourself. But then why didn't he use his bike to get down to the storage facility, especially when he thought time was of the essence?"

"Maybe it was broke or in the garage and he thought I'd see him take it. Or maybe he didn't think he could get it over the back fence without being seen."

"Yeah, maybe. I sure thought the way he was recruited was interesting. I always figured hit men started out in the Mafia or maybe just working for some local crime boss. Guess nowadays you just need to build an impressive rap sheet and then wait for prospective customers to come to you."

"I hate to say it, but that gives his recruitment a law enforcement flavor. Which reminds me, we need to get the details of these other two incidents to the Fairfax and Loudoun County police. Knowing that they are hits may open some avenues of investigation for them. Or maybe make them look a little harder at some they've already covered. In the mean time, we need to get with the Boss and plan on where to go from here. Hopefully our forensics guys can determine something from Furlong's email program that he said is on his flash drive."

"Or maybe there's something on the web sites he mentioned. They keep those blogs for a long time, but I'm not hopeful. Sounds like they were really careful."

"Everybody makes mistakes, Nita. Sooner or later, everybody makes mistakes."

CHAPTER TWENTY-EIGHT

Bolling Air Force Base, DC, 22 November, 1230 hours

Juanita and JT had been working together so much lately that they decided to "car pool." This usually meant that Juanita drove after she picked up JT if his house was on the way to where they were going, or JT drove over to her house and parked and she drove from there. So here they were in her PT Cruiser on their way to Bolling. Hanson wanted a meeting of everyone who was not on assignment at the moment in order to discuss the latest developments in the Quarles case. He couldn't make it before 12:30 and JT and Juanita were meeting with Dr. Jay at one, so he asked them to conference in. Juanita had both JT and Hanson calling her that now.

"Well, Team, we certainly have some things to look into here, don't we?" Hanson commented. "We need to see if we can track down this Blessing fellow. We have his emails to Furlong that are in Furlong's email program contained on his flash drive, and we have the website blogs that Blessing set up to communicate details of his meetings with Furlong. Our forensics guys are going to see if these can be traced back to the original email site to figure out where this guy is located. If they can't do it, they're going to ask the NSA for help. We're keeping Furlong's arrest low profile, so maybe there's some way we can get a message back to the originator and trace it that way. Josh, I want you to honcho that effort. Charles, I want you to look at the unfortunate implication of law enforcement involvement with the method that Furlong was recruited. I'm not sure how in the hell we go about tracing that, since access to that database is so widespread and contact with Furlong in that regard was by letter. In any event, see if you can trace any access to his record prior to his being contacted that first time. I would be especially interested in any other-than-LEO access to that database. Ronnie, I want you to get the relevant information on Furlong's earlier hits to the appropriate locals so they can revisit their cases on these homicides, if indeed that's how they are carrying them. They may be able to come up with something that points us in a specific direction. Phil, please check with the locations that Furlong identified as his meeting places with Blessing and see if they have any video. I know it's a long shot, but we have to pursue it. JT, how much do you think Doctor, ah, Jay, can be trusted and would she be willing to help us out?"

"Boss, both Juanita and I think she is on our side one hundred percent."

"Do you agree with that, Juanita?"

She responded affirmatively.

"Okay then, while you are over there, see if Arati can get a better handle on where these transfers into Styles' accounts that subsequently went to Furlong came from. I'd really like to bring him in for questioning based on that, but not with the level of confidence in the data that you've told me she has thus far. I would also like to have you and her take a lot closer look at the contractors involved with the DARPA efforts to see who may have been in a position to influence the contract selection and thus benefit from any kickbacks. I think that's it for the Quarles case for now." Hanson paused to see if there were any further questions or comments. "Okay, then. Brendon is coordinating our planned raid on the chop shop. I know today is Tuesday and Thursday is Thanksgiving. I'm assuming the place won't be open then, and maybe not Friday, and we believe they have a minimum compliment of employees on the weekend. I do *not* want to wait until next week and afford them the opportunity to heist more vehicles, so I would really like this pulled off tomorrow. Brendon, how we coming on that?"

"Sir, everything is on track for fourteen-hundred tomorrow. The FBI, the JTTF and Fairfax County are all ready. Charles and Josh are going after al-Hardar, and Phil and Ronnie are picking up Omar, also at fourteen-hundred."

"Excellent. I'm working on the warrants. JT, call me if you get anything good. So let's get to work."

Dr. Jay said she would meet them in the SCIF that they had talked in before, so Juanita drove directly there. The doc met them out front and escorted them back to the same room they were in last time. "You seemed anxious to relay the recent developments in the Quarles case," she began.

"Yes. We'd like to let you know where we are and maybe ask for your help," said JT.

"I would be delighted to help in any way that I can. I have been doing some research on the matter and have some items of information for you, as well. Would you like to go first?"

JT began by telling her what they had learned of Furlong's escapades: his description of how he was contacted originally and more recently for the last two hits, his revelation of prior "transactions," and his method of payment for the jobs. Juanita mentioned their concern about the potential law enforcement involvement because of his employer's knowledge of his rap sheet. Finally, JT relayed the boss' instructions to the team members.

"I see," Arati said slowly. "I believe your investigation into the email and webpage communications will be fruitless. It would be easy for a sophisticated user to utilize a different public access point for each message, such as a library or a coffee house, create a new account, send the information, and leave behind only the fact that the message was sent from there. Although ISPs have been trying to prevent that, there are programs that enable anonymous access, or a smart user could merely write his own. It could not be traced to an individual user unless you had time-dated video of the machines used. A smart user would avoid those places. For the web blogs, he need only sign the message for Mr. Furlong to know it was meant for him. As for the access to the criminal records, that also would be child's play. I could access them from here but then it could be traced to this system. If done in the aforementioned fashion, a trace would only lead to the public access point. I would ask that you let me know what you find out from your forensics team and from the NSA if they are utilized. I understand the latter does have some very good technicians."

"Of course we will. You said you had some things for us as well?"

"Yes. I have been using the Tomfoolery program—which, by the way, has had some major enhancements since the last time we talked—to trace the financial transactions that I believe are involved with your case. I must admit that I have learned only one thing: I cannot trace the origin of the transactions that placed the funds in Styles' account. I thought the transfer after Stefon's murder came from a dummy corporation, but I was wrong. I cannot tell where it came from any more than I can tell where the one after Crenshaw's murder came from. I can only conclude that they have been blocked; that is, the point of origin has either been erased or the program was not allowed to read it. I believe that there are only four people who would be in a position to accomplish that: myself, Stefon, William Arnold, who is one of the contractor programmers working on the program, and Dr. Briceman. If you are willing to exclude me, and of course Stefon, that leaves only Briceman and Arnold. I have done what I could from my end to check out these two. I found nothing untoward with either individual's account, but then I did not expect to. Both of these gentlemen would be likely suspects in Stefon's demise, but, as they say, my money would be on Briceman. I do not believe that Mr. Arnold has the requisite level of knowledge to implement such a sophisticated trapdoor."

"Wow! Arati," JT exclaimed as Juanita uttered a similar expression. "But why not hide the transfers out of the Styles' account, and likewise the transfers into the Mumford account?"

"To answer the latter question first, from what you have told me, Mumford/Furlong has been of little help in locating the individual that he has taken his assignments from. There would be no need to hide those transfers, as he is therefore expendable. Further, perhaps Briceman was not involved with those transfers. As far as the first possibility goes, I have drawn up a matrix of the possibilities to include Briceman ordering the hit himself, to being asked to transfer the funds and implicate Styles, to just being asked to transfer the funds. Included were the scenarios where Styles was complicit and not complicit. What I concluded was that Styles was either complicit and was being revealed as such, or he was not and was being set up. Or, finally, that Briceman was not involved with those transfers and just did not care one way or the other. In fact, the only thing that I am sure of is that if Briceman is involved, then he is convinced that Styles knows nothing of his involvement; otherwise, he would have hidden those transactions as well."

"Can you go any further with these?"

"Probably not at this time. But I have a suggestion."

JT was sure he saw a gleam in her deep, dark brown eyes. His respect for this woman, which was already considerable, was growing. He said nothing and waited for her to continue.

"Let me confront him with my suspicions." JT started to say something but Arati put her hand up to stop him. "I knew that you would object, but let me continue."

JT nodded. "I am certain that I could convince him that I am aware of what he is doing. Because, in fact, I am. Some of the details I am not sure of, but he is undoubtedly using a trapdoor program to hide specific transactions, presumably kickbacks from contractors. Further, I will tell him that I want to 'get in on the action.' This will not be hard for him to believe when I explain that I have several family members back in India whom I need to bring into this country. I will also inform him that I have detailed my findings in a manuscript that I have left with a friend in India to be given to the authorities should something happen to me. Do I not have all the bases covered?"

JT put his hand on his face and sat back in his chair. Juanita knew enough to be quiet at this point. JT and Arati sat there looking at each other for a few minutes. Finally JT said, "This could put you in some danger. I assume you have considered and would consent to wearing a wire?"

"JT, what he is doing is an abomination. I am willing to take some risk to put a stop to it, and I believe that the risk involved here is minimal, given that I will appeal to his inordinate ego. Further, he surely could not risk that my manuscript was possibly a reality. He would credit me with no less intelligence than to assure my own safety."

"What do you think, Nita?"

She looked at JT, turned and looked at Arati, and then with a smile on her face said, "Let's get the bastard."

"Arati, Briceman almost assuredly knows that we have been talking. He will be suspicious of your intentions."

"Ah, yes, but you would naturally talk to me as a colleague of Stefon. Further, you would discuss the program with me. This is how I would come to suspect his involvement, which I would not mention to you since I would have no proof, and of course I would begin to see an opportunity for myself and my family."

"Arati," said JT, "You are a brilliant woman, but you are not used to dealing with the criminal element. I believe that we can agree to this on several conditions: one, that you rehearse with us what you are going to say when confronting, excuse me, soliciting, Briceman, before you meet with him; two, you realize that he may want to search you; three, that we are within shouting distance just in case; and four, my boss agrees to this. You okay with these conditions?"

"In for a penny, in for a pound," she said.

"Now," said JT, "what kind of a case can we make against Styles? Can you now prove that he was the recipient of contract kickbacks?" They discussed the aspects of that for the next forty minutes before reaching an agreement on a course of action. They agreed to meet next Monday for Arati's dress rehearsal and to give her the micro-transceiver and recorder.

CHAPTER TWENTY-NINE

Springfield, Virginia, 23 November, 1355 hours

The team had gathered in the detention center, which luckily had a fairly large entrance room. It was located in a nondescript building on Boston Boulevard, a street that, for most of its length, ran parallel to Fullerton Road. The two roads curved to meet each other at the eastern end of Boston Boulevard. Ron's Auto Repair and Body Work was located on Twist Lane, a little side street off Fullerton Road. Although situated less than two hundred yards from the detention center, the team would have to go down most of Boston Boulevard and up a good deal of Fullerton Road to get to the chop shop. Hanson had asked the JTTF to help, and they provided the SWAT team for the entrance. The FBI had their forensic accountants there to get the books and computers, and another couple of men to record the vehicles. The Fusion Team's detention center couldn't hold the expected ten to twelve new residents, so the FBI agreed to put them up. Fairfax County had a couple of cruisers there to block the place off and provide traffic control. There were two rear exits to Ron's, so Hanson had four JTTF members in plain clothes stationed in the parking lot out back in case anyone inside noticed the rest of the team's approach from the front. It looked like everything was ready.

Hanson had anticipated getting the warrants that morning, which they did, and he and Brendon had coordinated with all the agencies involved ahead of time. He had Charles and Josh ready to pick up Ozawa, whom they identified as Shahzad al-Hardar from his Virginia drivers license, at The Sublette Shoppe in Springfield where he worked. Phil and Ronnie were picking up Sattar Omar at his place of employment, a Short and Feisty real estate office, also in Springfield. Hanson had hoped that they'd identify another procurer or two, but the last two nights were quiet at the shop, and the daytime traffic looked legitimate. They were all set for fourteen-hundred hours sharp.

At five before the hour, four cars headed down Boston Boulevard, caught the green light at Fullerton Road and headed up the hill turning left on Twist lane. Two Fairfax County police cars, one that approached from the east and one from the west, closed in behind them and blocked off the exit to Fullerton Road. The SWAT team was in front and entered the business first: six guys through the double glass front doors. The team leader waited until three of his guys maneuvered over to the door to the shop area and two made it to the stairs at the side of the waiting room and then announced to the folks in the office area, "This is a raid. Everyone put your hands where I can see them and don't move." "Everyone" included a receptionist and the shop foreman behind the front counter, and an apparent customer in their small waiting room. The team leader, along with Hanson and Brendon, who had followed the SWAT guys into the building, frisked the two behind the counter, read them their rights, let them get their coats after checking them for weapons, and then cuffed them. They then moved them to the front of the office area.

Hanson made the determination that the man reading the newspaper in the waiting room really was a customer, much to the man's relief, so after getting his information they let him go. Unfortunately, his car was not about to get fixed anytime soon, so he had to call his wife to come get him.

Giving the same advice to the people in the shop area that his team leader had offered the folks in the office, one of the SWAT members got the attention of the men there. Included in that group were six mechanics working on the various vehicles, and none of them offered any resistance. The team went through the same routine with them and had all six of the suspects ready to go in the front of the shop area in less than five minutes.

The two SWAT team members that had taken the stairs to the upper level found it empty, but there was a back door and a landing, obviously the top of a set of stairs on the outside of the building. As they approached the door one of the JTTF guys that had been stationed out back entered, followed by the apparent previous occupant of the room and another JTTF member. The "manager," as he called himself, had tried to make it out the back when he heard what was going on downstairs. The JTTF guys relieved him of the two large files that he had in his hands when they intercepted him. They got the keys to everything from him, then had him join the rest of the detainees.

The SWAT team leader indicated to the lead FBI guy that everything was in order, and he called for the two Suburban transport vehicles that had been standing by across the street in the State Department parking lot. Ten minutes later, the employees of Ron's Auto Repair and Body Work were off to an FBI processing center.

Hanson thanked the SWAT team and the other four JTTF members, and they packed up to leave after handing over the keys to the place and the files that they had retrieved from the manager. Hanson gave them to the techies and he and Brendon hung around to watch them work, making sure to stay out of their way. The accountants among them did a very neat and through job of packing and labeling the files, dozens of DVDs, a cash box, and four computer work stations. They located the floor safe on the lower level and the combination to it in the manager's desk. It was loaded with more files and more cash. The guys in the shop recorded the VINs for all the vehicles there along with their physical description. "What a haul," beamed Hanson. "What a haul."

At two o'clock sharp, Phil and Ronnie walked into the Short and Feisty real estate office on Commerce Street in Springfield. It was located in a two-story brick building next to an Italian restaurant. The complex also housed two dentists' offices and an escrow/title insurance company. They saw a well-dressed, middle-aged female employee helping a young couple at the desk near the front of the office. Ronnie proceeded to the back of the office as Phil waited to get the employee's attention.

"Excuse me, Miss, but is the manager in?" he asked.

Before she could answer, Omar walked out from a long hallway that led to several back offices. He didn't notice Ronnie as he approached Phil and said, "I'm the manager. Can I help you?"

"Sattar Omar, you're under arrest for grand theft auto," Phil said, as he moved toward him. "Put your hands on your head and don't move."

Omar looked around to find an avenue of escape and saw Ronnie staring at him from the back of the office with her side arm showing. A look of resignation came over his face.

"You're going to have to come with us. Can you leave this employee in charge here?"

Omar nodded and handed the woman some keys and said, "Lock things up when you leave. I have to go with these policemen to explain what is no doubt quite a mix up. I will see you in the morning." While Phil read him his rights, Ronnie retrieved his coat from the back room. After he put it on, she cuffed him and led him out of the building and into the back seat of their car.

"Well, that was easy," remarked Phil. "I wonder how the raid is going."

"Let's take this guy back to Fullerton and find out," Ronnie said, and they drove off as the employee and the young couple stared out the window at them.

At two o'clock sharp, Charles and Josh walked into The Sublette Shoppe on Backlick Road, also in Springfield. "Shahzad al-Hardar," Charles called out as he held his badge out and stepped behind the counter, much to the surprise of everyone there, "you are under arrest for grand theft auto. Put your hands on your head and come over here."

Josh had maneuvered to the other end of the counter but stayed on the outside.

Al-Hardar dropped the Italian herb and garlic bun he had in his hands and started running toward the back of the store. Josh had pulled his nine millimeter out and had it pointed right at al-Hardar, who apparently didn't think Josh would shoot, or didn't care if he did, because he kept on running. Josh didn't have a clean shot because of all the other people there, but Charles was hot on his tail and followed al-Hardar to the back room of the store after weaving his way through the other three employees behind the counter.

"Knife!" yelled Josh who noticed that al-Hardar had not dropped the ten inch knife he had in his hands to cut the buns. Jumping the glass partition separating the customers from all the bins of meats and veggies did not seem like an option, so he quickly ran around to the front and entered through the same swinging door that Charles had.

One of the employees was wet mopping the back room and al-Hardar slipped on the wet floor and went sprawling. Charles saw what happened and tried to avoid the wet spot and ended up running into the slop bucket, tripping and falling right on top of al-Hardar who consequently had the wind knocked out of him.

When Josh got to the back, he saw al-Hardar on the floor trying to catch his breath with Charles on top of him waving his .357. He could see that al-Hardar had dropped the knife.

"He slipped and fell," yelled Charles as he stood up and tried to regain his composure.

Josh approached the fallen man cautiously, kicked the knife further out of his reach, and proceeded to cuff him.

The manager thought the store was under attack and was cowering in the corner of the room yelling, "Oh my god, oh my god, call 9-1-1, call 9-1-1!"

Charles showed his badge to the manager and explained what was going on.

The manager calmed down enough to ask, "Will I have to pay him for the days he worked this week?"

Charles, trying to brush the water from his suit said something to the effect of al-Hardar not needing the money where he was going.

In the mean time, Josh helped al-Hardar get up, read him his rights, asked him where his jacket was, and then threw it over his shoulders.

Charles had recovered enough to walk calmly out of the store with Josh and al-Hardar right behind him. "You mention one word of this back at the office and I'll tell them about the time that you broke the mirror in the whore house."

"My lips are sealed, partner," said Josh laughing. "My lips are sealed." They loaded al-Hardar in the back seat of their car and headed back to Fullerton.

CHAPTER THIRTY

This is fucking unacceptable! A whole damn operation shut down! How did this happen? How did this happen? We've probably lost six operatives, including Sidiq and Shahzad. And there must have been a half a million in cash there and a dozen vehicles. These feds are just getting too damn smart for their own good. We must make some major adjustments now. It's certainly a good thing that we kept the operations separate from each other, and that only one was compromised. We must determine how they got wind of this—it could not have been happenstance. Farooq knew nothing of this; I do not think it could have been him. We must get together and determine if the other operations are in danger. This is fucking unacceptable!

Fusion Team Headquarters, 28 November, 1100 hours

"Ladies and gentlemen," began Hanson, smiling ear to ear, "I hope everyone had a nice Thanksgiving holiday. I certainly did. And a very well-deserved one too, after our successful raid last Wednesday. For those of you who don't know, we made quite a haul: $476,000 in cash, three boxes of files on the chop shop operations, four PCs also loaded with data, and nine employees— the manager, the shop foreman, a receptionist and six mechanics. We also picked up two procurers, Sattar Omar and Shahzad al-Hardar, and got a lead on five others, three of whom we have also nabbed. That's thirteen criminals off the streets with a potential for three more. And so far, it looks like ten of them are bona fide terrorists. Finally, we recovered eight stolen vehicles and got information on the disposition of dozens of others. Excellent, excellent work. We have not only closed a chop shop and removed a bunch of car thieves from circulation, we have captured at least eight terrorists and shut off a significant source of funding for their activities. The FBI is working on tracing the financial connections and we expect to nab some even bigger game. They believe that this will lead them to the warehousing facilities, shippers and buyers. Suffice it to say they are having a heyday."

"What about the people we apprehended in the raid?" asked Phil.

"So far, the receptionist and three of the six mechanics have posted bail, with one more given the option to. It appears as though they had sufficient knowledge to realize that some illegal activity was going on, but not necessarily in support of terrorist operations. The rest, I think, will be detained for some time. Included in the latter group are: (1) al-Hardar, the one that Charles and Josh picked up during the raid and, as it turns out, one of our original *S&S* Sticks; (2 and 3) the shop foreman and the manager, neither of whom was on the Watch List; (4) Omar, the procurer that Phil and Ronnie picked up who was not on the Watch List; (5 and 6) two of the mechanics, both of whom were on the Watch List; and (7 and 8) the two other procurers that we picked up subsequently, one of whom was on the Watch List. That's the eight terrorists I mentioned that we had. Two of the procurers and one mechanic are still missing and, although none of them are on the Watch List, I suspect the first two are dyed-in-the-wool members of this group. I know some of you were working last Friday and over the weekend to get us this far along, and I thank you. Any other questions on this operation?" There were none, so he continued on to the next subject. "So, with that said, we do have an update on the Quarles case for all of you who are involved with that. Josh, what do you have for us?"

"We traced the emails that Furlong kept, the ones on his flash drive, to their origins. His laptop did not even have an email program—he kept it all on his flash drive. And it was as we suspected—they were sent via freshly created accounts from public locations, mostly libraries. Each one was from a different account with no traceability to the originator. The same thing with the blogs to the web sites. The NSA guys told us the same thing. We checked for video at each of the locations and only one had any—the county library in Fairfax. Although we're pretty sure we got the sender of one of Furlong's messages on camera, it really does us no good as far as identification goes. And the NSA guys said there was a possibility that the time stamp was altered. We even talked to the library employees and they remembered nothing about the guy. I'm afraid that's a bust, Cap'n."

"Okay. Phil, did you get something on the videos from the meeting places?"

"We checked every place he mentioned, including revisiting the *Starbucks* in South Riding, and we got nothing. The only two that had any video were the *Starbucks* at Tysons and the *Coastal Flats* in Fairfax, but they both had long since dumped the date in question. Sorry."

"We really didn't expect anything there but had to check. Thanks. Charles, what about the access to his record?"

"The only access we found was, as far as we could tell, for legitimate law enforcement purposes. The forensic guys told me that a really sharp user could access it and leave no trace. So, thank goodness, that turned out to be a dead end."

"Alright, thanks Charles. Ronnie, what about our boy's prior activities?"

"That proved to be very interesting, Sir. One was listed as an unexplained death, probably an accident, and the other was listed as an unsolved homicide. The 'accident' one was in Fairfax County and they want all our case files and also want to interview Furlong to see who contracted the hit. They were happy to let us handle Furlong's future, however. We did get some blowback from the other one up in Montgomery County—they wanted to reopen the case and prosecute Furlong and were not happy with our agreement. They'll get over it, though. They also want the files and the chance to interview Furlong in order to trace the source of the hit. Phil and I reviewed both of the case files and didn't find anything relevant to our two cases, other than the similar MOs. So if it's okay with you, I'll copy the files for them and authorize the interviews."

"No blowback from Fairfax?" Hanson asked.

"Well, at first, yes. But then JT talked to them and they withdrew their objections."

"I see. And they're cool now, JT?" he asked, casting a sideways glance at the former Fairfax County police officer.

"Yes, Sir. When I explained our current case and the likely extent of his period of incarceration, they were pacified. I must admit that I did commit to letting them know if Furlong got less than life without parole. I should also mention that Baltimore was more than happy to let us handle the Crenshaw situation, especially after they were so unwilling to admit the possibility of malice aforethought in the first place. And, finally, as you know, Loudoun has been willing to let us run with the Quarles case all along."

"Okay. Ronnie, go ahead and transfer the files and let them interview Furlong. Now let's discuss the matter of these funds transfers."

Arlington, Virginia, 29 November, 1530 hours

"Doctor Jabornae, how nice to see you again." You could not ask for a better person than Lou Callas to run your Visitor Control Center: he oozed civility and never forgot a name or a face. Of course, Arati was a standout in most any crowd. "I'm sorry about Doctor Quarles," Lou offered. He also remembered whom each person normally came here to see. "Will you be seeing Doctor Briceman this visit?"

"Yes, Lou," she replied. "And thank you. That was certainly a tragedy and he will be missed."

"Yes Ma'am. Here is your badge. If I recall, you don't usually carry a cell phone, let alone one with picture taking capability." Cameras and picture phones were not allowed above the first floor.

"You have a good memory, Lou," she said as she nodded agreement.

"Have a fruitful visit."

"Thank you," she said as she headed out to the elevator banks while attaching her badge to her blouse. She had removed her jacket and draped it over her left arm, partially covering the small leather satchel that she used in lieu of a purse. Arati had been here several times before, once early on to meet Quarles and discuss the project with him, and then a few times subsequent to that to serve on the source selection evaluation board for the Coltrane contract. Once it was awarded, Stefon always came to see her at NRL. She was quite sure he liked getting out of the office. She got off the elevator on the seventh floor and proceeded to Briceman's office. Stationed outside his office, as usual, was Jessie, his research assistant. "Good afternoon, Jessie. Is he ready to see me yet?"

"Yes, Ma'am," she replied. "He said for you to go right in."

"Thank you." The door was open and Briceman had heard the exchange and was walking over to greet her. "Good afternoon, Rick," she said as she extended her hand. They had become acquainted working together on the Coltrane SSEB and were on a first name basis.

"Arati, how good to see you again." He motioned her to one of the chairs facing the windows and then walked over to close his door—his way of letting Jessie know that he didn't want to be disturbed. He walked back and sat down directly across from her. "I am so sorry about Stefon and I must apologize for not talking to you sooner. I know it's been a month now since his passing and we have not met to discuss the prognosis for the program. I am so glad that you called last week and suggested this meeting, and that you have carried on with the program in good DARPA tradition."

"Thank you. It was not only my pleasure, but also the least that I could do under the circumstances. Actually, there are a couple of things I would like to discuss with you."

"Of course, but I would like to start with something. I have reviewed the program with TT and he has agreed that, in his words, 'We should press on with Arati leading the charge.' In fact, he would like me to offer you Stefon's position here at the Agency."

This surprised Arati, and, for a moment, pleased her. *In spite of what I think of him, he is still quite intelligent and he would also need the Director's approval for the hire. That is two people placing significant confidence in my abilities. Then again, he probably thinks I am not clever enough to figure out what he is doing, so what better place to have me.*

Her thoughts were interrupted with Briceman's continuing dialogue. "We could only offer you a GS-15 at this time. The Pentagon has already asked for Stefon's SES position back. But we could probably come up with an ST position at a later time."

A GS-15 would be about a six percent raise, and an ST somewhat more. But then, what do I need the money for other than to bring my "fake" family back here.

"So what do you think, Arati?"

"I must say I am flattered. And since that is a perfect segue into the reason for my visit, I will get right to the point—I need more money." Briceman's offer of a job had thrown her off script. She'd just have to adlib it from here. *JT must be squirming in his car seat.*

"I don't understand. I thought that we had fully funded Stefon's program, Arati."

"Rick, I have worked with Stefon on this program almost from the beginning. While the original idea was certainly his, and indeed the solutions to some of the recalcitrant problems were also his, I am very well-versed in its intricacies and its operation. In fact, I have been tracing financial transactions of various DARPA contractors and subcontractors, and have come to the conclusion that someone has found a way to mask them from the program that we developed. Now, I believe that in order to do that, one would not only have to be exceptionally clever, but also have access to and have been involved with the program's development. You and I are the only two people that fit in that category."

Briceman, rather than deny the accusation or even get excited, just sat there gently stroking his red goatee for several moments. Arati knew enough to let him think. He got up and started toward his desk and said, "My dear Arati, I'm having a hard time processing what you said. Whatever do you mean by that and whatever does it have to do with me?" He leaned over and flipped a switch on a little gray metal box on his desk and grabbed a piece of paper and wrote something on it. He sat back down and handed it to her.

"JT, this damn thing's not receiving. Something happened to our signal. What do you want to do?"

"She mentioned that this might happen. Let's just hope that he hasn't discovered the plant and that the onboard recorder is working. Relax. She said if he finds it, she'll just say that she was covering her bases, and we'll end up without a recording."

"He may not believe that she could get such a sophisticated device except from a federal source."

"Relax. She's in a very public place. And besides, if he believes that then he'll also believe that we know exactly where she is and who she's with."

Arati glanced at the note and then said, "Look, Rick. I understand your concern and the reason for the note. But there is no wire and there is no reason to disguise our conversations. Besides, we both know that with the locks and sweeps you have on the door and the noise makers on the windows that you just activated, discussions up to top secret could be held in this room and a wire would be useless." She had indeed mentioned to JT that this was a possibility. Briceman grabbed the note from her and wrote something else on it and handed it back to her.

As she read the PROVE IT he had written there he said, "I'm afraid you are making no sense here at all. You're talking all over the place and have me confused."

"You are a cautious man, Dr. Briceman. How would you like to go about this?"

He got up and grabbed her jacket and her leather satchel and spent some minutes examining them very carefully. He then walked over to the window that looked out on the building next door and drew the blinds shut. He turned to her and said, "So far, so good." Arati removed her blouse and handed it to him. He held it up to the light, felt every part of it, especially the seams. When done he turned and looked at her expectantly. She sighed and removed her bra and handed it to him. "Oh my god," he exclaimed as he looked at her full, dark breasts. Forgetting for the moment that he was still trying to be careful about what he was saying just in case she did have a wire on, he blurted out, "I'm sorry for staring, but you don't see one black and one white nipple every day. At least not on the same person."

"My left areola has albino pigmentation. It is a genetic trait of the women in my family. Can we get on with this?"

258

"Oh, ah, yes." He then examined the bra in the same fashion as the other items. She handed him her skirt before he asked for it. After examining that, he asked her to stand. "I can examine them on or off," he said looking at her panties, "your choice." He was definitely aroused now but hoped she didn't notice. She didn't like the thought of him touching her, so she removed her panties and handed them to him. He took a minute to refocus and then checked the seams. "Almost done," he said as he pointed to her earrings while trying to keep his eyes on the task at hand. She removed them and handed them to him. "That's a lovely hair tie." She removed the hand woven Indian tie that her mother had given her that gathered her pony tail and handed that to him as well. He went over and set them on his desk and placed a glass upside down over them. "And finally...," he said as he pointed at her shoes. They were plain black ballet style flats with a thin rubber sole. She had actually slipped them off earlier so she just bent over and picked them up off the floor. Briceman wasn't sure whether he was more aroused because he had a naked lady standing in front of him, or because he felt like she was under his complete control. He refocused once again and examined the shoes. "Now turn around once please." After she complied, he handed her back the stack of clothes that had piled up next to him and said, "I apologize for this but a man can't be too careful. Please, ah, get dressed."

"Thank you. It is getting rather chilly in here." *I hope he appreciates the double entendre.*

As Arati redressed herself, Briceman, now embarrassed, walked over to his desk and did not watch her. When she was done, she cleared her throat and he walked back over to her. "Okay, he said. I apologize again, but there is a lot at stake here. So tell me what you know."

"As you know, I suppose, two government agents came to talk to me about Stefon. From my conversation with them, I got the impression that they thought Mike Styles was somehow complicit in Stefon's demise. So I started looking into his finances using the Coltrane program. It became obvious to me that a DARPA subcontractor had transferred money into an offshore account for him, apparently in payment for directing one or more contracts their way. That had nothing to do with Stefon, of course, but it was interesting nonetheless. This was a couple of weeks ago. As I mentioned earlier, I started looking into other DARPA contractors and subs and noticed that a number of monetary transfers had been made from contractors or subs that you were involved with, but I could not tell where the funds were transferred to. So a few days ago, I used the beta version of Tomfoolery that was just delivered and the transactions were still not traceable. I could not believe that the program did not work as it should. It occurred to me that only I, Stefon, and you knew enough about the programming involved to implant a subroutine that was designed to ignore certain transactions. I determined that some of the programming changes were made only recently, after Stefon's demise. I know I did not do it and Stefon was out of the picture, so—"

"What about Bill Arnold?"

"I did indeed think of him, and decided that he is not clever enough to engineer something like this. My conclusion is that, in recompense for sending business their way, you are secreting money from contractor kickbacks into one or more hidden personal accounts."

"I see. So tell me, Arati, what did you mean earlier when you said you would be needing more money?"

"I have an extended family in India, several of whom I have been trying to secure passage for to the United States. That, unfortunately, requires a good deal of money. There are bribes to be made to various officials back in India, the transportation costs themselves are substantial, fake documentation fees are required, there are considerable set up costs when they get here.... Need I go on?"

Briceman shook his head.

"So I considered this clever little setup that you have here and hoped that you would not mind sharing. I could be very useful to you. I understand the program like no one else, except maybe you, and perhaps could be put in a position to control the access and use of the program."

"I see. You are a clever woman." He pondered the idea for a few minutes. "Yes, I think something like that could be arranged. However, under these new circumstances, I don't think it would be a good idea for you to take Stefon's place. We would need to get you into the operations arena over at DIA once we're up and running with this thing. The current plan is for the program to be monitored out of Joel Henning's new shop. I think with a little friendly persuasion he could be convinced to take you on. I mean, there would likely be several possible program glitches that you could conveniently contrive and then fix. We could milk this thing for several years. Certainly long enough for us to get what we need out of it."

"Excellent. So what do we do now?"

"I do need some time to process everything that we have discussed. You have, after all, put me in an awkward position, and I need to make some arrangements. TT will not be happy with this and I'll have to think of some way to put a good spin on it. How about if we set up another meeting when we can get more into the details of our 'partnership'?"

"Absolutely. But I must tell you one last thing. The details of what I revealed to you this afternoon are contained in a manuscript in the hands of one of those members of my extended family in India that I mentioned. This is merely an insurance policy for me that I am sure I will never need to utilize."

"I would have expected no less, Arati. We are in this for the duration. I'll call you after I've checked out a few things and we can get back together, perhaps at your place this time."

"I look forward to it."

As Arati got up and walked to the door, Briceman reopened his blinds and turned off the window noise. He was convinced that he could hear the high pitched hum and it irritated him. "Could you please close the door on your way out? I have some thinking to do."

"Hey. We just got a signal back," Juanita blurted. Sounds like... Yep, it's Arati saying goodbye to Briceman's secretary. So I'm guessing she pulled it off. Let's go pick her up." JT had parked near the end of the park that was in direct line of site from Briceman's office. Well, there were a few trees in between them and his office that still had some leaves on them, so there was no danger of them being spotted. They swung around to the back side of the Metro stop—their prearranged meeting spot and a place not visible from the DARPA building. Arati walked up not two minutes after they arrived and jumped in the back seat.

"Wow! I must say that was exciting. It was, as you say, a little touch and go for awhile, but I accomplished the mission, I believe. Do you often have this much excitement?" Arati was quite beside herself. They had not seen this side of her before and were both amused with her considerable enthusiasm.

"Arati, you had us worried when we lost the signal. And it sounded like you went off script. What happened?"

"Well, you heard the part where he offered me Stefon's position. That threw me off stride. And, as I suspected, he had noise dampeners on the window that he switched on when the conversation got 'delicate.' Speaking of delicate, he did insist on a search. I must implore you not to give the recording, if it worked, broad dissemination. Oh my, I think that is a pun."

I took JT and Juanita a second or two to get it, but then they all laughed, probably due more to the release of tension than from the unintentional pun. "I am so glad you are okay and that everything turned out okay," gushed Juanita.

"Likewise," uttered JT. "Well, the transmitter obviously worked, and there's no reason that the recorder in your shoe wouldn't, as well. I just talked to Hanson and he wants to meet us nearby to review the tape. Do you want to come along with us and see if it worked?"

"Most definitely!" Arati exclaimed. "I would *not* want to miss that."

CHAPTER THIRTY-ONE

Clarendon, Virginia, 29 November, 1800 hours

Hanson had a dinner date in Rosslyn a little later in the evening and asked that JT and Juanita meet in the office that the Fusion Team maintained in the DIA building in Clarendon. It was close to DARPA where the three of them were and a short hop down Wilson Boulevard for Hanson to get to Rosslyn when they were done. The nondescript, twelve-story brick highrise had underground parking for which they had passes. JT and Juanita arrived early and helped themselves to the coffee mess until Hanson got there at six sharp. JT had already removed the transmitter that the forensics team had put on Arati's scalp by applying a special release solution to it. The transmitter was only ten millimeters long and three wide, and stuck up only two above the surface of her head. The forensics team had placed it in the middle of her head about three centimeters back from where her hairline met her forehead, and they did have to shave a portion of her head in order for it to adhere to her scalp better. Colored the same as her hair, it would have been impossible to notice unless you were looking for it. The digital receiver/recorder—one centimeter square and three deep—had been implanted in the sole of her left shoe. Juanita used an exacto knife to extricate it.

After being introduced to Hanson, Arati said, "Mr. Hanson, I hope you will be discreet with the information about me that you are about to hear."

"Doctor Jay, I most certainly will."

Arati looked at JT.

"He has trouble with foreign names. Don't pay him any mind."

By this time, Juanita had connected the appropriate leads and executed the play command. They listened to the tape, which had indeed recorded every word uttered by Arati and Briceman, in addition to the annoying hum of the air handlers. Juanita did her best to tune out the hum until finally they could actually hear Briceman walking around and closing the blinds and Arati removing her clothes. When they got to the part where she removed her bra, all three of them couldn't help but glance at her breasts.

"This is the delicate part I mentioned," she remarked.

When the tape was finished, Hanson looked at Arati and said, "Doctor Jay, you are a trooper. And your anatomical peculiarities are safe with us. I am very pleased that you didn't bring up his possible involvement with the two murders. Do you think he suspects?"

"He is a very intelligent man, and after our meeting today, I feel that he has a newfound respect for me. He might believe that I have not made that connection yet, but will no doubt consider that I am aware of it before our next visit. I think it would be wise for me to bring it up and indicate that I am not happy with the situation, but that I understand the necessity for it."

"Good," replied Hanson. "However, if he's as smart as everyone says he is, he'll probably figure this out and make a run for it. I'm going to ask for a warrant based on his admission of contract tampering but leave its execution open, and we'll put him under surveillance to forestall the opportunity of his escape. If he stays put, then you can have another meeting with him as he suggested. I believe a jury would have no trouble believing that he was involved with illegal contract activities, but we all think he was also complicit in the two murders. Can you reconstruct the financial transfers after the murders now that you know the program was jimmied?"

"The program change that he made does not destroy the data; it merely ignores it. If he did not alter the raw data, then yes, I could rerun the program and track the transactions. But if I were him, given the time that he had and the importance of the data, I would have destroyed it. The raw data *is* resident in my database that he has access to. Then the question is whether or not NSA maintains a copy of the data that they send to us. I must admit I do not know, but I rather doubt it since it is voluminous and they would have no use for it."

"Can you work on that and check with NSA if you need to? I can run point with them if you need that."

Arati nodded.

"If that doesn't work out, then you'll definitely need another sit down with Briceman in order to get him to admit to the murders. Now, what do we do about Styles?"

"Well, Boss," JT began, "according to Arati, we can probably get him for accepting bribes. She can definitely show that funds were transferred from various DARPA contractors to an account that appears to be his. The problem would be getting access to the offshore bank records to show that the account really belongs to him. So far the only withdrawals from that account didn't go to any of his known accounts, but rather Furlong's fake Mumford account. The timing of the transfers in and out suggests his involvement with the two murders, but he could have been set up. I'm on the fence as to whether or not we bring him in and sweat him, or let him out there to make a mistake, except that—"

"If we bring him in, that might spook whoever else is involved," Juanita finished. And we don't want that to happen before Arati talks to Briceman again."

"Exactly."

"Arati," Hanson said, recalling JT's mild rebuke of a few minutes ago and finally becoming comfortable with pronouncing her first name, "I hate to impose upon you anymore than we already have—"

"We are all paid by the people," she interrupted.

"True, but through different channels. The additional help that I want to ask for is whether or not you could trace the financial transactions made by the chop shop. The FBI is of course handling all that, but if they run into any blank walls, I was thinking that maybe your program could point us in the right direction."

"I would be delighted. Just let me know whom I should talk to if the situation arises."

"Alright. But if you get any flack from your boss, just let me know."

She nodded and indicated that that would not be a problem.

"I'm looking forward to a night on the town. You guys carry on or whatever. It was very nice meeting you, Arati. And thank you again for all your help, delivered and forthcoming."

"My pleasure, Sir. So now what?" she asked as she turned to Juanita and JT.

"I think we need to bring you up to speed on everything we found out about these terrorists," Juanita said. She started with the original meeting at S&S Enterprises, what they had heard that they thought connected the Quarles case and the terrorists, the report on the IED used, and the murder of Ashan in front of the Marriott. JT continued with the showdown at Mustafa's and his debriefing, the strikeout on Aimal over in upper Marlboro, and finally the tracking of Omar that led to the chop shop.

"You have indeed been busy," she said. "That is a lot to process. Let me consider all of this data and see if anything presents itself. Perhaps a different set of eyes will offer a new avenue of research. But I must say I think you have covered all the possibilities that I can think of off-hand, given the manner in which you are processing the data from the automotive repair facility. In the mean time, I do have a few questions about Mr. Furlong's activities that I thought of after talking to you the other day." She asked them and Juanita and JT took turns answering them.

"Oh damn, it's after 8:30. I'm going to miss putting Andy to bed another night if I don't get out of here now. Nita, can you give Arati a lift home?"

"No problem, *amigo*. I'll see you in the morning?"

"Yeah, but how does ten o'clock sound?"

Juanita gave him a thumbs up, so he closed up shop quickly and left. "Arati, I'm hungry, how about you?"

"Yes. I have not eaten since lunch."

"How about if we pick a place on the way to your house— any suggestions?" Juanita started packing up her stuff and in short order they were walking out the door. "By the way, where do you live?"

266

"I live in an apartment building on Chesapeake Street just off South Capitol Street. That is an easy commute to NRL and the rent is reasonable. I really could not recommend any good eating establishments near there. And besides, that would keep you out rather late and I would not want to impose."

"That's probably not the safest neighborhood in town. How about if I pick out a place a little closer to here? There's a great Italian restaurant practically across the street from here. And don't worry about keeping me out to late. I've got nothing else to do and would love the company."

"I am ready and Italian sounds wonderful."

Juanita finished cleaning up the area, shut off the computer and turned out the lights. Arati grabbed her coat and followed her out the door.

The restaurant was the Café Italia, one of Juanita's favorites, and one of the few that was open past nine o'clock. Since it was a weeknight and rather late, there would be parking right out front, so Juanita drove the few blocks rather than walk and have to go back to the garage later for her car. They agreed on a Tuscan antipasto salad and a glass of Chianti each. Juanita ordered the lemon dill shrimp ravioli and Arati the lasagna verdi. With that out of the way, Juanita began the conversation. "Arati, you have me at a disadvantage: you checked me out and know all about me. So tell me about yourself."

"Well, that is not entirely true. I do know what was in the public records about you. And that is probably the same data that you were able to gather on me, at this point. My family, all three of us, came to this country after I graduated high school, but by that time I had already learned to speak fairly good English, since my father worked for an American company and thought it wise to teach it to my mother and me. My father is exceptionally smart and expected no less of me, so he continually challenged me to do better. I guess I would have to say that he succeeded, since I did get my Ph.D. and have a responsible position."

"You do have other family back in India, right?"

"My father was an only child, as am I, which is actually somewhat unusual, although becoming less so. My mother has a brother who is still back in India, but her sister died when my mom was very young. My Uncle Harshad does have two offspring, a male and a female, Mahesh and Dhara, who are close to my age, but they have expressed no interest in coming to America."

"So what about your friends?"

"I am afraid that I am a workaholic and have no social life. I know none of my neighbors, my few cohorts at work are all married and do little socializing, at least not with me, and the people that I worked with at China Lake are still back there. I did have a roommate in college, Carlie Wilkins, and we do keep in touch, but she moved to Washington state and works for Microsoft. And that is all there is to Arati Jabornae. Now it is your turn."

"No men in your life?"

"As I said, I have no social life."

"Well, let's see. I'm sure you know my mom is Mexican and my dad was a pilot in the U.S. Air Force. I am also an only child, but do have a number of cousins in Mexico and the southwest U.S. I've got an undergraduate in criminology and I'm working on my masters. All of this you probably already know."

Arati nodded.

"I've had a few boyfriends, one serious one that I broke up with a year or so ago. Nothing serious since then."

"You seem to be very close to JT. I realize he is your colleague, but if you do not mind my asking, is there anything between you two?"

"We are very good friends. My boyfriend and I palled around with JT and Sara before she died, so we got to know each other pretty well. But no, we are just friends, and partners."

"How can you be so close and not have 'romantic' feelings for him?"

"I do, on occasion, but try to think of him as my brother. Or at least how I think I would feel about a brother. Romantic entanglements at work are a bad idea, especially in the law enforcement arena. I know you read all about them in the mystery novels, but I've actually seen very few in real life, but then I haven't really been looking for them either."

"JT is from a large family. Have you met them?"

"Yes, and it's really neat. He has a sister and two brothers, and his mother is the oldest of seven, so he has lots of aunts and uncles, not to mention nieces and nephews and cousins. Their family get-togethers are lots of fun and always interesting. I've always envied his extended family. Actually, they are so friendly that they make me feel like I'm part of the family, which is why I guess I feel like he is a brother. His mother is generous to a fault, and his dad is a stitch. He used to work for NASA and has great stories to tell of his time as a flight controller for the Apollo missions. But enough of JT. Tell me something funny that happened to you in college."

"Okay. There was the time when Carlie was pledging a sorority, and she was asked to get some of the recruiting posters for a rival sorority and 'doctor them up' as a joke. She mentioned it to me and I suggested that we affix a hidden message on them that would only appear after passing a magnetic field over the ink that we used. That way we could let the other group post their recruiting posters and she could change them after they were up and behind glass fronts in many cases. I created a half a liter of ferrofluid ink, Carlie and a few of the other pledges 'borrowed' two dozen of their posters, and they stenciled a hidden message on them. The other sorority was Sigma Phi Nu by the way, and their message advertised their next mixer. After we changed the posters, they read 'Signa Phi Nutin wants you.'"

Juanita laughed and then asked, "You *made* the ink?"

"With some materials I borrowed from the chemistry lab. So tell me something that you did in college."

"There was a rivalry between the all-male dorm and the all-female dorm that I lived in when I went to Maryland U. They faced each other across the main pavilion on campus. My boyfriend at the time managed to program the football scoreboard to say 'Maynard Hall sucks,' which stayed lit for about thirty minutes before the campus police turned it off. Of course, Maynard Hall was my dorm. Not to be outdone, I coordinated with all the women in our dorm and at exactly eleven o'clock that same evening, we got everyone to open their drapes and turn their room lights either on or off so that the side of our building facing Clements Hall read 'fuck you.'"

"Oh, you did not! That is great," Arati laughed. By now, their meals had come but this hardly interrupted their conversation.

"So what was it like growing up in India?"

It was almost eleven before they finished up and Juanita drove Arati home.

CHAPTER THIRTY-TWO

Downtown Washington, DC, 1 December, 1030 hours

Hanson thought it best if they went to the FBI to learn what results they had obtained so far on their review of the records from the chop shop. He decided to keep the crew that he brought along with him down to a reasonable size: Brendon, since he had organized the raid, Arati, so she could ask any questions about the financial transactions, and JT. Besides, most of the others were busy tracking down leads or on surveillance duty. The J. Edgar Hoover Building is located at 935 Pennsylvania Avenue, NW, and was constructed in what's termed the Brutalist architectural style: the exterior consisting entirely of poured concrete and glass windows. In fact, it has suffered much criticism for its lack of aesthetics and functionality, and was even named one of the "Ten Buildings That Should Be Torn Down in D.C." by a prominent Washington magazine. JT's dad had taken him and his two brothers and sister on the FBI tour when they were young, and it was still being conducted, and he still remembers watching a submachine gun being fired in one of the basements. He thought the building was beautiful, and everything in it neat. He was so taken with it and the tour that he had his mom take him to the local library the next day and he checked out and read the FBI Story, the 1956 book written by Don Whitehead. He found it fascinating and exciting even though it was twenty-five-years old when he read it as a boy of twelve. It no doubt influenced some of his career decisions, and he was delighted to be back in the building again which, he thought, still looked beautiful.

They met the FBI team in a corner conference room on the seventh floor from which you could see a good portion of the Federal City, including the Capitol. The FBI personnel included Raymond Parsons, one of the forensic accounting supervisors, and three members of his team. Parsons reminded JT of a scarecrow—he wore a beige suit with a light-brown, plain tie, had a slim build and thinning blonde hair, and wore wire-rim spectacles. Except for his gauntness, you might think he was a well-to-do CPA of some large firm.

After introductions, Parsons started. "I have to admit that you have provided us with a plethora of material to go over. And I might add that your good work has eliminated a significant source of illegal funding that I suspect has been used to finance terrorist activities. Over the past year, this one operation alone has provided 8.2 vehicles per month at an average take of $13.5 thousand each for an annual revenue of over 1.3 million dollars. Their records indicate expenses of $412 thousand, which includes about $500 for each of the stolen cars to the 'procurers,' for a net of $916,400. Almost a million dollars, and we think this is one of several setups in the Baltimore/Washington area and who knows how many in the country." Parsons keyed a remote and a pictorial showing a summary of the calculations he just mentioned appeared on an overhead screen. "Unfortunately, we couldn't find any connections to other similar operations, but we did find out how they are getting the vehicles out of the country. Which is what they are doing—taking them to a loading dock in Annapolis and shipping them to Europe and the Middle East, mostly, we think, aboard container ships owned and operated by *Olsen Svelvik Industries, ASA*, a Norwegian firm."

Parsons looked around to see if he still had everyone's attention, and was somewhat surprised to find that he did. *Perhaps this is a sharper bunch of folks than I thought,* he mused. He changed the overhead picture to one detailing the shipping company, and continued. "We have agents looking into them, but preliminary findings are that they obtained apparently clear titles, fake though they were, and probably have no legal liability. They actually buy the cars from *Ron's Auto Repair and Body Work* and then sell them overseas to various dealers and individuals. We did a quick look into their other businesses and they all appear to be legit. They are not getting cars from any other source as we had hoped, at least not in the states. While we suspect that there may be many of these shops connected somewhere near the top, they have apparently compartmentalized them to prevent the discovery of one from affecting the operation of the others."

"Then the parties they are selling them to won't have any liability, either?" queried Brendon.

"I'm afraid not. Nor do I think that it will have any bearing on your case, given that it appears to be a number of companies and individuals."

"How were they making the titles?" queried JT.

Parsons nodded to one of his team who answered, "From blank purloined D.C. Government titles. We're looking into possible sources, but let me tell you, that place is a mess."

"The profits from this enterprise have been going through two dummy corporations and then finally into a bank account located in the Maldives." Parsons changed the screen image to a geographic one of the Republic of Maldives. "This is an island nation consisting of a group of atolls stretching south of India's Lakshadweep islands, between the Minicoy and the Chargos Archipelagoes, and about 435 miles southwest of Sri Lanka in the Laccadive Sea of the Indian Ocean. The twenty-six atolls which constitute the Republic of Maldives encompass a territory of 250 inhabited islands out of 1,192 islets. It is the smallest Asian country in terms of both population and area, and it is the smallest predominantly Muslim nation in the world. They do have a relatively stable government and it is not hard to figure out why they have the funds transferred there."

Parsons paused at this point and Arati looked over at Hanson expectantly. He nodded, so Arati asked a question. "Were the funds from the chop shop transferred to any other account besides the one in the Maldives?"

"Not in the past year," replied Parsons. "All the money that went into these two dummy corporations recently ended up in the Maldives. However, prior to that, a number of transfers were made to two accounts in Andorra. "

"As in the little country between France and Spain?" asked JT.

"That's the one." Anticipating this line of questioning, he had a pictorial of Andorra ready to display. "It's a landlocked country located in the eastern Pyrenees Mountains. It is the sixth smallest nation in Europe, and for most of its history, it was isolated from mainstream Europe because of its inaccessibility. Modern developments in transportation and communication have removed it from its isolation, and today it is a prosperous country mainly because of tourism and its status as a tax haven. Interestingly enough, the people of Andorra have the highest life expectancy in the world: 84 years at birth. Its political system was thoroughly modernized in 1993when it joined the United Nations and the Council of Europe. They have no military, surely a boon to their economy, and rely on France and Spain for protection. It would be interesting to know if they pay for that. I might note that neither one of these countries has signed an extradition treaty with us."

"Were you able to track the disposition of the funds that were deposited into the accounts in either the Maldives or Andorra?" Arati asked.

"We did not feel that we had sufficient justification to attempt that," said Parsons, somewhat defensively. "Funds for the operation of the shop were originally obtained from a loan from an overseas source that we were not able to identify, but for the last several years the shop has been 'self-supporting,' with revenues generated from its own vehicle sales and its legitimate repair work."

"Were you able to identify the owners of *Ron's Auto Repair and Body Work*?" Hanson asked.

"We traced it back through three holding companies and ultimately to a company called *Aeronautics Alectrona, LLC*. I have the information that we were able to obtain on them listed here in this handout." He handed them an eight-page computer printout and projected another image on the screen. "The first couple of pages there, after the cover page, are what I've shown you already on the overhead. Page six is on the screen now and concerns *Aeronautics Alectrona*. The last two pages are on the holding companies and the two dummy corporations I mentioned previously."

After reviewing them for a few minutes, JT asked, "What about the warehousing facilities they used to store the cars in?"

"Those are owned by the shipping company, *Olsen Svelvik Industries*, so, as I said, I doubt that we'd have any recourse there."

There was a pause in the briefing, so Hanson looked around and asked, "Do we have any more questions for these gentlemen?" Getting no response, he continued, "Thank you very much, Mr. Parsons, gentlemen. It was a pleasure meeting you and we are very grateful for your assistance. Could I have one of your cards?"

"Our contact information is on the cover page that we gave you. But if you wouldn't mind, could we have an update on the personnel captured in the raid?"

"Oh, by all means. Thank you for asking and I apologize for not volunteering it. I thought you would have been briefed." Hanson spent several minutes giving them the rundown that he had provided the team the previous Monday. Luckily, he had his notes with him as it was indeed a good deal of information. "Now, for an update to that, we located the missing mechanic: he was out sick on the day of the raid. He's already out on bail, as is the other mechanic that hadn't come up with the bail when we last discussed their status. So, of the seven mechanics employed there, we're pretty sure that only two of them really knew what was going on—the other five are out on bail, as is the receptionist. *She* appeared to be totally clueless. Frankly I'm not sure how she even functioned in that job. Although, she was a looker. Everybody else, except Omar and al-Hardar, both of whom are in our facility at Fullerton, are being held by your guys pending deportation or trial. The two missing terrorists who were part of the operation's pickup team are still in the wind. We traced down their living quarters fairly quickly from records recovered in the raid and sent some of our guys around to what turned out to be empty apartments. Although they were not on the Watch List or in TIDE before, they are now."

Hanson Paused here for a drink of water. He thought it would be a good idea for interagency relations to give the feebs a little credit, as they certainly did help in this operation. "I understand that your guys have questioned all the detainees relentlessly, and it appears as though the kingpin in the whole operation was the shop manager. The procurers got their directions from him, although we have not as yet determined how he came up with the potential vehicles for heisting. We don't know if he hacked into the DMV database, tracked dealer sales, or just drove around looking for temporary tags, but all the vehicles were relatively new. Unfortunately, I think he is the only one that we might get some useful information from, and I don't think he's gonna crack. Oh, incidentally, they were using one fancy electronic alarm-disabling device which your guys are trying to track down. They told us it's probably homemade, or should I say chop shop made."

"Speaking of which, how many cars did you recover?" asked one of Parsons' coworkers.

"There were eight in the shop that have been or will shortly be reunited with their owners. Your guys located another seventeen in the *Olsen Industries* warehouse that will take a little longer to process. By the way, their last shipment out was the end of August and there were two dozen of these stolen vehicles on board that one. Who knows where they ended up. I suspect it would be impossible to trace and recover them at this point. Actually, our raid was well-timed, as one of their ships was due in the Port of Annapolis just five days later, or two days ago. It appears as though they were trying to get up somewhere close to that two dozen number by then. I guess *Olsen Industries* will have less cargo than normal this trip. In summary, eight terrorists are off the streets; two were sent further underground, hopefully back to their homeland; twenty-five cars were recovered; and one chop shop is out of business."

"Appreciate the update. Do you have any more questions for us?"

"Two things," Hanson said. Could we get a copy of the data that you worked with, and would it be okay if we use the room for a while longer?"

"As for the data, here it is." He handed Hanson three DVDs. "As for the room, no problem. I reserved it until two o'clock, and it could even be available after that. I'll check if you'd like."

"We'll be long gone by then. Thanks again."

Parsons nodded and he and his team left the room.

"Okay, Troops. Sounds like we'll have to proceed from here on our own. Arati, were you able to rerun your data and trace the transactions that occurred after the murders?"

"As you know, the data is gone, erased no doubt by our perpetrator. I called the contact at NSA that you gave me and he verified that they do not keep the data after they send it to us. So, I cannot prove Briceman made the transfers or the changes to the programming or the data set. However, if we could gain access to the machine that he uses to interface with the data, and maybe place him there with security tapes—"

"We've had lesser PC aficionados than him jimmying that security data already, Arati. And besides, he would most likely have covered his tracks," said JT.

"Okay. Nice try on the data, Arati," Hanson said. "I do have someone verifying the owner of the account in the Bahamas that we think is Styles'. When that comes back positive, I'll probably send someone out to pick him up, but not before you see Briceman again, which I guess is now necessary. Do you think you can provide any further direction, in or out, to the funds in the Maldives and Andorra that they were talking about?"

"Actually I believe that I can. I will let you know when I have examined the data they provided to me on these discs," Arati said as she waived the discs in the air.

Southeast Washington, DC, 1 December, 1248 hours

Farooq was supposed to get out of the hospital five days ago but took a turn for the worse—something about a bed sore, of all things. Not that Hanson minded, as this kept him in a confined place where he could be watched over, and the MPD were still willing to accept the overtime payments for keeping him that way. Farooq also seemed to be coming around and more willing to talk. Hanson believed that with just the right offer, they could get him to give up everything he knew. He was going to give JT another shot at Farooq. Another day or two of hospital food and he should be ready.

He had the proper badge displayed and looked like a nurse—just one of the many that were taking care of this special patient. He delivered Farooq's lunch as well as his meds at the appropriate time, so the cop on duty thought nothing of it. Today's dessert was Farooq's favorite, too: ice cream. He had developed a fondness for it in his almost four weeks here—at least the last two when he was a little more coherent than when he arrived—and requested it for every meal. After lunch, he started feeling woozy and sick to his stomach. By the time another nurse showed up and he mentioned it to her, he was feeling really bad. He started convulsing and the nurse called for a doctor and a crash cart. But it was too little too late, and Farooq went on to meet whatever fate awaited him in the afterlife.

CHAPTER THIRTY-THREE

Arlington, Virginia, 2 December, 0930 hours

"I'm walking over to the company for a short meeting and stopping by the cafeteria for something on the way back. Would you like anything?" Jessie asked.

"No, thanks anyway, Jessie. Close my door would you please? I'm going to make a long distance conference call and also work on the budget figures for next week's meeting."

Jessie closed the door while Briceman reached for the phone. She saw one of his lines light up on her instrument panel before she walked off. He set the receiver down on his desk and walked over and drew the blinds on the windows facing the building next door. Grabbing the bag from behind his desk that he had brought in that morning, he pulled out his electric shaver and used the trimmer feature to cut his beard down to stubble level, then shaved that off. He got out the light brown suit and tan shirt that he had placed in the bag last night after his wife went to sleep. He removed his dark blue suit and light blue shirt and changed into the tan clothes. He folded the discarded garments neatly and packed them into the bag. Luckily, it was warm enough last night and this morning that he could get between his house and the car and the office without putting his tan overcoat on, which he had left hanging in his office. He donned it now along with a tan rain hat that did not look too conspicuous. He opened his door a crack and saw that the coast was clear to the hallway door. With bag in hand, he went into the hall and quickly to the stairwell door. *So far, so good; it would be nice to get out of here without running into anyone.*

On the first garage level, the stairs exited onto the automobile ramp that went out the back side of the building. The guards left the garage door open during the day, so he walked up the ramp as casually as he could and turned left up Tenth Street. It was a sunny day, so he had his sunglasses on and strolled the five blocks up to the Ballston Metro stop. He figured that if he used the Virginia Square/GMU stop that was across the street from DARPA, there was a much higher risk of being spotted, even clean-shaven and with a hat covering his red hair. At the Ballston/MU station, he'd take the orange line to New Carrollton, knowing that this one went through Metro Center. There he'd switch to the red line to Glenmont and get off at Union Station.

The train arrived in less than five minutes and he hopped on. He felt much better now, his confidence level in the plan increasing. He sat back and started thinking. *That damn woman is just too damn smart. I hadn't planned on that. Now I'm stuck trying to get out of the country before I reached my goal of ten million. Hah! Just have to make do with six-point-two. In Andorra, I think that will keep me more than happy. Can't wait to get there and get some skiing in. The skiing in this country sucks. I am going to miss Jennifer, but then the excitement's been gone for awhile. Besides, I don't think I'll have any trouble finding a smart, fun-loving woman in Andorra—not with my money. A lot of things have to come together, but I think I've got everything worked out. Damn that Arati anyway! If I had more time, I could've gotten a fake passport and this would have been a whole lot easier. Hopefully they won't even notice that I'm gone for a couple of hours. I should be in BWI by then.*

Josh had parked on Monroe Street such that they could see cars exiting from the garage at the back of the building and people from the front of the building—the exit they'd use to go to the Metro. He and Sal caught the early morning surveillance shift and they'd been on the job since before Briceman left for work at 6:30. His car had a GPS tracker on it and was easy to follow, and their display showed it now parked in the DARPA garage. "I didn't see our boy come out for his usual lunchtime walk around the park," remarked Sal. The team had been on his tail since last Tuesday and noted that he had a fairly consistent daily routine. "I'm going to call Lou Callas and see where he shows him at."

Sal dialed Lou's cell phone and asked about Briceman's whereabouts.

Lou checked his monitor and then walked out into the lobby so as not to be overheard. "I show him entering the building at 7:14 and the seventh floor east door at 7:19. Then again the seven east door at 9:15 and no activity since then."

"So it looks like he's been in his office for several hours now?"

"Yes, but you know, we only require card use on the way in and even then you can tailgate."

"Got it. Okay, thanks, Lou." Sal hung up and relayed the conversation to Josh, who recommended he call Briceman's office. Sal made the call and when Jessie answered the phone said, "Hi. This is Doctor Dominico, from Innova Fairfax Hospital. Is Mister Briceman in?"

"Yes, sir," Jessie answered, "but Doctor Briceman is on the phone and has been for some time. I believe he's on a conference call. Could I take a message?"

"Actually, this is very important and he's been expecting my call. I'm sure he would want you to interrupt him for just a second. Would you, please? I know he'll appreciate it."

"Yes, sir, I will. Just a second while I buzz him." Jessie hit the intercom button and waited for her boss to pick up. When he didn't, she got a little concerned that he didn't want to be bothered, but the man on the phone was rather persistent. She buzzed a second time but again to no avail. She thought it might be best to relay the message in person so got up and knocked on his door. When there was no reply, she became quite concerned thinking that he may be in some sort of medical difficulty—he had never before ignored a knock on the door. She reached for the doorknob and found that the door was unlocked so she stepped in. Briceman was nowhere to be seen. Jessie checked all around the office but there really wasn't much room to hide. The phone receiver was on the desk and when she picked it up found the line was dead. She punched the other line and said, "I'm sorry, sir, but he has apparently left the office without my realizing it. Shall I take a message?"

"He wasn't on the other line?"

"Well, no. The receiver was off the hook but there was no one on the line."

"Is there any way you could page him? It is rather important that I speak to him now."

"I'm sorry, but no. I can take a message and text it to his Blackberry if you'd like."

"Thank you. I'll do that myself." As Sal hung up, he looked at Josh and shook his head. "This doesn't look good, Josh. I think our bird may have flown the coop."

"Call Lou again and get him to do a walk by," said Josh.

Lou did the walk by while being as discreet as he could be. He called back with the results and Sal asked him for Briceman's Blackberry number. Lou retrieved it from his database and called Sal back one more time.

"Thanks, Lou. If he shows up, can you give me a heads up on this number?"

Lou agreed and Sal hung up.

"I'm calling in for a trace on his Blackberry." After a few minutes, he got a call back and was told that it was located not fifty yards from his position and stationary.

"Okay. Time to call his PDA," commented Josh.

Sal did and let it ring. After about twelve rings, it was answered.

"Doctor Briceman's office," a female voice said.

"Is this his secretary?" Sal asked.

"Yes. Are you the gentleman who called for him a few minutes ago?"

"Yes. I gather he left his Blackberry in the office."

"I'm afraid so. You sure you don't want to leave a message?"

"I'll catch him at home. Thanks for your help." Sal looked at Josh and said, "He's in the wind, Partner . He's in the wind. I'll call the Boss."

Fusion Team Headquarters, 2 December, 1245 hours

Hanson wanted Arati to present the results she had garnered in her research on the financial transactions of the DARPA contracts and the chop shop. JT, Juanita, Phil, Ronnie and Brendon were also available and they settled in Hanson's conference room. Arati had worked on the DARPA connections a couple of days ago and spent most of yesterday afternoon and evening working on the FBI data. "I've asked Arati to hit the highlights of what she's uncovered," Hanson said. "Then I'll summarize what I think has been happening based on that data." He nodded at Arati.

"I will begin with the DARPA data but will not go into a great deal of detail," Arati began. "I will only be reporting on those activities in which I have a high confidence level. Remember that most of my data only goes back about one year. In that time, however, I have uncovered a host of financial transfers from three DARPA subcontractors made through several dummy corporations to accounts that appear to belong to various individuals. One of those subcontractors worked for two different primes, so there are four prime contractors involved. As I mentioned before, I was sure that one of these individual accounts belonged to Michael Styles, the Assistant Director for Administration at DARPA. Using his connections in the State Department, Mr. Hanson has verified that the Bahaman account does indeed belong to him. There were transfers out of this account into a local Bank of America account registered to a Mr. John Mumford, AKA Jonathan Furlong."

JT smiled to himself when he noticed that Arati had put just the slightest emphasis on the acronym.

"Transfers out of the other subcontractor accounts that I reviewed went through two dummy corporation accounts and finally into two accounts in Andorra. I was not able to identify the owners of these accounts, although I am reasonably confident that there have been no recent electronic transfers made from them to any other accounts, but I could not discount any cash withdrawals being made from them."

"Could you identify who made the transfers out of the contractor or subcontractor accounts?" queried JT.

"Not individuals. But these are most often approved by the CFO, and can be effected by him or her, although the actual transfer is usually accomplished by company accounting technicians." She turned to Hanson. "Do you want me to go into the FBI data now?"

"No. Let's discuss this first. Based on the information we now have, I believe we can arrest Mike Styles for the acceptance of bribes and for the solicitation of murder. JT, I want you and Juanita to do that as soon as we have something solid on Briceman. Speaking of whom, Arati, when do you meet with him?"

"I talked to him and set up a meeting with him at my place at three o'clock on Monday."

"Okay. Do we have the goods on anyone else at this point with regards to the illegal contract activities?"

He got a chorus of head shakes.

"Then we need to subpoena the records of the four contractors and the three subcontractors and go from there. I'll ask Charles to do that. We need to take a quick look at these then I think that we should turn over this whole contract fraud mess to the FBI. By the way, what about the information you got from them, Arati?" She was not even a minute into her explanation of the FBI data when she was interrupted by Hanson's phone ringing. He looked at the caller ID, held up a finger to Arati indicating he needed a minute, and picked it up. "What's up Sal? Could you be a little more specific?" He listened intently for a few minutes, occasionally nodding or saying okay. Then, "Stay there until you are absolutely sure that he isn't in the building anymore or you find out where he is. Then call me." He put the phone down and then looked out at an expectant audience. "Seems you won't be meeting with Mr. Briceman after all, Arati. Sal and Josh believe he's on the move—gave them the proverbial slip. His car is in the garage but he's not in the building. There is nothing on his schedule for this afternoon and nobody seems to know where he is. I think we need to decide what to do about this before we continue our previous discussions. Arati, you probably know him better than the rest of us. If he's running, where is he running to?"

"He had to know that this day was coming and prepared for it with a fake passport and credit card. I suspect he has already purchased a ticket out of the country. Probably to Andorra or the Maldives, but my money would be on the former given his ethnicity."

JT smiled to himself again and wondered if she had ever used that colloquial a phrase before. She was picking up the lingo fast.

Hanson looked at JT.

"Boss, as smart as this guy is, he's got a bigger ego. I don't think he worried about an exit plan prior to Arati talking to him the other day, because he thinks he's playing this smart enough to stick around longer for a bigger take. So he's got to get out of the country without using his passport or credit card. He knows a cash airline purchase, especially overseas, will trigger an alarm with TSA. So he has to use resources like a private jet or boat."

Juanita chimed in with, "I could check on the contractors he's been dealing with to see if any of them have a corporate jet and where it's located, and more importantly, on their flight plans over the next day or so."

Hanson's phone rang and it was Sal again. "Josh just came back from talking to Lou Callas, the head of the DARPA Visitor Control Center, who said he found red hair clippings in Briceman's office. He must have shaved his goatee. Josh also questioned the guard stationed just outside the front door and the one in the plaza. The plaza guy said he saw a man in a tan trench coat and hat carrying a fair-sized bag walking up Tenth Street about ten or 10:15."

"And you guys didn't see him??"

"We wouldn't have seen a pedestrian exit the garage, sir, only a car."

"What's up Tenth Street?"

"There's a Metro stop as well as a cab stand."

"Get up there and question the cabbies there and the Metro folks, then call me." Hanson hung up the phone and was visibly upset. He took a minute to collect himself and then relayed Sal's information to the group. He concluded with, "Okay, Team. Briceman is definitely running. And he's got about a three-hour lead on us. Sounds like he's taking either the Metro or a cab—to one of the airports would be my guess. Juanita, check on those corporate jets like you suggested. Phil, Ronnie, start calling cab companies. JT, I want you to check on any possible water escape routes. Maybe one of those companies has a seagoing vessel. Damn, he could've jumped in a car with anybody leaving the building and gotten a ride out right from under our noses."

"Boss, he's a loner," offered JT. "I think he'd be doing this by himself and even if he did get a ride, it likely wouldn't be to the airport—just the Metro or cab stand. I'll put out a BOLO at the airports, just in case."

"Okay, good. *What* are we forgetting?"

"If I were at work, I could check on whether or not he closed his local bank account," suggested Arati.

"I don't think so—too obvious," said Hanson. "What else?"

"The train station. That would get him to BWI or even West Virginia for that matter. I'll put out a BOLO for him at the train station," said JT.

"I'll put out one on his wife's car, and I'll try to locate her while I'm at it," Brendon proffered and Hanson nodded.

"All right, I want everyone back here at 4:30 for an update. Phew!" Hanson exhaled. "Some days are not as good as others," he said to Arati as the team departed.

"What can I do to help?" Arati asked.

"I guess while everyone else is tracking down our suspect, we could go over what you gleaned from the chop shop data."

"As you recall," Arati began, "the monies from the shop were going to an account in the Maldives. I was able to verify the FBI data with the Tomfoolery program and further identified transfers out of this account back to one registered to Aeronautics Alectrona, the company that ultimately owns Ron's Body Shop. Monies were transferred from this account to a host of accounts, but one that I found interesting is owned by Sidiq Haq, the manager of Ron's. It seems as though he paid for many if not all of the illegal activities from this personal account. It is a non-interest-bearing account and transfers in and out were all below $5000, so it would remain off any federal or state radar screen." Arati paused to make sure Hanson was with her.

Hanson thought about this for a minute and then stated, "I guess we've come full circle here, with nothing pointing to anybody we haven't already rounded up." Arati nodded. "In other words, nothing to connect Briceman to any of this?"

Arati shook her head, "Not yet."

"What about the owners of Aeronautics Alectrona? Did anything stand out there?"

"I was hoping to use your facilities to check on them, since you have permission to access those databases."

"Of course. I guess I've been treating you as a member of the Team and making some assumptions. Perhaps we should discuss that at some point. I did look over the list of owners provided by Mr. Parsons and none of the names reached out to grab me. How about if I set you up so you check those out for us?"

"I would love to do that. Perhaps I should also mention what I found out on the Andorran accounts?"

Hanson nodded.

"As you know, a little over a year ago, several transfers were made into two accounts in Andorra. Since my database did not contain data from that far back, I could not verify the FBI information, but I have no reason to discredit it. However, whereas they were not willing to examine disbursements from those accounts, or perhaps could not, I discovered that one of those accounts was closed, but I do not know where the money went. The other account had a more recent final electronic disbursement to a separate Andorran account owned by a company called Fusion MicroElectronics, and then the remaining funds were apparently cashed out and the account closed. I can also check out that company when I do the check on Aeronautics Alectrona."

"Okay, Arati." Hanson sat back in his chair and looked like he was making every effort to collect his thoughts and calm himself. "I think it's time that we get serious about this. How about if I request that you be detailed to us for a year? Would that be okay with you? I wouldn't want it to have any detrimental effect upon you or your current position or your career, for that matter."

"Mr. Hanson, I would very much like to do that, and I do not believe that ONR would disapprove." Hanson knew that the Office of Naval Research was the parent organization of the Naval Research Lab. "In fact, I believe that a practical assignment like this would enhance my ability to determine potential avenues of research, not to mention ways to improve the program, but I do need to see the Tomfoolery effort to fruition. I could devote part-time to your organization, seventy-five to eighty percent at this point in the program, and then become full-time at some later point; I would estimate six months from now. Would that be acceptable?" she asked sheepishly.

"Yes, it would, and if you agree I'll make that happen."

Arati nodded her head enthusiastically.

"But more importantly, we need your help now with these fund transfers and with tracking down the connections between all these companies and dummy corporations and people, and lord it makes my head spin. I'd like to get you over to the National Counterterrorism Center this afternoon and get you a crash course in doing just that. That will be far easier, in my estimation, than trying to bring one of their folks up to speed on our complicated situation. Of course, you have the required top secret clearance, and, I'm sure you realized that we ran some additional checks on you when you became involved with this program."

"Yes, sir, I knew that. And I can do that. But I need to make one phone call first and clear this with the Director of Research. He may desire to speak with you."

"You make your call and I'll make mine. When we get this squared away, do you have transportation?"

"I do."

"Let's get the ball rolling."

CHAPTER THIRTY-FOUR

Fusion Team Headquarters, 2 December, 1700 hours

"Guess I'll start this off," Hanson said as people gathered in his conference room. "I heard from Josh and Sal a few minutes ago and they got zip on their canvass of the Metro and the cab stands. Nor have we gotten any hits yet on any of the BOLOs that we put out. I hope some of the rest of you have better news. I know Charles is working on those subpoenas, but where's Juanita?"

"She was on the phone, Boss, and said she'd be here in a few," responded JT.

"So what do *you* have for me?"

"I put BOLOs out at the airports and the train station, and even managed to get a decent picture of Briceman faxed to them, albeit with a goatee and in a sport coat and tie. Marine-wise, there's nothing commercial leaving the entire northeast for the next three days, except for one cruise liner out of New York to the Western Caribbean leaving tomorrow. They checked their passenger list for me and I faxed them the picture, as well. There are, however, a number of ships leaving Florida tomorrow. I'll get the info out to them shortly." JT finished with a shoulder shrug indicating that he was sorry he couldn't be more encouraging.

"I got a hold of his wife at work," offered Brendon, "who said he called earlier today and told her he had one of those 'dinner meetings with the Director' this evening and wouldn't be home until late. She had her car with her at work and I admit I had a hard time explaining to her why I wanted to know that."

"Ronnie, what were you looking into again?"

"Phil and I called all the cab companies that operate over near DARPA and they had no pickups from DARPA itself, and the only two within a ten-block radius were both for women. That doesn't mean he didn't get a ride with some independent, but most of them operate up near the Ballston metro stop where Josh and Sal were checking."

Juanita came charging into the room at this point with her hair flying and her eyes twinkling.

JT thought, *Damn, she looks good when she's excited.*

"Boss, we may have something here. A company called Pangborn Total Solutions Group, the parent company of Avique, one of the DARPA contractors that we suspect of illegal activities, has a corporate jet they fly out of BWI, which is just outside their headquarters in Baltimore." She took a breath. "I got a whole lot of flak from them, so I finally called the FAA at BWI and found out that their jet filed a flight plan from BWI to Atlanta taking off at three o'clock."

Juanita was talking a mile a minute but Hanson managed to interrupt. "And their landing time is?"

"The flight plan listed it at 4:20, but they have no record of them landing in Atlanta. When I called, they would have been twenty minutes late. I called airport operations and told them I was law enforcement, but they said they would call me if and when the plane landed."

"Unbelievable!" Hanson exclaimed.

"I got a buddy at the FAA," said Phil as he reached for a phone. After a few minutes he said, "Gonzo, ole Buddy, I need a favor. Yeah, I know. The whereabouts of a plane that filed a flight plan out of BWI for Atlanta supposedly landing at 4:20. Hold on. Juanita, type plane, tail number, whatta ya got?"

"A Lear Jet 31 belonging to Pangborn Total Solutions Group, hangared at BWI. I was kinda in a hurry," she muttered defensively.

Phil smiled and repeated the information to his buddy. He put the phone down and enabled the speaker function.

Just short of seven minutes later, they heard, "Okay, Fill-ups, here's the story. They filed a revised flight plan en route with a new destination of Tamiami. Landed at 1633, dropped off a passenger, taxied right back out and headed home to BWI with an ETA of 1900. Anything else I can do you for?"

"Gonzo, I owe ya. I'll get back to you later. Thanks."

"Good work, Phil, I mean, Fill-ups," Hanson said with a smile on his face.

"It's a long story, Boss."

Hanson looked at the clock hanging on the wall of the conference room. "I'd say our boy has a good thirty or forty minutes on us and is out of the airport by now. Probably headed up to Miami to catch an international flight or, I don't know, maybe a cigar boat to Cuba."

No one was sure if he was making a pun or just confused, and didn't want to ask.

"JT, get a hold of some of your TSA buddies and see if they saw anything or can get a track on him at all. Put a BOLO out with Miami-Dade and get his picture down there. I doubt if he'll rent a car so he'll probably take a cab. See if you can get the locals interested enough to canvass the place. I'll call the local FBI agent and see what he can do for us. And soon as you're done with that, I want you and Juanita on a flight to Miami to see if you can catch up with our guy. Good work, by the way, Juanita. While JT's on the phone, can you call Arati over at NCTC and see how she's doing? Just give her a little encouragement and the ole team spirit thing. She's going to be a valuable resource and I don't want her feeling isolated from us. I've got her number at my desk."

"No problem, Cap'n. I was going to do that anyway."

"Good. Phil, I want you and Ronnie to arrest Mike Styles. If he's not in his office at the Pentagon, then hook him wherever he's at. I know you two wanted to do that," he said as he looked at JT and Juanita, "but you guys have the best chance of recognizing Briceman, so I need you on that."

"Okay, Boss," replied Juanita. "I'll check out the flights now."

Both JT and Juanita had overnight bags at the office, so they were both good to go. Luckily, there was a late flight out of Reagan direct to Miami International leaving at 8:10, and they were only fifteen minutes for the airport. JT phoned Carmen before he left the office to let her know he'd be gone for a while and to talk to Andy for a few minutes. They got out of the office at 6:30.

291

Hanson was still at his desk an hour-and-a-half later trying to coordinate everything. He thought twice about calling the Miami office of the FBI since, just before he and Juanita left for Quantico, JT mentioned that the FAM guys had Miami International covered. The Tamiami folks remembered a passenger deplaning earlier from the Lear jet but had no further information on him. A canvas of the cabs and rental companies yielded a number of pickups and rentals, but none of the passengers or renters looked like the picture of Briceman that they were shown. Further, none of the cabs went to Miami International and all the rental cars were paid for with credit cards. There were only two flights scheduled out of Tamiami that evening, one to Dallas and one to Pensacola: seemingly unlikely destinations for someone trying to escape the U.S. Hanson wondered if Briceman had changed his appearance even more, or worse, *did* have a fake passport or other ID. He figured he'd head home and take care of anything that came up the rest of the evening from there.

Cabin John, Maryland, 2 December, 2005 hours

It was late enough that Ronnie, who was driving, figured the traffic wouldn't be that bad on the Beltway. She had just crossed over the American Legion Bridge into Maryland when Phil asked, "Have you lived in this area long?"

"Pretty much all my life. Why?"

"I was wondering if you knew what they did at the Naval Surface Warfare Center back there in Carderock."

"You're the one in the Navy. You tell me."

"It's a big organization, and I never did learn much about the research side of it. I thought maybe since you lived here awhile..."

"Criminee sakes, Phil. There are so many government organizations and military installations around here that no one can keep track of them. And they're changing all the time. I have a hard time remembering that we just passed over the American

Legion Bridge because when I was growing up it was the Cabin John Bridge."

"It must be neat staying in one place long enough to see it change and grow with it. My dad was in the Navy and we moved around a lot. Hell, I've been on a ship for three years and been stationed at five different places in the states. I think I might settle down here, though. The wife likes it, and both my kids are in high school and looking at local colleges."

"You got your twenty in, right?"

"Oh yeah—twenty-two, actually. And getting a job here apparently wouldn't be a problem, what with my background and all. My mom and dad are down in Norfolk, and Nancy's folks are in Rehoboth. My brother and Nancy's sister are both in Baltimore, believe it or not. Guess we've pretty much decided now is the time and the place."

"You tell the boss yet?"

"We talked about it. My assignment here is up in a few months and he may be able to get me a permanent position."

"That sounds too settled for me, but then I don't have a family to worry about. I like getting different jobs every couple of years, but I wouldn't want to move around like you did. Guess I'm lucky that you can do that here. So, have you met this Styles guy? Sounds like a real pistol," Ronnie commented as she steered left onto Interstate 270.

"No. And asshole is more like it if you believe half of what JT and Juanita have said about him. We gotta remember everything about this 'cause they're gonna want to hear it. You know, I've got no idea where his place is. Are we close yet?"

"We take this Democracy Boulevard exit and then it's another three miles or so. Does the boss really think he can get you a permanent slot? I mean, we're all detailed, except for him and JT and the other team leaders, and I thought that was the idea."

"He told me that if this whole Fusion Team idea works out that DHS may authorize up to three or four permanent positions per team. Having different folks come and go does lend varying expertise to the task, but he thinks you need a little more stability than just a permanent team leader. Wow, this is really the high-rent district up here, isn't it? I'll bet some of these folks pay more to run all their outdoor lighting than I do for my whole electric bill." Phil continued to marvel at the size of the houses for the next few minutes.

Ronnie took a left on Iron Gate Road and passed three estates before seeing the address she was looking for. "I Googled this place and it's got a tennis court and a swimming pool out back. I'll bet it's two acres and the house is five-thousand square feet," she estimated as she pulled into the huge circular driveway. "I'm surprised it's not a gated community. Good thing I didn't ride my Harley up here. I'd probably get shot." A two-foot-high brick wall lined the driveway and an array of flowers, shrubs and small trees adorned the area between the wall and the street. The doors to the attached three-car garage were located on the side and not visible from the front. Ronnie had checked with his office at the Pentagon and they indicated that he had left for home at 6:30. They hoped he had come straight home and not yet decided where to go out for the evening, if anywhere. The house itself was a huge, two-story, rectangular-shaped place and had a well-lit alcove that served as the front entrance way. The brown and white flagstone finish complemented what appeared to be functional brown shutters. Two good-sized balconies wrapped around the front and side at either end of the house, probably outside two corner master bedroom suites, Ronnie surmised. She entered the alcove, rang the bell and stood back.

"What do you two want?" came a gruff voice over a speaker located just beside the door but concealed by some lattice work with ivy growing through it. It was obvious from his remark that there was a hidden camera there, as well. "My name is Ronnie Hamilton and this is Phil Ellis. We're agents with DHS and we need to talk with Michael Styles."

"You can talk to my lawyer. Call me at the office and I'll give you his number."

"That's not the way it works, sir. You talk to us here and now or we go to our office in Arlington and talk forty-five minutes from now."

"Where's your warrant and what's this about?"

"We don't need a warrant to question you, sir. We have a few more questions regarding one of Dr. Quarles' contracts. Can we come in and get this over with, please? It's late and I'd like to get home sometime tonight."

"All right, damn it. Come in," he said as he buzzed the door open. The entranceway contained a fountain and a small pool full of water plants and koi, and the floor and walls were tiled. The room was actually not that big, but then this was just the entranceway. The doorway led to another large room that was probably the living room. In there were two settees with a large glass top table between them covered with potted plants. Styles motioned for them to have a seat and said, "Make this quick. We have plans for this evening."

Without sitting down, Ronnie said, "I promise this won't take even five minutes. Michael Styles you are under arrest for the solicitation and acceptance of a bribe and…"

"Holy shit! You guys are fucking crazy!" he interrupted. "You can't prove a single thing and I ain't saying a word until I get my lawyer." His outburst had apparently attracted his wife's attention, as she appeared in the doorway leading to another room.

"If I may finish," Ronnie continued, "and for two counts of solicitation of murder. You have the right…." Ronnie finished reading him his rights but doubted that he heard much of it, his whole demeanor now indicating disbelief.

His wife just stood there and shook her head until Phil turned to her and said, "Can you get a coat for him as we're taking him to our detention facility." He handed her a card. "This is where he'll be and where you can tell his lawyer to catch up with him. From what I understand, it's doubtful that he'll make bail, but then that's not my call."

Styles finally came out of his stupor by the time his wife had retrieved his coat. "Lizzy, do something. Don't let them take me. I didn't do anything. Call that lawyer of yours." He put his coat on and Phil cuffed him.

"You might want to take one last look around," Phil added for good measure as he headed him out the door.

His wife never said a word and was still shaking her head.

295

CHAPTER THIRTY-FIVE

Miami International Airport, Florida, 2 December, 2250 hours

The plane landed right on schedule and they were met by two land-based FAMs stationed at Miami International named Drew Paulson and Ron Kratowicz. After introductions, Paulson asked if they had talked to their home office lately. JT said he'd talked to Hanson about eight o'clock while he and Juanita were in the air, and that he had passed on what information he'd gotten so far from the local DHS and Miami-Dade folks.

"Sure glad I brought my coat. What is it, seventy degrees here?" Juanita asked.

"No, ma'am. It's actually only sixty-seven," replied Paulson cracking a smile. "We got you two rooms in the Wyndham here at the airport but thought you might want to come by the operations center first."

"Yes, that would be great."

The two agents led them in and out of several corridors and then up two floors to the mezzanine level of the hotel where their office was located. "When we're done at the center, you can just go upstairs to your rooms or downstairs to the garage. We also got you a car," Kratowicz said as he handed JT the keys. "It's a plain wrapper company car parked in the first garage level in space 1C4. Tag number is on the key chain there. Let's see if we have anything else for you." As they entered the center, the receptionist stationed out front said she had a message from a Miami-Dade officer that she handed to Paulson.

"Well, this may be something. Cabbie that they interviewed said he made a pick-up at Tamiami fitting your general description and the guy asked to be dropped off at the entranceway to the Turnpike. Said the guy gave him an extra twenty to keep it quiet. That was at 5:15."

"And where would that take him?" asked Juanita.

"Well, north is Miami and pretty much the rest of Florida and the whole east coast for that matter; south is the Keys."

"If you were trying to get out of Dodge. what would you do?"

Paulson thought for a minute before answering. "I'd catch a tour boat over to Nassau and then a flight to England. He'd need a fake ID and passport though, since if we put out a BOLO for him with their airport, they'd let us know if he used his real passport; however, I've heard they are easier to come by over there."

Kratowicz chimed in with, "He could try to catch a boat ride down to Cuba, which is not too hard. Getting out of there without some good solid contacts could be dicey, though."

"Okay, Drew, could you put out a BOLO for him with the Nassau airport, and then check with the Port Authority and see what sort of ships are scheduled out of here for the next twenty-four hours?"

"Will do. What's your and Juanita's cell phone numbers?"

Juanita gave them their business cards and he headed out.

"And Ron, I don't guess there's any way you could check if he was catching a ride to Cuba as you suggested."

"No, sir, not practically."

"Okay. Could you show me how to review all the input you've got from the airport cameras from, say 5:30? And then maybe you and Juanita could canvass the ticket agents again."

"The place is shutting down, so we probably better hurry." Kratowicz gave JT a quick tutorial on the video system and then he and Juanita headed back down to the airport.

JT was still reviewing the data when they came back an hour-and-a-half later. "I've looked at these twice and I didn't see our guy, but Nita, why don't you give it a shot for awhile. I concentrated on the international ticket counters, but I did look at all of them. Did you get anything from the troops downstairs?"

"No," responded Juanita. "We talked to everybody still on duty and showed them Briceman's picture. There's nothing else out of here until morning now, so hopefully our guy didn't get out of here today. Do these cover all the airlines?" she asked Kratowicz.

He said they did and then showed her how to work the video equipment while JT made some notes.

She was about ten minutes into reviewing the evening's activities when Paulson came back with his findings. "Luckily there was nothing out of the Port after 3:30 today. There is, however, a good deal of traffic starting at 5:30 tomorrow morning—a couple of container ships leaving at that time, four tours over to the islands leaving between eight and 9:30, then two Caribbean cruises and two more trips to the islands shipping out in the afternoon. Of course, lots of stuff not scheduled could be heading out, as well, but that would be mostly fishing boats, private and commercial, and any amount of pleasure boats. Those would most likely be out and backs though."

"Thanks. While Juanita finishes reviewing the video I'll call the boss before it gets too late. Then I'd like to lay out a plan for tomorrow. Will you guys be here and can you get some more help?"

"We're at your disposal and I can have another five or six agents here if you'd like."

JT gave him a thumbs up and then picked up the phone.

They were up and at 'em early and finished their breakfast in the hotel restaurant by 5:30. They met Paulson and Kratowicz and the five agents they had rounded up at the main entrance to the airport a few minutes later. JT had donned a fake mustache and beard, Horatio Caine sunglasses, and a Dolphins' ball cap; Juanita had pulled her hair back in a bun and also had sunglasses and a ball cap.

"Ladies and Gentlemen, these are agents Dunkirk and Singletary from Headquarters," Paulson said as he introduced JT and Juanita. "We're here to give them as much help as we can. JT, it's all yours."

"We have reason to believe that Doctor Richard Briceman, a scientist employed at DARPA, is trying to leave the country from here. He is wanted for solicitation of murder, association with terrorists, and contract fraud. One of the victims was developing an anti-terrorist software program that Briceman was apparently trying to sabotage." JT gave them all a photograph of

Briceman, explained the appearance changes that he was aware of, and described his general physical characteristics. "I'd like you all to be on the lookout for him down here on the floor while Juanita monitors the video surveillance from back in the office. If you get a good feel for someone, call and let her know where you are. Our cell phone numbers as well as the office number here are on the back of your picture. Do not try to apprehend anyone without my or Juanita's okay. I know you'll be as unobtrusive as you can be, as we don't want to spook him if he is here. We'll likely be here most of the day, unless we're lucky, so plan on eating here while you are observing. When the last flights are out of here this evening, we'll reconnoiter and plan tomorrow's agenda. Any questions?" There were none and the troops spread out in the airport. He turned to Paulson and asked about the container ships that left that morning.

"The Port Authority checked the manifests of both ships, and verified that every person was a valid crew member and there were no paying passengers, and, further, that none of the crew resembled the picture of Briceman. Do you want to head over there now and check out the Port in general and the island tours in particular?"

"Yeah, let's do it."

Port of Miami, Florida, 3 December, 0650 hours

Twelve minutes and four miles later, they were at the Port of Miami. Touted as one of the more modern port facilities in existence, it had, among the many special design features and amenities of Passenger Terminals D and E, a VIP lounge, a high-tech security screening facility for embarkation, airline counters and an airport-style conveyor baggage system. Additionally, each featured a one-stop federal multi-agency facility for passenger processing. It seemed unlikely that Briceman could have gotten through here without being noticed, since upon entering you are subject to a search of your person, vehicle, and any container in your possession. And a government issued photo identification is required at all times. On the other hand, something or someone could be missed in a place where four million passengers and over eight million tons and a million twenty-foot equivalent units of cargo transited each year. The Port of Miami advertised that they served more than twenty shipping lines that call on more than 250 ports in 100 countries across the world. Paulson took JT to the SOC, or the security operations center of the Port, and introduced him to the supervisor in charge. They had been advised of the need for increased surveillance and had also rounded up an extra five agents to help out, in addition to the two that were normally stationed there. JT gave them the same pep talk he had given the airport guys and they seemed just as enthusiastic. Like Juanita, JT decided to monitor the video cameras and have the agents call him if they saw anything.

"Can I get you something to drink, Agent Dunkirk?" Supervisor Franks offered. Franks had a rather senior position for his age, thirty-two, and had a lot on the ball. He stood six-foot even and kept his weight down by daily exercise and a healthy diet. He had wavy brown hair and a chiseled face that gave him a John Wayne look.

"Please call me JT, and it's Tom, right?" Franks nodded. "Yes, if you wouldn't mind, I'd love some nice strong coffee. It was a short night."

"We've got a small coffee bar right here in the center if you'd like to fix it yourself."

"Great. Do you get much action down here?" JT asked as he walked over to the bar.

"You know, all the usual stuff—drunk passengers and sailors, a few weapons, and an occasional shipment of drugs. We did have a large cache of money come through here a few months ago—part of a drug payment. And about a year ago we intercepted a couple of pounds of C-4."

"Bet that had your bomb appraisal unit on their toes."

"Yeah. Never seen those guys so excited. The Coast Guard gets a lot more action than we do—they're checking on the private boats all the time." He showed JT how to switch between cameras and access the playback feature. "I'll be in the next room most of the day, kind of in and out, you know. If you need someone to spell you, just give one of these guys a holler," he said pointing to the two agents nearby.

"Right, thanks." JT settled in for what he hoped was not a long day, but knew it was likely to be exactly that. He gave Juanita a buzz. "I'm all set up over here. You doing okay?"

"Everything is just peachy keen, partner. What time are you gonna call in today?"

"I guess after all the tours get off at nine o'clock or so. How about if I give you a call then?"

"Okay. Stay awake."

JT did a radio check with the agents on the floor and got them to identify where they were so he could locate them on the cameras. After a while, he got fairly good at manipulating the cameras and identifying the agents. He really didn't want to bother the two agents manning the cameras, so he shot the breeze with Tom Franks every time he came back and discussed the details of the case with him.

"I think Paulson has it right," Franks commented. "It would be easy to hop on one of those daily cruises—they don't manifest them, and they see so many IDs and passengers that they couldn't identify anyone if their life depended on it. If your guy has a fake ID, he could get a flight out to London and we'd be none the wiser."

"That's what we're afraid of and why we need to get him before he gets over there. That is if it's not too late already."

JT's recent late hours were catching up with him and he almost nodded off a couple of times. He called Juanita but she said the airport was so busy that she really didn't really have time to talk. So he got up and stretched, fixed himself more coffee, and went to the head a lot. He called home and checked on Andy and Carmen and apologized for waking them up early on a Saturday morning. Between eight and 9:30, he was fairly busy helping to check out the passengers on the four ships leaving on day cruises to the Bahamas. There were two false alarms called in by the agents on the floor: both times the guy did fit the general description and could indeed have been Briceman, but it turned out otherwise. At 10:30, he called the boss and let him know what was going on. Hanson let him know that they had Styles in custody in Fullerton and that as of yet no lawyer had shown up inquiring about him. JT got a kick out of his wife's reaction and laughed when Hanson told him it took Styles almost ten hours before he figured out no one was coming and called his wife and then phoned for his own lawyer. After JT hung up, he remembered reading Styles' wife's resume and then seeing her picture on Styles' desk in the Pentagon and wondering how such a smart, good-looking woman could have gotten mixed up with such a loser. JT figured Styles was probably capable of being a charmer long enough to convince her there was something there. He could just picture her standing there shaking her head with a disgusted look on her face. Franks and two of his agents came in and jogged him out of his reverie.

"Probably won't be much action around here until after 12:30 when the passengers for the Caribbean cruises start showing up. It's after eleven—you want to catch an early lunch?"

"Great idea. Let me check in with Juanita real quick." He did and she had no news but did say she was still quite busy. "Got anyplace good but quick?" he asked Franks.

"As a matter of fact, I'll show you this taco place that's close, cheap and has great food."

"Who could ask for more?" They walked out of the SOC with the two agents that were manning the monitors who had swapped places with the two just in off the floor. Within ten minutes, they were at the little taco place that Franks had mentioned. Franks asked for a quick description of working at the headquarters level, which JT tried to make sound at least somewhat exciting. When he found out JT used to be a Federal Air Marshall, he was really interested and wanted to know all about it. Franks was obviously interested in doing something more interesting than the Port job. "If you like to fly, it's the place to be," commented JT, and mentioned some of the many overseas flights he'd been on. "The training is tough but fun, and the first couple of years I really enjoyed it. But advancement opportunities are rather slim and will be until the raft of upper level guys recruited from the Secret Service and other organizations retire. At least they did learn a few things and it's easier being an agent now than it used to be. The FLEOA actually got a lot of the nutty procedures changed—just about the time I left naturally."

"The 'flee-o-a'? What is that?" Franks asked.

"Stands for the Federal Law Enforcement Officers Association."

"Oh, yeah. I heard of them before but never checked them out. Sounds like a good group." He asked a few more questions then they finished up.

"It's still going to be slow for awhile so how about a short walking tour?" Happy to be moving about, JT readily agreed and they headed down the main corridor connecting the several terminals. He had removed the sunglasses to eat lunch, and wished he could remove the fake beard because it itched. As they passed by another small eating establishment, JT thought he noticed, at the outer periphery of his vision, an individual turn quickly away. The area was cordoned off by metal poles with wide nylon straps running between them at the top and midpoint to give the impression of an enclosed eating area. The guy was sitting at the inner row of tables such that he was away from the corridor but could still see people walking along it. But now his face was turned inward—away from the corridor—like he was avoiding eye contact. JT put his arm up to stop Franks and asked him to pretend like he was getting something out of his pocket to give him. Franks caught on quickly as JT slowly maneuvered the two of them so that Franks had his back to the subject and JT was looking just past Franks' shoulder. The guy cast another furtive glance in their direction.

"I'm going to approach this guy from the front. Let's shake hands like we're saying goodbye and then you continue on and position yourself on the other side of those poles. If he runs toward you then stop him. Are you carrying?"

"No. I left it in the office."

"Well I am, so if he doesn't draw down on me then tackle him or trip him if you have to." They shook hands and said their pretended farewells and Franks continued on down the corridor. JT looked around like he was trying to decide on where to eat and opted for the place right in front of him. He then entered the cordoned off area but bypassed the food counter and headed directly for the suspicious character. He removed his ball cap. The guy was looking down like he was paying attention to his

303

food until JT was only about a foot away. At that point, the guy looked up and JT saw the glint of recognition in his eyes. "Doctor Briceman, I presume."

The guy jammed the table into JT's mid-thigh nearly causing him to lose his balance. The suspect stood up quickly with his small flight bag in hand, causing his chair to fall over backwards. He turned abruptly and headed away from JT. On the fly, he put his foot on the top strap of the barrier and pushed it to the floor as he hurdled over the fence. The poles attached to either side came crashing down and were followed by several of the poles connected to them in a cascading effect that rang throughout the whole place. He took two steps past the downed fence and almost ran into Franks, who was standing there with his feet positioned in a brace, his left hand held out in front of him and his right hand on his hip like he was ready to draw a weapon.

"Port Authority Police! Stop right there and put your hands in the air."

JT walked up to them with his weapon drawn just in case the guy was armed.

"Drop the bag and put your hands up," Franks ordered.

Briceman knew he was caught and complied with the order.

"I've got him covered. Put these cuffs on him," JT said as he threw Franks his manacles.

As Franks reached for his arm, the suspect grabbed Franks' arm instead and flung him around behind him and right into JT's line of fire and almost into JT. He then grabbed the bag and took off like a bat out of hell—surprising JT with his agility.

JT looked around and saw a stack of magazines in the newsstand ten feet away from where they were. Taking careful and deliberate aim and making sure everyone knew what he was about to happen he fired into the stack. "The next round goes into your right thigh Briceman," shouted JT.

Briceman stopped running and put his hands on the back of his head.

"Put 'em up higher—all the way up."

Once again, Briceman complied. Franks had picked himself up and recovered the cuffs. They walked over to the suspect and this time Franks got the cuffs on him and picked up the flight bag.

"Tom, you okay?" JT asked.

"Fine," he replied, "just fine. Don't you love it when they rabbit?"

"I do indeed. Let's see what kind of ID he has on him." JT searched and found a wallet in one inner coat pocket, and a passport in the other. "Well, if it isn't the one and only Doctor Richard Alan Briceman. You look a little different than your passport picture. Doing a makeover? Doctor Briceman, you have the right to remain silent...."

Franks had radioed for help earlier as soon as he was out of the suspect's sight, and by this time, two of his agents had arrived. The first agent looked down at the large wet mark all over the front of JT's pants from the coffee that went flying off the table that Briceman had shoved into him. "Were you a little nervous, agent?" he asked.

JT, who hadn't noticed this, looked at himself and laughed. "I've simply gotta quit drinking so much before a bust."

The guys all laughed and Franks directed the agents to disperse the crowd and make amends with the restaurant and newsstand operators.

With Briceman in tow, they headed back toward the SOC where JT had left a few things. On the way, he called Juanita and gave her the good news and said he'd meet her back at the hotel in about an hour. "Can you call the boss with an update?" he asked her.

She agreed and then congratulated him.

As he looked at Franks, he asked, "Do you have a detention facility here?"

"We have *excellent* accommodations for our guests. Would you like me to get you three on the first thing back to D.C?" He looked at JT's clothes and then amended his last statement. "Say, one leaving in about two hours?"

"Actually, I'm thinking more like tomorrow morning. I'll talk to Juanita, but I think we could use a little winding down. I'll get our troops to handle the flight."

Franks turned to his two agents that had returned to the SOC when they heard the search was over and said, "Please escort the good doctor to his room. Do you have any baggage you want taken back?" he asked Briceman.

"Just the bag that you picked up from the restaurant back there," he replied.

"You mean this one with all the cash in it?" Franks asked as he picked the bag up and waived it in the air. As the two agents led Briceman out of the room, Franks turned to JT. "That's the most excitement I've had in over two years. I'm sorry about your clothes, though."

"I shouldn't have gotten so close, but I wanted to see the whites of his eyes.
He knew it was me and that I recognized him from the look he gave me. That's why he bolted. Thanks for all your help. I'll see that there's a letter from the Assistant Secretary put in your file."

"That's not necessary," Franks offered.

"I know that. That's why I'm gonna do it. Will you get any blowback about the discharged weapon?"

"Nothing I can't handle from this end. By the way, think you could omit the part about my leaving my piece in the office?"

"I distinctly remember you with your hand resting on it when you stopped the suspect," JT said smiling. "But seriously, why didn't you?"

"I usually use a shoulder holster but I've got a rash under my arm right now that it irritates. And I don't like carrying it on the hip. So...."

JT laughed. "Think I could get a ride back to the hotel? I thought I might take advantage of it for one more night."

Franks nodded.

On the way back, JT asked, "Would you be available to join us for dinner tonight? Then I could give you our flight info and let you know when we'll need the prisoner."

"Be glad to. Just give me a call."

"Thought I'd ask the two FAMs to join us as well."

Bud Durand

"Sounds like a plan."

CHAPTER THIRTY-SIX

So they have the brilliant Doctor Briceman in custody. I'll bet the greedy little bastard got rid of Quarles because he figured out what he was doing. Quarles was irritating, that's a fact, but at least he was an honest man, unlike a good bunch of the rest of us. I almost hated to see him go. By the way, thank you Rick, you saved us the trouble, but now I'm sure you'll spill how the program can be manipulated, so your usefulness has come to an end. Looks like they have him in Arlington County—that shouldn't be too hard. We'll have to pick someone expendable though, just in case. And time is of the essence.

Clarendon, Virginia, 5 December, 0915 hours

JT and Juanita arrived at the Arlington County Detention Center located on Courthouse Road right at 9:15, more than early enough for their first interview with Briceman and his lawyer at 9:30. The white concrete building stood twelve stories above the street in the Clarendon section of the county and also housed the sheriff's office, the courthouse and other county facilities. Although accused of a federal crime, there was not a nearby federal facility available, so Arlington graciously agreed to hold the prisoner until arraignment, which would be in federal court. As JT and Juanita showed their creds to the guard, they asked for directions to Interview Room 2. He handed them a floor plan of the tenth floor of the building, circled the interview room, and then called the guard at that station to let her know that they were coming up. After going through security and checking their weapons, they entered the room and saw the two occupants look up expectantly.

JT recognized Briceman's lawyer, Dennis Byerly, who he knew by reputation: he had won over ninety-two percent of the cases that he had actually taken to court and the others resulted in plea bargains that were generally a good deal for his clients under the circumstances. He looked like the quintessential high-priced attorney with his pin-striped suit, A. Testoni shoes, power tie and Rolex watch. Although he was mild mannered out of court, and reminded JT of Jerry, the lawyer with Asperger syndrome on the old *Boston Legal* TV show, JT still felt just a bit antsy, as he had seen this guy in court and knew he was worth every penny he charged. *But then we have righteousness on our side,* JT thought. "Good morning, Dr. Briceman. How nice to see you again," JT began. I'm sure you remember Agent Singletary. And who is this?" he asked as he looked at Briceman's lawyer.

"Dennis Byerly, representing Dr. Briceman. When can we expect him to be arraigned?"

"I just thought we'd chat a little bit first and see where that goes."

"We've got nothing to say until we get to court, where we'll plead not guilty. If the judge thinks you have enough for a trial then we'll ask for my client to be freed on his own recognizance and see you in court."

"Well, that's rather unlikely, given that he was on the run when we caught him. Nonetheless, let me tell you where you stand, as we certainly owe you that."

Both Byerly and Briceman raised their eyebrows, as they did not expect this tactic.

"You know, Dr. Briceman, we brought you in here because we have fairly conclusive evidence that you were involved with contract kickbacks. And, of course, you were apparently trying to leave the country as you had changed your appearance and were in the Port of Miami. While the latter is relatively minor and not necessarily a crime, the former can carry a hefty fine and jail sentence. You've no doubt 'confided' in your lawyer and told him what you've done and not done, explained away the evidence against you, and given him your reason for fleeing. If you were truthful, then he may be able to set up a reasonable defense. What you probably forgot to mention to him, however, is that we have Doctor Jabornae working on uncovering more evidence against you. We were thinking that you might want to come clean now while you still have some room to negotiate."

"We believe that all your evidence is circumstantial at best, and we'll take our chances in a court of law," said Byerly.

"We've talked to the Justice prosecutor and he is ready to deal if there is some cooperation here."

"If you want to offer a deal, we'll look at your proposal, but I must tell you we are disinclined to accept anything that results in actual jail time."

JT smiled to himself at this tacit admission of guilt.

"Now, when can I expect my client to be arraigned?"

"We need to talk to Justice again, and to our boss. We'll get back to you before what, 12:30 tomorrow?" he asked looking at Juanita.

She nodded.

"You sure you don't want to take one last shot at cooperation before we find anything else out?"

"I think we're done here, Agent. We'll see you tomorrow."

JT and Juanita walked out, leaving Briceman to confer with his counsel.

"That didn't really go anywhere," commented Juanita as they rode down in the elevator.

"No, but it was worth a shot. Besides, I wanted to get a feel for him and his lawyer before we confer with the boss and the prosecutor. So I guess it's back to the shop now, huh, *compañera*?"

"Guess so."

Tysons Corner, Virginia, 5 December, 1540 hours

Hanson decided that he would visit Arati at the National Counterterrorism Center rather than have her come back to Fusion Team Headquarters. He hadn't been to Liberty Crossing since before the DNI moved there. While most intelligence agency locations are purposely rather drab on the exterior, the anti-terror center had adopted a "spy agency" look: it was a sleek, six-story, modern white building, although the external windows were bullet- and blast-proof, cast to standards set after the Oklahoma City bombing. Collocated in the center on Tysons McLean Drive, along with the Director of National Intelligence, were the CIA and FBI Watch Centers, DoD's Joint Intelligence Task Force-Counterterrorism and the NCTC. This was probably one of the better ideas that the intelligence community had come up with in years. Arati was located on the fourth floor near the rear of the building and indicated on the phone that she could not wait to tell him what information she had learned in her short time there. He called from the lobby and asked if he could bring up a soda from the canteen. She said that a tea would be nice, so he got one for her and a coffee for himself. Since each office is essentially a vault with a coded lock to get in, she met him in the corridor outside her office.

"So, did you hear that we have Briceman in custody?" he asked after she ushered him in and he handed her the tea.

"Yes, I did. Juanita called me from Miami and described what happened. I think she was concerned that I might be apprehensive about him."

"That is a consideration with these criminal types. So tell me, Arati, how are you getting along with everybody over here?" he asked, changing the subject.

"They have been very nice and very helpful. I told them what I was looking for and they showed me how to bring up the information from several different databases, correlate it and even draw some conclusions via a sophisticated application they have for just that purpose. I have been very impressed with the capabilities here and am looking forward to learning more about them. Pull up a chair so you have a good view and let me show you what I have uncovered."

Hanson pulled up close to her screen and got as comfortable as he could.

"You asked me to develop a list of contractor suspects that have been or may still be offering bribes to DARPA and CIFA officials. By looking at the financial transactions between the agencies and the contractors and correlating those with contract amounts, billing requests, transfers to individual accounts, and some other data points, I can say with a ninety percent confidence level that this group of companies has been involved with rendering bribes to government officials, whether solicited or otherwise." She displayed a list of seven companies with twelve transfer amounts and dates. "Further, I have identified the individuals in five of those companies that were responsible for the transfers. I am working on the remaining two, but they are well-disguised and may not lend themselves to discovery." Five individual names appeared on the screen beside eight of the individual transactions.

"Arati, that's marvelous. I admit that that this will keep us busy for a while, but I'm a little disappointed that I don't see Briceman's name there." He sensed that Arati was saving the best for last as she beamed and moved back to the keyboard.

"That is true. But look at this. When I added the transfers in and out of Styles' accounts, which as you know were made just after both incidents, I noticed that they correlated with transfers made by this individual."

Hanson looked at what Arati had displayed on her screen. "Arthur Heilig, the CFO of Avique. What sort of research do they do?"

"Information technology: that is the DARPA contractor working on the Coltrane contract and I am sure anticipating an award from the Tomfoolery program. I understand that they did some earlier work for CIFA as well."

"So let me get this straight—he authorized the transfers that went out of his company and into the Styles account that then went to Furlong? Are you quite sure about this?"

"Well, sir, I am sure about the timing. In both instances, the transfers were made from his company to one of those dummy corporations. Then within forty minutes, he made a phone call to Briceman, and very shortly after that the same amount was transferred from the dummy corporation account, through Styles' account, and minutes later to the Mumford account. That much I can say with some confidence."

"So is that all you have for me, Arati?"

Arati was crestfallen. "Well, sir, I have only been at this for a couple of days and...." Then she noticed the smile on Hanson's face and said, "Oh, you are teasing me."

"Yes, I am. I don't think we could get a warrant based on that, but it does give us something to look into further. You actually learned how to trace phone calls already?"

"That is one of the easier procedures."

Hanson nodded his head approvingly. "By the way, I've talked to all the right folks and the detail is yours if you still want it."

"I do. I feel like I am contributing more directly to my country here than I was as a researcher. Not that that was not important, but this is at least as important and certainly more exciting. Besides, I believe that the director wanted to hire another researcher in order to pursue what he thinks is a more fruitful avenue of research, and he can now do that."

"All right, then. You actually started working for us today. Can you bring up the information on Mr. Heilig for me? Also, can you come into the office about ten o'clock tomorrow and we'll get some details worked out and maybe a tentative schedule, at least until you've gotten all your training and things smooth out a little bit?"

"You bet, Boss," she said with a smile from ear to ear, as she handed him a printout on Heilig.

Hanson enjoyed the way she said that and couldn't help but smile in return. With that done, he decided that it was too late in the day to go back to the office, but he probably should at least call in. He got a hold of JT and told him what Arati had discovered.

"Boss, there's something about that name that rings a bell—hang on a second."

Hanson raised his eyebrows and started twiddling his thumbs, much to Arati's amusement. She knew it was JT on the phone and thought he might be telling another one of his jokes. Hanson was thinking that his chance to miss some of the rush hour was fast dwindling away.

When JT finally got back on the line a couple of minutes later, he was rather excited: "Holy shit Cap'n! Furlong's first victim was Heilig's mother-in-law! That, sir, is no coincidence."

"Arthur Heilig? Spell it. You got an address?"

JT found the address in the file and read it off to Hanson.

"That's the guy. I think we need to give his place the once over. I'll call Krolick and tell him we have a request for a warrant

313

for this guy's house, car and office coming. Who's up on the board?" he asked.

JT put the phone on hold and went over to Hanson's office. He checked the board and then picked up Hanson's phone and hit the blinking button. "Looks like Charles and Josh from our side of the house, and Scotty Westfield from Bravo Unit, and Chuck Forsythe from the JTTF are also available."

"Okay. Work out the logistics and get one team on the way to Heilig's office and the other to his house. I'm forwarding the information that Arati found to you for inclusion in the warrant. If you don't hear back from me by the time you're ready, then go ahead and forward it to the judge from my account. Tell the guys that you'll forward the approved warrant electronically as soon as you get it. Call me on my cell when it's done. And oh, good work, JT, and," he looked over at Arati, "good work Arati. I think we caught a break here."

Luckily, Krolick was available and agreed to the warrant. Pleased with himself, Hanson decided to go home after all and await JT's call. As he walked out the door, he was thinking what a tremendous asset to the team Arati was going to be. "See you tomorrow, Arati."

Vienna, Virginia, 5 December, 1840 hours

Thus it was that Charles and Josh were on their way to Vienna. Scotty had called from Heilig's office and said they had just missed him and found out that he had left at his usual time and would be home around 6:30. Charles had obtained his DMV picture and found what appeared to be a more recent one on his company's website. Figuring there was probably no good way to get from Crystal City to Vienna at this time of day, Josh had decided to go up to Rosslyn and catch Route 66. Although probably no worse than any other route, it was certainly no better, either. Heilig lived on Westview Court just off Beulah Road, so Josh took the Nutley Street exit to approach from the south and thus avoid the Tysons Corner area, which was a mess anytime, but especially in December with all the Christmas shoppers.

314

"Why do we always have to do these things at rush hour?" asked Charles. "We've been on the road for almost an hour now."

"Did you want to wait until ten to avoid the 'rush hour'?"

"Good point. I remember Dad was assigned to a few big cities during his FBI career, but the traffic is worse in this one— except for LA, maybe. Of course, I wasn't really driving in some of those, so maybe I just didn't notice. At least the trip back home should be easier. I see this guy is fifty-one. Hopefully that means there's not any young kids at home. That's never a good scene. Wives are bad enough to deal with."

"Alright, there's Westview Court," said Josh, "so what's the address?"

"There it is on the left. Looks like both cars registered to him are there so he should be home. Do you want to do the honors?"

"Unless you'd rather, I'll do it," offered Josh.

Charles shook his head.

"Okay then, if we end up arresting him, be ready to cuff him if he's not cooperative." Josh turned around at the end of the court and pulled up in front of the Heilig residence. The modest-looking, two-story place fit in well with the rest of the neighborhood—vinyl siding, two car garage, well-kept yard with several mature trees. "These guys never think about what they'll be giving up if they get caught. I've done this enough to guarantee you that I'll never be in this position," he said as he rang the doorbell.

A rather homely young woman in her mid- to late twenties answered the door. "May I help you?"

"Good evening. We're looking for Mr. Arthur Heilig. Is he home from work yet?"

"Yes. May I say who's calling?"

"I'm Josh Paxton and this is Charles Burton. We're federal agents with Homeland Security and we have a few questions for him regarding some people that work with him," Josh said as they both showed her their badges.

"Come in. Daddy, there's two gentlemen here to see you," she called out to the back of the house.

Heilig walked in from the kitchen with a beer in his hand. "I'm Artie Heilig. What can I do for you?"

Josh handed him the warrant and said, "Arthur Heilig, we have a warrant to search your house, including your computer, and your car."

Heilig had a deep voice befitting of the two-hundred pounds on his six-foot frame. "What the hell for?" he bellowed as his daughter looked at the two agents in disbelief.

"To search for any evidence relating to the solicitation and payment of bribes on several government contracts."

"That's totally nuts!"

"Then you don't mind if we look around, do you? And could we have your car keys?"

Heilig shook his head, said the cars were unlocked, and then started toward the back of the house.

"I'm afraid that I'll have to ask you and your daughter to stay in here while my partner searches your place and your cars. Is there anyone else in the house?"

Heilig shook his head again. Then he and his daughter started to sit down.

"Actually, this would go a lot quicker if you and your daughter showed me where your computer is so I could start looking at it."

Heilig showed Josh to the den and he and his daughter took seats right across from him as he began his search. It wasn't password locked, so Josh got right to it.

About forty minutes later, Charles walked into the den carrying a small tote bag. "Find anything, partner?"

"Yes, a few rather interesting websites."

Charles looked and nodded.

"How about you?"

"Found a few interesting things myself when I searched the back of his bedroom closet." As he reached into the paper bag he asked, "What have we here, Mr. Heilig? Looks like a fake mustache and wig, some amber vision sunglasses and an REI rain hat. What do you think, partner?"

"That's more than enough for me," Josh said as he stood up. "Mr. Arthur Heilig, you are under arrest for the murder of Stefon Quarles and Donald Crenshaw. You have the right...."

As Josh continued reading him his rights, Heilig, who had just stood up to stretch his legs, almost fell backwards. He fumbled a bit and then slumped in the nearest chair with what was left of his beer spilling out on his arm and the chair.

His daughter screamed, "What? You must be mistaken. Daddy, what's going on here?"

Heilig shook his head, looked at his daughter and regained some of his composure. At this point, Josh asked him if he understood his rights. He nodded and then said, "It's alright, sweetie. I'm sure there's been some mistake. We'll have this straightened out in no time."

Charles handed the daughter a business card and indicated that she and his lawyer could get in touch with him there. "Where is Mrs. Heilig?"

"Huh? Oh, no. I mean she passed away a few years ago. Daddy, I'll call Stanley and let him know what's going on."

"It's okay. This will work out okay. Let me get my coat."

"If you could please get it for him, Miss," directed Josh as he turned off the computer and prepared it for transport.

Heilig seemed resigned to going in, so Charles didn't cuff him in front of his daughter but waited until they were outside just before they put him in the car. It was a company car and had the back door lock controls but no screen between the front and back, so Charles sat in the back with Heilig. They put the computer and the tote bag in the trunk. Charles explained that they were going to a detention center in Fullerton but the prisoner was nonresponsive. Except for a short phone call that Charles made to Hanson, it was a long, silent drive back to Fullerton.

CHAPTER THIRTY-SEVEN

Fullerton, Virginia, 6 December, 0700 hours

Heilig's daughter had called the family lawyer, Stanley Walton, and he was there with his client. Although only thirty-seven, Walton had considerable experience defending criminal suspects. He had a slight build and very light short hair; in fact his eyebrows were barely noticeable. That, combined with his conservative dress and slow, determined speech pattern, made him appear older and ostensibly more experienced. JT and Juanita walked in to the interview room and introduced themselves. "I read your search warrants," began Walton, "which I must say seemed rather flimsy, as I believe that your evidence is circumstantial at best."

"Perhaps we should inform you and your client what we determined from the fruits of our warrant," Juanita offered. "From your work computer, we noticed numerous visits to political blog sites, the same ones that a confessed hit man said he received his instructions on. On your home computer, we found URLs for sites that explain how to make IEDs—again the same ones that our hit man said he was given in order to construct the bomb that he used to murder Dr. Quarles. That would be the same Dr. Quarles who was threatening to expose the contract bribes that you were involved with. As you know, we found this hidden in your bedroom closet." As she said that, she threw the wig, fake mustache, sunglasses and rain hat on the table. "I especially like the Amber Vision glasses and REI hat, which match the description of the obvious disguise that the hit man's contact wore when they met. Would you like to try them on? We have Mr. Furlong in a cell just down the hall, and I'm sure he would be glad to come over here and pick you out of a lineup of gentleman wearing the same getup. Or perhaps he'll recognize your voice. He certainly described your general build accurately. If that wasn't enough, we also have Dr. Briceman in custody. He was trying to flee the country and we have charged him with some of the same crimes. If I were you, I really don't believe I'd trust him to keep you out of this. Oh, and one last thing. We found out that Mr. Furlong's first victim was your former mother-in-law. What do you say, Mr. Heilig?"

Walton looked at his client, who had laid his head down into his hands.

"Would you two like some time to confer?" asked JT. Walton nodded, so JT and Juanita got up and headed out the door. JT said, "We'll be back in fifteen minutes." Outside he said, "Well, that went pretty well. You ran over him like a tank. I think I would have led him on a bit first, but then that's my style. Think he'll go for it?"

"Sure he will. That's why we have the offer from the Justice Department with us, isn't it?" They got something to drink and talked about how well Arati was getting on in the department. Juanita mentioned that she thought Hanson showed a little too much interest in Arati JT offered that it was strictly professional as she had certainly earned everyone's trust and praise.

Twenty minutes later, they walked back into the interview room. "So, what's the verdict," queried Juanita, placing emphasis on the last word.

"We'd like to see if there is anything in the offing here, Agent."

"We thought you might, and here it is," she said as she gave them the plea agreement that they had worked out with Justice. "Would you like a little more time?"

Walton responded positively, so Juanita indicated that they'd be back in another fifteen minutes as she and JT left the room for the second time.

A half hour later when they came back in Walton said, "Mr. Heilig has agreed to abide by the terms of this agreement, specifically the waiving of the death penalty for complete and total disclosure of all previous contracted homicides, but with the exception of the potential fine. He does not want his daughter hurt financially as a result of his criminal activity. He does agree to the return of his ill-gotten gains, as they are almost all still available. Is that acceptable?"

"Well, Mr. Heilig, you should have thought of that a long time ago. I don't have the authority to change the agreement, but I can tell you right now that that would be unacceptable to the Justice Department. Based on the quality of your information and the extent of your cooperation, DHS can certainly recommend a lessening or even a removal of the potential fine, but you know that the final determination on that will be made by a judge. So do you want to play ball under those circumstances or not?"

Walton looked at Heilig and he nodded.

"Okay, then. Let's get this underway." Juanita started the recorder and gave him the standard preamble.

Mr. Heilig, as it turns out, had an excellent memory. He recalled a considerable amount of detail, including dates and amounts of dollar transfers. He described how he bribed a police officer to get him arrest data on several criminals convicted of assault and other serious felonies, and found one—Furlong—on his second try, who would be willing to operate as a hit man. He laid out the meetings with Furlong, and his details agreed with the scenarios they had heard from the now former hit man. "When I got this anonymous letter suggesting that Quarles was about to spill the beans, I already had this relationship with Furlong, although he didn't know who I was, and I used him to eliminate the problem. Same thing for the Crenshaw problem. Of course, I knew Rick Briceman was on the take, so I asked him to transfer the funds because this problem was too close to home and I knew he could hide the transfer. Not to mention that I couldn't come up with the cash at the time. Took some convincing on my part and I had to appeal to his ego."

"But he did agree?"

"He took care of it."

"Why did you request Furlong make the hit look like a terrorist activity?"

"I figured that if the folks funding the Coltrane and Tomfoolery programs thought that terrorists wanted the programs derailed, they'd redouble their efforts to make them work. Also, it would help to deflect suspicion away from anyone involved with the program."

"You never intended to have any actual terrorists take care of this 'problem'?"

"I don't *know* any actual terrorists!"

"And you decided to have Furlong make the Crenshaw murder look like a robbery gone bad because...?"

"The opposite reason—I didn't want it connected to the programs."

"We may have some further questions on these later, but can you detail the other 'contracts' that you were involved in?"

"Like you figured, the first one was my mother-in-law."

Everyone in the room shook their head.

"She had a substantial amount of savings from investments that her husband had made and I needed that money to seed my first business venture. She was pretty sick and the hospital and doctor bills were eating it all up, not to mention the suffering that it was causing my wife. She was spending all her time taking care of her mother. So I made a desperate move to solve both problems and established this relationship with Furlong. The second one was a business rival who had the only other viable bid on a government contract that we were both trying to win. With him out of the way I won the contract, made a shitload of money, then sold the company for a killing."

JT and Juanita winced at that wording.

"Sorry, that wasn't intended—poor choice of words."

"These two and Quarles and Crenshaw; any others?" asked Juanita.

"No."

"Give us some more detail on these last two and then we'll get this transcribed."

Heilig went on for another ten minutes describing the first two contract killings. When he was done, Juanita turned off the tape and she and JT took it out to one of the admin assistants for transcription. Less than forty minutes later, they brought it back and Heilig and Walton both read it and concurred. Heilig signed it and then said, "I know I deserve life in prison for this, maybe several times over, and that'll be bad enough I guess. But what will really hurt is what my daughter will think of all this. I mean, I had her grandmother killed. She'll probably suspect me of killing her mother too. I want you to know that I had nothing to do with that—it was a car accident. I loved her and miss her terribly. Now I'll be spending the rest of my life without either one of them."

Juanita said, "Don't worry, Artie, you'll have lots of close friends in prison."

On the way back, JT opined that the boss would not be happy about the law enforcement involvement resulting in the selection of Furlong.

Clarendon, Virginia, 6 December, 1200 hours

It had been almost seventy-two hours since they arrested Briceman in Miami, and now he had his lawyer with him and was expecting an arraignment sometime within the next few minutes. When JT and Juanita walked back into Interview Room 2, Byerly and Briceman were obviously upset at having been kept waiting. "So, do you have something from Justice," began Byerly, noticing that Juanita had a folder in her hand, "or are we going for arraignment now?"

"As we mentioned in our first little chat," JT began, "you've no doubt discussed with your counsel what you've done and not done, given him a reason for your attempt at fleeing, and otherwise explained away the evidence against you, but did you mention that we suspect you of being an accessory to murder?"

This did not have the effect that they had hoped for as both Briceman and Byerly seemed nonplused. "Actually, my client and I did discuss possible accusations in that area, and we know that you have no evidence to that effect."

"I see. What I'm sure he didn't mention, and it's understandable as we only just found out ourselves, is that we have a witness willing to testify that he asked your client to transfer money to the account of the hit man that murdered Dr. Quarles and Mr. Crenshaw."

"You're bluffing," Briceman quickly but calmly offered before his lawyer could say anything, "because I never did any such thing."

"Really? That's not what Artie Heilig said. In fact, his sworn confession says that you knew exactly what the money was for as the two of you were in cahoots with the contract kickbacks and knew that those two men were about to expose you." Byerly rolled his eyes to the ceiling and Briceman started to say something but was interrupted by Juanita.

"Of course you don't have to take our word for it," she said as she slid the folder across the table toward Byerly.

He picked it up and gave it a quick once over and then looked at Briceman who had slumped down in his chair.

"Could we please have a few minutes to discuss this turn of events?"

"What's to discuss?" JT asked. "By the way, Mr. Briceman, you are under arrest for murder as an accessory after the fact. You've already been read your rights once; would you like me to repeat them?"

He shook his head.

"Then we'll see you at the new arraignment. Have a nice day."

"Agent Dunkirk," Byerly called out as JT and Juanita started to leave the room, "I believe there may be some room for maneuvering here. This does change the dynamics of the case. Perhaps we could come to some accommodation. A few minutes, please?"

"Alright, we'll hang around. Just let the guard outside know when you're ready. But I don't have all day, Counselor," JT said as they closed the door behind them.

It was forty minutes before Byerly called for the guard and requested that the two agents return. "We noticed that Mr. Heilig's confession accuses my client of contract tampering in two specific cases and transferring funds for a hit man in two specific cases. Hypothetically, if my client were aware of additional crimes that may have been committed and was willing to cooperate in their resolution, would that afford a mitigation of any sentence for the felonies he is currently accused of?"

"That's a pretty serious charge against your client," offered Juanita. "Not only is a jury going to be thinking megabuck contract bribes, but also premeditation, conspiracy, and murder by proxy to prevent their discovery. I honestly don't know if we're looking at a possible death penalty or maybe life without parole here. I think you'd have to have some heavy duty help in mind in order to reduce any sentence. I'll mention it to the prosecutor from Justice. Do you have something more specific to offer?"

Byerly looked at Briceman who almost imperceptibly nodded his head. "We were thinking of the names, dates and amounts of those involved with other contract improprieties. We certainly have no other information on any other murders."

"We'll pass it on," said Juanita. "In the meantime, Mr. Briceman will remain here until he can be arraigned on these new charges. We know how to get in touch with you if Justice has anything to offer. Stay as long as you like."

"Let's get back to the office," said JT on the way out. "So you think the prosecutor will go for a deal?"

"I don't know," replied Juanita. Guess when we get back we'll see how the boss wants to handle it."

Clarendon, Virginia, 7 December, 1030 hours

Hanson had met with the prosecutor from Justice and they agreed that getting a death penalty was iffy, but that they could put Briceman away for a long, long time. It was within their power to remove the death penalty, but they were pretty sure a judge would likely go with the maximum sentence, regardless of their recommendation, so they agreed to go with no death penalty and a recommendation of less than the maximum sentence, all depending upon the quality of Briceman's information. They wrote the deal up and Hanson said he'd try to meet JT and Juanita in Arlington as he really wanted to be there to hear what Briceman had to say. They got there before their boss and met him outside the same Interview Room 2 they were in yesterday and the day before, and read the agreement from Justice. Briceman and his lawyer were already in the room.

Juanita led off the discussion this time. "We managed to convince Justice that you might have something useful to say and they agreed to remove the death penalty *and* to recommend less than the maximum sentence. More than I think you deserve," she added as a sidebar. She handed the agreement to Byerly. After a few minutes he handed it to Briceman who also read it. "If everything's in order can we begin the debriefing?" queried Juanita.

Byerly looked at Briceman who nodded and said, "Let's get it over with."

Juanita started the recorder that had been set up and went through the preliminaries. Then, "It's all yours, Dr. Briceman, and, if you please, give us as many details as you can remember—names, dates, and so forth. Let's start with the contract maneuvering and go from there."

Briceman took a deep breath, leaned the chair back on its two hind legs, looked up at the ceiling and began talking. He went on for forty minutes detailing how he had solicited contract bribes from three DARPA contractors and two subcontractors over the last three years, and three other contractors when he worked for CIFA before that. He alternated leaning back in the chair and sitting upright with his elbows resting on the table and his head cradled in his hands. He told them how he had set up the numbered account in Andorra and was transferring the majority of his ill-gotten gains into it, hoping to get up to ten million before he moved over there. He gave the names of the individual contractors involved and approximate dates and for the most part exact amounts. "I destroyed the details but of course you can at least trace the dates and amounts of the transfers into my Andorran account." He paused for a minute shaking his head. "I certainly didn't give Dr. Jabornae enough credit as she is obviously as brilliant as Quarles was, and I realize now that she was working for you guys. By the way, where was the wire?"

"We had a small transceiver about the size of a dime glued to the top of her head."

"How did you get past my security devices? Was she wearing some sort of a storage device as well?"

"That was located in the sole of her shoe."

"Guess I should have searched her better," he said with a smirk on his face.

"When did you suspect her?"

"When she came to see me and suggested that she be cut in on the deal I started thinking that the whole thing was getting too complicated. I really didn't suspect her at first, but talked myself into being cautious. I have to admit that I just didn't want to go through that whole process again, and decided to run before I had to meet with her again. Is there anything about these transactions that I can add?"

"Have you mentioned *all* the contractors that you've solicited and accepted bribes from?" asked Juanita.

Briceman indicated that he had to the best of his recollection.

"Were there other government employees involved with these illegal transactions?"

Briceman rocked back to level with all four legs of his chair on the floor, thought about it for a minute and then responded, "Well, not that I could say for sure. If they were offering bribes to other government personnel it's unlikely they would let me in on that. I had some suspicions but that's all they were."

"Give us the names and we'll check it out. If they're clean, no harm done; if not, they're going down."

Briceman complied with four names, including, no surprise, Mike Styles.

"Okay. Now what about the two murders, Dr. Briceman?"

He took a drink of the water that they had provided for him, rocked back in the chair again and began. "About two months ago, when Stefon started getting suspicious, I sent anonymous letters to the same list of DARPA contractors and subcontractors that I previously mentioned. I indicated that he was about to blow the whole setup, hoping that one of them would take care of this problem. As I know now, Artie Heilig did, apparently via a hit man. Then, and this is certainly ironic, he asked me to anonymously transfer some funds into this Mumford person's account for a recent job he had completed for him. It seemed reasonable to assume that he was the one that took care of it, or knew who did, but I figured it didn't matter and I really didn't want to know. The funds were in a dummy account that could have been set up by any of them. This of course was my big mistake: up to this point I had plausible deniability. After Quarles was gone I grabbed his hard drive to see if there was any evidence there that I needed to get rid of. In going through the data there I found out that he had confided in Don Crenshaw who had similar suspicions. So why mess with success? I did wait a couple of weeks so that the two incidents hopefully wouldn't seem connected, and then sent another anonymous letter to the same group of individuals. Once again, the problem went away, apparently via a hit man. I get another funds transfer request from Artie similar to the previous one and transferred the funds. Oh, by the way, as much as I hate to admit it, I decided it would be fun, not to mention complicate things, if I transferred the money through Styles' account since he had a known dislike for Quarles and was such a perfect asshole. Everyone knew he was a crook and it wasn't hard to figure out where he was sending his money. I'm sure he never knew a thing about it, either time. I would love to have seen his face if you confronted him with that."

"We did and it made my day," responded Juanita. "But it is a shame. I was *so* looking forward to hitting him with a murder charge. By the way, in accordance with our agreement, if you haven't given us all the overseas accounts our deal is off. And you know, Doctor Jabornae *will* find them."

"I know, Agent, I know," he sighed.

"Then I guess we're done here. Unless you have anything further to add."

"I know it's kind of meaningless now that I'm caught, but I really am sorry about Quarles. Crenshaw too for that matter, but I understand that Quarles was just starting a family. If there was any other way...."

"Yeah, it's a little late," said JT as he glared at Briceman. "And there *was* another way: first off you could have been an honest individual and been *more* than happy with your *more* than adequate income. Barring that, you could have decided to leave at that point rather than wait until you thought that someone else might be on to you. By your own admission you already had some four million bucks socked away."

Briceman's remorse looked genuine at this point, as he hung his head rather than look them in the eye.

"I imagine you'll hear from the Justice lawyer in a couple of days, Mr. Byerly," said Juanita as she and JT got up to leave. Once in the hallway they met Hanson and she commented, "Greed: probably the worst of the seven deadly sins."

"I don't know," said Hanson. "I think I've seen more murders committed for lust than greed."

"I think maybe they were due to pride," offered JT. "You know, she had no right to deny him of her companionship, or worse, love, let alone offer it to anyone else less deserving."

"Yeah, you're probably right. I guess we have to let Styles' lawyer know that his client is no longer suspected of murder."

"Oh come on, Boss, do we have to?" pleaded Juanita. "A few years in jail for contract fraud is not anywhere near what that guy deserves."

"Maybe he'll lose his pension and his wife will take her money and leave. Besides, Troops, we did some really good work here today and should be happy with it. I think we have the Quarles and Crenshaw murders pretty well wrapped up. Now, let's get back to the office and see where we are on these terrorist connections. Which these were *not* a part of, which is also good news."

"There's still the intercepted communication mentioning Quarles and the program," commented JT.

"Yes, damn it. There is still that. There is still that," said Hanson shaking his head.

CHAPTER THIRTY-EIGHT

Fusion Team Headquarters, 7 December, 1435 hours

Everyone except Charles and Josh, who were out chasing down another NSA intercept, showed up for the team meeting Hanson called to pass on the good news. Arati had also come over from her perch at NCTC. "In case you haven't heard," Hanson began, "Briceman confessed to the solicitation of murder and aiding and abetting after the fact, in addition to soliciting and accepting bribes. He gave us quite a list of potential wrongdoers that agrees substantially with the list that Arati developed, so we are going to turn that whole ball of wax over to the FBI for their investigation. It appears that we have the three individuals responsible for the murder of Doctor Quarles and Don Crenshaw: Rick Briceman, who originated the idea in order to rid himself of two people who may have upset the transfer of his ill-gotten gains, as well as potentially expose his game, and who also transferred the funds to the actual killer; Artie Heilig, who contracted with the hit man and came up with the funds for same; and Jon Furlong, the hit man himself. Since we offered deals to all three of them, we are going to have Justice prosecute them. We're working with Fairfax and Montgomery Counties on Heilig's and Furlong's first two murders to close out their cases. I've called Styles' lawyer and let him know the 'good news' about his noninvolvement in the two murders, so he is now facing only the contract bribery charges. We've decided to let the FBI handle that one along with the others. Thus the Quarles case is basically wrapped up except for one detail—the mention of Quarles and his program by suspected terrorists. Not one of our three perpetrators has any discernable terrorist connection, and indeed deny the same, except that Heilig asked Furlong to make it look like a terrorist hit. But Furlong carried it all out himself, so that looks like an end that may remain loose. Is there anything else we need to discuss on these?"

"Well, Boss," said Phil, "I checked out Heilig's admission that he used a LEO to get his original information on Furlong. The guy he implicated was involved with his daughter and there were some substantial loans involved. Seems he was shot and killed at a traffic stop and got a hero's sendoff. I haven't passed any of this on to Fairfax yet."

"Don't see any reason to do that at this point, do you?" he asked the audience in general and got a collective head shaking. "Then let's discuss where we are on our terrorist investigations." Hanson pulled out a large sheet of paper that he brought into the conference room with him, and attached it to an easel in the front of the room. "So far, in the investigation stemming from the original meeting at *S&S Enterprises*, we have identified sixteen know terrorists, and we have taken eleven of them out of circulation. This includes the drive-by shooting at the Ahmadi residence where they attempted to kill Mustafa, and the raid on the chop shop that resulting from following up on a name overheard by Mustafa." He had placed the names of the suspected/confirmed terrorists on the paper along with info about them and their current disposition.

NAME	COO	EVENT	DATA	STATUS
Najam Aimal	Afghanistan	S&S	2nd generation citizen	At large
Shahzad al-Hardar	Iran	S&S, CS procurer	Naturalized citizen	In custody
Mahmoud al-Sadr	Iran	S&S, drive-by	Work visa	Deceased
Ali Fayadh	Unknown	CS procurer	Illegal	At large
Sidiq Haq	Iraq	CS manager	Naturalized citizen	In custody
Rasheem Haqqani	Pakistan	S&S	Illegal, Taliban	At large
Farooq Husna	Afghanistan	Drive-by	Work visa	Deceased
Sajid Hussain	Pakistan	CS procurer	Student visa	In custody
Talat Iqbal	Pakistan	Drive-by	Resident alien	Deceased
Ashan Khadija	Pakistan	S&S	Work visa	Deceased
Khalid	Unknown	S&S, drive-by	Illegal, Taliban	Deceased

Tariq Khan	Pakistan	CS procurer	Resident alien	In custody
Umar Nadeem	Pakistan	CS foreman	Naturalized citizen	In custody
Sattar Omar	Afghanistan	CS procurer	Naturalized citizen	In custody
Hishan Sarhan	Iraq	CS procurer	Work visa	At large
Mohammed Shah	Iran	S&S	Illegal	At large

"As you can see, we have six in custody, all of whom are facing a trial and sentencing or deportation if found guilty. The FBI are continuing to question this group, and are hopeful that one or more of them will yield some additional actionable information. There are five dead: one killed we believe by the terrorists themselves—that was Ashan, the cab driver; the two shot by JT and Brian at the drive-by at the Ahmadi residence; one who was wounded by Brian there and then killed himself by jumping out of the ambulance; and the other one there who was wounded by his own guy and who later died under mysterious circumstances in the hospital right under the noses of the MPD. Five are still at large and we are going to concentrate on this group. Brendon, do I need to add any of the mechanics from the chop shop to my list?"

"Boss, everything points to them just working there. Besides their obvious connection to the shop and the fact that they all knew that what they were doing was illegal, they either did not realize that they were aiding and abetting terrorists, or at least have plausible deniability. I guess they will face whatever charges their involvement dictates."

"Phil, what about those two missing procurers, ah—" Hanson turned to look at his sheet, "—ah Fayadh and Sarhan? There was nothing in all that data we got from the shop to point to their whereabouts?"

"We got Sarhan's address from ICE since he had a work visa, but he hasn't shown up there since the raid. It's been two weeks now so I rather suspect he's not coming back. I recommend we call off the surveillance. They had nothing on Fayadh other than his name, so we listed him as illegal."

"I know we've followed every lead we have on these Sticks, so I guess we'll have to work harder on what we've got or turn up some new leads. Arati, were you able to make any connections between the contract bribe/murder funding transactions of Briceman and company and the terrorist funding transactions of the chop shop?"

"No, sir, not yet, but I am still working on it. I may have a lead on the original funding for the chop shop and hope to have something on that for you by tomorrow."

"Alright then, if there's nothing new, let's get back to work."

Clarendon, Virginia, 7 December, 1540 hours

Hishan climbed the steps of the county building on Courthouse Road and opened the front door. As he walked up to the entry point with the electronic walk-through and the guard sitting behind the scanner, he unbuttoned his coat with one hand and then placed it back in his coat pocket. When the person in front of him went through the screener, he flung his coat open and at the same time removed his hands from his pockets. In his one hand was a detonator and in the other a Smith and Wesson .38. He brandished the gun toward the guard in front of the screener and yelled in a Middle Eastern accent, "Take me to floor ten and no one get hurt."

A third guard approaching the scene for a shift change reached for his weapon and was shot in the chest for his efforts. He was wearing a vest but the force knocked him back and he dropped his gun.

"Do not make me use this," Hishan shouted as he opened his coat wider and raised the hand with the detonator. "I move thumb, we all die."

"Holy shit!" the nearby guard screamed. "He's got dynamite sticks strapped to his body."

"You, you, you in elevator," Hishan said waving the gun back and forth at one of the guards and two nearby civilians.

"Leave gun," he demanded pointing at the guard. The guard carefully unholstered his gun and set it down on the floor. Then the three of them approached the elevator with the assailant maintaining his distance from them. As the elevator doors opened, Hishan motioned them to the front corner near the buttons while he took the opposite one and said, "Push ten." The guard maneuvered himself in front of the two civilians and started to say something, but quickly shut up when the assailant pointed his gun at the officer's head. As the elevator doors opened on ten, it was obvious that one of the guards downstairs had called up because no one was surprised to see them and they were maintaining a decent distance from the new arrivals.

The tenth floor housed the Arlington County detention center and the assailant hit the stop button after the doors opened and the others exited. The day-shift supervisor addressed the apparent terrorist as he exited the elevator behind the other three. "Just tell us what it is that you want and we'll try to comply so that no one gets hurt." He was a good fifteen feet away and was almost yelling over the alarm noise from the elevator.

Hishan took in the scene: he saw the thick plate-glass partition separating the entrance way from the detention cells, noticed that the two guards in front of the glass partition were armed and on either side of the room, saw two more behind the glass that appeared unarmed, and determined that there were two exit doors at either end of the room, both of which opened in. He did not see any place that anyone could be hiding except behind those two exit doors, or maybe under the small reception desk in front of him. He had the gun shoved in the lower back of the downstairs guard, a young man who looked rather cool under the circumstances. The two civilians, a middle-aged woman who had her hands clasped and her eyes closed, and an elderly man who had trouble walking, were not faring as well.

"You, you, you, put guns on desk," he motioned at the two guards and the supervisor. The supervisor and one of the guards complied. One guard didn't and was given a look by the supervisor that could have accomplished the same thing as the bomb strapped around the man's waist. After the last guard complied, Hishan pointed at the exit doors and motioned to the two guards saying, "Sit on floor in front of door. You over there too and you over there," he demanded shoving the two civilians towards the two exit doors. Keeping the gun pointed at the lower back of the guard he looked at the supervisor and said, "Get guns of men inside there and put on desk here."

The supervisor said that the men inside were not armed.

"Tell them to put up hands and turn around."

The supervisor motioned for the men inside to raise their hands and do a three-sixty.

Satisfied, Hishan asked the supervisor, "What your name?"

He responded with "Sam."

"Sam, you go get Briceman and bring him here." He enunciated the name very carefully as if he'd been practicing saying it and did not want it to be misunderstood.

Sam opened the partition door and headed back toward the cells.

"Briceman," he called as he approached the detainee's cell. "You've got a visitor. And I thought you didn't have any friends."

"Who is it?" Briceman queried with furrowed eyebrows and an upturned nose. "Another one of those federal agents?"

"You know, I didn't catch his name or occupation, but I do know he's rather a pushy type. Just come with me," he said as he unlocked Briceman's cell door.

As they approached the entrance door Briceman saw the man standing behind the guard and all the guns on the desk. As he stepped out he noticed the people sitting on the floor in front of the doors. "What's going on?" he asked.

"I guess your buddy is here with the bail," Sam commented as he maneuvered Briceman toward the terrorist.

As Briceman approached his "visitor," Hishan pushed the guard in front of him out of the way and pointed the gun at Briceman. Tipped to his intention, Briceman dropped to the deck just before it went off, and the bullet missed him and lodged in the plate glass. Briceman then rolled toward the reception desk and managed to get behind it before his attacker got off another round that lodged itself in the floor where Briceman was just a split second before. Hishan then ran toward the desk and rounded it just as Briceman dove towards him. Briceman hit his attacker in the lower legs and Hishan fell forward on top of him.

Sam dove for the cover of the plate glass, and everyone else in the room except the two antagonists hit the deck, turning away from the conflict and covering their heads with their arms and upper body. The two were now grappling and Briceman managed to grab his assailant's gun hand with his left and started pounding on his face with his right. After a few blows, his opponent's fight diminished. That's when Briceman realized his assailant had a free hand he wasn't using in the fight and heard the clicking sound. He looked down and saw the man's thumb pressing in and out on a button on some sort of hand-held device, and noticed the sticks of dynamite strapped around the man's waist. In a mighty effort aided by a surge of adrenalin, he wrenched the gun from the attacker's hand and rather than take the time to point and shoot he rammed it full force into the guy's face. The battered man groaned, dropped the detonator and slumped lifeless. Briceman figured that if this self-annihilation technique hadn't worked yet it wasn't going to.

About this time, the guards and the supervisor reached the same conclusion.

Briceman started to get up and turned the gun to grab it by the grip with his right hand at the same time that the supervisor reached for him. Briceman was quicker and pointed the weapon right at the man's head.

"Alright, you and I are getting out of here," he said positioning himself behind the supervisor with his left hand on the man's collar and his right hand pointing the gun at his neck. By now one of the guards on the floor had come up in front of the desk and grabbed one of the guns.

"Looks like what we have here is a Mexican standoff," Briceman offered as soon as he noticed him.

"Not quite," replied the supervisor. "You see, your friend there was willing to blow up a whole lot of innocent people if he had to in order to get to you. All my man has to do is shoot you and sacrifice me. Shoot him, Tony."

"Can't do it, Boss. He ain't worth dying for," he said as he put down the gun.

Briceman made his way toward the elevator so he would have better control of the room. Thankfully the alarm had finally stopped. "Call downstairs and have a car waiting for us," he said to the guard at the desk. At this point, the female civilian let out a blood-curdling scream that had obviously been bottled up for some time. Distracted by the noise, Briceman turned and the supervisor jerked down and away from the gun. Briceman was pushed off-balance somewhat by the supervisor's maneuver and the gun went off with the bullet finding the shoulder of the guard still seated by one of the doors. The guard at the desk grabbed back the gun he had just put down and swung it up toward the inmate. Briceman was still a little off-balance but fired at the guard and missed. The guard's bullet found Briceman's heart and his arm drooped, he fell to his knees, and finally crumpled in a heap on the floor.

Sam jumped up, retrieved Briceman's gun, and checked for his pulse. There wasn't one. He started issuing orders to his men: "Larry, check on our terrorist there and make sure he's dead. In fact, put the cuffs on him whether he's dead or not and make sure he can't touch that damn detonator thing. Then see if Ralph's okay and escort him and the two civilians there downstairs pronto. Joe, go in there and help Hank and Jerrod transport the prisoners out of here. I'll join you as soon as I call downstairs and let them know what's going on and that we need the bomb squad up here and have to evacuate the building." Everyone recovered their weapon and executed the boss' orders. After his phone call, Sam went over and checked on the terrorist himself, and although it appeared that he was dead, he nonetheless made sure his was securely fastened.

The employees at the front entrance to the building had already called 9-1-1 and the bomb squad. The Arlington County First Responders found that the downstairs guard was only bruised, thanks to his vest, and the guard from upstairs had only a superficial shoulder wound. They also treated the two civilians for shock and then asked if they could hang around and give a statement. Briceman, whom they evacuated with the last of the prisoners, didn't make it.

The bomb squad arrived as the last occupants departed the building. Sam escorted the squad up to ten, explaining what they were going to find when they got there. It only took them a few minutes to disconnect the detonator, determine that it was defective, and realize that that was real TNT strapped to the terrorist's waist. They cleared the scene for the EMT team, who then came upstairs and indeed found the terrorist dead. Once they got all the prisoners back in their cells and the place somewhat orderly again, Sam reached for JT's business card and picked up the phone.

CHAPTER THIRTY-NINE

Tysons Corner, Virginia, 8 December, 1035 hours

The Director of National Intelligence asked Hanson for a special brief on his on-going cases, having moved up a couple of days from his normal biweekly meeting with her, most likely due to the attempted murder of one of his prisoners by a dynamite-laden assassin. So he met with her and her staff early in the morning. It actually went fairly well, under the circumstances, with the DNI expressing interest in the disposition of the suspected terrorists that were in custody, any developments on the possible attack on a DC train station, and Briceman's connection to all of this. Hanson promised to keep her and her staff fully informed and thanked them for the use of their facilities and personnel for the training of Doctor Jabornae. Speaking of whom, since she was only a few floors down and he was already here, he decided to drop by and see. She was busy at her terminals and didn't see him approach. "Surfing the web, are you?" he asked.

"Why, no, I am—" Then seeing who it was she said, "You are teasing me again."

Hanson nodded and added, "So, how's it going?"

"I have uncovered something very interesting. Look at this."

"First, I need to let you know what happened yesterday afternoon," he said, giving her a rundown on the incident at the jailhouse.

"That is a conundrum, is it not?"

"Yes, it is. We'll have to work on that. What did you want to show me?"

She moved over a bit so Hanson could view her screen better. "Do you recall how we earlier determined that monies from the Maldives accounts were transferred to a company called

Aeronautics Alectrona, LLC, and that this was the company that owned *Ron's Auto Repair and Body Work*?"

Hanson nodded as he looked at her PowerPoint display.

"The FBI mentioned that *Aeronautics* transferred funds to two Andorran accounts, one of which I determined was closed out after transferring funds to a company called *Fusion MicroElectronics*."

Hanson again nodded.

"Guess who the owner of that latter company turned out to be."

"I'm all ears, Arati."

"Joel Henning."

"Jesus Christ! Did you say Joel Henning, my ex-boss at CIFA who is now over at DIA and was on the source selection evaluation board for some of the DARPA contracts?" Hanson looked at Arati and realized that she was taken aback. Embarrassed at his uncustomary outburst, he then looked around to see if he might have been overheard by anyone. Business seemed to be progressing as usual in the room, so he turned his attention back to Arati. "Sorry about that. It's just that that comes as quite a shock. I mean, I even discussed the case with him."

"One other thing, if you promise not to yell at me," she said smiling.

Hanson shrugged apologetically.

"*Fusion MicroElectronics* is the source of the original funding for *Ron's Auto Repair*. This puts Mr. Henning right in the middle of things, does it not?"

"It certainly does, Arati. I'll be asking for search warrants for his house and office. But you couldn't tie him into any of the illegal contract activities?"

"I know he was involved with those same contracts that others received bribes for, and that he was on the SSEB as you mentioned, but I can find no proof that he accepted any bribe money, although that is not a definitive no."

"I understand. But tying him in with the terrorist activities is a lot more important. You know, I always thought there was something odd about him. He was pretty much a loner and I often wondered how he got as high up in the government as he did. He doesn't have a family, except for his adoptive parents, and he never talked about them. He certainly was intelligent and seemed to understand the terrorist mentality—duh. We've got to move on this right away. Can you call JT and let him know what's going on and ask him to gather up the troops back at the office this afternoon, say about one?"

"Yes, sir. Would you like me to download the warrant form for you first?"

"Indeed, let's get this together. Oooh whee, this is exciting."

Bolling Air Force Base, DC, 8 December, 1615 hours

Hanson received the warrants by 3:30 and told Phil and Ronnie to show up at Henning's residence at exactly 4:15. He, JT and Juanita were here where he worked on Bolling AFB. Hanson had contacted a friend in the Director's office at DIA and determined that Henning was at work today, so the plan was for Juanita to get his keys and search his car, while JT and Hanson took care of his office. If any of them found anything incriminating, either here, at Henning's house or in his cars, they'd arrest him. They had already looked at his financials and found nothing untoward there. Hanson knew his ex-boss was involved with terrorists based on the information that Arati had uncovered but didn't think that was enough for a conviction. Phone taps would most likely not be fruitful, as Henning would be too smart for that. Nor did Hanson think that putting him under surveillance would prove useful, as he probably had little if any direct involvement. *No,* he thought, *we need to strike now.*

They were met at the front door by the head of security and two of his guards. The locals insisted on being part of the action and Hanson figured they could keep Henning occupied while he and his troops completed the search. When they got to his eighth-floor office, there was no one outside in the reception area where his assistant was usually located. And his door was closed.

JT went up and knocked loudly. "Mr. Henning, it's JT Dunkirk with Homeland Security. Are you in there?" There was no answer, but JT thought he heard something, like somebody sobbing softly. "We need to talk, Mr. Henning. Can you let me in?"

"Go away or there could be trouble!"

JT and Hanson looked at each other. "That's definitely him," said Hanson. "I'll look around for a coworker and see if we can learn anything," offered one of the guards. Juanita accompanied him. Two offices down, they found a woman and asked about Henning's assistant.

"Her name is Mary and she was outside his office earlier. I think she went in there, I'd say, about fifteen minutes ago. Sounds like Mr. Henning's upset with her, because I heard some yelling. That's very unlike him."

"Thanks," they both said and then rejoined the group to relay the information. "Bad news, sir," said the guard. It sounds like he's got his assistant in there—her name is Mary."

"Christ, Boss. I think she's in there sobbing," said JT. "I'm thinking our boy has really lost it. Maybe he plans on using her to get out of here," he offered. "Do we know if he has a weapon?"

"Yeah, most likely. He had several hanging on his wall at CIFA. Far as I know that was his one hobby—shooting, not collecting." Hanson looked at the head of security who forlornly nodded his head in agreement. "Alright, we need to play this cool. Let me see if I can reason with him." Hanson approached the door and carefully tried to turn the handle—it was locked. "Joel, this is Tom Hanson. Look, we only want to discuss a few things."

"Well, Tom, how are you? Long time no see."

There was a definite change in his tone of voice. Hanson thought he seemed calm enough so he said, "I'm sure we can clear this all up in a matter of no time, Joel. It's probably all just a big misunderstanding."

"Give me a break, Tom. The fact that you're here tells me you've got something actionable. I don't see any reasonable way out of this. I'm afraid that I'm going to have to settle this my way."

They heard a scream and then a gunshot. Everyone in the room drew their weapon. Hanson took a step back and threw his body into the door. The jamb gave way and the door flew open. He managed to keep his balance as he rushed in with his gun raised. JT was only two steps behind him with the rest of the entourage behind him. What they saw was not a pretty sight: Henning sprawled back in his chair with blood and brain matter splattered all over the window behind his head. His arm had dropped down by his side with the gun still clutched in his hand. Mary was in a chair in the corner of the room sobbing hysterically. The head of security went over to retrieve the gun while Juanita started to comfort Mary. She grabbed her up and with JT's help half-carried her out of the room, assuring her she was safe and it was all over now.

Hanson stood a few feet away looking at his ex-boss and shaking his head. "How did he go so wrong? What a waste of such a promising life. I guess you just never know what's inside someone's head," he said—more to himself than anyone in the room. One of the guards offered to call for a wagon and went to use the phone outside the office. Hanson decided to join his troops and Mary. She had calmed down somewhat with the assistance of the lady from down the hall. "Mary, when you're ready, we need to talk about what went on in there," Hanson said.

Juanita got Henning's keys and proceeded to search his car, but, as it turned out, to no avail. Hanson and JT secured his hard drive and gathered up all the non-classified documents, DVDs and flash drives that were in his office, with Juanita pitching in toward the end. In the mean time, the security force had gotten the body removed and had the place relatively clean. They were all through about an hour later, some of which time Hanson had spent talking to the base commander and the ranking officer at DIA. They agreed to let Hanson's team have the classified stuff, including his hard drive, as soon as they could.

Hanson asked Mary if she felt up to talking now, and she agreed. The security troops provided a recorder which they turned on and recited a short preamble into before Mary began.

She said her boss had asked her to come into his office and then locked the door behind her. He pulled a gun out of his desk and started waving it around. She said it was like he was talking to someone else in the room—not her. He kept mentioning something about some sort of plans going wrong, people with foreign sounding names, sources of revenue, someone named Rick something, and other things that didn't make any sense to her. Mary admitted that she was probably too scared to make any sense out of it. They went on for ten minutes but got nothing more substantial from her. She did agree to be hypnotized and questioned about the incident, and Hanson set that up for the next day back at headquarters.

The DIA protocol officer agreed to make the family notification, so Hanson figured they were done here. They used a cart to carry the four Xerox boxes of material out to the car.

"Well, troops, this hasn't been one of my better days," Hanson complained. "I think I'll just head on home now. You guys get all this stuff back to the office, okay?"

"Sure, Boss," JT replied, "but you sure you don't want to come out and have a drink with us?"

"No. Appreciate the offer but I'm okay. Just need to go home and think about all this. I'll see you tomorrow." With that he got in his car and drove off.

JT and Juanita pressed on to JT's Highlander and loaded the stuff in the back. "I think that hit him pretty hard," offered Juanita. "I didn't think he liked Henning that much, but I could be wrong."

"I think it's more like he feels betrayed. You know, you work for the guy carrying out an antiterrorist mission and then find out he was on the other side. That's got to be a lot to deal with. Why don't you push the cart back up to the entrance and I'll pick you up there?"

Juanita nodded and headed toward the front of the building.

On the drive back, they tried to piece together a scenario that fit what information they had. "Hopefully we can get something useful out of all his stuff," said Juanita. "Maybe Phil and Ronnie got some good information from his residence. I wonder how close he was to his parents, or vice versa, I guess."

"I don't think that even Hanson knows that. I have a feeling that it's going to be a lot of guess work from here on out."

"This could be just one more time that you're wrong, *amigo*."

"I certainly hope so."

Fusion Team Headquarters, 14 December, 0910 hours

"I see everyone is here," said Hanson. "I thought this might be a good time to lay out where we are on everything. Phil, how about an update on the folks we're still looking for."

"Sure, Boss." Phil gave the Team an update on the progress in tracking the whereabouts of the Sticks that were still at large. He also mentioned that they had a good lead from one of the FBI agents that regularly attended the *"Afghans in America"* meetings and had some surveillance ongoing. And the FBI had found a link to another chop shop in the records of the shop that the Team had hit three weeks ago and were closing in on it. "Seems there's some high level government discussions on the dispositions of the vehicles that were identified as moved through the chop shop. The ones they could locate that is."

"Glad we're not involved with that," said Hanson. "So JT, what did we get from all the Henning stuff?"

"We're still piecing this together from his notes, what we got off his hard drive, and some information that Mary gave us when she came in for her hypnotism session. He also maintained a journal of sorts that he kept at home. Some of this stuff was rather cryptic, Cap'n, but here's what we think so far. Seems Henning wanted to kill Quarles because he would have detected the backdoor program that he wanted to build into the Tomfoolery program. That would have enabled him to hide future transactions that could have funded his terrorist activities. Apparently he thought he would be given purview over the program operation in his new post at DIA. As we know, Briceman beat him to Quarles. He had nothing to do with the Crenshaw murder, however; that was all Briceman. Actually,

Crenshaw, who worked for Henning at CIFA, did tell him of Quarles suspicions about contract fixing. We think this may be what got Henning on to Briceman, and why he finally decided that he had to go. Briceman, of course, had already added the backdoor to the program and was using it to hide kickback payments. When he was caught, that drew even more attention to the program and is the reason that the current contract action was finally stopped until all the bribery activity can be sorted out. So he was responsible for the terrorist attack on Briceman. He and his cell were indeed planning a hit on Metro Center, and we think that has been sufficiently disrupted, at least for the time being. It's possible that he was actually the leader of two cells, maybe three, or at least a member of a group of men that ran them collectively. Unfortunately, we only have definitive data on the one. The State Department is still wrangling with the Maldivian and Andorran governments regarding the ill-gotten gains of these two characters."

"What was his motivation for all of this?" asked Ronnie.

"When Juanita and I checked on him due to his involvement with the contract evaluation group, we found that he was adopted at the age of ten by Howard and Thelma Henning. His adoption records were sealed and, given his age, we let it ride at the time. It took some persuasion and a federal warrant, but we got his earlier records. Seems he was born in this country but his parents were both illegals from Pakistan. By the time Immigration figured this out, he was seven and they were gone. They left him unattended and disappeared. He was in a foster home for three years before his adoption. We think his real parents may have kept in touch with him, coloring his outlook on society, and resulting in his pro-terrorist leanings. Dr. Bosworth says he thinks the guy was so conflicted between what his adoptive parents were teaching him and what he got from his biological parents that he just couldn't take it anymore."

"Yeah, that's believable. And we have nothing solid on these other cell leaders?"

"No, sir. And Arati's been working on that."

"Okay, okay. What about that guy that you've been tracking, Josh? What's the story there?"

And they went on.

EPILOGUE

Mustafa Ahmadi is in the witness protection program and is working as the assistant manager of a convenience store somewhere out west. His cousin's family was relocated to Florida and his cousin is working as an interpreter for the JTTF under a new identity.

Shahzad al-Hardar was convicted of three counts of aiding and abetting terrorism and is serving a twenty-four year sentence in a maximum security federal penitentiary.

Mrs. Don Crenshaw is enjoying the proceeds of a large insurance policy and is currently living in a condo in St. Petersburg. She no longer wears a watch.

Jonathan Furlong was convicted of four counts of murder in the first degree and is serving four consecutive life-without-parole sentences in a federal penitentiary. Since the person who hired him is also incarcerated, his request for witness protection was denied.

Sidiq Haq is serving a fifty-six-year sentence in a maximum security federal penitentiary after being convicted of eight counts of aiding and abetting terrorism.

Artie Heilig was convicted of four counts of soliciting murder and is serving four consecutive life-without-parole sentences in a federal penitentiary. His daughter has not spoken to him since his conviction and has moved to Indiana.

Charles Macey is out on parole from a federal penitentiary after serving only one year of a five-year sentence for theft of blasting caps and providing them to a known felon. JT testified at his trial.

Sattar Omar was killed in a convict riot within the first two months of arriving at a federal penitentiary. He was convicted of three counts of aiding and abetting terrorism and was sentenced to twenty-four years.

Martha Quarles is working as a paralegal in a Reston, Virginia law firm. Her parents moved down from New York and are staying with her. She is the proud mother of baby boy that looks remarkably like her deceased husband.

Michael Styles was convicted of two counts of soliciting and accepting bribes and was fined $250,000 and sentenced to six years in a federal minimum security facility. He will be eligible for parole in two years. His wife, Elizabeth Falworth, sued for divorce and sole custody of their little boy and won. She has since remarried.

LIST OF ACRONYMS

AFB—Air Force Base
AFIS—Automated Fingerprint Identification System
AFOSI—Air Force Office of Special Investigations
ARU—Accident Reconstruction Unit
ATF—Bureau of Alcohol, Tobacco, Firearms and Explosives

BOLO—Be-on-the-Lookout
BPD—Baltimore Police Department
BRAC—Base Realignment and Closing (commission)

CA—Commonwealth Attorney
CFO—Chief Financial Officer
CIA—Central Intelligence Agency
CID—Army Criminal Investigation Division
CIFA—Counterintelligence Field Activity
COLTRANE—Collection, Transmission and Analysis Enterprise (program)

DARPA—Defense Advanced Research Projects Agency
DHS—Department of Homeland Security
DIA—Defense Intelligence Agency
DNI—Director of National Intelligence
DoD—Department of Defense

FAA—Federal Aviation Administration
FAM—Federal Air Marshall

FBI—Federal Bureau of Investigation
FCPD—Fairfax County Police Department
FRS—Face Recognition Software (program)

IAD—Internal Affairs Division
ICE—Immigration and Customs Enforcement
IED—Improvised Explosive Device
IG—Inspector General
INFER—International Financial Enterprise Referendum
(program)
IT—Information Technology

JTTF—Joint Terrorist Task Force

LCSO—Loudoun County Sheriff's Office
LEO—Law Enforcement Officer

ME—Medical Examiner
MPD—Metropolitan (D.C.) Police Department

NCIC—National Crime Information Center
NCIS—Naval Criminal Investigative Service
NCTC—National Counterterrorism Center
NRL—Naval Research Laboratory
NSA—National Security Agency

ONR—Office of Naval Research
OSI—See AFOSI

SCIF—Sensitive Compartmented Information Facility

SEC—Securities and Exchange Commission
SSEB—Source Selection Evaluation Board
STICK—(Person with) Suspected Terrorist Involvement or Connections
SWAT—Special Weapons and Tactics

TIDE—Terrorist Identities Datamart Environment
TSA—Transportation Security Administration

UAV—Unmanned Aerial Vehicle
USCIS—United States Citizenship and Immigration Service (formerly INS)